Cat Schield has been reading and writing romance since high school. Although she graduated from college with a BA in business, her idea of a perfect career was writing books for Mills & Boon. And now, after winning the Romance Writers of America 2010 Golden Heart® Award for series contemporary romance, that dream has come true. She loves to hear from readers. Find her at www.catschield.com. Follow her on Twitter: @catschield.

Lauren Canan grew up listening to her dad tell stories of make-believe and was always encouraged to let her imagination soar. The multi-award-winning author and recipient of the 2014 Golden Heart® Award happily spends her days penning her favorite kind of stories: those of two people who, against all odds, meet, fall in love and live happily ever after—which is the way it should be. In her spare time she enjoys playing guitar, piano and dulcimer in acoustic club jams and getting lots of kisses and wags from her four-legged fuzzy babies. Visit Lauren's website at www.laurencanan.com. She would love to hear from you!

Ellie Darkins spent her formative years devouring romance novels, and after completing her English degree she decided to make a living from her love of books. As a writer and editor her work now entails dreaming up romantic proposals, hot dates with alpha males and trips to the past with dashing heroes. When she's not working she can usually be found at her local library or out for a run.

Mum's the Word!

CAT SCHIELD
LAUREN CANAN
ELLIE DARKINS

MILLS & BOON

First Published in Great Britain 2018
by Mills & Boon, an imprint of HarperCollins*Publishers*
1 London Bridge Street, London, SE1 9GF

MUM'S THE WORD! © 2018 Harlequin Books S. A.

Royal Heirs Required © 2015 Catherine Schield
Lone Star Baby Bombshell © 2015 Sarah Cannon
Newborn on Her Doorstep © 2015 Ellie Darkins

ISBN: 978-0-263-26801-0

05-0618

MIX
Paper from
responsible sources
FSC˚ C007454

This book is produced from independently certified FSC™
paper to ensure responsible forest management.

For more information visit: www.harpercollins.co.uk/green

Printed and bound in Spain
by CPI, Barcelona

ROYAL HEIRS REQUIRED

CAT SCHIELD

For Delores and Jerry Slawik.
Thank you for making me feel like part of your family.

One

"She's the perfect choice for you," Gabriel Alessandro's brother joked, nudging his shoulder.

The two princes were standing at the edge of the dance floor watching their father, the king, sweep Gabriel's future bride through a series of elegant turns while their mother concentrated on keeping her toes from beneath the prime minister's clumsy feet.

Gabriel released an audible sigh. With his future bride's father building a high-tech manufacturing plant just outside the capital, Sherdana's economy would receive the boost it badly needed. "Of course she is."

Lady Olivia Darcy, daughter of a wealthy British earl, was just a little too perfect. While she exuded poise and warmth in public, in private she never relaxed, never let down her guard. This hadn't bothered him at all in the days leading up to their engagement. From the moment he'd begun looking for a wife he'd decided to listen to his head and not his heart. Past experience had demonstrated losing himself in passion led to nothing but heartache and disappointment.

"Then why are you looking so grim?"

Why indeed? Even though Gabriel didn't have to pretend to be besotted with his fiancée in front of his brother, he wasn't about to admit his regret that his personal life would have less passion and drama once he was married.

Until the wedding planning had begun in earnest, he'd considered himself well and thoroughly lucky to have found a woman who wouldn't drive him mad with her theatrics and demands. It was in sharp contrast to his affair with Marissa, which had been a tempestuous four-year romance with no future.

Gabriel was not a world-famous musician or a dashing Hollywood actor or even a wealthy playboy. He was the heir apparent of a small European country with strict laws that dictated his wife must be either an aristocrat or a citizen of Sherdana. Marissa had been neither.

"How happy would you be if you were marrying a virtual stranger?" Gabriel kept his voice soft, but there was no hiding his bitterness.

Christian's grin was positively wicked. "The best part about being the youngest is that I don't have to worry about getting married at all."

Gabriel muttered an expletive. He was well aware that neither of his brothers envied him. In many ways that was a relief. In centuries past Sherdana had seen its fair share of plots against the crown both from without and within. It would have been awful if either of his brothers had schemed to keep him off the throne. But that was highly unlikely. Nic lived in the US, building rocket ships that might someday carry regular—wealthy—citizens into space while Christian was very happy buying and selling companies.

"…hot."

"Hot?" Gabriel caught the final word his brother had spoken. "What's hot?"

"Not what." Christian shot him a wry glance. "Who. Your future bride. I was just remarking that you should spend some time getting to know her. It might be more enjoyable than you think. She's hot."

Lady Olivia Darcy was many things, but Gabriel wouldn't label her as hot. A gorgeous package of stylish sophistication, she had the fashion designers competing to dress her. Her features were delicate and feminine, her skin pale and unblemished. She was slender, but not boyish, with long legs, graceful arms and an elegant neck. There was a serene expression in her keen blue gaze.

And it wasn't as if she was a frivolous socialite, spending her days shopping and her nights in clubs. She worked tirelessly for almost a dozen charities all focused on children's causes. The perfect future queen of Sherdana.

Gabriel shot his brother a narrow look. "You just referred to your future sister-in-law and queen as hot. Do you think Mother would approve?"

"I'm her baby boy." The youngest of the triplets, Christian had played the birth-order card all his life. "She approves of everything I do."

"She doesn't approve of your antics, she simply feels bad for all those times she had to leave you to the nanny because she could only carry Nic and me."

Ignoring his brother's gibe, Christian nodded toward the queen. "She's hot, too, you know. She'd have to be to keep Father interested all these years."

Gabriel had no interest in discussing his parents' love life. "What has you so determined to stir up trouble tonight?"

Christian's expression settled into severe lines. "Now that Mother has you all settled, she going to turn her sights to Nic and me."

"Nic is more interested in fuel systems than women," Gabriel said. "And you've made it clear you have no intention of giving up your bachelor ways."

In the five years since his car accident, Christian had become guarded and pessimistic when it came to his personal life. Although the burn scars that spread down his neck and over his shoulder, chest and upper arm on the right side were hidden beneath the high collar of his formal blue tunic, the worst of Christian's hurts were below the skin, deep in his soul where no healing reached. The damage was visible in those rare moments when he drank too much or thought no one was watching.

Gabriel continued, "I don't think either of our parents hold out any hope that the two of you will settle down anytime soon."

"You know Mother is a romantic," Christian said.

"She's also pragmatic."

But Christian didn't look convinced. "If that was true, she'd accept that you will father all the heirs Sherdana could ever want or need and leave Nic and me alone. That's not the impression she gave me earlier this evening."

A knot of discomfort formed in Gabriel's chest as he thought of his future bride. Once again his gaze slid to Olivia, who was now dancing with the prime minister. Although her smile was lovely, the reserve in her blue eyes made her seem untouchable.

His days with Marissa had been sensual, wild and all-consuming. They'd awaken before dawn in her Paris apartment and make love in the quiet hush of the early morning. After which they'd sit by the window, gorge themselves with pastries washed down with strong coffee and watch the sun paint the rooftops with golden light.

"Your Royal Highness."

Gabriel turned to his private secretary, who'd appeared out of nowhere. Usually Stewart Barnes was the calm eye in the middle of the hurricane. At the moment, sweat shone on his forehead.

The hairs on the back of Gabriel's neck rose. "Problem?"

Stewart's approach had caught Christian's attention, as well. "I'll deal with it," he said, stepping away from his brother's side.

"No, sir." The private secretary moved to block Christian. He gave a small shake of his head and met Gabriel's hard gaze with a look that conveyed the seriousness of the issue. "I know the timing is bad, but a lawyer has arrived with an urgent message for you."

"A lawyer?"

"How did he get into the palace?" Christian snapped, eyes blazing.

Gabriel barely registered Christian's words. "What could possibly be so important?"

"Did Captain Poulin give you a reason for granting this man entrance at such an inappropriate hour?"

"Can't it wait until after the party?"

Stewart's attention bounced between the two men as they fired questions at him. "He wouldn't tell me what it's about, Highness, only the name of his client." Stewart's tone was low and urgent. "I think you'd better speak to him."

Unable to imagine what could have rattled his unflappable private secretary, Gabriel shared a glance with Christian. "Who is his client?"

"Marissa Somme."

Hearing his former lover's name aroused a hundred emotions Gabriel would have preferred not to feel. He was a little surprised that Marissa had waited so long to contact him. He'd expected her to pull a stunt five months ago when he'd announced his engagement. To say she had a flare for the dramatic was like describing the Himalayas as tall hills.

"What mischief is she up to?" Gabriel demanded.

Christian cursed beneath his breath. "Something newsworthy, no doubt."

"I can't afford anything to interfere with the wedding." Sherdana's future was riding on the deal he'd struck with Lord Darcy. A deal that wouldn't be sealed until Olivia became a princess.

Gabriel glanced around to see if anyone had noticed their exchange and met Olivia's level gaze. She was beautiful, his future wife. But he'd chosen her for more than her appearance. She had a purity of spirit he knew would charm the Sherdanian people and her efficient, calm way of handling problems would see her through the hectic days ahead.

Beside her his father was laughing at whatever story she was telling him, looking years younger. Recent economic difficulties had taken their toll on the king. Once vibrant and strong, he'd begun to tire faster in recent months. It was why Gabriel had taken on more and more of the day-to-day running of the country.

Although she returned her attention to the king, the slightest lift of her delicate eyebrows let Gabriel know her curiosity had been aroused by his exchange with Christian and Stewart. Awareness surged through him. It was the first time that they'd connected at a level deeper than politeness. Anticipation sparked. Perhaps they would be able to share something more than a bed.

"Please, Your Highness."

Glancing toward Christian, he said, "Will you go entertain my fiancée while I discover what's going on?"

"Don't you mean distract?" Christian countered, his expression sour.

"Just make excuses for me until I can get back."

And then he was slipping through the multitude attending the ball honoring Sherdana's independence from France back in 1664, smiling and greeting the guests as if nothing in the world was wrong. All the while two words pounded in his head: *Marissa Somme.* What could this be about?

Since it first declared itself a principality, Sherdana had survived as an agrarian economy. But Gabriel wanted his country to do more than survive, he wanted it to thrive.

Tucked between France and Italy on a verdant plane resplendent with grapevines and fertile fields, Sherdana needed an active technological culture to move the economy into the twenty-first century and beyond. Olivia's father, Lord Edwin Darcy, held the match that would light the fuse. Nothing must interfere with that.

Entering the green salon, Gabriel strode over to greet the man who'd barged in unannounced. The lawyer wore his gray hair short, making no attempt to hide the bald patch that caught the light from the wall sconces behind him. His clear gray eyes had few lines at the corners. This was not a man who smiled often. Dressed in a navy suit and black overcoat, the only spark of color about him was a thin line of yellow in his striped tie.

"Good evening, Your Royal Highness," the gentleman said, bowing respectfully. "Forgive me for interrupting, but I'm afraid the matter is quite urgent."

"What mischief is Marissa up to now?"

"Mischief?" The man looked dismayed at Gabriel's harshness. "You misunderstand the reason I'm here."

"Then enlighten me. I have guests waiting. If you have a message from Marissa, then deliver it."

The man straightened his shoulders and tugged at his coat lapel. "It's a little more complicated than a message."

"My patience is wearing thin."

"Marissa Somme is dead."

Dead? Gabriel felt as if he'd been clobbered with a poker. For a second he couldn't process the man's words. Brilliant, beautiful, vivacious Marissa dead? His gut twisted.

"How?"

The older gentleman nodded in sympathy. "Cancer."

Even though he hadn't spoken with her in a very long time, the news rocked him. Marissa had been the first woman he'd ever loved. The only one. Their breakup three years before had been one of the most painful experiences of his life. But nothing compared to knowing she was gone for good. Wounds he'd thought healed were reopened, the pain as fresh as it had ever been. Never would he see her again. Hear her laugh.

Why hadn't she called him? He would have helped her out.

"You came all this way to deliver the news of her death to me?" Had she still cared about him? Despite her final angry words? Impossible. She'd never once tried to contact him.

"And to bring you something she said you should have."

"What?" Gabriel demanded. Had she returned the diamond heart pendant he'd given her for their first anniversary? He'd been a romantic fool in those days. Young. Rebellious. Caught up in a passionate affair that had no future. And a fool. "What did you bring me?"

"Your daughters."

"Daughters?" *As in more than one?* Gabriel wondered if he'd heard the man properly.

"Twins."

"Marissa and I had no children together."

"I'm afraid that's not true."

The man pulled out two birth certificates and extended them. Gabriel gestured to Stewart to take them and watched as his private secretary scanned the documents. Stewart's blue eyes were awash with concern as he glanced up and met Gabriel's gaze.

"They bear Marissa's last name, but she listed you as the father," Stewart said.

"They can't be mine," Gabriel insisted. "We were careful." Perhaps not careful enough. "How old are they?"

"They will turn two in a month."

Gabriel quickly did the math. They'd been conceived in the week he'd been in Venice shortly after their breakup.

Marissa had come and thrown herself at him in one last attempt to make him abandon his duty. They'd made love all night, their kisses frantic, embraces feverish. When she'd awakened to find him departing the room before dawn, she'd lashed out, claiming that he'd led her on, accusing him of indifference. Despite her antagonism, regret had stuck with him for months afterward.

They'd had no future. His duty was to his country. She couldn't accept that and he'd let the relationship go on too long. She'd begun to hope he would give up everything for her and he'd enjoyed shirking his responsibilities. But it couldn't last. Sherdana always came first.

What would he have done if he'd known she was pregnant? Set her up in a villa nearby where he could visit? She would never have put up with that. She'd have demanded his complete and total devotion. It was what had torn them apart. He belonged to the people of Sherdana.

"This could all be a huge hoax," Stewart said.

"Marissa might have loved drama, but pulling a stunt like this goes beyond anything she'd do."

"We'll know for sure after a DNA test," Stewart said.

"And in the meantime? What am I to do with the girls?" the lawyer asked impertinently.

"Where are they?" Gabriel demanded. He crackled with impatience to see them.

"Back at my hotel with their nanny."

He didn't hesitate to ponder the consequences. "Get them."

"Think of your upcoming wedding, Highness," Stewart cautioned. "You can't have them brought here. The palace is crawling with media."

Gabriel aimed a disgusted look at his secretary. "Are you telling me you're not clever enough to transport two toddlers here without being seen?"

Stewart's spine snapped straight as Gabriel knew it

would. "I will see that they are brought to the palace immediately."

"Good."

"In the meantime," Stewart said, "I suggest you return to the gala before you're missed. I'm sure the king and queen will wish to discuss the best way to handle things."

Gabriel hated every bit of Stewart's sensible advice and the need to play host when his attention was shackled to reckless urges. He didn't want to wait to see the girls. His instinct demanded he go to the lawyer's hotel immediately. As if by taking one look at the toddlers he could tell if they were his. Ridiculous.

"Find me as soon as they're settled," he told Stewart.

And with those parting words, he exited the room.

Knowing he should return immediately to the party but with his mind racing, Gabriel strode into the library. He needed a few minutes to catch his breath and calm his thoughts.

Twins. His heart jerked. Did they have their mother's clear green eyes and luxurious brown hair? Had she told them about him? Was he insane to bring them into the palace?

A scandal could jeopardize his plans for stabilizing Sherdana's economy. Would the earl still allow Olivia to marry him if word got out that Gabriel had illegitimate twin daughters? And what if Olivia wasn't willing to accept that her children wouldn't be his only ones?

Gabriel left the library, burdened by a whole new set of worries, determined to make sure his future bride found him irresistible.

From her place of honor beside the king of Sherdana, Olivia watched her future husband slip through the guests assembled in the golden ballroom and wondered what was so important that he had to leave the Independence Day gala in such a hurry.

It continued to bother her that in less than four weeks, she was going to become a princess, Gabriel's princess, and she had very little insight into the man she was marrying. Theirs was not a love match the likes of which Kate had found with William. Olivia and Gabriel were marrying to raise her father's social position and improve Sherdana's economic situation.

While that was great for everyone else, Olivia's London friends wondered what was motivating her. She'd never told anyone about the dream conceived by her three-year-old self that one day she'd become a princess. It had been a child's fancy and as she'd grown up, reality replaced the fairy tale. As a teenager she'd stopped imagining herself living in a palace and dancing through the night with a handsome prince. Her plans for the future involved practical things like children's charities and someday a husband and children of her own. But some dreams had deep roots that lay dormant until the time was ripe.

Before Olivia considered her actions, she turned to the king. "Excuse me."

"Of course," the handsome monarch replied, his smile cordial.

Released, she left the king and headed in the direction her fiancé had gone. Perhaps she could catch Gabriel before he returned to the ballroom and they could spend some time talking, just the two of them. She hadn't gone more than a dozen steps before Christian Alessandro appeared in her path.

His gold eyes, shadowed and wary around most people, warmed as he smiled down at her. "Are you enjoying the party?"

"Of course," she replied, bottling up a sigh as the youngest Alessandro prince foiled her plan to speak to his brother alone.

She'd encountered Christian several times in London over the years. As the wildest Alessandro brother, in his university days, Christian had spent more time partying than studying and had barely graduated from Oxford. He'd earned a reputation as a playboy, but had always treated her with respect. Maybe because Olivia had recognized the clever mind he hid beneath his cavalier charm.

"I noticed Prince Gabriel left the party in a hurry," she murmured, unable to conquer the curiosity that loosened her tongue. "I hope nothing is wrong."

Christian had an impressive poker face. "Just some old business he had to take care of. Nothing important."

"He looked a bit shaken up." She stared at her future brother-in-law and saw the tiniest twitch at the corner of his eye. He was keeping something important about Gabriel from her. Olivia's pulse skipped. Seemed she wasn't the only one with secrets.

Since Gabriel had opened negotiations with her father a year ago, Olivia hadn't had much opportunity to get to know the man she would marry. The situation hadn't improved since she'd arrived in Sherdana a week ago. With the wedding only a month away and parliament in session, they'd barely spent an hour alone together and most of that had been divided up into one- to five-minute snippets.

A stroll in the garden the day after she'd arrived, cut short when they'd met the queen's very muddy vizsla. Gabriel had commended Olivia's nimbleness in dodging the dog and retreated to the palace to change his trousers.

A moment in the carriage before the parade yesterday. He'd complimented her hat.

A whole five minutes during the waltz this evening. He'd told her she looked lovely.

Their exchanges were polite and cordial. At all times

he'd been the perfect prince. Courteous. Gallant. Cultured. And she'd been seized by the absurd desire to muss his hair and shock him with outrageous remarks. Of course, she would never do that. The daughter of an earl, she was acutely conscious of her image and position.

Christian refocused her attention on the crowd around them and began filling her ear with all sorts of salacious gossip about the local nobility. Normally she'd be amused by his outrageous slander of Sherdana's wealthy and powerful, but with each new dance the air in the ballroom grew stuffier and she wanted to spend time getting to know her fiancé.

What did Gabriel expect from her? A political partner? Or an attractive figurehead that he could trot out for state occasions? She hoped it was the former.

Firstborn, he'd won the right to inherit the throne by a mere forty minutes. But there was no question in anyone's mind that he was utterly and completely suited to the role.

His commitment to Sherdana was absolute and apparent to all. He'd been educated here and rarely left, except on official business. While in contrast, his two younger brothers had both chosen to spend as little time in their native country as possible.

Drawn by a magnetic pull too great to resist, her attention returned to the ballroom doors that Gabriel had passed through. What could have taken him away in the middle of the party? As if her thoughts had summoned him, she spied the prince coming through the crowd toward her.

Her gaze traced the sculpted breadth of his shoulders, the way his white jacket stretched across his broad chest, providing an abundance of room for the medals pinned there. A blue sash cut diagonally from shoulder to hip.

"Forgive me for neglecting you," he said as he came to a stop before her. "I hope my brother has kept you sufficiently entertained."

"Christian has been filling me in on your guests."

For the first time in her company, Gabriel's courteous mask slipped. He shot his brother a hard look. "What have you been telling her?"

"Things most people, including you, wouldn't. If she's going to be Sherdana's princess, she needs to know where the bodies are buried or she'll be no help to you at all."

Gabriel shook his head. "She doesn't need to know all the ins and outs of our politics to help out the country or me."

Olivia's heart sank. Now she knew what he expected from her. There would be no partnership, no working together. She would attend ceremonies and support charities while he ran the country and dealt with its problems alone.

"She's smarter than you're giving her credit for, Gabriel. You should use her to your best political advantage."

"Thank you for your opinion, brother." And his tone said that was the end of the conversation.

With a mocking bow, Christian retreated. While part of Olivia regretted his departure, she was glad for a moment alone with Gabriel. Or she was until he began to speak.

"I know you haven't seen much of Sherdana since your arrival," he said, his polite formality pushing her to greater impatience. "But maybe that can change in the next week or so."

"That would be lovely." She bit back her thoughts on how unlikely it was. With the wedding only a month away she would scarcely have the opportunity to sleep, much less take a tour of the countryside. "I'm eager to visit the wine country."

"Sherdana takes pride in its wine as you well know."

"As it should," she murmured, her boredom coming through in her tone. "I'm glad you were able to get your business resolved so you could return to the party so quickly."

"Business?" There wasn't the least suggestion of understanding in his manner.

"I saw your private secretary approach you with some news. It seemed to be something unpleasant. And then you left. Christian explained it was old business you needed to take care of."

"Ah, yes. Just a misunderstanding with Stewart. It was nothing."

"I'm glad." But her mind was busy cataloging all the nuances of his tone and expression. Her future husband was skilled at deflection.

"Would you care to dance?" he asked, his deep voice rumbling through her like distant thunder.

Not really. She was tired and her shoes pinched. But she smiled. "Of course."

A waltz began to play as Gabriel took her hand and led her onto the dance floor. Keeping her expression pleasant and neutral was torture as his palm slid against her back. The gown she wore had a modest cut, showing no cleavage or bare shoulders, but the material was silk and the heat of Gabriel's hand burned through the fabric and set her on fire.

"Are you feeling compelled to marry because your father wishes it?"

The abruptness of his question was so unexpected, she almost laughed. "Why would I need to be compelled by my father? You're rich, handsome and going to be king one day. What girl wouldn't wish to be queen?"

"You didn't answer my question."

"I'm not being forced to marry you. I have been given an opportunity many would envy." She assessed his expression, curious where this line of questioning originated. "Are you worried that down the road I'll regret my choice?" She cocked her head and regarded him intently. "Or are you looking for an excuse to break our engagement?"

"Nothing like that. I am just wondering if perhaps you'd have preferred a different life."

"I'm sure many people wish every day that they'd done something different. Mostly, we must play the hand life deals us. For some, it's struggling with poverty. For others raising a child on their own or dedicating themselves to their career and forgoing a family." She pitched her voice into sympathetic tones for the next example. "For you it's ensuring your kingdom's economic security. I get to marry a prince and someday become a queen."

For some inexplicable reason, he grew short with her. "But is that what you want?"

"To marry you and become a queen?" She let her surprise show. "Of course."

Gabriel didn't appear convinced. "We haven't had much time to get to know each other," he said. "I hope that will change over the next month."

"Perhaps we could begin now. What is it you'd like to know?"

"Let's begin simply. How do you come to speak French and Italian so fluently?"

"I had a whole army of tutors from the time I was small."

"Your accent is quite good."

"I've been told I have an aptitude for languages. I speak quite a few."

"How many?"

"Six, but I understand three more."

"That will come in handy when dignitaries visit us."

Once again it hit her that she would never return to her home in England for anything more than a short visit. As princess, she would be expected to spend most, if not all, of her time in Sherdana. At least she would see her father frequently because he would want to keep an eye on his investment.

"You don't smile much, do you?" His question was more reflective than directly aimed at her.

His observation caught her off guard.

"I smile all the time."

Gabriel's gaze slipped intently over her features, arousing a frantic thrumming in her chest. "Polite smiles. Political smiles, but I'm not sure I've once seen you smile because you're happy."

"I assure you, I'm quite happy."

"Stop telling me what you think I want to hear. That's not what Sherdana needs of its princess and definitely not what I expect from my wife."

The intensity of his tone and the nuances of his observation did not belong to the man she'd known up to this point. His frank speech loosened her tongue.

"Are you giving me permission to argue with Your Highness?"

He made a face. "Gabriel."

"Of course."

"Olivia." Tone commanding, he somehow managed to caress her name in a way that vibrated through her. "It would make me very happy if you would start thinking of me as a man and not a prince."

His demand sent a ripple of excitement up her spine. She decided to speak her mind.

"I will if you stop thinking of me in terms of economic gain or financial dealings and realize I'm a woman who knows exactly what she wants."

At her words, Gabriel blinked. Surprise quickly became curiosity as he regarded her. For the first time she believed he was seeing her as a person instead of the clause in the contract he needed to satisfy so her father would build a plant in Sherdana and create technical jobs to bolster the economy.

"I'm beginning to think there's more to you than I realize," Gabriel remarked, executing a turn in the dance that left her breathless.

"Thank goodness." It was an effort to get out more than those two words.

Perhaps marriage might hold more of an adventure than she'd first thought. She hadn't expected her husband to excite her. Even seeing how handsome Gabriel was, he was always so in control. She never imagined passion. And growing up sheltered from the experiences an ordinary girl would have with boys such as dating or even just hanging out, she'd never experienced desire. Until this moment, she wasn't sure she could.

Relief made her giddy. Tonight she'd glimpsed a very important and unexpected benefit this marriage would have for her and for the first time in months, she faced her future with a light heart.

TWO

Olivia lay on the blue velvet chaise in the bedroom she'd been assigned at the palace, a heating pad taking away the discomfort of cramps. She stared up at the touches of gold leaf on the ceiling's ornate plasterwork twenty feet above her. From the tall, narrow mirrors between the wide cream silk-draped windows to the elegant chandeliers, it was a stunning, yet surprisingly warm, space.

It was a little after two in the morning. She'd felt the first twinge of pain not long after the king and queen left the gala and had taken the opportunity to slip away. The attack had been blessedly mild. A year ago, she would have taken a pain pill and retreated to bed. Thank goodness those days were behind her. A princess couldn't avoid public appearances because she wasn't feeling well. She must have a spine of steel and prove her value was more than the economic boost her father's new technology company would provide.

As if to mock her optimism, a fresh ache began. She'd first started suffering with sharp cramps and strong periods when she was fifteen. Frightened by the amount of blood she lost each month, Olivia had gone to see a doctor. She'd been diagnosed with endometriosis and had begun taking oral contraceptives to reduce the pain and shorten her periods. Yoga, massage and acupuncture had also helped her cope with her symptoms, but none of these could correct the problem.

She'd needed surgery for that.

Olivia couldn't explain why she'd been so reluctant to have the growths removed when the pain grew progressively worse in her early twenties. She couldn't share her fears with her mother—who'd died giving birth to her—so she'd hidden the severity of the problem from everyone, including her father. Only Libby, her private secretary, knew how debilitating the pain could get. Libby had helped Olivia keep her doctor visits out of the press and made excuses when she had bad days. Olivia wasn't sure what she'd have done these past eight years without Libby's help.

It wasn't until a year ago, when she'd confronted the connection between endometriosis and infertility, that she began to rethink her plans for coping with the disease. If she was marrying a wealthy businessman, a politician or even one of her own country's nobles, she could discuss this issue with him and together they could decide what to do about her potential barrenness. But she was marrying the future king of Sherdana and would be expected to produce an heir.

So, she'd had the surgery and had been living pain free for almost twelve months.

With a sudden surge of impatience, Olivia set aside the heating pad and got to her feet. Brooding over her medical condition was the quickest way to doubt herself and that wasn't the way she faced things. Despite the late hour, the luxurious king-size bed held no appeal. She needed some fresh air and exercise. Perhaps a walk in the garden.

Although she'd removed her ball gown upon returning to her room, she'd not yet dressed for bed. Slipping off her robe, Olivia pulled on a sleeveless jersey dress and found a pair of ballet flats that would allow her to move soundlessly through the sleeping palace.

The room she'd been given was in the opposite wing of the palace from the royal family's apartments and used for housing dignitaries and visitors. Her father slept next door, his room as expansive and substantially furnished as hers. Olivia tiptoed past his door, aiming for the stairs at the far end of the hall that would deposit her close to the pink receiving room and the side gardens beyond. With her limited time in the palace, Olivia hadn't had a great deal of time to explore, but she'd taken this route her second day to meet with the queen.

When she got to the end of the hallway, the high-pitched shriek of an unhappy child caught Olivia's attention. The sound was muffled and it came from somewhere above her. She reached the stairs and paused to listen. She waited no more than a heartbeat before the cry came again, only this time there were two voices.

In an instant Olivia's destination changed. Instead of going down to the ground level, she headed up to the third floor, following the increasingly frantic exclamations of the children and the no less agitated voice of an adult trying to quiet them.

At the top of the stairs, Olivia spied two shadows racing toward her down the darkened hallway. Curious as to what was going on, she'd taken several steps in their direction when a voice cut through the shadows.

"Karina. Bethany. Come back here this instant." The shrill command provoked the children to faster flight.

Worried that at the speed they were going, they might pitch down the stairs, Olivia knelt and spread her arms wide. With their path blocked, the children stopped abruptly. With eyes wide, arms around each other for comfort, they stared at Olivia.

"Hello." She offered them her gentlest smile. "Where are you two going so late?"

"You girls are nothing but trouble."

The scolding woman hadn't spied Olivia in the dimness or she wouldn't have spoken so rudely. The two little girls shrank away from their pursuer, obviously afraid, and sidestepped in Olivia's direction. Now that they were closer, Olivia could see them better. She blinked, wondering if she might be seeing double.

The two little girls, two frightened little girls, were mirror images of each other with long brown hair and large dark eyes in their pale faces. They were dressed in identical dresses and tears streaked their matching cheeks.

Olivia wanted to snatch them into her arms, but feared upsetting them still more. Although her childhood had lacked a loving mother, Olivia had developed a strong maternal instinct. Being warned by the doctor that unless she had surgery she might never have her own children had been a sharp knife in her heart.

"You'd better learn to behave and fast or the people who live here will kick you out and you'll have nowhere else to go."

Having heard enough, Olivia surged to her feet to confront the woman and was surprised when the girls raced to stand behind her. They gripped her dress with strength born of fear, and protectiveness surged through her.

"Stop speaking this instant," Olivia commanded without raising her voice. "No one deserves to be threatened like that, especially not children."

The nanny stopped dead in her tracks and sneered. "You don't know what they're like."

"Whom do you work for?"

The woman looked wary. "I take care of these two."

"Yes, yes." Olivia put one hand on each of the toddlers' heads. The hair was silky beneath her fingers and she longed to give the girls her full attention, but this woman must be dealt with first. "But who are their parents?"

"Their mother is dead."

Olivia sucked in a short breath at the woman's lack of compassion. "That's awful."

The woman didn't respond.

"In heaven," the child on her left said.

Olivia liked the girls' nanny less and less. Had the woman no heart? Did the father know how badly his daughters were being cared for? "Perhaps I should speak to their father. What is his name?"

"A lawyer hired me a week ago to take care of them." The woman stared at Olivia in hostile defensiveness.

"Well, you're not doing a very good job."

"They're terribly spoiled and very difficult. And right now they need to be in bed." Eyes on the children, the nanny shifted her weight forward and her arms left her sides as if she intended to snatch the little girls away from Olivia.

The little girl on her right shrank back. Her sister, emboldened by Olivia's defense, fought back.

"Hate you." She hung on Olivia's skirt. "Wanna go home."

Although she'd been too young to know the shock of losing her mother, Olivia remembered her lonely childhood and ached for the sadness yet to come for these girls. She wanted to wrap her arms around the toddlers and support them through this difficult time, but these were not her children and she shouldn't get attached.

With a heavy sigh, Olivia knew it was time to extricate herself from the situation. She would summon a maid to get the girls settled and return to her room. In the morning she would find out to whom they belonged and fill him in on his employee.

"If I make this mean lady go away," Olivia began, gazing down at the dark heads. "Would you go back to your room and go to sleep?"

"No." Only one of the pair seemed to be verbal. The

other merely gave her head a vehement shake. "Stay with you."

Oh, dear. Obviously she'd defended the girls a little too well. But maybe it wouldn't hurt for them to spend one night with her. There was plenty of room in her big bed and in the morning she could sort them out.

"Would you like to come to my room to sleep tonight?"

In unison, the two dark heads bobbed. Olivia smiled.

"You can't do this," the nanny protested.

"I most certainly can. I suggest you return to your room and pack. I will send someone to escort you out shortly." Olivia extended a hand to each girl and drew the children toward the stairs. Once they were settled in her room, she would send a maid up for their nightgowns and things.

It took time to descend to the second floor. The toddlers' short legs made slow work of the steps, giving Olivia time to wonder who in the palace would raise a cry that they'd gone missing. She looked forward to having a conversation with their father in the near future about the sort of person he'd employed to take care of his children.

When Olivia entered her room, she was surprised to find it occupied by a maid. The girl looked up in surprise from the desk items she was straightening as the trio entered. Although the palace had provided Olivia with maids to tidy up and assist with whatever she needed, she hadn't expected to find one in her room during the middle of the night. And from the expression on the woman's face, she wasn't expecting to be caught at it.

"Lady Darcy, I was just tidying some things up for you."

"At two in the morning?"

"I saw your light on and thought you might be needing something."

Not wanting to make a huge scene in front of the little girls, Olivia scanned the maid's face, confident she'd be able to recognize her again from the hundred or so servants that maintained the palace. She had a small scar just below her left eye.

"Could you run down to the kitchen and get glasses of warm milk for these two?"

"Hate milk," the talkative one said. "Ice cream."

Recalling the nanny's assessment that the girls were spoiled, Olivia hesitated a moment before giving a mental shrug. Again she reminded herself they weren't her responsibility. She could indulge them to her heart's content. "With chocolate sauce?"

"Yeah!"

Olivia nodded. "Please fetch two bowls of ice cream with chocolate sauce."

"Of course, Lady Darcy."

The maid scooted past her, eyeing the odd group before disappearing through the doorway.

Olivia half sat, half collapsed on the sofa near the fireplace and gestured to the girls. "Let's get acquainted, shall we? My name is Olivia."

They hesitated for a moment before coming toward her. Olivia kept her warmest smile fixed on her face and patted the seat beside her.

"Please sit down. The ice cream will take a little while. The palace is very big."

The girls held hands and stared about the enormous room in wide-eyed silence. Now that she could see them better, Olivia noticed the Alessandro family resemblance. In fact, they looked like the pictures she'd seen of Gabriel's sister, Ariana, at a similar age. Were they cousins? She frowned. Her extensive research on Sherdana had included all the royal family. She recalled no mention of young cousins.

"I've only been here a few days and I've gotten lost a dozen times already," she continued, her voice a soothing monotone. "I was very scared when that happened. But I also discovered some wonderful places. There's a library downstairs full of books. Do you like stories?"

They nodded at her, their movements identical as if choreographed.

"So do I. My favorite stories when I was a little girl were about princesses. Would you like to hear one?" She took their smiles as assent. "Once upon a time there were two princesses and their names were Karina and Bethany."

"That's us."

Gabriel paced his office, impatient for Stewart to arrive with news that the twins had been settled into the palace. In his hand was the single photo he'd kept of Marissa after they'd broken up. He'd sealed it in an envelope and shoved it in the back of a drawer. Why he'd kept it was a question he was brooding over now.

After a long, unproductive strategy session with Christian regarding Marissa's daughters, he'd sent his brother home. Although he had rooms for his use in the palace, Christian liked his privacy and only rarely stayed in them. Sometimes Gabriel suspected that if either of his brothers had a choice they would give up their titles and any claim to Sherdana's throne. As it was they spent almost no time in Sherdana. Nic had gone to university in the US where he'd met his business partner and only returned when he absolutely had to, while Christian spent most of the year out of the country pursuing his business interests.

As close as the triplets had been growing up, the distance between them these days bothered Gabriel. While he'd known, as eldest son, that he'd be in charge of running the country someday, he'd never expected that his brothers wouldn't be around to help.

Stewart appeared as Gabriel was returning Marissa's photo to the envelope. Glancing at the clock he saw it was almost three in the morning. He'd sent his private secretary to check on Marissa's daughters half an hour earlier.

"Well?" he demanded, pushing to his feet.

"They arrived at the palace a couple hours ago and I arranged to have them escorted to the nursery in the north wing." It had seemed prudent to squirrel them away at the opposite end of the palace, far from where the royal family was housed.

"Have you seen them?" He wanted to know if the girls bore any resemblance to him, and could scarcely restrain himself from asking the question outright. Christian had cautioned that a DNA test would have to be performed before Gabriel let himself get emotionally involved. It was good advice, but easier agreed to than acted upon.

"Not yet."

Gabriel's temper flared. "What have you been doing?"

The private secretary wasn't fazed by his employer's impatience. "I went to the nursery, but they appear to be missing."

"Missing?" He couldn't imagine how that had happened. "Didn't the lawyer say they had a nanny? Did you ask her where they are?"

"She's gone. Apparently she was escorted from the palace by one of the guards an hour ago."

"Escorted...? On whose authority?"

"Lady Darcy's private secretary."

Unable to fathom how she'd gotten involved, Gabriel stabbed his fingers through his hair. This business with Marissa's daughters was fast spiraling out of control. "Have you spoken with her?"

"It's three in the morning, sir."

And if two little girls weren't missing, he might be inclined to leave his questions until morning. "Tell her I want to speak to her."

"Right away."

His private secretary wasn't gone more than five minutes. "Apparently she's in Lady Darcy's room, sir." Stewart paused. "With the girls."

Dismay shouldered aside irritation as Gabriel headed for the wing that housed his future bride. An encounter between Olivia and Marissa's daughters was a problem he hadn't anticipated. No doubt she would have questions about them. She was proving more troublesome than he'd expected based on their limited interaction before he'd proposed. Christian had warned him there was more to Olivia than a pretty face and polished manners, but she'd done an excellent job keeping her agenda hidden. The question was why.

Gabriel knocked on the door of Olivia's suite, agitation adding sharpness to the blows. His summons was answered more quickly than he expected by a pretty woman in her early thirties, wearing a classic blue dress and a frown. Her eyes widened as she spied him standing in the hall.

"I'm here looking for two little girls who've gone missing from the nursery," Gabriel said, his tone courteous despite the urge to push past her. "I understand they are here. May I come in?"

"Of course, Your Highness." She stepped back and gestured him in. "Lady Darcy, Prince Gabriel is here to see you."

"If you'll excuse us," Gabriel said, gesturing her out before entering the dimly lit suite and closing the door behind him.

His gaze swept the room in search of his fiancée. He spied her by the fireplace. She looked serene in a simple cotton dress, her hair in the same updo she'd worn to the gala. So she hadn't yet gone to bed. This thought made his attention shift to the large bed where he spied a lump beneath the covers.

"Sorry for the late visit," he told her. "But two children have gone missing."

"Bethany and Karina."

She knew their names. What else had she found out?

"What are they doing here?" he asked the question more sharply than he'd intended and saw her eyes narrow.

"They each had a bowl of ice cream and fell asleep." Her sweet smile had a bit of an edge. "They were terrified of that horrible woman who'd been hired to look after them and refused to sleep in their own beds. So I brought them here."

"And plied them with ice cream?"

"Their mother just died a few days ago. Strangers tore them from the only home they'd ever known and brought them to this big, scary place. Do you have any idea how traumatic all that was for them?"

"The nursery is not scary."

"It was for them. And so was that awful woman who was taking care of them."

"Is that why you had her escorted out of the palace tonight?"

Olivia's eyes flashed. "I suppose you're going to tell me it wasn't my place to fire her, but she reminded me of the villain in every children's story I've ever read."

Her outrage was charming and Gabriel found his annoyance melting away. "How did you come to meet them?"

"I couldn't sleep so I thought I'd go for a walk. When I got to the stairs I could hear their cries and the nanny's scolding. They were running down the hall away from that woman and the things she said to them." Olivia's lips tightened. "I would like to speak to their father about her. First thing tomorrow morning if at all possible."

"The situation with them is a little complicated," Gabriel told her, his gaze once again drawn to the lump in the center of the mattress.

"Then explain it to me."

This was what Gabriel had been wrestling with all evening. What he was going to tell the world about Marissa's daughters was a small issue compared to how he would explain things to his parents and the woman he would soon marry.

"Some matters need to be cleared up first."

Olivia's hard stare searched his expression for a long silent moment before she spoke. "What sort of matters?"

He couldn't tell her that the girls were none of her business when she'd already taken their care upon herself. At the same time, he didn't want to claim the girls before the matter of their heritage was cleared up.

"Perhaps you're referring to a DNA test." She laughed at his surprise. "They look like your sister when she was young."

"They do?"

"Didn't you notice?"

"They only just arrived. I haven't seen them yet."

Heart thumping hard against his ribs, Gabriel moved toward the bed. Since finding out about the twins, he'd been impatient to see them, but abruptly his feet felt encased in concrete. Caught between dread and hope that the girls belonged to him, Gabriel stared down at matching faces, peaceful and so innocent in sleep.

The breath he'd taken lodged in his chest as recognition flared. Marissa hadn't lied. They were his. He traced each of the children's delicate cheeks with his finger and his muscles slackened as relief washed over him.

"They're yours, aren't they?" Olivia's voice swelled with emotion, but when he glanced at her, her expression was as serene as if they were discussing the weather. "I had hoped they belonged to Christian."

"I just learned about them tonight."

"Their mother never told you?" Olivia sighed. "And now she's dead."

"Things ended badly between us." He couldn't face Olivia with his emotions this raw, so he kept his gaze on his daughters. "I didn't know she was ill." For a moment he was consumed by despair. He pressed his lips into a tight line. Then, feeling her watching him, he settled his features into an impassive mask.

"You loved her."

He and Olivia had never spoken of love. Their marriage was about politics, not romance. But if she suspected he'd given away his heart to another woman, she might not be so happy.

"We were together a long time ago."

"Karina and Bethany aren't even two. It wasn't that long ago."

Despite her neutral tone, Gabriel suspected she wasn't thrilled to have his past thrown so fully in her face. If the truth about the twins got out the press would speculate and create drama and controversy where there was none. Olivia would become the unwitting victim of their desire for ratings.

"This has to remain a secret," he told her.

"Impossible. The minute you brought them to the palace you risked word getting out."

"Perhaps, but I'd like to postpone that as long as possible so we can strategize how we're going to control the damage."

"If you're worried about my father's reaction, don't be. He's committed to opening a plant here."

"And you?"

"They're two precious little girls. I'll support whatever decision you make, but I think you should proudly claim them as yours."

Her eyes were clear of hesitation or deceit. Did she

realize this would make her a stepmother to his former lover's children? Would another woman have been so understanding?

"I can't figure you out."

"Your Highness?"

"Gabriel," he growled, amused rather than annoyed. "I'll not have you calling me Your Highness in bed."

The underlying heat in his voice reached her. Her cheeks flared pink.

"Gabriel," she echoed, her soft voice low and intimate in a way that warmed his blood. "I promise to remember never to refer to you as Your Royal Highness, or Prince Gabriel, while we're making love."

For the first time he glimpsed the Olivia beneath the enigmatic, cultured woman he'd decided to marry. Impish humor sparkled in her eyes. Intelligence shone there, as well. Why had she hidden her sharp mind from him? Gabriel considered how little time they they'd spent together and shouldered the blame. If he'd gotten to know her better, he'd have seen the truth much sooner.

"All of a sudden, it occurs to me that I've never kissed you." He took her hand and dusted a kiss over her knuckles.

"You kissed me the day you proposed."

"In front of a dozen witnesses," he murmured. He had asked her to marry him in front of her father and close relations. It had been a formality, really, not a true proposal. "And not the way I wanted to."

"How did you want to?"

She'd never flirted with him before and he discovered he liked the challenge in her gaze. Anticipation lit up the room as he set his finger beneath her chin and tilted her head, bringing her lips to a perfect angle to align with his. He watched her long lashes drift downward.

Her breath caught as he stopped just shy of brushing Olivia's lips. The disturbed rush of air awakened his senses with fierce urgency. He longed to crush her against him and feast on her soft mouth. Instead, he concentrated on the scent of her, a delicious floral that reminded him of a spring evening when the roses were in full bloom, while he reined his urges back under control.

What was happening to him? Her body's tension communicated across the short distance between them, the trembling of her muscles, a siren call that demanded he claim her. He was a little startled how compelling that desire was.

Ever since they'd danced, he'd been preoccupied with investigating the chemistry that had sparked between them. He hadn't expected to find passion in his marriage. But now that the sexual chemistry had flared, he couldn't wait to explore her every sigh and moan.

From the start she'd intrigued him. Every time they shared the same room, she'd claimed and held his attention. But he'd chosen her because of what her father's investment could mean for Sherdana rather than for any emotional connection between them. And then tonight she'd revealed that her tranquil exterior camouflaged a quick mind and determined nature.

"This might not be the best place for our first kiss," he told her, his voice raw and husky. Body aching in protest, Gabriel stepped back.

"I understand." She glanced toward his sleeping daughters.

But he doubted that she did because he barely understood his own actions.

No woman before or after Marissa had made him feel like losing all control, and it was logical to assume that no one ever would. Earlier he'd thought of Olivia as cool and untouchable. He'd been very wrong.

This abrupt and overwhelming craving to make love to her long into the night until she lay sated in his arms wasn't part of the plan. He needed a woman who would grace his side in public and warm his bed at night.

The operative word being *warm*.

Not set it on fire.

"I think they should stay here tonight," Olivia murmured, her words wresting him back to the other complication in his life. "In the morning, we can get them settled upstairs." She must have seen a protest building because she shook her head. "They're staying put. They've been through enough for one night. I want to make certain someone familiar is with them when they wake."

Gabriel's eyebrows rose at her adamant tone. "And you're that someone familiar?"

"I fed them ice cream," Olivia said, her expression lightening. "They'll be glad to see a friendly face."

"You certainly have that." He glanced toward the sleeping girls. "And a very beautiful one, as well."

Three

Olivia didn't sleep well on the couch. But she wasn't sure she'd have slept any better in her bed alone. She kept running through her evening. Rescuing the twins, discovering they were Gabriel's illegitimate children and finally, the kiss that had almost happened.

Why had he hesitated? Had she imagined the desire in his eyes as they'd danced earlier that night?

Doubts had begun to plague her as soon as Gabriel left. Her experience with men wasn't extensive. Indulging in lighthearted affairs wasn't something she'd ever done. Her friends accused her of being overly conscientious about her reputation, but in fact, she hadn't been attracted to the men in her social circles. She might have worried about her inability to feel physical desire if she hadn't experienced something magical her first year of university.

She'd attended a masquerade party with one of her friends. The event's host was one of London's most notorious bachelors, and it was the last place she should have shown her face. Fortunately, the costumes and masks had enabled her to remain anonymous. The crowd had been racier than she was used to. Drinking and drugs had led to some boisterous behavior and Olivia had made the mistake of getting cornered.

The man had used his size and strength to pin her against the wall and run his hands beneath her skirt. She'd struggled against the hateful press of his moist lips against her throat, but couldn't free herself. And then it had been over and he'd ended up sprawled on the floor some distance away, the hands he cupped over his bloody nose muffling the obscenities he launched at the tall stranger who'd stepped in.

The hallway was too dark for her to see her rescuer clearly and she was still shaken up by the violence of the encounter, but she managed a grateful smile. "Thank you for helping me."

"You don't belong here," the stranger had told her, his English lightly accented. "It isn't safe for someone as young as you are."

Her cheeks had grown hot at his words because he was right and she had felt foolish. "When is it safe for any woman when a man won't stop when she says no?" She peered through the guests, searching for her friend. "Next time I will carry a stun gun instead of lipstick in my purse."

He'd smiled. "Please don't let there be a next time."

"You're right. This isn't my crowd." She had spotted her friend halfway across the room and decided it was time to leave. "It was nice to meet you," she had told him. "I wish the circumstances had been different." Impulsively she rose up on tiptoe and touched her lips to his cheek, before whispering, "My hero."

Before she moved away, he had cupped her cheek and dropped his lips to hers. The touch electrified her and she swayed into his solid strength. His fingers flexed against her skin, pulling her closer. The kiss had been masterful. Demanding enough to be thrilling, but without the roughness that would make her afraid.

Magic, she remembered thinking, as she'd indulged in a moment of reckless daring.

Olivia released a long slow exhale at the memory. Seven

years later it continued to be the most amazing kiss she'd ever had. And she'd never even known his name. Maybe that's why it dwelled so vividly in her memory.

Lying with her forearm across her eyes, Olivia pushed aside the emotions stirred by that singular event. No good would come from dwelling on a romantic moment. The man who rescued her was probably as vile as the rest of the guests and had merely suffered a momentary crisis of conscience. She was marrying an honest, good man and needed to stay focused on the here and now.

As the room began to lighten, Olivia gave up on sleep and pulled out her laptop. During her research into Gabriel and his family, she'd focused on all things Sherdanian. Now she searched for his past romance and discovered a couple articles that mentioned him and Marissa Somme, a half American, half French model he'd dated for several years.

Olivia scanned the news stories. A few mentioned rumors that Gabriel had been considering abdicating the throne to one of his younger brothers, but ultimately, the affair ended instead.

Awash in concern, Olivia went looking for images of the couple. What she saw wasn't reassuring. The news outlets had gotten it right. The couple had been very much in love. Olivia stared at Gabriel's broad grin and Marissa's blinding smile and guessed if she hadn't been a commoner and an unsuitable candidate to give birth to the future king of Sherdana, they would have married and lived happily ever after.

Obviously Gabriel had chosen his country over his heart. And Marissa had vanished.

Hearing soft whispers coming from the bed, Olivia rose from the sofa. Sure enough, the twins were awake. They'd pulled the fluffy cream comforter over their heads, encasing themselves in a cozy cocoon.

For a moment, Olivia envied them each other. An only child, she'd always longed for a sister to share secrets with. If her mother had lived, she could have had a second child and Olivia might not have grown up so isolated from other children. Because her world had been filled with adults—nannies and various tutors—she'd never had a best friend her own age to play with. In fact, playing wasn't something she'd been given much freedom to do.

Multiples obviously ran in the Alessandro family. Did that mean she could expect a set or two of her own to be running around the palace in the years to come?

Olivia tugged on the comforter, pulling it down little by little to reveal the twins. They lay with noses touching, intent on their communication. Their first reaction as the comforter slid away was fear. Olivia saw their hands come together, as they took and received reassurance from each other.

Then, they recognized her and smiled.

"Someone's been sleeping in my bed," she teased, her words bringing forth giggles. "And they're still here."

Then she growled like a big bad bear and reached down to tickle them. Squeals and laughter erupted from the girls, a vast improvement over last night's terrified protests.

Olivia sat down on the bed. The prince would be back soon and the girls needed to be prepared to meet him. No doubt he'd informed the king and queen and they would be interested in meeting their grandchildren. It would be an overwhelming day for the girls and Olivia wanted to prepare them.

"Today you are going to meet many new people," she told them. "I know you might be scared, but you don't need to be."

"A party?"

"Sort of." If that was what it took to keep the twins from being afraid, then so be it.

"A birthday party?"

"No."

"Mommy said."

Bethany's mention of their mother reminded the girls that she was dead. Olivia saw Karina's lip quiver and rushed to distract them.

"Are you this old?" She held up two fingers and was rewarded with head shakes.

"We're this old." Bethany held up one finger.

"But you're too big to be one. I'll bet you have a birthday coming up soon."

"Get pony," Bethany said with a definitive nod.

Olivia rather doubted that, but clever of her to try to sound convincing. "I'm not sure you're old enough for a pony."

Karina spoke for the first time. "Puppy."

That seemed more doable.

"Pony," Bethany repeated. "Mommy said."

"There might be a pony in the stables," Olivia said, aware she was already caving to their demands. She hadn't pictured herself the sort of mother to give in to her child's every whim.

Bethany nodded in satisfaction. "Let's go."

"No." Karina shook her head. "Puppy."

"Oh, no. It's too early to go to the stables. We have to get dressed and have breakfast. Then we have to get you settled in your own room."

"No." Karina's large green eyes brimmed with anxiety.

Immediately Olivia realized what was wrong. "It's okay," she assured them. "The mean lady is gone. You will have really nice people taking care of you."

"Stay here." Bethany had an imperious tone well suited to a princess.

"I'm afraid you can't do that."

"Why not?"

"This is my bed and you two take up way too much room."

"Slept with Mommy."

Somehow they'd circled back to Marissa again. Olivia held her breath as she watched for some sign that they would get sad again, but the girls had discovered the mattress had great springs and they started bouncing and laughing.

Olivia watched them, amusement taking the edge off her exasperation. The challenges confronting her were coming faster than she'd expected. She wasn't just going to become a wife and a princess, but now she was going to take on the role of mother, as well. Not that she couldn't handle all of it. Maybe it was just her sleepless night and her anxiety about marrying a man who might not be over his dead former lover.

While the girls jumped off the bed and raced around the room, looking out the window and exploring the attached bathroom, Olivia heard a soft knock. Assuming it was Libby, she opened the door. To her intense surprise, Gabriel stood there, looking handsome and elegant in a charcoal pinstripe suit, white shirt and burgundy tie.

"I hope it's not too early," he said, entering the room. His gaze slid over her hair and silk-clad body.

Several maids followed, one pushing a cart loaded down with covered plates. Delicious smells wafted in their wake.

Olivia smoothed her hair, acutely aware of her makeup-free face, knowing she wasn't looking her best after such a rough night. She hadn't even brushed her teeth yet.

"No, of course not. You're eager to meet the girls."

"I am." His gaze went past her shoulder, golden eyes intense and a little wary.

Olivia's heart gave a little start as she realized he must be thinking about their mother. Chest tight, she shifted her attention to the twins. "Bethany. Karina. Come meet…" She wasn't sure how to introduce the prince.

Gabriel supplied the description. "Your father."

Beside him, Gabriel felt Olivia tense in surprise. In the hours since leaving her room, he'd contemplated what the best political move would be regarding his daughters and decided he didn't give a damn about the fallout. He intended to claim them.

Olivia held out her hands to the girls and they went toward her. She introduced them one by one, starting with the little girl on her right. "This is Bethany. And this is Karina."

Gabriel could discern no difference between their features. "How can you tell?"

"Bethany is the talkative one."

Neither one was verbal at the moment. They stood side by side wearing matching nightgowns and identical blank stares.

Deciding he would appear less intimidating if he was at their eye level, Gabriel knelt. "Nice to meet you." As much as he longed to snatch them into his arms and hug the breath from their bodies, he kept his hands to himself and gave them his gentlest smile.

The one Olivia had introduced as Bethany eyed him suspiciously for a moment before declaring, "We're hungry." Her imperious tone made her sound like his mother.

"What would you like for breakfast?" he asked them. "We have eggs, pancakes, French toast."

"Ice cream."

"Not for breakfast," he countered.

Olivia made no effort to hide her amusement. Her grin and the laughter brimming in her blue eyes transformed her from an elegant beauty to a vivacious woman. Gabriel felt his eyebrows go up as her charisma lit up the room.

"Wit' chocolate."

Bethany's demands forced Gabriel to refocus his attention. "Maybe after lunch." He'd met some tough negotiators in his time, but none had shown the sort of determination exhibited by his daughters. "If you eat everything on your plate."

"Want ice cream."

"How about waffles with syrup?" He tried softening his words with a smile. The twins weren't moved.

"Olivia." Bethany's plaintive, wheedling tone was charming, and Gabriel found himself struggling to restrain a grin.

"No." Olivia shook her head. "You listen to your father. He knows what's best." She gently propelled the girls toward the table the maid had set for breakfast and got them into chairs. "There aren't any booster chairs so you'll have to kneel. Can you do that?"

The twins nodded and Gabriel pulled out the chair between them, gesturing for Olivia to join them, but she shook her head.

"You should spend some time alone with them. I'm going to shower and get dressed." With one last smile for the twins, she headed toward the bathroom.

As the door shut behind her, Gabriel turned his full attention to the toddlers. "Have you decided what you want to eat?"

Their green eyes steady on him, they watched and waited for some sign that he was weakening. Gabriel crossed his arms over his chest and stared back. He was not going to be outmaneuvered by a pair of toddlers.

"Pancakes."

The word broke the standoff and Gabriel gestured the maid forward to serve pancakes. Having little appetite, he sipped coffee and watched them eat, seeing Marissa in their gestures and sassy attitude.

The girls ate two large pancakes before showing signs of slowing down and Gabriel was marveling at their appetite when the bathroom door opened and Olivia emerged. Her long blond hair framed her oval face in soft waves and she'd played up her blue eyes with mascara and brown eye shadow. She wore a simple wrap dress in seafoam that accentuated her tiny waist and the subtle curves of her breasts and hips. Nude pumps added four inches to her five-foot-six-inch frame and emphasized the sculpted leanness of her calves.

Gabriel felt the kick to his solar plexus and momentarily couldn't breathe. Her beauty blindsided him. Desire raged in his gut. He hadn't expected to feel like this when he proposed. She'd been elegant, poised and cool, inspiring his admiration and appreciation.

In a month she would be legally his. But he was no longer content to wait until his wedding night to claim her. Such had been the heat of his desire for her last night that if the twins hadn't occupied her bed, he would have made love to her.

The strength of his desire gave him a moment's pause. Wasn't this feeling what he'd hoped to avoid when he chose her? Craving something beyond reason was what had gotten him into trouble with Marissa. But desire wasn't love and didn't have to become obsession. He should feel a healthy desire for his future wife. Surely, he could prevent himself from getting in too deep with her and repeating his past mistakes.

He'd sunk into a black depression after his breakup with Marissa. Knowing they couldn't have a future together hadn't prevented him from letting himself be lured into love. He'd come through the other side of losing Marissa, but the fight to come back from that dark place wasn't something he wanted to go through ever again.

"Coffee?" he asked, shoving aside his grim reflections.

He just needed to be certain that he kept a handle on his growing fascination with her. He'd lost his head over Marissa and look what it got him. Two beautiful, but illegitimate, daughters.

"Yes." she gave a little laugh, seeming more relaxed with him than ever before. "I'm afraid I'm in desperate need of the caffeine this morning."

"Rough night?"

"The couch is not as comfortable as it is beautiful."

"Did you get any sleep?"

"Maybe an hour or so." She dished up scrambled eggs, fruit and a croissant. She caught him watching her and gave him a wry smile. "Your pastry chef is sublime. I will need plenty of exercise to avoid becoming fat."

"Perhaps after we speak to my parents about the girls we could take a walk in the garden."

"That would be nice, but I don't think there's time. My schedule is packed with wedding preparations."

"Surely if I can let the country run without my help for half an hour you can delegate some of the wedding preparations to your private secretary. We haven't really had a chance to get acquainted, and with our wedding less than a month away, I thought we should spend some time alone together."

"Is that a command, Your Highness?"

He arched an eyebrow at her playful tone. "Do you need it to be?"

"Your mother is the one who determined my schedule."

Suspecting his fiancée needed no help standing up to the queen, he realized she was chiding him for his neglect during her first week in Sherdana. "I'll handle my mother."

"A walk sounds lovely."

"Go see pony," Bethany declared, shattering the rapport developing between the adults.

"Pony?" Gabriel echoed, looking to Olivia for an explanation.

"Apparently Bethany wants a pony for her birthday. I told her she was too young, but I thought maybe there was a pony in the stables they could visit."

"None that I know of." He saw the bright expectation in their faces vanish and couldn't believe how much he wanted to see them smile again. "But I could be wrong."

He made a mental note to have Stewart see about getting a pair of ponies for the girls. He and all his siblings had all started riding as soon as they could sit up. Ariana was the only one who still rode consistently, but Gabriel enjoyed an occasional gallop to clear his mind after a particularly taxing session of cabinet.

"Do you ride?" he asked Olivia.

"When I visit our country house."

A knock sounded on the door. Olivia's private secretary appeared, Stewart following on her heels. They wore duplicate expressions of concern and Gabriel knew the morning's tranquillity was about to end.

"Excuse me a moment." He crossed the room and pulled Stewart into the hall. "Well?"

"The king and queen are on their way here."

He'd hoped to be the one to break the news to his parents. "How did they find out?"

"The arrival of two little girls in the middle of the night didn't go unnoticed," Stewart told him. "When your mother couldn't find you she summoned me."

"So, you felt the need to spill the whole story."

"The king asked me a direct question," Stewart explained, not the least bit intimidated by Gabriel's low growl. "And he outranks you."

"Gabriel, there you are. I demand to see my granddaughters at once." The queen sailed down the hallway in his direction, her husband at her side. Lines of tension bracketed the king's mouth. After nearly forty years as a queen, nothing disturbed her outward calm. But discovering her son had fathered two illegitimate girls was more stress than even she could graciously handle.

"They've been through a lot in the last few days," Gabriel told her, thinking she would upset the twins in her current state of agitation.

"Have you told Olivia?"

"Last night." He held up a hand when his mother's eyes widened in outrage. "They spent the night with her after she stumbled upon them fleeing their nanny."

The king's light brown eyes had a hard look as they settled on his son. "And how does your future bride feel about it?"

As diplomatic as his parents were with the outside world, when it came to family, they were blunt. It wasn't like them to dance around a question. Of course, they'd never come up against something this enormous before.

"What you want to know is if she intends to marry me despite my having fathered two children I knew nothing about."

"Does she?"

The king's deep frown made Gabriel rein in his frustration. As much as he disliked having his carelessness pointed out, he had let passion overwhelm him to the exclusion of common sense. Marissa had made him wild. She was like no other woman he'd ever met. And because of that their relationship had made his parents unhappy.

Gabriel exhaled harshly. "So far it appears that way."

"Does her father know?" the king asked.

"Not yet. But the girls are living in the house. It won't be long before the truth comes out."

His mother looked grim. "Will Lord Darcy back out on the deal?"

"Olivia doesn't think so. He wants his daughter married to royalty."

"Have you figured out what we're going to say to the press?"

"That they're my daughters," Gabriel said. "We'll send out a press release. Anything else would be a mistake. Olivia noticed the resemblance immediately. They look exactly like Ariana did at that age. Coming clean is a good offensive and hopefully by doing so we can minimize the scandal."

"And if we can't?"

"I'll ride it out."

"We'll ride it out," the king said.

"Have you considered that Olivia might not want to raise Marissa's children?"

Gabriel had already entertained those doubts, but after what he'd seen of Olivia, he'd discovered layers that might surprise everyone. "I don't think that will be an issue. She's already very protective of them and they trust her."

The queen sighed and shook her head. "It *will* be wonderful having children in the palace again. Let's go see your girls."

Four

Olivia was standing with her hands relaxed at her sides as the door opened to admit the king and queen. Libby had warned her they were coming and she'd made sure the girls' hands and faces were clean. The arrival of more unfamiliar people had revived the toddlers' shyness and they hid behind Olivia.

"This is your father's mother," Olivia explained to them, using gentle pressure to nudge them into the open. "She's come to meet you."

Karina shook her head, but Bethany peered at her grandmother. The queen stopped dead at the sight of the girl and reached out a hand to her husband.

"Gabriel, you were right. They look exactly like your sister at that age." She took a seat nearby and gestured Bethany toward her. "What is your name?"

To Olivia's delight Bethany went to the queen.

She stopped just out of arm's reach and studied the queen. "I'm Bethany."

"It's nice to meet you." The queen looked toward her sister. "And what is your name?"

Bethany answered again. "Karina."

"How old are they?" the king asked.

"They'll be two in a few weeks," Gabriel answered.

"Puppy." Karina had finally spoken.

"I have a puppy you can meet. Would you like that?"

The queen smiled as Karina nodded. "Mary," the queen said to the maid who'd brought the twins' clothes from upstairs. "Go get Rosie." The Cavalier King Charles spaniel loved people, especially children, and was a great deal calmer than the queen's vizsla.

In five minutes the maid was back with the dog and both twins were laughing as Rosie licked their cheeks. "Gabriel, why don't you and Olivia make yourself scarce for a while. I'll see the girls are settled."

Recognizing an order when she heard one, Olivia let Gabriel draw her from the bedroom and down the stairs.

"Let's get out of here while we can," he murmured, escorting her through a side door and into the garden.

The late May morning had a slight edge of coolness, but when he offered to send someone upstairs for a sweater, Olivia shook her head.

"Let's walk in the sunshine. I'll warm up fast enough."

He took her hand and tucked it into the crook of his arm. Olivia gave herself up to the pleasure of his strong body brushing against her side as they strolled along the crushed granite pathways.

"Thank you for all you've done with the girls," he said.

"It breaks my heart that they'll grow up without their mother, but I'm glad they have you."

"You never knew yours, did you? She died when you were born?"

She'd never told him that. "I guess we both did our research."

"I've treated our engagement like a business arrangement. For that I'm sorry."

"Don't be. I knew what I was getting into." She heard a touch of cynicism in her tone and countered it with a wry smile.

Gabriel didn't smile back. "I don't think you have any idea what you're getting into."

"That sounds intriguing." Olivia waited for more, but the prince didn't elaborate.

"Starting now I intend to learn everything there is to know about you."

While she was sure he meant to flatter her with the declaration, Olivia froze in momentary panic. What if he found out she hadn't come clean about her past fertility issues? Even with the problem solved, he might be angry that she hadn't disclosed such an important fact.

"A girl needs to keep a little mystery about herself," she countered, gazing up at him from beneath her lashes. "What if you lost interest once you discovered all my secrets?"

"It never occurred to me that you'd have secrets," he murmured, half to himself.

"What woman doesn't?"

"I'd prefer it if we didn't keep secrets from each other."

"After the surprise you received last night, I understand why. So, what would you like to tell me?"

"Me?"

Olivia congratulated herself on turning the conversation back on him. "Getting to know each other was your idea. I thought you'd like to show me how it's done."

Gabriel's eyes gleamed with appreciation. "What would you like to know?"

"Why did you pick me?"

"Your passion for issues relating to children and your tireless determination to make their lives better." Gabriel stopped and turned her to face him. "I knew you would be exactly the sort of queen my country would love."

As his words sank in she stared at the pond, watching the ducks paddle across the still water. "Your country."

At times like this it amused her to think of how many girls longed to be her. If they knew what her life was like, would they still want that? Marriage to a prince might seem like a fairy tale come true, but did they understand the sacrifices to her privacy or the responsibility she would bear?

But marriage into Sherdana's royal family would offer her the opportunity to focus on things near and dear to her heart and to advocate for those who needed help, but who had no one to turn to. Earlier in the week she'd had an opportunity to speak with a local hospital administrator about the need for a more child-friendly space to treat the younger patients. The woman had a lot of ideas how to change the children's ward to make a hospital stay easier on the children as well as their families.

Olivia was excited about the opportunities to help. Sherdana would find her an enthusiastic promoter of solutions for at-risk and underprivileged children. She was proud of the money she'd raised in London and loved the hours she'd spent visiting with children in the hospitals. Their courage in fighting their illnesses always inspired her. She intended to inspire others to help.

As Sherdana's princess and future queen, she would be in the perfect position to bring children's issues to the forefront of public awareness.

"I will do my best to never let your country down."

"I knew you'd say that."

Her knees trembled as he slid his hand beneath her hair, fingertips drawing evocative circles on her nape.

Cupping her cheek in his palm, Gabriel turned her head until their eyes met. Her heart skipped a beat. He wanted her. The expanding warmth in her midsection told her so and she basked in the certainty.

His gaze held her entranced until the second before his lips skimmed hers. Wrenched free of anticipation, relief rushed through her like a wildfire. A groan built in her chest as his tongue traced the seam of her lips. Welcoming the masterful stroke of his tongue into her mouth, she leaned into him, pressing her breasts against his chest, needing his hands to cup their weight and drive her mad.

A throat cleared somewhere behind them. "Excuse me, Your Highness."

Gabriel stiffened and tore his mouth free. Chest heaving, he drew his thumb across her lower lip. "We will continue this later," he promised, his voice a husky rasp against her sensitized nerve endings.

"I look forward to it."

She received the briefest of smiles before he turned to face his private secretary. Released from the compelling grip of his gaze, Olivia had a hard time maintaining her composure. The kiss, although cut short, had been everything a woman craved. Passionate. Masterful. A touch wicked. She locked her knees and moderated her breathing while she listened to Gabriel's conversation with his secretary.

Stewart cleared his throat again. "Sorry to interrupt, but the media found out about your daughters and Lord Darcy is meeting with your parents."

Distantly, she became aware that Stewart was filling in Gabriel rapid-fire style about what had been on the television this morning.

"How did they get wind of it so fast?" Gabriel demanded.

Not even the ice in his voice could banish the lingering warmth Olivia felt from his kiss.

Stewart came up with the most obvious source. "The lawyer might have gone to them."

"Unlikely. He had nothing to gain."

"Someone in the palace, then."

"Who knew last night?"

"The maids who were tasked with preparing the nursery," Stewart said. "But they've worked for the palace for over a decade."

Olivia considered the one who'd been straightening her room at two in the morning. The strangeness of it struck her again, but surely the palace staff was carefully screened and the woman had merely been doing as she said.

"The nanny." Olivia knew with a sinking heart that this had to be the source of the leak. "The one I had escorted off the property."

Stewart considered this. "The lawyer assured me she'd been kept in the dark about the twins' parentage."

"But that was before they'd been brought to the palace," Gabriel said.

"I'm sorry," Olivia murmured, aware she'd committed her first huge mistake as Gabriel's fiancée. "I shouldn't have taken it upon myself to remove her."

"She was the wrong caretaker for the girls and you had their best interests at heart." Gabriel offered her a reassuring nod. "Besides, it was going to be impossible to keep the twins hidden for long."

Although she was accustomed to life in the public eye, she'd never been the focus of such frenzied interest on the part of the media, and the upcoming wedding had stirred them like a cane striking a wasp nest.

"If we present a united front," Olivia said, feeling like his partner for the first time, "I'm sure everything will blow over."

Gabriel took her hand and scorched a kiss across her knuckles. "Then that's exactly what we'll do."

Hand in hand, Olivia and Gabriel entered the salon most often used by the family for its proximity to the back garden and the views of the park beyond. They found Christian and Ariana there. Gabriel caught sight of the television and heard the reporter. The amount of information the news channel had gleaned about the twins' arrival late last night revealed that someone inside the house must have been feeding them information. Gabriel went cold as the reporter speculated on whether or not the powerful Sherdana royal family had paid Marissa to go away or if all along she'd hidden her daughters to keep them from being taken away from her.

"They may be painting us as the bad guys," Christian commented, "but at least they're not claiming we're weak."

Gabriel didn't reply to his brother's remark as Marissa's face came on the screen. As the narrator gave a rundown of her career, Olivia moved as if compelled by some irresistible force, stepping closer to the television. Dismay rose in Gabriel as one after another, the photographs of his former lover on the covers of *Vogue, Elle* and *Harper's Bazaar* flashed on the screen. Her legs looked impossibly long. Her face, incredibly beautiful.

Gabriel knew his daughters would be as exquisite. Would they follow in their mother's footsteps and pursue careers in fashion? Photographers would stand in line to take their picture. They'd make an incredible pair. But was that any way for an Alessandro to make a living?

The question forced Gabriel to consider his daughters' place in his household. They were illegitimate. With their mother's death, that situation could never be rectified. An ache built in his chest for Bethany and Karina. At their age they would retain few memories of their mother. They'd never again know her love.

When the television began showing images of Gabriel and Marissa together, laughing, arms around each other, looking happy and very young, he realized Olivia had gone still. Picture after picture flashed on the screen, and many of them weren't paparazzi shots. There were photos taken of them in private at friends' homes, even a couple when they'd vacationed on a private island in the Caribbean.

Gabriel's disquiet grew as Olivia's attention remained

glued to the news footage that recapped his turbulent years with Marissa. Naturally the reporters made their relationship sound more dramatic, the end more tragic than it actually had been.

While he watched, Olivia's private secretary approached her and spoke softly in her ear. She nodded and came to stand before Gabriel.

"My father wishes to speak to me."

"I'll walk with you."

"You should stay and discuss what is to be done now that the story is out."

Her suggestion made sense, but he wasn't sure it was good to let her leave without clearing the air. "I'd like a moment alone to speak with you."

"I have a fitting for my wedding dress at ten. I should be back a little before noon."

Once again their schedules were keeping them apart. "I have a lunch meeting with my education adviser."

"Perhaps Stewart and Libby can find us a moment to connect later this afternoon."

Gabriel wanted to proclaim they should make time, but had no idea what he was committed to for the rest of the afternoon.

"This shouldn't wait until later. Let's go to my office and discuss this situation in private."

"Whatever you wish."

Disliking the polite calm of her tone, he guided her from the room with a hand at the small of her back. Beneath his palm, her spine maintained a steady inflexibility that marked the change in her mood from their earlier interlude.

As pointless as it was to resent the timing of recent events, Gabriel couldn't stop himself from wishing he and Olivia had been given a month or two to form a personal connection before their relationship had been tested to this extent. But that wasn't the case and as he escorted her into his sanctuary and shut the door, he hoped they could weather this storm without sustaining permanent damage.

His office was on the first floor of the palace, not far from the formal reception room. Originally the space had been one of the numerous salons set aside for visiting guests. Five years ago, he'd appropriated it for his own use, tearing down the lavender wallpaper left over from the late 1970s and installing wood paneling and bookshelves that he'd filled with his favorite authors. The room was his sanctuary.

"You're upset."

"Just concerned about the twins." Her quiet voice and dignified demeanor were at odds with the passionate woman who'd melted in his arms a little while ago. Gabriel felt something tighten in his chest. "I think it might be a good idea to have them in the wedding. I thought I would talk to Noelle Dubone. She's creating my wedding dress and I'm sure she would be happy to design matching flower-girl dresses for Bethany and Karina to wear."

Gabriel leaned back so he could stare into her eyes. "Are you sure?"

"Completely. The world knows they're here. Hiding them would be a mistake."

"I agree. I'll speak with my parents about it." He could tell that Olivia's anxiety over the twins' welfare had been sincere, but surmised more than that was bothering her. "The news coverage about my relationship with Marissa—"

At his slight pause she jumped in. "You looked very happy together." She seemed to have more to say, but remained silent.

"We had our moments." Gabriel drew a deep breath. "But much of the time we fought."

"The paparazzi must not have caught any of those moments on film."

She sounded neutral enough, but Gabriel sensed she

wasn't as tranquil as she appeared. "We fought in private." And then made up in spectacular fashion.

His thoughts must have shown on his face because her eyebrows rose.

She moved toward the French doors and looked out. Gabriel stepped to her side. For a moment he wanted nothing more than to take her in his arms and relive the kisses from earlier. The compulsion to be near her tested his composure.

Her gaze slid in his direction. "Passion can be addictive."

How would she know that?

He knew of no serious romances in her life. Her private life was without even a whiff of scandal. No boyfriends. No lovers.

"Do you have firsthand knowledge of this fact?" Lord in heaven, he sounded suspicious. And yet, he couldn't stop himself from probing. "Have you...?" Realizing what he'd almost asked, he stopped speaking.

"Taken a lover?"

Damn the woman, she was laughing. Oh, not outwardly where he could see her mocking smile and take offense. But inwardly. Her eyes sparkled and her voice had developed a distinct lilt. Had his expression betrayed an unanticipated flare of unfounded jealousy? Or was she reacting to the revelation that for all his sources, he knew nothing about her?

Gabriel turned her to face him, but she wouldn't meet his gaze. "Have you?"

"No." She shook her head. "You'll be my first."

Desire exploded as she met his gaze. Wild with satisfaction that she would be completely his, Gabriel lost touch with his rational side. Surrendering to the need to kiss her senseless and show her just how addictive passion could be, he cupped her cheek in his palm, slid his other hand around her waist to hold her captive and brought his lips to hers.

He gave her just a taste of his passion, but even that was enough to weaken his restraint. Breathing heavily, he set his forehead against hers and searched her gaze.

"Your only." He growled the words.

"Of course."

Her matter-of-fact tone highlighted just how fast he'd let his control slip. His hands fell away, but his palms continued to burn with the heat of her skin. He rubbed them together, determined to banish the lingering sensation.

The need to spend some time alone with her had just grown more urgent. He was concerned that the media storm surrounding the arrival of the twins would make her father consider changing his mind about letting his daughter marry Gabriel. No wedding. No biotech plant on the outskirts of Caron, Sherdana's capital. Gabriel needed to hedge his bets with Olivia.

As long as she still wanted to marry him, everything would proceed as planned. He just needed to reassure her that marrying him was a good idea. And he knew the best way to convince a woman had nothing at all to do with logic.

Some private time should do the trick, just the two of them. A chance to present her with a small token of his affection. Thus far her engagement ring was the only jewelry he'd given her. He should have had a gift ready to present on her arrival in Sherdana, but he'd been preoccupied. And if he was honest with himself, he hadn't been thinking of Olivia as his future bride, but as a next step in Sherdana's economic renaissance.

"I'll arrange for us to have a private dinner in my suite."

"I'll look forward to it," Olivia said, her expression unreadable. Gabriel had chosen her partly because of her composure when dealing with reporters and her public persona. Now, he wasn't happy at not being able to read her.

Shortly after she departed, Gabriel summoned Stewart and had him reschedule his morning appointments so Gabriel could meet with his jeweler. Half an hour later, he entered the reception room where Mr. Sordi waited with two cases of sparkling gems. Despite the wide selection, Gabriel wondered if he'd have trouble selecting the perfect piece for his bride-to-be. In the end, he chose the first bracelet that caught his eye, believing the fanciful design of flowers rendered in diamonds and pink sapphires would please her.

Business concluded, he let Stewart show the jeweler out while Gabriel slipped the bracelet into his office safe. He dashed off a quick note to Olivia, inviting her to dinner, and got one of the maids to deliver it. Then he went off to his lunch meeting with his education adviser, but his thoughts were preoccupied with the evening to come.

After a short conversation with her father to assure him that she'd already known about the twins and was perfectly happy that they'd come to live with their father, Olivia went to change her clothes, but ended up standing on the stone terrace outside her room, staring at the garden below. The euphoria of those passionate moments in Gabriel's arms were misty memories.

Olivia's heart sank to her toes. Caught up in the romance of kissing Gabriel in the beautiful garden, she'd been on the verge of doing things in public she'd never even done in private. While on a subconscious level she'd begun to think in terms of love. In reality she was embarking on an arranged marriage.

Being told Gabriel had loved the mother of his children and being confronted by the hard truth of it were very different animals. The pictures playing across the television screen had complicated her emotions. She'd been besieged by thorny questions.

Had he been thinking of Marissa as he kissed her? Had he been wishing that the woman he'd loved wasn't dead? Or that her ancestry had permitted them to be married? Marissa had been every man's fantasy. Vivacious, sexy, breathtakingly beautiful. In her eyes danced promises she might or might not keep. A man could spend a lifetime wondering which way she would go. How could Olivia hope to compete?

She couldn't.

But she wasn't marrying Gabriel because he loved her. She was marrying him because as a princess her voice advocating for children would reach further and she could fulfill her dream of becoming a mother. Her children would be the next generation of Alessandros. Still, it hurt to see the way Gabriel had stared at the screen as his former lover's face was shown in photo after photo. Her heart had ached at the way his expression turn to stone while his eyes looked positively battered.

Suddenly Olivia wasn't sure she could do this. Sucking in a sharp breath, she glanced down at her engagement ring. Sunlight fell across her hand, lighting up the large center diamond like the fireworks at a centennial celebration. She'd come to Sherdana to marry a prince, not a man, but after tasting passion and realizing she wanted more, she didn't think she could settle for marrying a man with a past that still haunted him.

A man still in love with the mother of his illegitimate twin girls.

Maybe this marriage wasn't meant to be.

But so much was riding on it. So many people were counting on the jobs her father's company would bring to Sherdana. And the wedding was less than a month away. She had a fitting for her dress in less than an hour. Olivia stared at the slim gold watch on her arm, her mother's watch.

A short time later, Olivia stepped out of the car that had driven her and Libby to the small dress shop in Sherdana's historic city center. She'd pushed aside her heavy heart, averse to dwelling on something over which she had no control. She was her father's daughter. Raised as a pragmatist, she knew it was impractical to indulge in pretty dreams of falling in love with her prince and living happily ever after.

The shop door chimed as Olivia entered. Wide windows provided a great deal of light in the small but elegant reception room. The walls had been painted pale champagne to complement the marble floors. There was a gold damask-covered sofa flanked by matching chairs in the front room. The glass-topped coffee table held a portfolio of Noelle Dubone's previous work. Some of her more famous clients were not featured in the book, but on the walls. Stars, models, heiresses, all wearing Noelle's gorgeous gowns.

Almost before the door shut behind them, Noelle was on hand to greet her. The designer offered Olivia a warm smile and a firm handshake.

"Lady Darcy, how delightful to see you again."

Noelle had a lilting Italian accent. Although Sherdana shared borders with both France and Italy, it had chosen Italian as its official national language. With her dark hair and walnut-colored eyes, Noelle's lineage could have gone back to either country, but from earlier conversations Olivia knew the designer's ancestry could be traced back to the 1500s. Noelle might not be one of Sherdana's nobility, but the church kept excellent records.

"It's good to see you, as well," Olivia said, warming to the willowy designer all over again. Choosing to have a dress made by Noelle had been easy in so many ways. Although her London friends had counseled Olivia to go with a more famous designer and have an extravagant gown made, Olivia had decided she much preferred Noelle's artistry. Plus Noelle was Sherdanian. It made political sense for Olivia to show her support of the country where she would soon be a princess, especially taking into consideration how hard-hit Sherdana's economy had been in the past few years.

"I have your dress waiting in here." Noelle showed Olivia into a dressing room.

For her more famous clients, Noelle often traveled for fittings. She would have brought the dress to the palace if Olivia had requested. But Olivia liked the shop's cozy feel and wasn't eager to entertain anyone's opinion but her own.

The dress awaiting her was as beautiful as she remembered from the sketches. It had stood out among the half dozen Noelle had shown her six months ago; in fact, the rendering had taken her breath away.

With the help of Noelle's assistants, Olivia donned the dress. Facing the three-way mirror, she stared at her reflection, and was overcome with emotion. It was perfect.

From the bodice to her thighs, the dress hugged the lean curves of her body. Just above her knees it flared into a full skirt with a short train. Made of silk organza, embroidered with feathery scrolls over white silk, the gown's beauty lay in its play of simple lines and rich fabrics. Although Noelle had designed the dress to be strapless, Olivia had requested some sort of small sleeve and the designer had created the illusion of cap sleeves by placing two one-inch straps on either shoulder.

"What are planning to do for a veil?" Noelle asked.

"The queen is lending me the tiara she wore on her wedding day," Olivia said. "I'm not sure I want to use a veil with it."

"Good. When I designed the dress, I didn't picture it with a veil." Noelle stepped back to admire her handiwork.

"You have lost a little weight since we measured you. The waist needs to be taken in a little."

Olivia turned sideways to peer at the way the short train looked behind her. "I will try not to gain before the wedding."

For the next hour, Noelle and her staff worked on minor alterations to the fit. While Olivia thought the dress fit well enough that she could have worn it as is, Noelle was obviously a perfectionist.

"I have another project that I'd like to talk to you about," Olivia said as Noelle handed off the dress to her assistant.

Ever since arriving, she'd been thinking about including the twins in the wedding. While Gabriel seemed okay with the idea, she wasn't sure how his family would react, but after this morning's media coverage of the girls' arrival at the palace, hiding them from public scrutiny would be impossible and counterproductive.

"Come into my office," Noelle said. "Tell me what you have in mind."

Sipping the coffee Noelle's assistant had provided, Olivia contemplated the best way to begin, then decided to just dive in.

"Did you happen to see the news this morning?"

"About Prince Gabriel's daughters?" Noelle pressed her lips together. "The royal family hasn't given them much fodder for stories in the last few years. I'm afraid the level of coverage on this particular item so close to your wedding is just too huge for them to use restraint."

"Dealing with the media comes with the territory," Olivia said. "You'd know that."

Noelle looked startled for a second. "I only design for the stars," she demurred. "I'm not one of them myself."

"You are making a name for yourself. Don't be surprised when you become as big a story as your clients."

"I hope that doesn't happen. I like my quiet little life."

Noelle's gaze touched a silver frame on her desk. It held the photo of a small dark-haired boy. The angle didn't offer a very good view of his face, but Olivia could tell from Noelle's expression that he was very special to her.

"Is he your son?"

"Yes. Marc. He was two in that picture. The same age as the prince's daughters."

Olivia felt a clenching low in her abdomen. A cry from her empty womb. "He's beautiful. How old is he now?"

"Almost four."

Olivia didn't ask about the boy's father. She knew Noelle wasn't currently married and wasn't sure if the question would arouse difficult memories.

"I would like to include Prince Gabriel's daughters in the wedding and want you to make dresses for them."

"I'll work on some sketches and send them over to the palace. Did you have a color in mind?"

"White with pale yellow sashes. To match Princess Ariana's gown." The color suited the dark-haired princess and would her nieces, as well.

"I'll get to work immediately."

At the sound of a light knock, both women looked toward the door. Noelle's assistant hovered on the threshold.

"I just wanted to let you know that there are media outside."

Although the announcement of her engagement to Gabriel had briefly made Olivia newsworthy in England, the future princess of a small country hadn't interested the British press for long.

In Sherdana, however, it was a different story. She'd found the citizens were very curious about her. When she'd visited three months ago, she'd been besieged by requests for interviews and followed wherever she went. Numerous public appearances had filled her daily schedule from ribbon-cutting ceremonies to attending sessions of parliament.

But when Olivia emerged into Noelle's reception room, she understood the assistant's concern. At least a hundred people crowded the streets, most of them armed with cameras. Surely not all these people were reporters. David, her driver, and Antonio, the enormous man Gabriel had assigned to accompany her whenever she was out in public, had called in five others from palace security to create a corridor of safety between the front door of the wedding shop and the car.

Olivia shot Libby a look. "I think life as I knew it has come to an end." Then she turned to Noelle. "Thank you for everything. The dress is perfect."

"You're welcome."

Squaring her shoulders, Olivia put on her public face and stepped toward the front door. Noelle held it open for her with a whispered, *"Bon courage."*

"Olivia, how are you dealing with the discovery of the prince's illegitimate children?"

"Lady Darcy, can you tell us if the wedding is still on?"

"How do you feel about raising another woman's children?"

"Do you think the prince would have married Marissa if he'd been able?"

The questions rained down on Olivia as she headed for the car, smiling and waving as she walked, but responding to none. She slipped each query into its own special cubbyhole for later retrieval and didn't realize she was holding her breath until the car had pulled away from the curb. Libby watched her in concern.

"I'm fine."

"You look...unhappy."

"I'm just tired. The twins slept in my bed and I wasn't able to get comfortable on the couch. That's all."

The excuse pacified her secretary and gave Olivia the space to sort through the highs and lows of the last twenty-four hours. While she wasn't naive enough to think that Gabriel was marrying her for anything other than business, Olivia had hoped that he'd grow fond of her. But while they'd kissed in the garden, she'd let herself believe that their future could be filled with passion and romance.

The photos of him with Marissa that the media had broadcast this morning had been a wake-up call. That was love. Olivia stared out the window at the old town slipping past.

She needed time to adjust to sharing him with a ghost.

Five

When Olivia returned to her room after the fitting, she discovered an invitation and a small, slender box wrapped in ribbon. Heart pounding, she opened the envelope and recognized Gabriel's strong handwriting.

A quiet dinner, just the two of them. In his suite. She clutched the stationery to her chest and breathed deep to calm her sudden attack of nerves. Except for the brief time last night and this morning, they hadn't been alone together. Did he intend to seduce her? Olivia certainly hoped so, but what did she wear to her deflowering? Something demure that matched her level of experience in all things sexual? Something that bared her skin and invited his touch?

Her fears that he didn't find her attractive had melted beneath the heat of this morning's kiss. But he was accustomed to women with far more experience than she possessed. Apprehension made her nerves buzz like a swarm of angry hornets.

Leaving her worries to sort themselves out, she tugged at the ribbon holding the box closed. The pale blue silk fell away. Her fingers brushed the hinged lid as she savored the anticipation of her first gift from Gabriel. From the box's shape, she knew it was a bracelet.

Olivia took a deep breath and opened the lid. Lying on a bed of black velvet was a stunning free-form emerald an inch and a half wide and almost two inches long that dominated the design. The rest of the band was diamonds, set in a diamond-shaped pattern. Bold and contemporary, it wasn't the sort of thing she'd wear, being a little too trendy, but she couldn't fault Gabriel's taste.

Ignoring a pang of disappointment that he'd chosen something so not her taste, she draped the wide cuff over her wrist. As she admired the sparkle, she couldn't shake a nagging sense of familiarity. It was a unique piece, something one-of-a-kind, yet she was certain she'd seen it before. But where? The answer eluded her and she set aside her musings as Libby arrived and helped Olivia decide on the perfect outfit to highlight Gabriel's extravagant gift.

Around midafternoon she went up to the nursery and found the twins eager to visit the stables. But she listened with only half her attention as Bethany chattered on the short walk to the stables. Olivia was having a hard time thinking about anything except her dinner with Gabriel and the hope that they could forget all about Marissa and begin their lives together. Comparing herself to Gabriel's former lover would only lead to trouble down the road. She'd be smarter to put that energy into keeping Gabriel's mind fixed on the present.

While a pair of grooms took Bethany and Karina to look at the ponies their father had ordered to be delivered to the stable, Olivia drifted along the barn's center aisle, stroking a soft nose here and there, lost in a pleasant daydream. The soothing sounds of the barn wrapped her in a cocoon of stillness that allowed her ample privacy to relive the moments in the garden that morning.

Her blood heated and slowed, flowing into the sensitive area between her thighs that Gabriel's fervent kiss had awakened earlier. She leaned her back against a stall and closed her eyes to better relive the delicious caress of his hands against her back and hips. Her breasts had ached for his possession. She'd never felt anything like the powerful craving his kiss aroused. She'd been seconds away from begging him to touch her everywhere. He'd been her master. Her teacher. And she, a very willing student.

The memories disturbed the smooth rhythm of her breathing. How was it possible that just thinking of Gabriel aroused her?

"Are you okay?"

Olivia's eyes snapped open. A groom peered at her, concern in his brown eyes.

She offered a weak smile, feeling heat in her cheeks, put there by her sensual daydreams. Had she really been standing in the middle of a barn, imagining how it would feel to have Gabriel's large, strong hands roaming over her bare skin?

"Fine." The word came out a little garbled. What magic had he wrought to make her forget her surroundings so completely? "I'm fine."

From outside came the twins' high-pitched voices lifted in childish delight. Olivia pushed away from the wall and went in search of them. In the stable yard, beneath the watchful eyes of the grooms who'd taken charge of them, they each stood on a mounting block in order to better acquaint themselves with their new pony.

Olivia fought anxiety as she watched the girls, but soon she calmed down. These ponies had obviously been chosen for their placid demeanor; otherwise the excited movements of the twins would have startled them. The geldings were well matched in size, color and markings. Bethany's had a long, narrow blaze that stretched from forehead to right between his nostrils. Karina's had a wider stripe of white that spread out as it reached the nose. Both ponies had two white front socks and one back.

Bethany was the first to notice Olivia. She threw her

arms around the pony's neck and said in an excited voice. "Look at my horse. Her name is Grady."

Olivia started to correct Bethany on the gender of her new pony, but Karina jumped in before she could speak.

"Peanut." The quieter twin looked so delighted that Olivia wondered if she would still demand a puppy for her birthday.

"They're lovely," Olivia said. "But I think they're both boys."

The girls were too excited to listen and went back to petting and chattering to their ponies. The head groom came over to where Olivia stood.

"They will make fine horsewomen."

"I believe you're right."

"Would you like to see the mount His Highness chose for you?"

It had never occurred to Olivia that she would receive a horse as well when she told Gabriel how she loved to ride whenever she spent time at Dansbrooke. The park around the palace wasn't as extensive as the lands surrounding her family's country estate, but she welcomed the opportunity to get whatever exercise she could.

"I'd love to see him." She laughed. "Or her."

"It's a mare. A Dutch Warmblood. I heard you've done some eventing. You'll find Arioso is a wonderful jumper and an eager athlete."

The beautiful chestnut had large, soft eyes and a gentle disposition, but before she had time to do more than stroke the mare's long neck, the twins had finished with their ponies and joined her at the stall.

Deciding they'd had enough for one day, Olivia gathered them together and bid the grooms goodbye. After depositing them with a pair of maids in the nursery, she returned to her room to bathe and dress.

Olivia took a long time preparing for the evening. She

played with hairstyles for an hour before settling on a softly disheveled updo that required only a couple of pins to keep it in place. The gown she'd chosen was a simple black sheath that bared her arms and appeared demure in the front but dipped low in the back.

Anticipation began to dissolve her calm as she zipped up the dress and fastened simple diamond dangles to her earlobes. Boldly eschewing panty hose, she slid her feet into elegant patent leather pumps.

She wanted everything about her to say "touch me."

And surveying her appearance in the full-length mirror, Olivia felt confident she'd done just that. That left only one more thing to do. Olivia popped the top on the jewelry box and laid the wide bracelet across her wrist. Libby helped by securing the clasp.

"Is this all for my brother's benefit?" Ariana had slipped into the room after a soft knock.

Olivia felt her cheeks heating. "Do you think he'll approve?"

Ariana smiled. "How could he not?" Her gaze slipped over Olivia, stopping at the diamond-and-emerald bracelet. She reached for Olivia's hand, as the color drained from her face. "Where did you get that?"

"Gabriel sent it to me." Concern rose in Olivia. Why was Ariana looking as if she'd seen a ghost? "Why? Do you recognize it?"

"Gabriel sent it?" Ariana echoed. She shook her head. "I don't understand."

"You recognize it?" Olivia felt her heart hit her toes. "It's cursed, isn't it?"

"You might say that."

"Tell me."

"It's none of my business."

There was no way she was letting Ariana get away

without an explanation. "If there's something wrong, I need to know."

"Really, I shouldn't have said anything." Ariana backed toward the bedroom door. "I'm sure everything is fine."

It wasn't like Ariana to hedge, especially when it came to things that distressed her. And seeing the bracelet had obviously upset the princess.

"What do you mean everything is fine? Why wouldn't it be? What aren't you telling me about the bracelet?"

Olivia caught Ariana's wrist in a tight grip. Startled, the brunette looked from the hand holding her, to the bracelet on Olivia's wrist and finally met her gaze.

"I don't want to upset you."

"And you think that's going to persuade me to let you walk out of here without spilling the truth?" Olivia tugged her future sister-in-law toward the wingback chairs flanking the fireplace. She didn't let go until Ariana sat down. "Tell me what about the bracelet upset you."

Releasing an audible sigh, the princess leveled her pale gold eyes on Olivia. "The last time I saw that bracelet was the night before Gabriel broke things off with Marissa."

Pain lanced through Olivia, sharper than anything she'd experienced this morning as she'd watched the pictures of Gabriel and Marissa on the television.

"He bought it for her."

"Yes. It was…for their second anniversary."

The cool platinum burned like acid against Olivia's skin. She clawed at the clasp, blood pounding in her ears. Her excitement over having dinner alone with Gabriel vanished, replaced by wrenching despair. The first gift he'd given her had been the bracelet he'd bought to celebrate two years with Marissa?

The clasp popped open beneath her nails. Olivia dropped it on the mantle and sat in the chair opposite

Ariana, unsure how much longer her shaky legs would support her.

"How did he get it back?"

"I don't know. Maybe she returned it when they broke up."

Olivia felt sick. It was bad enough that Gabriel had given her the trinket he'd bought for another woman, it was worse that it was a returned gift. "I thought I'd seen it before," she murmured.

Ariana leaned forward and placed her hand over Olivia's. "I'm sure this is all a huge misunderstanding. Maybe I'm thinking of a different bracelet."

Olivia drew comfort from Ariana for a moment, before sitting up straight and bracing her shoulders. "The only misunderstanding is mine. I thought tonight was supposed to be the beginning of something between us." She offered Ariana a bitter smile. "I forgot that our marriage is first and foremost a business arrangement."

"I don't believe that's true. I saw the way Gabriel watched you this morning. He was worried by how you reacted to the press coverage of the twins' arrival and all the scandal it stirred up."

"He's worried about losing the deal with my father."

"Yes, but there's more to it than that. He had other opportunities to secure Sherdana's economic future. He chose you."

Ariana's words rang with conviction, but Olivia shook her head. The sight of the bracelet made her long to hurl it into the deepest ocean. She felt betrayed and yet she had no right. She was marrying Gabriel because he was handsome and honorable and she would one day become a queen. Her reasons for choosing him were no more romantic than his.

"Ask him to tell you about the first time you met."

"The party at the French embassy?" Olivia recalled

his stiff formality and their brief, stilted conversation, so different from their exchange in the garden this morning.

"Before that."

Olivia shook her head. "We didn't meet before that."

"You did. You just don't remember."

How was that possible? Every time he drew near, her stomach pitched and her body yearned for his touch. His lips on hers turned her into an irrational creature of turbulent desires and rollicking emotions. If they'd met, she'd have recognized the signs.

"Your brother is very memorable," she argued. "I'm certain you are mistaken."

Ariana's eyes glowed. "Just ask him."

Abruptly filled with uncertainty, Olivia looked down at her gown and noticed the brush of cool air against her bare back and arms. She'd dressed to entice Gabriel. She'd wanted his hands to go places no man had ventured before. Even after learning that he'd given her a bracelet that once belonged to his former lover, she still wanted him. She ached with yearning. Burned with hungers unleashed by an hour in the bath tracing her naked skin with her fingertips, imagining Gabriel doing the same.

"Damn it." The curse shot out of her and startled Ariana.

"Oh, I've really done it," the princess muttered. "Please don't be mad at Gabriel. That was five years ago. I'll bet he doesn't even remember the bracelet."

Olivia's gaze sharpened into focus as she took in Ariana's miserable expression. "You remembered."

"I'm a woman. I have an artist's eye for detail." Ariana shook her head. "Gabriel is a man. They don't notice things like fashion. Now, if he'd given you a set of antlers off a buck he'd shot, that he'd recall."

Olivia recognized that Ariana was trying to lighten her mood, but the damage had been done. She wasn't half as angry with Gabriel as she was with herself. For being a fool. For not realizing that she never would have agreed to marry Gabriel unless she was already emotionally engaged.

But it was too late. She was already in too deep. The only thing she could do now was keep her wits about her and not allow herself to be disappointed again.

To his intense shock, Gabriel was second-guessing himself.

As he towel-dried his hair. As he shaved for the second time that day. As he dressed in gray slacks and a black collarless button-down shirt.

All he could think about was what a mistake he'd made with the bracelet he'd chosen for Olivia's first present. As beautiful as the item was, he couldn't help but think she'd appreciate something more romantic with a little history attached.

He was grimly amused with himself. Since when had he devoted this much time and energy to a gift for a woman? In Marissa's case, he'd always zeroed in on the most flamboyant piece available, the more expensive the better, and been richly rewarded for his generosity.

Gabriel slid a watch onto his wrist and checked the time. He had half an hour before Olivia was due to arrive if he wanted to fetch a particular piece from the vault. "I have a quick errand to run," he told Stewart. "If Lady Darcy arrives before I return, serve her a glass of champagne and assure her I won't be long."

With that, he exited his suite and headed to the vault, his mind on the perfect thing to present to his fiancée. It took him exactly ten minutes to find the necklace and return. Stewart was alone when Gabriel returned.

"Dinner is set to be served at eight."

"Perfect." Gabriel had no interest in rushing. At the

same time, he wanted plenty of the evening left over for getting to know Olivia thoroughly. "You ordered all her favorites?"

"Of course." Stewart's head turned at the light knock on the door. "That must be Lady Darcy. I'll let her in, then make myself scarce."

Gabriel grinned, glad she was as eager to begin their evening as he. Stewart went to answer the door. With his pulse kicked into overdrive, Gabriel found himself holding his breath in anticipation. Realizing what he was doing, he exhaled, wondering how long it had been since the idea of spending time alone with a woman had excited him. But Olivia wasn't just any woman.

She aroused him faster and more intensely than anyone since Marissa. To look at her, it made no sense. She was elegant, cool and poised. Not the sort of sultry, lush temptress that turned men's heads. But today he'd discovered an inner core of vibrant, sensual woman hiding within her. The little he'd sampled explained his craving for a more prolonged taste.

A tense conversation was taking place near the door. Gabriel frowned as he spied the petite woman standing in the hall. Not Olivia. Her private secretary. Although curious about the content of their discussion, Gabriel made no attempt to listen in. He would learn what it was about soon enough.

The exchange at the door came to an end. Stewart came toward him, wearing a frown.

"What's wrong?"

"Your Highness." Stewart looked as if an elephant had stepped on his toes. "Lady Darcy has declined your invitation."

Dumbstruck, Gabriel stared at his assistant. Declined his invitation? Outrageous.

He'd anticipated their evening alone and the chance to learn more about her. "Is she ill?"

Stewart hesitated. "I didn't…get that impression."

"What impression did you get?" he demanded, impatient at his secretary's caginess.

Stewart squared his shoulders. "That perhaps she was unhappy…with you."

"With me?" When they'd parted this morning she'd been all dreamy eyes and feminine wiles. What could have possibly happened in the past twelve hours?

Without another word to Stewart, Gabriel exited his suite. Long, determined strides carried him down the hall toward the rooms assigned to Olivia. He barely noticed the maid scurrying out of his way as he passed her. He did, however, notice Ariana stepping out of Olivia's suite.

"Gabriel, what are you doing here?"

"I'm here to collect Olivia for dinner."

Ariana's gold eyes widened. "Didn't you get the message? Olivia's not up to having dinner with you tonight."

He leaned down and pinned his sister with a steely glare, wondering what mischief she had been up to. "What's wrong with her?"

Ariana set her hand on her hip and regarded him with annoyance. "She's not feeling well."

"Then I'd be remiss in not checking on her," Gabriel intoned, sounding as suave as he could through gritted teeth. "Step aside."

But his sister didn't budge. "Leave it tonight, Gabriel," she coaxed. "Give her a little time."

"Time for what?"

"Honestly," his sister fumed. "You can be so insensitive sometimes."

What was he missing? "Enlighten me."

Ariana pressed her lips together, but Gabriel kept up his

unrelenting stare and she finally sighed. "She's had your affair with Marissa thrown in her face all day."

He remembered the expression on Olivia's face while the footage of him and Marissa had played on the television. But he thought they'd cleared the matter up in his office. Why was she letting the past bother her? Gabriel nudged his sister aside and reached for the door handle.

"Gabriel—"

"This is none of your concern. It's between me and my future bride."

"Fine." Ariana tossed up her hands. "But don't say I didn't warn you."

With her dire words ringing in his ears, Gabriel entered Olivia's suite. Some impulse prompted him to slip the lock before scanning the space. His fiancée was not in the bedroom. After his encounter with Ariana, he'd expected to find Olivia sulking over some perceived slight. Then he noticed a slight billowing of the sheer curtains over the French doors leading out onto the terrace.

Olivia stood near the terrace railing staring out over the pond and the park, her gaze on the path where they'd walked and kissed this morning. She wore a black dress that bared her back in a plunging V. She'd knotted her hair on top of her head, exposing the nape of her neck. The sight of all that bare skin did unruly things to his body. He'd always been a sucker for a woman's back, finding the combination of delicacy and strength an intoxicating combination.

Gabriel shoved aside desire and refocused on the reason he'd come here in the first place.

"We're supposed to be having dinner in my suite."

"I don't feel up to it," she replied in a cool tone, not bothering to turn around.

"Then you're not upset."

"Of course not."

He didn't believe her. For the briefest of moments he wondered if she was trying to manipulate him with some feminine trickery. He almost laughed at the notion. Marissa was the only other woman who'd tried to best him with her wiles. He'd quickly set her straight.

Time to set Olivia straight, as well. "I thought this morning you understood that whatever was between Marissa and me has been over for three years."

"What sort of evening did you have in mind for us tonight?" She turned around and faced him and he got his first glimpse of her expression. Genuine anger shimmered in her gaze. "Were we to sip champagne and become lovers or did you plan to educate me on Sherdana's upcoming social and economic challenges?"

What had gotten into her? This morning she'd been like warm honey in his arms. Tonight she'd become an ice sculpture. All this because a few reporters dredged up old news from three years ago?

"I'd hoped we'd spend some time getting to know each other tonight, but I had no intention of rushing you into bed." Tired of sparring with her, he stepped within touching distance. "I thought that we'd reached an understanding this morning."

"So did I," she murmured, the fire fading from her tone.

"Then what's wrong?"

"Our marriage is an arrangement."

"Yes." He grazed his fingertips up her sides from her hips, letting them coast along the side of her breasts. The hitch in her breath told him the fight was over. "But it doesn't have to be all business between us."

"And it isn't," she agreed. "It's just that I'm not really sure what's happening."

So, he wasn't the only one struggling to find his way. Ever since last night, he'd found himself drawn to her as never before, but he wasn't sure she felt it, too. And now that he knew she did, he wasn't about to let her run away from it.

"We have strong sexual chemistry," he told her, and then in a softer voice confessed, "I wasn't expecting that."

Her scent flowed around him, feminine and enticing. As desire began to assert itself, he noticed the details his anger had blinded him to. For a woman intent on denying him her company, she'd dressed with care. He dipped his head and drank in the feminine scent of her. She'd dabbed a light floral perfume behind her ears. His lips found the spot and made her shiver.

"Gabriel, please." Her hand on his chest wasn't going to deter him now that he'd gotten wind of her imminent surrender.

"Please, what?" he inquired. "Stop?"

Knowing it was what she had in mind, he tugged the pins from her hair and tossed them aside. The golden waves spilled around her face and shoulders.

"Yes." But the word lacked conviction.

"You're lying," he pressed. "And badly. This is what you wanted when you dressed tonight." He took her stiff body in his arms and immediately the fight began to drain from her muscles. "My hands on you." He dipped his head and drew his lips across her cheek, finishing his thought with his breath puffing against her ear. "My mouth tasting your skin."

Her body was limp against him now, all resistance abandoned.

"We're meant to be together." He was more convinced of that than ever. "You know it as well as I do."

She'd closed her eyes to hide from him, not realizing how futile her actions were. "Yes."

Six

Without sight, all her other senses came to life. The unsteady rasp of Gabriel's breath told her he too was disturbed by the attraction between them. But was it enough? Hadn't she discovered less than an hour ago that she wanted more from him? So much more.

His fingertips grazed along the sensitive skin inside her arm, from the hollow behind her elbow to the pulse jerking frantically in her wrist. Gently he laced their fingers and began to pull her along the terrace. Her eyes flew open.

"Where?" Her gaze found his and she saw feverish hunger blazing in the bronze depths.

"To bed, of course," he teased, but there was nothing lighthearted about the determined set of his mouth or the tension that rode his muscles. Tension that communicated across the short distance between them.

"What about dinner?"

Inside the suite once more, he drew her close, sliding a hand over her hip to pull her against the hard jut of his erection, and bent to whisper in her ear. "You made me hungry for something besides food."

His lips dropped to hers, lingering at the corner of her mouth for too long. His unproductive nuzzling wasn't getting the job done. She wanted a kiss. A real, hard, deep kiss with no possibility of interruption. Growling low in her throat, she lifted on tiptoe and framed his face with her hands, holding him still while she pressed her mouth to his. Her tongue tested the seam of his lips as she flattened her breasts against Gabriel's broad chest, eager to convey her desire, letting her hunger shine through.

Gabriel captured handfuls of the dress near her shoulder blades and pulled the edges forward and down, baring her torso to the waist. Olivia gasped at the sudden rush of cool air over her breasts.

He slid his hands up over her rib cage until his fingers reached the undersides of her breasts. Smiling with male satisfaction, he cupped her and kneaded slightly.

She arched into the pressure of his hands, offering herself to him. Reaching behind, she found the dress's zipper and slid it down. With a determined stroke of her palms against her hips, the dress pooled at her feet, leaving her wearing nothing but her black pumps and a white lace thong.

He had tracked the progression of the dress to the floor, his gaze sliding over her legs as the falling black fabric bared her to him. Liking the way his nostrils flared at the sight of her nakedness, Olivia stepped out of the dress and kicked it aside.

Pressure built inside her as she hooked her fingers in the thong, determined to rid herself of it, as well. Gabriel's hands covered hers, halting her actions.

"This is your first time." His voice sank into rich, warm tones that did little to equalize her pulse or diminish her hunger. "I want to take this slow."

"I don't."

His lips moved into a predator's smile, slow and lazy. "You'll thank me later."

And with that, he swept her feet off the floor.

Placing her in the center of the big bed, Gabriel stepped back to rid himself of his clothes. Olivia raised herself on her elbows to better catch the unveiling of all that amazing bronze skin. From the little contact she'd had with his body, she knew he was lean and well-muscled, but nothing prepared her for the chiseled perfection of his torso as his shirt buttons gave way. She goggled at the sheer beauty of his broad shoulders and the sculptured magnificence of his chest.

He raised his eyebrows at her obvious curiosity, his hands going to the belt buckle. As he unfastened the top button, he kicked off his shoes. His pants hit the floor, followed by his socks.

He left on his boxers, but Olivia's eyes were drawn to the way they bulged in front. Her obvious curiosity and lack of concern turned him on and sped even more blood to his groin. Making this the most amazing night of her life might prove challenging. She certainly wasn't playing the part of nervous virgin.

He climbed onto the bed.

"What's this?" His finger grazed a black Chinese character in the hollow beside her hip bone and her stomach muscles twitched.

"A tattoo."

His elegant British fiancée had a tattoo? And in a very sexy spot, he might add. He frowned.

"What does it say?"

"Hope." She bent the leg opposite him and braced her foot on the mattress so she could cant her hips toward him. "I got it in college. My one wild act freshman year."

He imagined her baring her body for the needle, sliding down jeans and underwear. And the thought of another man touching her there made him want to roar in outrage.

His emotions must have shown on his face because she rushed to say, "It was done by a woman."

His shoulders relaxed at her words. She was his, or would be soon. And he wasn't the sort of man who cared to share. Living with two brothers had turned him into a possessive madman when anything encroached on what he believed was his.

"In that case, it's very sexy."

She grinned at how grudging his words sounded. It continued to both infuriate and delight him that she was not even remotely close to the type of woman he thought he'd chosen to make the next queen of Sherdana and his wife.

He hadn't anticipated surprises. He'd expected gracefulness and composure, not this wanton creature with her disheveled hair, bare breasts and body marked by the word *hope*. But now that he had her, she turned him inside out with wanting. She fired his imagination and his blood in the span of a heartbeat. Life would not be dull with her.

Which was the problem. He'd had passion once, crazy desire. It had consumed him and compelled him to think with every part of him but the one that mattered for the future king of Sherdana: his head. He didn't need a wife who made him feel out of control. He needed someone sensible, who kept him focused on matters of state.

Yet deep down he knew Olivia would do that.

And then, behind the closed doors of their private suite, she would make him forget everything but the sweet rush of carnal pleasure.

The best of both worlds.

What was there to worry about?

Taking her leg in his hand, he caressed upward from her knee to the place where her thighs came together.

"That's…" Her voice faltered as he slid one finger beneath the scrap of lace hiding her hot, wet center from him. She balled her fists into the coverlet, holding her breath as the tip of his finger grazed her warmth.

"You are incredibly wet," he said, delighted by the quickness of her arousal.

"Stop talking and touch me."

"Like this?" Stripping off her underwear, he did as she

asked, dipping between the folds that concealed her core and riding the river of wetness toward the knot of nerves. He circled it slowly, listening to her pant, smelling the waves of her arousal. Her hips rose off the mattress, pushing into his hand.

Gorgeous.

With her eyes closed, her knuckles whitening as she held on to the bed linens for dear life, she was as deep into the throes of sensual pleasure as any woman he'd ever known. She writhed against his hand, mindless in her pursuit of her ultimate goal. He watched her face, absorbing each tremble and jerk of her body as he carried her closer and closer to orgasm. Her brow knit as she concentrated. He picked up the pace and watched her mouth open, her back arch.

It was the sexiest thing he'd ever seen.

And it was his name that escaped her lips as she climaxed.

Panting, she opened her eyes. "That was incredible."

He grinned. "It gets better."

"Better?" She sounded doubtful. "I can't imagine that it could get better than that."

He loved a challenge. "Hold your opinion for another hour or so."

"An hour?" She stared at him, her eyes wide with uncertainty. "I don't think I could possibly survive that long."

He didn't think he would survive that long, either. But he was determined to try.

Forking his fingers into her hair, he brought his mouth to hers. Desire continued to claw at him, and tasting her eagerness only made it that much harder for him to maintain control.

He wanted to claim her, make her his. The notion that he was the first man to put his hands on her made him wild. The uncivilized part of him that had run wild with

Marissa roared within its cage, demanding to be free. Gabriel turned his back on those impulses.

Making this first time perfect for her was the only thing that mattered. And for him to do that, he must stay in control.

Her hands left the mattress and moved up his sides. Caresses like fire swept over his skin as she explored the contours of his shoulders and back.

His tongue delved between her parted lips, tasting her passion, capturing the soft cries she made as his fingers found her breasts, nails raking lightly over her taut nipples. Her legs tangled with his. Her wet curls dampened his boxers. He rocked against her heat and broke off the kiss to take her nipple in his mouth.

Her head fell back as he suckled her. Cupping her butt in his hand, he guided her undulating rhythm until they were in sync. A groan collected in his chest as her fingers speared beneath the waistband of his boxers and found him.

Olivia gasped at the first contact with Gabriel's erection. The silken feel of his skin. The steel beneath. The sheer size of him made her whimper with fear and excitement. How was she supposed to take all of him inside her?

"It's okay," he murmured, easing her fingers away. Somehow he'd understood what was in her mind. "I'll take it slow. You'll get the chance to get used to me little by little."

"But you aren't little, so little by little isn't how I see this happening," she retorted, twisting one hand free so she could touch him again.

A groan burst from him as she wrapped her hand fully around his length and measured him from tip to base.

He pulled her hand away and pinned it on the pillow by her ear. "It certainly isn't going to happen that way if you don't stop touching me."

"But I like touching you," she countered, lifting up to kiss his chin. She'd been aiming for his lips, but with his chest pressed against hers, she couldn't lift up that high. "Kissing you." She could barely gain the breath she needed for speech as his body slid down hers. "I've been waiting a long time for this."

"Then let's not delay."

Further conversation became impossible as Gabriel kicked off his boxers and slid between her thighs. Olivia felt his erection against her skin and wiggled her hips to entice him to bring their bodies together in the way they both wanted. Her entire focus consisted of this powerful man and the ache only he could satisfy. Despite her inexperience, she knew exactly what she wanted. Gabriel inside her. She needed to be connected to him on that elemental level and she needed it now.

"Gabriel, please," she murmured, her body shuddering as his mouth slipped over her skin, licking, nibbling, kissing. He seemed determined to investigate every inch of her when there was only one place she wanted his attention focused. "Take me."

Her voice broke on the plea. But it had its effect. He kissed her one last time on the hollow beside her hip bone and settled the tip of his shaft at the entrance to her core. The feel of him there was so amazing. She lifted her hips and took him a little way in.

"We'll get there," he murmured, framing her face with his hands.

Surrendering to the ride was part of the excitement. Forcing him to move faster would get her to satisfaction quicker but wasn't the journey worth some patience?

"You're extremely tight." Capturing her lips in a hot, sizzling kiss, Gabriel flexed his hips forward, sliding into her a little deeper. "It will go easier the first time if you relax."

She was a mass of anticipation and tension. How the hell was she supposed to relax? Olivia gripped his wrists and focused on his expression. His rigid facial muscles and intense concentration told her that this slow loving was taking its toll on him, as well.

"I have no idea how to do that." The heavy throb in her womb grew more powerful as she held her breath and waited for him to join with her completely.

His low chuckle sounded near her ear.

"Breathe."

"I can't." Her words were garbled, starved for air.

His teeth nipped her throat and she gasped. Then he was sucking on the spot where he'd administered the love bite, his tongue laving the tender area. Her mouth fell open as an electric charge shot from where he'd placed his mouth to the place where he was claiming her in the most elemental way possible. Her body stretched as he rocked against her again, his movement driving him a little deeper into her.

The sensation was incredible. She focused on the joy of being filled by him and her muscles unwound. Relief swept through her and she gave herself over to wonder with a murmur.

"Or maybe I can."

"That's it," he coaxed, withdrawing with the same deliberate motion only to move into her again.

The sensation was incredible. She loved the way he filled her.

It took a moment of concentration before she shifted her hips into sync with his slow rhythm. Which was too slow as it turned out. He might have all the patience in the world, but she didn't. His gentleness wasn't getting him where she needed him most. So, as he began his next measured, torturous thrust into her body, she arched her back, drove her hips forward and sunk her nails into his tight rear, accepting all of him. They cried out in unison. If she hadn't been so shattered by the feel of him so deeply buried in her, Olivia might have giggled. Utterly possessed, she had no breath to laugh or speak.

Gabriel licked his lips and slowly his gaze refocused. The transformation of his features from rigid concentration to outright shock magnified the pleasure inside her.

"What happened to slow?" he murmured, fingertips grazing her cheeks with reverent gentleness.

Olivia's body had adjusted to his. A contented purr rumbled in her chest. She ran the soles of her feet down his calves and drifted her hands along his spine.

"You were taking too long."

"It's your first time," he grumbled. "I was trying to be gentle."

"What happens now?" Her inner muscles flexed as he rocked his hips against hers.

"Watch and see."

With those cryptic words, Olivia turned herself over to the dazzling display of fireworks in Gabriel's eyes as he began to move against her, gauging her every response. Then he thrust back inside her and pleasure began to build once more.

He captured her hips in his hands and helped her find his rhythm. To her astonishment her body caught fire. Pleasure radiated outward from her core, spreading in waves of sensual hunger that climbed higher and higher, reaching outward with an intensity that made her feel as if she was on the verge of splintering into a million pieces.

And then it began, the breaking. Yet this time, unlike the last, she had Gabriel with her, climbing beside her. She held on to him, glorying in his strength and the power of the pleasure he gave her.

Her breath caught as the sun exploded behind her eyelids. Ecstasy blasted through her, detonating with all the power of a volcano. She cried out and clung to Gabriel as his movements increased. Everything went dark for a second, then she heard her name on Gabriel's lips and he thrust one last time, shaking with the power of his orgasm, before collapsing on her.

Olivia tunneled one hand through his hair while her other unlocked from his shoulder. His chest heaved against her, as he dragged air into his lungs in great gulps. Their hearts thundered in unison, as matched in the aftermath as they'd been during their loving.

She scrambled for words, but nothing could describe her emotions at the moment. Instead, she settled for silence and let her fingers talk for her. She ran them soothingly across his skin, conveying her profound thanks.

"Are you okay?" Gabriel asked, rousing himself enough to slide out of her and roll onto his side.

The loss of him from her body hit her like a sledgehammer. The connection they'd had, now severed, made her realize just how intimate the act of making love was. For those few minutes, she'd not just taken him into her body, into her womb, but into her heart, as well. He'd possessed her body and soul.

"Never better," she replied, unable to mask the smile in her voice.

He gathered her close and dropped a chaste kiss above her brow. Beneath her palm, his heartbeat returned to normal.

"That makes two of us." His thumb moved against her shoulder in an absent fashion as if his mind was somewhere besides the two of them naked in this bed. "You're sure that wasn't too rough?"

"Since I have nothing to compare it to, I'm going to say it was just rough enough."

He stopped staring at the canopy overhead and sliced a sharp look her way. His mouth tightened for a second until he realized she was teasing him.

"I had hoped to initiate you in a more civilized manner."

"There's a civilized way to make love?" Despite her best intentions, she giggled. "Do tell." Lifting onto her elbow, she walked her fingers down his stomach. "Better yet, why don't you show me?"

Gabriel growled and captured her fingers in a tight grip, placing their clasped hands on his chest. "Behave."

"Or what?" She had no idea what demon had possessed her but suddenly she felt more free and alive than any time in her life. Keeping her virginity intact all these years had obviously created a powder keg of trouble. Like a genie in a bottle, once released, her sexuality was ready to cause as much mischief as possible before she stuffed it back in and replaced the cork. "You'll spank me?"

Gabriel's eyes widened at her outrageous suggestion, but temptation danced in their bronze depths. His pupils widened, a sure sign of sexual arousal, and his erection flared to life again.

And shockingly enough, she felt herself awakening, as well. What did this man do to her?

"You led me to believe you were cool and composed," he complained as she wiggled around until she got a thigh on either side of his hips. His erection prodded her from behind. He looked pained as she extricated her hand from his grasp and raked her nails down his chest and over his abdomen, smiling as his muscles twitched beneath her touch. "What's gotten into you?"

She leaned forward to grin at him. "You."

His hands bracketed her hips as she poised herself over his shaft and slowly lowered herself downward. Taking him deep, adjusting the angle to give herself the most pleasure, she watched his face contort with delight and his eyes glaze over.

When she sat on him, savoring the feel of him buried inside her once more, she watched his gaze come back into focus. He reached up to capture her breasts in his hands, kneading gently, pulling at her nipples while she rose off him, mimicking the slow way he'd tortured her.

For a while he let her control the action, and she appreciated the chance to learn how the feel of him sliding in and out of her could be different if she leaned forward or backward. She liked taking him deep until the tip of him nudged against her womb.

But her education would not be complete without a little tutoring, and Gabriel's patience couldn't last forever. His fingers bit into her hips, changing her cadence. He began to move powerfully, driving himself into her. The bite of her nails created half-moons in his shoulders as his hand slid between their bodies and touched the knot of nerves hidden in her hot wet lips. Sparks exploded behind her eyes as her body began to pulse with ever stronger pleasure. She threw her head back and her mouth fell open in a keening cry as pleasure spun through her like a cyclone.

Gabriel thrust into her, his pace frantic, his own mouth open to expel a groan of acute pleasure. Olivia watched him climax, watched him become completely hers. Panting, she trembled in the aftershocks of her orgasm, her inner muscles clenching around his shaft as he poured his seed inside her and she welcomed this essence of him she could keep.

For the past two hours, Gabriel had lain beside Olivia and listened to her deep regular breathing while his thoughts retraced the evening. As morning light began to come in through the windows, he rolled out of bed, moving carefully to avoid waking Olivia. While he dressed he kept his eyes off her to avoid succumbing to the temptation to return to bed and wake her. Again. A full-fledged grin engaged every muscle in Gabriel's face. He couldn't help it.

Making love with Olivia had demonstrated his life would be spectacularly entertaining from here on out.

As he exited her room, he wondered if she'd done it on purpose. Picked a fight with him that ended in spectacular lovemaking. It was something Marissa had done often enough. Sex with her had been mind-blowing, hot, passionate, animalistic. She'd scratched long welts on his back and marked his shoulders with love bites. She'd possessed him as much as he'd possessed her.

But although their sex had been out of this world, it had many times left him feeling empty. And in typical male fashion, he'd ignored the emotional vacuum because what did he care if his carnal needs were satisfied.

Then, last night, he'd discovered what he'd been missing all those years. Spectacular sex and a deep emotional connection that left him more than a little rattled. With her curious innocence and startling sensuality, Olivia had slipped beneath his skin as if she'd been there all along. As if she was the answer to a prayer he hadn't even realized he'd breathed.

He hadn't liked the sexual power Marissa had held in her delicate hands. He liked Olivia's ability to influence his emotions even less.

Which was why he was heading for his suite of rooms rather than face her in the moments before dawn.

An hour later, Gabriel found Stewart in the office on the first floor. His private secretary had a cup of coffee at his elbow and wore a troubled frown.

"You're up early," Gabriel commented, settling himself behind the intricately carved cherry desk.

"I think you might be interested in seeing this." Stewart extended a jewelry box in Gabriel's direction.

He frowned at it. "What is that?"

Stewart nudged his chin at the box. "When Lady Darcy's secretary delivered her message that she wasn't joining you for dinner, she gave me this. You left before I had a chance to open it."

With an impatient snort, Gabriel cracked open the box. The hairs on the back of his neck lifted as he stared at the contents.

"Where the hell did this come from?" he growled, staring in shocked dismay at the bracelet he'd given Marissa for their second anniversary. "Why did Olivia have it?"

Stewart shook his head. "I spoke with her secretary this morning and apparently it was waiting in her room when she got back from her fitting."

"No wonder she was so angry." He closed the box with a snap. "Ariana must have told her I'd bought this for Marissa."

"Who would have done this?" Stewart asked, refocusing Gabriel on the real trouble spot.

"Whoever it was wanted to create trouble between Olivia and me." Gabriel sat back and steepled his fingers.

"Someone could have entered her suite and left it for her. Staff is coming and going all the time."

"That means someone in the palace is playing a dangerous game." Gabriel poked at the box with a pen. "Time to give Christian a call. This sort of intrigue is right up his alley."

Seven

Finding Gabriel gone when she awoke didn't surprise Olivia. A quick glance at the clock told her it was past eight. He had probably been up for hours. She eased into a sitting position, taking inventory of every strained and aching part of her. Nothing a hot shower wouldn't cure.

When she stepped from the bathroom a short time later, she discovered a visitor. Gabriel sat beside a table laden with an array of breakfast offerings. With his long legs stretched out in front of him and his hands clasped around a steaming cup of coffee, he hadn't yet noticed her.

Olivia leaned her shoulder against the door frame and let her gaze drift over his strong features and muscular torso clad in a tailored midnight-blue suit, white shirt and shimmering burgundy silk tie. For the moment his powerful energy was banked. But Gabriel in a contemplative state was no less arresting than him fully engaged.

Some small sound, probably a dreamy sigh, alerted him to her presence. He straightened and came toward her, his movement fluid, and before she knew it, he'd wrapped her in a snug embrace and given her the lusty morning kiss she'd been hoping for when she'd first awakened.

Desire stirred at the firm press of his mouth against her. He tasted of coffee and raspberries. Olivia dipped her tongue in for a second taste, murmuring approval.

"Good morning," he said, breaking the kiss, but not

ceasing the slow advance of his hands up her spine. "I'm sorry I left without doing that earlier."

"Why didn't you wake me?" She snuggled her cheek against his chest, savoring the unsteady pace of his heart and the hoarse timbre of his voice.

"Because I would have wanted to pick up where we left off last night," he retorted, his voice soft and deep. "And the palace would have been fully awake by the time I left your room."

That wrenched a laugh out of her. "You don't think everyone knows what happened last night?" Her cheeks heated despite herself. She'd always known there would be no privacy for her in the palace, but facing his parents and siblings when she knew they'd be apprised of what had happened between them last night would take a little getting used to.

"Perhaps, but I'd prefer to at least give the appearance of propriety until we're married." Gabriel gave her a wry smile that enhanced the devilry in his eyes. "Are you hungry?"

Her hands snaked around his waist, to tug his crisp white shirt from his pants. "Starving."

With a deep, rumbling laugh he caught her wrists. "I meant for breakfast. We missed dinner last night."

She waited until he'd dusted a kiss across her knuckles before answering. "I'd quite forgotten about dinner."

His eyes glowed with fierce delight as he drew her toward the table and poured a cup of coffee. "I didn't know what you liked for breakfast so I ordered some of everything."

"Usually I have an egg-white omelet with mushrooms and spinach, but today I think I want pancakes with lots of syrup."

To her astonishment, Gabriel served her himself. Olivia found it quite difficult to concentrate on her delicious breakfast while he watched her through eyes that danced with fondness and desire.

"Aren't you eating?" she asked.

"I had something an hour ago." He glanced at his watch. "The girls are going for their first ride this morning. I thought we should go watch. I already checked with your secretary and she said you're available until ten."

Considering his busy schedule, Olivia was delighted that he'd made time for such an important event. "They'll be thrilled. I took them to the stables yesterday afternoon. They loved the ponies. I predict they'll be enthusiastic equestrians."

"I have something for you." He pulled a small box out of his pocket and set it on the table between them.

Olivia eyed the black velvet case on the crisp white linen and shook her head. "I don't want it." The memory of yesterday's gift had made her more blunt than polite.

Gabriel didn't look at all surprised or insulted by her refusal. "You don't know that until you open it."

More of his mistress's leftovers? Olivia heaved a sigh. "You really don't need to give me anything."

"I need to explain about the bracelet."

She did not want to hear about the wretched thing ever again. "There's nothing to explain. It was beautiful. It was rude of me not to accept something you put so much thought into."

Gabriel leaned back in his chair, his expression a mask. But his eyes glittered like sunlight on water. "I'm not certain whether to be appalled or delighted that you are such a skillful diplomat."

She kept her lashes down and her lips relaxed. All her life she'd been watched for any sign of reaction or weakness. She'd mastered her facial muscles well before her fourteenth birthday. And she'd needed to. Her stepmother had enjoyed poking her with emotional sticks. Any reaction was sure to displease Lord Darcy, who wanted nothing more than for his two girls to get on. He was fond of reminding the women that he loved them both. And wished with all his heart that they would get along.

"You are marrying me because of my diplomacy and public image."

"In part." Gabriel turned over her hand and set the box on her palm. "I'm also marrying you because of your impeccable breeding and the fact that ever since the day I met you, I haven't been able to stop thinking about you."

Stunned by his admission, she stared at Gabriel's gift, knowing no expensive bauble could compare to the gift of knowing he was smitten with her. "That's lovely of you to say."

"Now back to the bracelet. Do you know where it came from?"

His question confused her. "From you."

He shook his head. "This is what I selected for you."

"Then where did the bracelet come from?"

"That's what I'd like to know."

Relief swept through her. "Then you didn't give me Marissa's bracelet."

"No." He gave her a stern look. "And I'm a little bothered by the fact that you think I'd be so cruel."

Olivia opened her mouth but had no ready response. Since dancing with him at the Independence Day gala she'd become foolish and irrational where he was concerned. With her hormones overstimulated and her emotions swinging from one extreme to the other, she shouldn't be surprised her brain was producing nothing but gibberish.

"Someone in the palace with access to my room played a cruel joke on me."

"Whoever it is, I don't think they are playing. This is a very serious breach in security. One that I will address." The determination in his voice matched the steel in his expression. After a second his gaze softened. "Please open my gift."

Olivia did as she was told.

Unlike the previous evening's trendy, emerald brace-let, this necklace was exactly something she would have chosen for herself. Olivia touched her fingertip to the large teardrop-shaped aquamarine, set into a frame of diamond-lined branches and suspended from a chain of faceted aquamarine beads and diamond-encrusted plati-num balls. Gabriel had picked out the perfect, unique gift.

"The necklace belonged to my great-aunt Ginnie. Her husband gave it to her as an engagement present. I believe it came from his mother who received it as her engage-ment present."

"I love it." And she did. More than any million-dollar diamond necklace he could have found in the treasury. It represented tradition and love. And it demonstrated a sen-timental side she would never have guessed Gabriel pos-sessed. Feeling bold, she picked up the necklace and sat down on her fiancé's lap. "Can you help me put it on?"

She lifted her hair off her neck and held still while his knuckles brushed her nape. The casual touch sent shiv-ers spiraling along her nerve endings. As the drop settled against her skin, she turned and planted a sweet kiss on Gabriel's cheek.

"Is that the best you can do?" he questioned, laughter in his voice.

Veiling her eyes with her lashes, she peered at him. "If I do much better we run the risk of not leaving this room in time to take Bethany and Karina for their first ride."

His response was to capture her lips in a sizzling kiss. Olivia sagged against him, surrendering to the firestorm of desire that had not burned out even after last night's love-making. She groaned beneath his lips as his hand found her breast, thumb coaxing her nipple to a hard point.

With a low growl, he broke off the kiss. "Perhaps you were right to be cautious." And with that, he stood with her in his arms and carried her to the bed.

In the end, they were in time to watch the twins circle the ring on the docile, well-mannered ponies, each led by an attentive groom. Although both were equally delighted by the ride, their individual personalities shone through. Bethany chattered incessantly as she rode, her every thought voiced. Karina was more circumspect and her seat was more natural. Of the two, Gabriel suspected she'd be the better rider.

Soon the twins' first riding lesson was done, leaving Gabriel free to turn his thoughts to the woman beside him and all that had transpired in the past twelve hours.

Since discovering last night how swiftly Olivia became aroused, he'd taken full advantage of her ardent responses and made love to her with fierce passion. Already his lust for her was dangerously close to uncontrollable. Telling himself making love to Olivia was a novelty that would soon wear off wasn't cooling his ardor one bit. Even now, as he watched her smile as her gaze followed the twins, he felt heat rise in his blood.

It shocked him to realize that he'd happily forgo the rest of his appointments to spend the time alone with Olivia in her suite. This was how he'd been with Marissa. Preoccupied. Distracted. Obsessed.

Then again, it was early in their relationship. The time of exploration when all things were fascinating and new. Their lust would eventually burn itself out and they could settle into companionable monotony. But even as he entertained this possibility his instincts rejected it. More than his blood hummed when she was near. This was a feeling he'd never known before. Besides being beautiful, Olivia was intelligent and caring. He'd been right the first time he'd pronounced her perfect. But he'd underestimated how deep that flawlessness went.

"Gabriel?" Olivia said, returning him to the here and now. "I was just explaining to Bethany and Karina that we can't have dinner with them tonight."

"Because we are…" He had no idea what was scheduled that evening. How was that possible? He usually knew his itinerary backward and forward.

"Going to the ballet," Olivia prompted.

"That's it." He smiled at her.

"But perhaps we could visit before we leave to read you one quick bedtime story."

"That we can do."

The twins' chorus of happiness sent a bird winging off through the trees from a few feet away.

"I think it's time to head back to the palace," Olivia said, shaking her head as the girls began to protest. "Your father has work to do."

Gabriel was impressed how well she managed the toddlers. The twins were darling but rambunctious. Marissa had done a fine job of blending discipline with love for they seemed to take direction well and had none of the fits of temper he had grown accustomed to with their mother. Despite losing Marissa recently, they were adjusting nicely to life in the palace. Of course, they had each other, something he could relate to with two brothers of his own. Sometimes it had seemed as if it was him, Nic and Christian against the world when in truth it was probably more reasonable to say it had been the three of them against their parents.

After leaving the twins in the hands of two young maids, Gabriel walked Olivia to her meeting with the wedding planner and bussed her cheek in a chaste kiss goodbye. He had fifteen minutes before his first meeting of the day and went in search of Christian.

His brother was nowhere near the palace. Christian had an office in the city that he usually preferred to work out of, claiming fewer distractions. Gabriel suspected he liked working without the king's or queen's "subtle" influence. With two brothers ahead of him for the throne, Christian had always enjoyed a lot of freedom. So had Nic. The middle brother didn't even live in Sherdana. He'd gotten his education in the States and resided in California while he pursued his dream of privatizing space travel.

Gabriel envied them both.

And he wouldn't trade places with, either. He'd been born to rule and had never wished to do anything else. But being king came with a price. He belonged to the people of Sherdana and owed it to them to do what was best for the country, even at the expense of his own desires. Breaking off his relationship with Marissa was only one of many sacrifices he'd made for Sherdana, but it had been his hardest and most painful.

It was why he was marrying a woman he admired instead of one he loved. And yet, hadn't last night and this morning proved that life with Olivia at his side would be the furthest thing from hardship?

Grinning, Gabriel headed into his father's office where the energy minister had come for a briefing.

Olivia yawned behind her hand as she surveyed Noelle's drawings for the twins' dresses for the wedding. It was almost midnight. She'd just returned from another event, this one raising money for an arts program for underprivileged children.

She wasn't insensible to the irony that what she intended to pay for these two dresses could probably fund the program for a year.

Behind her the door to her suite opened and closed. Her skin prickled in anticipation as muted footsteps advanced toward her. The faint scent of Gabriel's aftershave tickled her nose a second before his hands soothed along her shoulders.

"Waiting up for me?"

Gabriel placed a kiss on her neck, his lips sliding into a particularly sensitive spot that made her tremble.

Was it possible that less than a week ago their every private encounter had been stilted and awkward? Now she spent her days as a tightly wound spring of sexual anticipation and her nights in Gabriel's arms soaring toward the stars.

"Of course," she answered, setting aside the sketches and getting to her feet. She'd already dressed for bed in her favorite silk pajamas. They covered her from neck to toe. Not exactly seductive, but Gabriel never seemed to care.

"I'm leaving early in the morning," he explained, pulling her into his arms and dropping a sweet kiss on her lips. "And I will be gone for four days. I wanted a private moment with you before I left."

Four long days. And nights. She'd gotten accustomed to cuddling against his side, her cheek on his bare chest, his heartbeat lulling her to sleep.

She adored his intensity—making love with Gabriel was like being consumed by the sun—but these moments of stillness had their own rewards.

"Just a moment?" She tipped her head to grant him better access to her neck and ran her nails along his nape the way he liked.

"Did I mention I'm leaving very early in the morning?" Tender mockery filled his voice. He nudged his hips into her, letting her feel his erection. She smiled, no less turned on despite wanting to do nothing more than stretch out on her mattress and sleep for twelve hours.

"Of course," she murmured. "I just thought that perhaps you could give me a few minutes to say goodbye properly."

"Just a few minutes?"

Olivia's bones turned to water as he drew his tongue along her lower lip, tasting, but not taking. With his hands warm and strong on her lower back, she leaned into his powerful chest and savored the tantalizing slide of his mouth against hers.

"Take as many as you need."

She'd grown accustomed to sharing her bed with him and hated the thought of sleeping alone these next four nights. Every morning, after he woke her with kisses and made love to her in the soft light before day, she fell back to sleep wondering if once they were married, once she became pregnant, if he would share her bed every night. She already knew that a suite of rooms was being prepared for them in the family wing. They would each have their own space. Their own beds after the wedding. That wasn't what she wanted.

Olivia wasn't surprised when Gabriel swept her off her feet and carried her to the bed. The chemistry between them had skyrocketed in the days since they'd first made love. With their clothes scattered across the mattress, Olivia clutched at Gabriel as he brought her to orgasm twice before sliding into her. Being filled by him was a pleasure all its own and Olivia wrapped her thighs around his hips and held him close while he thrust into her.

He stayed for several hours, his large hands moving with such gentleness up and down her spine. Snuggled against his chest, with their legs intertwined, Olivia let herself drift. When she awoke several hours later, Gabriel was gone and she was already lonely.

Exhausted, but restless, Olivia left the bed and slipped into a robe. Her suite faced the gardens behind the palace so she had no hope of catching a final glimpse of Gabriel, but she opened the French door that led to the terrace and wandered across to the railing. At night the garden was lit up like a magical fairy tale, but dawn was approaching and the garden had gone dark. A cool breeze carried the scent of roses to her. Olivia leaned her arms on the cool stone. Vivid in her thoughts was the night Gabriel had found her out here and demonstrated that resisting him was a pointless exercise.

And now she knew it had been all along. When she'd agreed to marry him, she'd fooled herself into believing that sexual desire and mild affection would make her happy. After several nights in his arms she'd completely fallen under his spell. It was as if all her life she'd been moving toward this man and this moment.

Recognizing that her motivation for marrying Gabriel had changed, she had to ask herself if she was no longer concerned whether one day she'd become a queen...what did she really want?

Love.

The thought made her knees weak. Olivia braced herself against the stone railing. Deflated, she stared at her hands. At the engagement ring sparkling on her finger.

She couldn't be falling in love with Gabriel. He certainly wasn't falling in love with her.

This was an arranged marriage. A practical union for the good of his country. A sensible bargain that would lead to stability and children. She hadn't expected to fall madly in love with her husband or be deliriously happy. She expected to be content. To feel fulfilled as a mother and someday as a queen.

Sexual satisfaction hadn't entered into her plans—not until Gabriel had kissed her.

Olivia turned away from the softly lit garden and returned to her suite. As she closed and locked the glass door, her gaze fell on her desk and the locked drawer where she'd placed copies of important paperwork, including a file with some of her medical information. Had those scratches always marred the lock's brass surface? The idea that someone in the palace could have tried to break into her desk was ridiculous. And then she recalled the night the twins arrived. There'd been a maid at her dresser in the middle of the night. When nothing was missing she'd seen no reason to pursue it.

A few hours later, when Libby entered the suite, Olivia was still seated at the desk. She'd opened the locked drawer and hadn't found anything disturbed, but with the twins' arrival at the palace having been leaked to the press and the mysterious appearance of Marissa's bracelet, Olivia had checked each page of her thick file to make sure it was intact.

"Why are you looking through your papers?"

"I might be mistaken, but I thought I spotted fresh scratches on the lock and wanted to make sure my medical file hadn't been rifled." Olivia glanced up when Libby didn't immediately comment. "What's wrong?"

"Prince Christian is systematically interviewing the staff about the leaks to the press."

A chill chased across Olivia's skin. "He thinks someone inside the palace is providing information?" She remembered the photos of Gabriel and Marissa. Those hadn't been paparazzi shots. They had been taken among friends.

Olivia touched the lock again, wishing she could determine if the scratches were recent. If someone had gotten their hands on her medical records it could have catastrophic results. "Keep me updated on the investigation," she said, "and see if you can find a more secure place for these."

Gabriel was having a hard time keeping his mind on today's biotech plant tour. For the past several days he'd been touring manufacturing plants in Switzerland and Belgium in search of other businesses that would be interested in moving their operations to Sherdana. He probably should have sent Christian to do this. His brother had made a significant amount of money investing in up-and-coming technology. Christian would have been interested in the product lines and the way the manufacturing facilities were organized. Gabriel was finding it as dry as overdone toast.

That's probably how both his brothers felt about what went into the running of the country. These days, they had little in common. It often amazed Gabriel that three people could share a womb for nine months, communicate among themselves in their own language until they were teenagers and participate in a thousand childhood adventures together yet be so completely different in their talents and interests as they entered their twenties.

Nevertheless, this trip couldn't have come at a better time. The past few nights with Olivia had been some of the most passion-filled of his life. She'd slipped effortlessly beneath his defenses with her eager sensuality and curious nature. He'd become obsessed with the soft drag of her lips across his skin and the wicked suggestions she whispered in his ear as he entered her.

His constant craving for her company warned him he was fast losing touch with why he was marrying her. Cool, sophisticated elegance and a warm heart. Not feverish kisses and blazing orgasms.

Gabriel cleared his throat and tugged at his collar as the head of the factory droned on. He definitely needed some space from her. Unfortunately, the distance wasn't having the effect he'd hoped for. Being apart was supposed to cool him off. That was what he'd anticipated, but that wasn't the result.

He daydreamed about her at the oddest moments. Him. Daydreaming. Like some infatuated fool. He'd never expected her to preoccupy him in this way. She was supposed to be a sensible mate, an able partner in governing the country, not a hellcat in bed.

Hope.

The tattoo drove him crazy. Its placement. Its message.

It awakened him to possibilities. He wanted to throw sensible out the window and take chances. Because of Olivia he wanted to shake up the established way of doing things. She'd awakened his restless spirit that he'd believed he'd conquered after ending things with Marissa.

Every day he was finding out that Olivia was more than he'd expected.

And he'd be a fool not to worry about the power she now had over him. Yet he was helpless to stop what was developing between them. The best he could hope for was to slow things down until he shaped the relationship into something he was comfortable with.

But was *comfortable* going to make him happy in the long run? Was he really going to shortchange his future all for the sake of feeling safe and in control?

A few days after Gabriel left on his trip, Olivia was scheduled to have a private lunch with the queen. Ten minutes before the appointment, she slipped pearl earrings into place and stepped in front of the mirror to assess her appearance. She'd chosen a sleeveless pink dress edged in white with a narrow white belt to highlight her waist, and accessorized with a pair of floral pumps. The feminine ensemble required a soft hairstyle so she'd left her hair down and coaxed out the natural wave with a light blowout.

This morning she'd awakened to some discomfort in her lower abdomen and wasn't feeling on top of her game, but wasn't about to cancel on the queen.

Drawing a fortifying breath, she entered the private dining room that only the immediate royal family used. Pale blue had been chosen for the chairs as well as the curtains framing the large windows. It was the only splash of color in a room otherwise dominated by white walls and lavish plasterwork painted gold. More intimate than many of the other rooms on the first floor, it nevertheless didn't allow her to forget that this was a palace.

"You look lovely," the queen said as she breezed into the room. She wore a classic suit of dusty lavender and a stunning choker of pale round Tahitian pearls. Noticing Olivia's interest, she touched the necklace. "An anniversary gift from the king," the queen explained, her smile both fond and sensual.

"It's beautiful."

"Matteo has exceptionally good taste."

The queen gestured toward the dining table, capable of seating twelve, but set for two. As the two women sat down, a maid set a glass of soda on the table before the queen.

"Diet cola," she, sipping the fizzy drink with pleasure. "I got a taste for it when we visited the States two decades ago. It's my indulgence."

Olivia nodded in understanding. She wasn't much of a soda drinker herself, but she understood how someone could come to crave a particular item. Like a tall, bronze-eyed prince for example.

The servers placed plates of salad in front of the two women and the queen launched a barrage of questions to determine what Olivia knew about Sherdana's current political climate and their economic issues. Although Olivia had been expecting to discuss the wedding preparations, she was just as happy to share what she knew about the country she would soon call her own.

"Does my son know how bright you are?" the queen asked, her expression thoughtful as the maids cleared the main course and served dessert. She frowned at the plate in front of her and sighed. "Oh, dear. The chef is experimenting again."

Olivia stared at the oddest fruit she'd ever seen. About

the size of her fist with a leathery hot-pink skin, it had been sliced in half to reveal white flesh dotted with tiny black seeds. A hollow had been carved out of the center and filled with yogurt and sliced strawberries.

"Dragon fruit," the queen explained. "And from what I understand quite delicious."

Olivia took her first bite and was surprised at the wonderfully sweet flavor. It had a texture like a kiwi with the seeds adding a little crunch to each bite.

"You look pale." The queen pointed at Olivia with her spoon. "I expect you'll get more rest with my son away."

Olivia's entire body flushed hot. The queen had just insinuated that she knew where Gabriel had been spending his nights.

"Oh, don't look so mortified," the queen continued. "You are to be married and my son was determined to have a short engagement. Besides, there are no secrets in the palace."

"No, I suppose there are not." Olivia knew better than to think her nights with Gabriel were something between just the two of them. She'd grown up surrounded by servants who knew most everything about her daily habits.

"How are the twins' dresses coming for the wedding?" The queen had taken a few days to approve the idea of Bethany and Karina being a part of the ceremony, but Gabriel had at last persuaded her.

"They should be finished later this week. The lace Noelle has chosen is beautiful. I think you'll be pleased."

"Noelle is very talented. You will all look beautiful." The queen nodded in satisfaction. "I must say, you've accepted this situation with Gabriel's children much better than most women would in your position."

"It's hard to imagine anyone not adoring those precious two," Olivia admitted, but she understood what the queen was getting at. "I love children. Helping to make their lives better is the foundation for all my charity work. I would be a wretched person and a hypocrite if I turned my back on Bethany and Karina because of who their mother was." And what Marissa had meant to Gabriel.

"They certainly have taken to you," the queen said. "And you seem to have everything it takes to be an excellent mother."

"Thank you."

The queen's praise should have allowed Olivia to relax, but the tick of her biological clock sounded loud in her ears.

Eight
<u></u>

"How was the trip?" Christian asked as he and Gabriel crossed the tarmac toward the waiting limo. "I hope you brought me a present."

"Naturally." Gabriel hoisted his briefcase and deposited it in his brother's hands. "It's filled with all sort of things I'm sure you'll find vastly interesting."

"Unlike you?"

"Technology is more your and Nic's thing." Gabriel was aware that the trip had been less productive than he'd hoped. Mostly because he'd had a hard time concentrating. Thoughts of Olivia had intruded with a frequency he'd found troubling. "You probably should have gone instead of me, but it was something I needed to do. I want to encourage more technology firms to move to Sherdana. The best way for me to do that is to speak to companies that might be looking at expansion."

"I'll bet you hated it."

Gabriel shot Christian a quelling look. "I can't expect to enjoy every aspect of my position. Some things must be done no matter how painful. This was one of them."

"Is your future wife another?"

This time Christian laughed out loud at his brother's sharp look.

"How I feel about my future bride is none of your business."

"Come on, you've got to be a lot happier about having to get married these days. From what I hear, you two have been acting like a couple kids in love."

Gabriel growled in displeasure, but couldn't ignore the electric charge that surged through him at the mere thought of seeing Olivia again and feeling her soft lips yield beneath his. Each of the past four nights he'd gone to bed alone and found himself unable to sleep. Plagued by memories of Olivia's smiles and her sassy sensuality, he'd lain with his hands behind his head, staring up at the blank ceiling and doing his best to ignore his erection.

Cold showers had become his 2:00 a.m. ritual. How had she bewitched him in such a short time?

"Neither one of us is in love," Gabriel muttered. "But I won't deny we're compatible." He leveled a hard gaze at his brother, warning him to drop the matter.

"Not in love?" Christian cocked his head. "Maybe you're not. But are you sure about her?"

Christian's question roused a memory of the last evening before his trip. He'd almost succumbed to Olivia's plea to spend the night. She'd seemed so vulnerable, her characteristic confidence lacking. But that didn't mean she was in love with him.

"Ridiculous," he said. "We've only spent a couple weeks in each other's company."

"You don't believe in love at first sight?"

Gabriel regarded his brother's serious expression with curiosity. "Do you?"

"Absolutely."

"Is that why you do your best to chase every woman away who gets too close?" Gabriel wondered if his brother was taunting him or if he was offering Gabriel a rare glimpse into his psyche. "Have none of them made you feel as if you were clobbered by something beyond your understanding or control?"

Something flared in Christian's gaze but was quickly gone. His mocking smile returned. "Who wants to settle down with one woman when there's a banquet of lovelies to sample?"

"One of these days someone will appeal to your palate and you'll find that you can't get enough of that particular delicacy."

"Is that what happened to you?"

"I'm getting married because I have to." Gabriel was well aware that he'd dodged the question and not with any finesse.

Christian's eyes narrowed. "And if you didn't have to?"

"Since that's never been an option, I've never really thought about it."

And he didn't want to think about it now because it opened old wounds. Would he have stayed with Marissa if marriage to her had been possible? Had he loved her or had he inflated his feelings for her because circumstances made it impossible for them to have a future?

"Well, I certainly stirred you up," Christian taunted.

"Wasn't that your intention?" Gabriel countered, staring past the hedge that bordered the driveway to the palace. For a moment he glimpsed a pair of ponies and the two little girls riding them. Despite his tumultuous thoughts, he couldn't help but feel joy at the appearance of his daughters and feel sorry for Christian. His cynical attitude would undoubtedly prevent him from experiencing the wonder of holding his own children in his arms and feeling their enthusiastic kisses all over his cheek.

"God," Christian exclaimed, "you are smitten."

"I caught a glimpse of my angels out riding."

Christian snorted. "They're not exactly angels. In fact, they've been turning the palace upside down with their version of hide-and-seek, which entails them finding some tiny nook and not coming out until every servant is called upon to look for them. It's been worse these last few days with Olivia feeling unwell."

Gabriel frowned. "What did you say about Olivia? She's ill?"

"Didn't you know?"

"I spoke with her last night. She said nothing." Gabriel rubbed at the back of his neck. "How bad is it?"

"I don't know. She hasn't been out of her suite for the last two days."

"Has she been in bed that whole time?"

"I don't know," Christian sounded amused. "But if you'd hinted that you'd like me to check on your English flower in her bedroom, you should have said something."

Gabriel didn't even look at his brother as he exited the car and strode into the palace. Tension rode his shoulders as he entered the foyer, barely hearing the greetings from the staff on duty. Why hadn't Olivia told him she wasn't doing well? He took the stairs two at a time and turned in the direction of his fiancée's suite. His knock was answered by a maid.

"I'm here to see Lady Darcy," he told her, his scowl compelling the young woman to step back.

Three women occupied the room. Olivia sat on the couch with her feet up, her back to him while Ariana sat opposite her facing the door. Olivia's private secretary was by the desk. His sister's lilting laugh broke off as he entered.

"Good afternoon, ladies." He forced himself to approach Ariana first. His sister looked splendid as always in an evening-blue dress. The color flattered her golden skin and dark brown hair. She wore a simple gold bangle at her wrist and gold hoop earrings.

"Welcome back, Gabriel," she said, standing as he drew near and making her cheek available for a kiss.

"We missed you," Olivia echoed, turning to gaze up at

him. Her normally pale complexion lacked its customary healthy glow and there were shadows purpling the skin beneath her eyes.

Concern flared. He sat beside her on the sofa and touched her cheek with his fingertips. "Last night on the phone, why didn't you tell me you've been ill?"

"It's nothing."

"You're too pale. I demand to know what's wrong."

Olivia sighed and cast her gaze toward Ariana. Her eyes widened, causing Gabriel to turn his head. Ariana had vanished. The door to the bedroom was shut. They were alone.

Gabriel refocused on Olivia. "Answer me," he growled.

Red patches appeared on her formerly dull cheeks. "I've been having a particularly difficult period," she murmured.

Relief flooded him. She was embarrassed to discuss her body's natural process? Was that why she'd kept silent the night before? Amused, Gabriel dipped a finger beneath her chin and raised it.

"I'm going to be your husband. You better prepare to discuss all sorts of things like this with me."

"Be careful or you may live to regret those words," she muttered, but her lips were soft and eager beneath his. "Welcome home."

An endearment hung between them, unspoken. She'd promised not to call him Prince Gabriel or Your Highness as they made love, but she had yet to find a pet name for him. What would it be? Darling? Dearest? Sweetheart? My love?

"Did you have a successful trip?" she asked.

"It was very long." He leaned forward and kissed her neck below her ear, smiling as she trembled. "And lonely."

She framed his face with her hands. "I missed you so much. In fact—"

A knock sounded on the door, interrupting her. Heaving

a weary sigh, Gabriel kissed Olivia on the nose and then raised his voice to be heard in the hall. "Come."

Stewart poked his head around the door. "The king wondered if you'd gotten lost on your way to the meeting with the prime minister."

Gabriel stood and bent over Olivia's hand. "Duty calls."

"Of course." The bright smile she gave him didn't quite reach her eyes. "Perhaps we can have dinner together?"

Regret pinched him. "I'm afraid I can't tonight. I already have an appointment."

"Of course."

He'd grown familiar with the micro expressions that belied her thoughts and could see she was disappointed. He hated being the one who robbed her eyes of their sparkle, and the intensity of his desire to see her smile caught him off guard. Falling in love with his fiancée wasn't what he'd had in mind when he decided to marry Olivia.

"I'll stop back to check on you later," he said.

Her gaze clung to his face. "I'll be waiting."

The morning after Gabriel returned from his business trip, Olivia caught herself smiling almost as often as she yawned. True to his word, he'd returned after his dinner to check on her and they'd snuggled on the sofa until almost three in the morning while Olivia filled him in on the twins and he spoke of what he'd seen in Switzerland and Belgium.

In addition to talking, there'd been a fair amount of kissing, as well. Lighthearted, romantic kisses that left Olivia breathless and giddy. He'd treated her with tender patience, not once letting passion get the better of him. Olivia had found his control both comforting and frustrating. Four days without him had aroused her appetite for his hands roaming over her skin and she cursed her cycle's timing.

On the other hand, there would be nothing to get in the

way of their magical wedding night. Unless there wasn't going to be a wedding.

This was her first period since discontinuing the birth control pills that regulated her cycle. At first she'd been down because as amazing as her nights with Gabriel had been, she hadn't gotten pregnant. Soon, however, she began to worry as old, familiar symptoms appeared. Assuring herself everything was going to be fine became harder each day as her period stretched out. For the past two days fear had begun to sink deep into bone and sinew. She began to confront the very real possibility that her surgery might not have cleared up her problem. She had to face that getting and staying pregnant might be more difficult than she'd assumed.

Then, after seeing Gabriel yesterday, it became clear what she had to do. She needed to tell him the truth. Despite the connection they shared, she wasn't sure how he was going to react to her news. She could only hope he would act like his father and work with her to solve any issues that came up.

"Olivia?"

A soft voice roused her. With the paparazzi hungry for their first glimpse of Gabriel's daughters, Olivia had requested that Noelle bring their flower-girl dresses to the palace to be fitted. Blinking, she refocused on the slim, dark-haired woman.

"Sorry, Noelle. With the wedding two weeks away my mind tends to jump around a great deal these days. What were you saying?"

"I asked if you wanted me to bring your dress here next week for the final fitting rather than have you come to my shop."

"It would help me if you brought the dress by. I'm drowning in wedding preparations and that would save me time."

"I'd be happy to."

A moment later the twins appeared in their new finery. They looked like angels in their matching sleeveless white dresses with full lace skirts and wide satin sashes in pale yellow. Noelle's assistant had pinned up their hair and attached wreaths wrapped in pale yellow ribbons.

"These are merely to demonstrate one possible look for the girls," Noelle explained. "If you like it, I'm sure the florist could create beautiful wreaths with yellow roses."

"The dresses are perfect," Olivia breathed. "Thank you so much for making them on such short notice."

"I'm happy you like them."

While Noelle and her assistant made little adjustments to the dresses, Olivia distracted Bethany and Karina by explaining to them what their role in the wedding would be. They seemed to understand the seriousness of the event because they listened to her with wide eyes and their full attention.

An hour later, Noelle had left, taking the dresses with her, and Olivia was reading the twins a story when the door to her suite swung open without warning. Startled, Olivia swiveled on the sofa to face a very unhappy Gabriel.

"What's wrong?"

"It's time for the twins to head back to the nursery," he answered, his voice level and cool as he gestured to the nanny who jumped to her feet. "I think it's time for their lunch."

Olivia set the book aside and got to her feet to urge the girls over to their father for a kiss and a hug. His manner softened for them, but a minute later they were gone and Gabriel was back to scowling.

"Is it true?" he demanded.

Her stomach twisted at the hard suspicion in his eyes. "Is what true?"

"That you're infertile?"

Of all the things that had raced through her mind, this was the last thing she'd expected. How had he found out? Libby was the only person who knew about her condition and Olivia knew her private secretary would never betray her.

"Where did you hear that?"

He stalked across the room toward the television and snatched up the remote. Dread filled Olivia as he cued the power button. She'd not imagined he could look so angry.

"Sources inside the palace confirm that the future princess has little to no chance of producing an heir for Sherdana's throne. With her medical condition you have to wonder what the prince was thinking to propose."

The words blaring from the television were so horrifying that Olivia would have crumpled to the floor at his feet if Gabriel hadn't seized her arms in a bruising grip.

His gaze bore into hers. "Tell me the truth."

"I had a condition," she began, and at his dark scowl, rushed on. "But I had surgery to correct the problem. I should be able to get pregnant." But after these past few days and the return of her old symptoms, her confidence had waned.

"Can you or can't you?"

"Six months ago when you proposed I thought I could. At this moment I honestly don't know."

"You should have told me." He set her free as if the touch of her was distasteful. "Did you think you could keep this a secret forever?"

"I really didn't think it was going to be a problem." Olivia clasped her hands to keep them from shaking and looked up at Sherdana's crown prince, who stood there like a granite statue. Little about his current demeanor encouraged hope that he might listen to her with a rational ear. "I would never have agreed to marry you if I believed I couldn't have children."

"But your doctor warned you the chances were slim." It wasn't a question.

She didn't ask him how he knew that. The reporter on the television was divulging her detailed medical records. Her privacy had been violated and yet she was being treated like a villain.

"He never said slim. He said there was a good chance I could get pregnant, but to do so I had to stop taking the pill and he wasn't sure how my body would react since I've been on it almost ten years."

"But you were a virgin. I can attest to that. Why were you on birth control?"

"I had severe cramps and bleeding. It helps control those problems." Olivia wrapped her arms around herself. "I quit taking the birth control before I left London. I wanted to get pregnant as soon as possible. Provide you with your heir. I knew that's what you all would expect."

Gabriel's expression didn't change, but his lips tightened briefly. "We expected you to be truthful, as well."

She flinched at his sharp words.

"I intended to tell you tonight. I haven't felt right these last few days and thought I needed to discuss the situation with you."

"I need an heir, Olivia." His harsh tone softened.

"I understand completely." Their marriage was an arrangement, an exchange of her hand in marriage for her father's business. But she was also expected to be a mother. "I never would've agreed to marry you knowing I might not be able to have children."

He needed to marry someone who could provide the next generation of Alessandros. At the moment she wasn't completely convinced she could do that.

A sharp pain lanced through her and she winced. Her cramps had been a dull ache all through the morning, but now they gained in strength.

"Are you okay?"

She shook her head. "It's been a hectic morning and I've done too much. I should probably take something and lie down for a while. Can we continue later this afternoon?"

She barely waited for his agreement before heading toward the bathroom and the bottle of pain medication she hadn't needed earlier in the day. She shut the bathroom door, hoping that Gabriel wouldn't come to check on her, and braced her hands on the vanity top. The woman in the mirror had dark circles beneath her eyes and white around her mouth.

The pain in her body was vivid and icy, very unlike her usual cramps. The difference scared her.

Forcing herself to take deep, even breaths, she fought back nausea and swallowed her medication. Within minutes, the sharp edges came off the ache in her pelvis and she was able to return to the bedroom. There she found Libby waiting for her with the queen. Helpless tears filled Olivia's eyes. She blinked them away.

"Have you tried pineapple juice?"

The queen's suggestion confused Olivia. "No."

"There's something in it that will help with your cramps."

Olivia clasped her hands as her stomach flipped sickeningly. Why was the queen being nice, given the news?

"Thank you. I'll try pineapple juice."

"You aren't the first woman in this palace to grapple with reproductive issues. I was young when I came to marry the king and eager to give him the heir he needed. Unlike Gabriel, Matteo had no male siblings to take over the throne if something happened to him."

"You had trouble getting pregnant?"

"There's a good reason why Gabriel has two brothers so close in age." The queen gave a fond smile. "I wasn't able to get pregnant without help. We did in vitro fertilization twice before the procedure was successful. Gabriel, Nicolas and Christian are the result."

"And Ariana?" The princess was six years younger than her brothers, close to Olivia's own age.

"My miracle baby."

Olivia liked the sound of that. She hoped her own miracle baby was on the horizon. Because the way she felt at the moment, a miracle might be exactly what she needed.

"Do you love my son?"

She rolled the engagement ring around and around on her finger. "Yes."

"Good, then you'll do what's best for him."

And leaving Olivia to ponder what that was, the queen took her leave.

When the door opened a short time later, Olivia looked up, expecting Libby, and saw a maid instead. "I really don't need anything right now. Perhaps you could check back in later this evening."

"I thought you'd like me to pack your things. I'm sure you'll be heading back to England now that the prince knows you can't have children."

The woman's snide tone wasn't at all what Olivia was expecting and she sat up straighter, adrenaline coursing through her veins. Of average height and appearance with brown hair and hazel eyes, the woman looked like any of a dozen palace maids. But there was a frantic energy to her movement that made Olivia apprehensive.

"Don't be ridiculous," she said, feeling at a disadvantage as the maid stalked toward her. "I'm not leaving."

Olivia pushed to her feet. The sudden movement sent pain stabbing through her. She swayed and caught the back of the chair. Her breath came in labored gasps. Something was very wrong.

"Of course you are." The woman's hazel eyes burned

with a crazy zeal. "The prince won't marry you now that he knows you're damaged."

"That's for him to decide." It was hard to keep her mind on the conversation when it felt as if hot pokers were being driven into her lower abdomen. "Get out."

"What makes you think you can order me around?" the woman spat. "Because you have a title and your father has money?"

Step by deliberate step, Olivia backed away from the maid's furious outburst. It was then that she recognized the woman's face. She'd been the one who'd been searching the desk the night the twins arrived.

"Who are you?" she asked.

"My sister was twice the woman you could ever hope to be."

The woman made as if to rush at her and Olivia stumbled backward.

"Marissa was your sister?" Impossible. This woman was as plain and dull as Marissa had been beautiful and vibrant.

"My younger sister. She was beautiful and full of life. Or she was until Prince Gabriel destroyed her."

"What do you mean?"

Olivia knew she had to keep the woman talking. Somewhere behind her was the bathroom with a solid door and a lock. She just needed to get there.

"In the months following her trip to visit him in Venice, she grew more and more depressed. She couldn't live with the fact that he wanted nothing more to do with her." The sister glared at Olivia as if she'd been the cause of Marissa's heartache.

"I'm sorry your sister was upset—"

"Upset?" The woman practically spat the word. "She wasn't upset. She was devastated. Devastated enough to try to kill herself. I was the one who found her bleeding to death. She'd slit her wrists. It was at the hospital that she found out she was pregnant. She loved her girls. They were everything to her."

Olivia reached her hand back and found the bathroom door frame. "Bethany and Karina are wonderful."

"He doesn't deserve them. He doesn't deserve to be happy. And now he won't because you can't have children. He won't want you anymore." Marissa's sister was shouting now, her voice rising in unbalanced hysteria.

Another wave of pain made Olivia double over. She backed into the bathroom and clawed at the door. Blackness pushed at the edges of her vision. By feel alone she shut the door and slid the lock into place. The door rattled as Marissa's sister beat against it in fury and Olivia staggered back.

With her strength failing, Olivia slid to the floor and set her back against the vanity, hoping that the door would hold. Hoping that someone would come find her. Hoping that Marissa's sister was wrong about Gabriel.

Nine

Gabriel leaned forward in the saddle and urged his stallion to greater speed. Wind lashed at his face, and he focused on the thrum of hoofbeats filling his ears to slow his racing mind. He'd gone for a ride after leaving Olivia because he needed to sort through the conflict raging in him.

Although the powerful Warmblood had stamina enough for a longer run, Gabriel slowed him to a walk after only a mile. He passed the lake where he and his brothers had swum during the hot summers of their youth and wished he could go back to those innocent times.

Accusing Olivia of lying had been unfair. She wouldn't do that. If he'd learned anything about her, it was that she had a great deal of integrity.

What woman, when faced with the prospect of never becoming a mother, wouldn't deny the possibility? Especially someone who adored children the way Olivia did. He'd watched her with the twins. He'd seen how his daughters had bonded with Olivia. She'd won them over with her generous, kind heart. They'd been as helpless against her sweetness as he'd been.

By now his parents would be discussing damage control. And debating how to proceed. Olivia had understood the position this news report had put him in. They would advise him against marrying a woman whose fertility was in question. But he wouldn't make any decisions until he knew the extent of her problems.

And if she could never have children?

He would need to address the bargain he'd struck with her father. The deal with Lord Darcy was contingent on Olivia becoming Gabriel's wife.

Talk about being stuck between a rock and a hard place. No matter what decision he made, he would fail Sherdana.

Two hours later he entered the salon in the family section of the south wing and found everyone assembled.

His sister came forward to give him a hug. "Did you check on Olivia?"

"I went for a ride."

His father regarded him with a frown, his opinion clear. Gabriel ignored him and went to sit beside his mother. He'd come to a preliminary decision and knew it wouldn't meet with everyone's approval.

"I needed some time to think."

The king fixed Gabriel with a hard stare. "How do you intend to handle this?"

"Handle?" Gabriel hadn't considered how they should approach the press about this latest bombshell. "We could start by sending out a press release downplaying the serious nature of Olivia's problems, but I'm not sure with her doctor's records as proof, this is going to do us much good."

"I meant with Olivia," the king said, his voice a low rumble.

Gabriel became aware that his entire family was watching him and waiting for his answer. It was as if the occupants of the room had stopped breathing.

"What do you mean?" Gabriel asked, certain he knew where his father was going with the question, but needing to hear it asked out loud.

"You need a wife who can bear children."

In other words, he must break his engagement with Olivia and reexamine the dozen or so women he'd rejected when he chose her.

"And what am I to say to Lord Darcy? That his daughter's only value to me lies in her ability to produce heirs?" His father's glower told Gabriel he'd stepped into dangerous territory with his sarcasm. At the moment, Gabriel didn't care. What could his father do? For a moment, Gabriel reveled in rebellion. As a teenager, he'd been the best behaved of his siblings, getting into trouble rarely and then never with anything serious.

Nic had started a fire in his room at fifteen experimenting with rockets. Christian had "borrowed" their uncle's Ferrari when he was fourteen and gone joyriding. The expensive sports car had ended up half submerged in a ditch and Christian had been disciplined, but that had only temporarily slowed him down, not stopped him completely.

Gabriel had shouldered his future responsibility like a dutiful son and the newspapers had been filled with photos of him accompanying his mother on her visits to the hospital and various other charitable events and headlines about how lucky Sherdana was to have such a shining example of youth for their next monarch.

"I had fertility problems, as well," the queen reminded her husband, breaking the tension between father and son.

"But neither of us had any idea before we married," the king said, sending his wife a stern look.

"Yet despite your need for an heir, you didn't set me aside when my troubles came to light."

"We'd been married two years. How could I have let you go?"

Gabriel saw the unspoken communication that passed between his parents and felt a flare of envy. The emotion didn't surprise him. He'd felt twinges of it before when watching his parents in private. They were so in sync with each other. He'd hoped for just a little of that depth of intimacy in his own marriage and had begun to believe he'd find it with Olivia.

"Olivia and I will talk later this afternoon."

"You are intending to break off the engagement."

"I'm not sure that's necessary." He saw his father's brows come together. "She claims she had surgery to correct the problem. We need to discuss the situation in more depth and consult a doctor before I make such a radical decision."

The door flew open without a warning knock, catching everyone's attention. Stewart stood in the open doorway, his face stark with concern.

"Forgive my interruption," he said, bowing in apology. "Something has happened to Lady Darcy."

Gabriel's heart jumped in his chest. He surged to his feet and crossed the room in three strides. "What's wrong?"

"I don't know. Miss Marshall said she's locked herself in the bathroom and won't answer the door."

"What makes you think something has happened to her?"

"Her clothes are all over the suite and they've been shredded."

Cursing, Gabriel lunged past his secretary and raced down the hallway. Stewart's long legs usually made him a match for Gabriel, but he had to resort to jogging to keep up.

When Gabriel entered the suite, he registered the destruction in passing but didn't stop. He rushed over to join Olivia's private secretary, who was at the bathroom door, knocking and calling for her to answer. Shoving her aside, Gabriel kicked in the door.

When the door frame gave and the door shot open, the metallic tang of blood immediately hit him. Olivia lay on the cold tile, a large crimson patch on her pale blue skirt. Panic tore through him.

"Call an ambulance!" He dropped to his knees beside her and was relieved to see her chest rise and fall. "When did you enter the suite?" he demanded of her private secretary.

"Perhaps ten minutes ago. I called to her but she didn't open the door or answer. And from what had happened to her clothes I knew something had to be wrong."

How long had she been bleeding like this? Gabriel clenched his teeth and fought the fear rising inside him. She couldn't die. He wouldn't let that happen.

"Get me a blanket off the bed. We're going to take her to the hospital."

Libby did as she was told. "What about the ambulance?"

"There isn't time." Besides, he didn't think he could sit around and watch Olivia slowly bleed to death without going crazy. He'd always prided himself on thought before action, but right now, he was thinking of nothing but saving the woman he'd been yelling at no more than three hours earlier.

Forget that. Focus on getting Olivia to the hospital.

He wrapped her lower half in the blanket and scooped her into his arms. His family had arrived in the hallway just outside the suite. He brushed past his father and brother without answering their offers of help. Olivia was his fiancée. His responsibility.

And he blamed himself for her current crisis. Somehow he knew that if he'd been more approachable, if so much pressure hadn't been brought to bear on her, Olivia might have talked to him about her fertility problems and a safe solution might have been reached.

The limo was waiting at the bottom of the stairs. He settled her into the backseat and cradled her body in his lap. Only then did he become aware of the thundering of his heart. The painful pounding in his chest wasn't caused by carrying her through the palace, but by the sight of her utter stillness and pallor. As the car raced through the palace gates, it finally hit home just how bad this situation was.

"Faster," he growled to the driver as he hooked his finger around a strand of her blond hair and pulled it away from her lips.

The car's powerful engine roared as they sped through the city, but the fifteen-minute drive had never felt so long.

Gabriel brushed his lips across Olivia's forehead and silently pleaded with her to hang on and fight. *Like you fought for her?* Gabriel tried to tune out the mocking inner voice, but guilt sliced at him.

At the hospital's emergency entrance, five people in scrubs crowded the car as soon as it stopped. Stewart must have called ahead and warned them he was coming. They got Olivia situated on a stretcher and took her away before he had a chance to say a word. He rushed toward the glass doors in their wake, catching bits of medical jargon as they sped the unconscious woman inside.

He'd expected to be allowed into the treatment room with her, but a nurse blocked his way.

"Let the doctors work," she said, her voice kind but firm.

He might have ten inches and eighty pounds on her, but Gabriel sensed that the nurse could stop him if he tried to go past.

"How soon will I know something?"

"I'll make sure someone keeps you informed."

"She's lost a lot of blood," he said.

"We know."

She herded him into a private waiting room and offered coffee. Gabriel stared at her, unable to comprehend why this woman was behaving in such a mundane manner while Olivia was down the hall struggling for her life.

"No," he snapped, and then moderated his tone. "Thank you. All I need is information."

She nodded and headed off.

Left alone, Gabriel dropped his head into his hands and surrendered to despair. She couldn't die. She couldn't leave him. He wasn't sure how to step into the future, to become king without her by his side. They would figure a way around her infertility. He recalled his mother's words. She, too, had struggled to produce the heir her husband so desperately needed. When natural methods had failed, she'd gotten help from specialists. And now, she had four children to show for it.

He and Olivia would find specialists, as well. They would have children together.

"Gabriel?"

A hand touched his shoulder. He lifted his head and stared up into his sister's face. She touched his cheek and her fingertips came away with a trace of moisture.

"Is she?" Ariana gasped, seeing his expression.

He shook his head, guessing what conclusion she'd leaped to. "They're working on her now."

"Any word how she's doing?"

"No. The nurse said they'd keep me informed, but she hasn't been back." He glanced at his watch. "That was thirty minutes ago."

What had been happening while he'd been lost in thought? Anxiety flared that he'd had no news. How bad had things gone since she'd been taken away from him?

"She's going to be all right, Gabriel," Ariana said, moving toward him.

Standing, Gabriel wrapped his arms around his sister. She pushed her body against his to offer comfort.

"Your Majesties. Prince Gabriel. Princess Ariana." A

solemn man of average height in pale green scrubs stood five feet away from the royal pair. "I'm Dr. Warner."

Gabriel felt Ariana's tight embrace squeeze his ribs even harder and appreciated her support. "How's Olivia?"

"I won't sugarcoat it. Not good. She's lost a lot of blood." The doctor looked even grimmer as he delivered the next bit of news. "She's still hemorrhaging. We've sent her up to the OR."

A primal cry of denial gathered in Gabriel's chest. "What aren't you telling us?" he demanded.

"The only way to save her may be a hysterectomy. Naturally we will do everything possible to avoid such a drastic procedure."

"Do whatever it takes to save her life." Gabriel pinned the doctor with his gaze, making sure the man understood. "Whatever it takes."

Ten

The first time Olivia opened her eyes, she was aware of nothing but pain. It stabbed at her like slivers of broken glass. Then, something changed. The hurt eased and she fell backward into darkness.

The next time she surfaced, she kept herself awake longer. But not by much. Voices reached her ears, but the speakers were too far away for her to catch individual words. And the pain was back. All she wanted to do was escape into numbness.

They said the third time's the charm. Olivia wasn't sure she agreed when next she regained consciousness. Her body ached. No. Not her body, her abdomen.

Breathless with fear, she stared around the hospital room. It was empty. She was alone.

She felt hollow. Like a balloon filled with air.

The last thing she recalled was fighting with Gabriel. Where was he? Did he know she was in the hospital? Did he even care? Her heart contracted.

"Good to see you awake," a nurse said as she entered the room. "How's your pain?"

"Manageable." Her mouth felt stuffed with cotton. "May I have some water?"

The nurse brought a cup close and placed the straw between Olivia's lips. She sipped gratefully, then sagged back against the pillow, exhausted by the simple movement.

"I feel so weak."

"You've been through a lot."

"What happened to me?"

"The doctor will be along in a little while to talk to you."

Without energy to argue, Olivia closed her eyes and let her mind drift. The silence pressed on her, heightening her tension. She fought to clear her head, sought her last memory. Her period had been heavier than ever before. And the cramping... She'd been afraid, depressed. Gingerly she sent her fingertips questing for the source of her discomfort. Pain shot through her as she pressed on her lower abdomen.

Just then, the door opened again and a handsome older man in scrubs came in. "Good afternoon. I'm Dr. Warner."

"I wish I could say it's nice to meet you."

"I understand. You've been through a tough time."

"What happened to me?" Her mind sharpened as anxiety filled her.

"You were hemorrhaging, and we had a difficult time stopping your blood loss." He plucked her chart out of a pocket attached to the foot of the bed and scrutinized it. "How's your pain?"

"About a six." She waited while he jotted something down on her chart before asking, "How did you stop the hemorrhaging?"

"Surgery." He met her gaze. "It was an extensive procedure."

He hadn't said anything specific, but his expression told her just how extensive the surgery had been.

"I'm never going to have children, am I?"

"I'm sorry. The only way we could stop the bleeding was to remove your uterus."

Olivia shut her eyes to escape the sympathy in the man's face. Denial exploded in her head. She clutched the bed rails, desperate for something to ground her as the world tipped sideways. A wail began in her chest. She clenched her teeth to contain it as a lifetime of discipline and order asserted itself. She would grieve later. In private.

"I know that this will be a difficult adjustment. You are very young to have undergone such a drastic change."

"Who knows?" she whispered.

He looked taken aback. "Your father. The royal family."

"The media?"

"Of course not." Dr. Warner looked appalled.

"Is my father here?"

"He's in the waiting room with Prince Gabriel. I spoke with him an hour ago."

"Could I see him, please? No one else, just my father."

"I'll have the nurse fetch him for you."

But the man who showed up next wasn't a sixty-year-old British earl with gray hair and a neat beard, but a tall, hollow-eyed man with a dark shadow blurring his knife-sharp jawline. Olivia's heartbeat accelerated as Gabriel advanced into the room, his clothes rumpled, his face a mask. He reached out to cover her hand with his, but she moved it away just in time.

"I'm sorry," she said, unable to lift her gaze higher than the open collar of his white shirt. "I should have told you about my medical issues. I just thought that everything was going to be okay."

"You gave us a scare." He pulled a chair beside her bed and lowered himself into it. This put him at eye level with her and made avoiding his fierce golden gaze that much harder. "When I found you on the floor of the bathroom unconscious." His tone made it hard for Olivia to breathe. "I thought…" He shook his head.

"I'm sorry. I had no idea that quitting the pill was going to cause this much…" To her dismay a sob popped out. Just like that. No warning. No chance to swallow it or choke on it. Then tears were streaming down her face and Gabriel was stroking her hair and squeezing her hand. His gentleness only made her feel worse.

"Olivia, I'm so sorry."

He placed her palm against his cheek. The warmth beneath her fingers spread up her arm and drifted through her entire body as she took in the aching sadness in his eyes.

"I'm going to be fine," she lied, hating how much she wanted to lean on him for support. Choking on her misery, she barreled on. "At least now there's no question whether I can have children. You'll never have to wonder if by marrying me you made a huge mistake."

"Marrying you would never have been a mistake."

But if she'd had difficulty getting pregnant, he couldn't help but blame her.

"That's a moot point." She willed herself to be strong and to make the break quick and final. "We can't marry now."

"I'm not giving up on us." He covered her hand with his and regarded her with somber eyes.

"There is no more us, Gabriel." She tugged her hand free. "You are going to be king of Sherdana one day. You need to put your country's needs first."

"I have two brothers—"

"Please." She couldn't bear to hear any more. Anything he said would encourage her to be optimistic and the last thing she needed to do was hope everything was going to be okay. "I'm really tired. And I'm in pain. I just want to see my father."

He looked as if he wanted to argue with her. She shook her head and closed her eyes. Another tear trickled down her cheek, but she ignored it.

"And I think it would be better if you don't visit me again."

"I can't accept that."

"Please, Gabriel."

He exhaled harshly. "I'll get your father."

She waited to open her eyes until his soft footfalls receded. Her fingers tingled from contact with Gabriel's cheek. It brought to mind all those times when her hands had roamed over him, exploring his masculine contours, learning all the delightful ways his body differed from hers.

Reaching toward a nearby box of tissues exhausted her. The weakness was frustrating. Before she had the chance to lose herself in the black cloud of misery that hovered nearby, her father entered the room. His embrace stirred up her emotions again and Olivia began to cry once more. This time, however, she didn't feel the need to hold back. His shirt was soaked by the time she ran out of tears.

"I want to go home," she told him, making use of the tissue box once again.

"The doctor wants to keep you in here for at least a week."

"Can't I be transferred to a hospital in London?"

"You are in no shape to travel." He patted her hand. "It's just a week. Then I'll take you home."

A week. It was too long. More than her body needed to heal and that wouldn't be possible until she was miles and miles from Sherdana and its prince.

Shortly after speaking with Olivia, Gabriel returned to the palace alone, his emotions in turmoil. Staff scattered as he crossed the expansive foyer, heading for his office. The way they disappeared he must have looked like the devil himself had come calling.

It had shocked him that after she'd survived her brush with death, her first act would be to end their engagement. She'd done it gracefully, shouldering the responsibility, leaving him free to move on with a clear conscience.

"Move on."

He spat out the words like the foulest curse. No matter how angry he'd been when he found out about her medical condition, he'd not really considered ending things. How could he ever replace Olivia in his life after making love with her? Watching her with his daughters? Seeing that damned tattoo. *Hope.* He could sure use some right now.

Entering his office, he flung himself into a chair near the cold fireplace. He'd been up all night. Exhaustion should be eating into his bones and muscles, but rage burned white-hot in his veins. He massaged his temples where a headache had begun the minute he'd walked out of Olivia's hospital room. Or perhaps it had been there all along. Up until that moment, he'd been completely focused on Olivia.

But after leaving her bedside, he realized that his role in her life was over. As was her role in his. From now on they would be nothing more than familiar strangers. He would probably not exchange a dozen words with her before she left for England and her old life.

God, his chest ached.

"Your Highness?" Gabriel's secretary had poked his head in the door.

"Not now, Stewart."

He needed some time to adjust. How much time, he didn't know. He'd never imagined having to live without Olivia and he wasn't going to pretend that he could just shake off this tragedy and continue on.

"Your Highness," Stewart persisted. "Your father, the king, wants to speak with you."

"I know my father is the king," Gabriel said, taking his annoyance out on his private secretary. He pushed out of the chair, deciding to face whatever his father had to say now rather that make the king wait until he'd showered and changed.

He found his father on the phone in his office and went

to pour himself a shot of scotch while he waited for him to conclude the call.

"A little early for that, isn't it?" the king demanded as he hung up.

"I think a man's entitled to a drink after his fiancée breaks up with him, don't you?"

The king shot him a hard glance as he rose to his feet and crossed to the tray with the coffeepot and cups. Pouring a cup, he plucked the crystal tumbler from Gabriel's finger and replaced it with bone china.

"I just got off the phone with Lord Darcy. He told me you and Olivia ended things."

Ah, so the old man was pulling his offer to set up a company since his daughter was no longer going to be Sherdana's queen. Gabriel shrugged. He didn't really blame the earl for changing his mind.

"She ended it," he said. "But don't worry. Christian will find us some other prospective investors." He sipped the coffee and regarded his father over the brim. "Perhaps one of them will even have an eligible daughter since apparently I'm back on the market."

The king let Gabriel's bitter comment pass unanswered. "Naturally, I would like to continue pursuing other companies, but the need isn't urgent. Darcy is going forward with his plans."

Gabriel's cup hit the saucer with a clatter. From his contact with Lord Darcy, he knew the man was a hardheaded businessman. Sherdana was a good choice for expansion, but not his only and not necessarily his best.

Olivia.

This was her doing.

The exhaustion he'd expected to feel earlier washed over him now. Gabriel wavered on his feet. "Olivia must have told him to honor the commitment. There's no other reason for Darcy to proceed."

"But if she knows you're not getting married, why would she persuade her father to honor his commitment to us?"

"Because that's the sort of woman she is," Gabriel said. "Honorable. The sort who doesn't go back on a promise. Unlike me," he finished in an undertone.

This time, his bitterness was too much for his father to ignore. "You are not reneging on a promise to Lady Darcy," the king said. "She understands she will never be able to give you an heir and has graciously ended your engagement."

That's when it hit him. He didn't want their engagement to end.

Olivia had promised to marry him. And if she was as honorable as he'd just described, she still would.

After six endless days in the hospital, with pain and grief her constant companions, Olivia was an empty shell in both body and soul. For the majority of her stay she'd lain with her eyes closed, floating on a tide of pain medication that dulled the ache in her lower abdomen but couldn't blunt the agony in her heart. With her ability to bear children ripped from her, she shrank from her future. Abandoned by optimism, tears filled her eyes and ran unheeded down her cheeks. Her losses were too much to bear.

On the third day of her incarceration, Libby had smuggled in her favorite chocolate. Olivia had put on a show of courage for her private secretary, but left alone once more, she'd retreated to the dark place where she contemplated what her life had become.

Then, this morning, twenty-four hours before she was scheduled for release, she instructed Libby to bring her files so she could compile a list of all the things she'd committed to in the past month.

"Are you sure you should be taxing yourself with this?" Libby protested, a dozen files clutched to her chest.

Olivia indicated that she wanted the files placed on the rolling tray positioned over her bed. "I've got to find something to keep my mind busy, or I'll go completely mad."

Libby did as she was told and then retreated to the guest chair with her laptop. "Prince Gabriel…" the private secretary began, breaking off when Olivia shook her head.

"How are Bethany and Karina?"

"They miss you." Libby opened the laptop and stared at the screen. "Everyone at the palace misses you."

Not wishing to go down that path, Olivia changed the subject. "Have they found Marissa's sister yet?"

"I'm afraid not."

The memory of the woman's attack had resurfaced a couple days after Olivia had woken up. It hadn't struck her as odd that no one asked about the incident because she'd assumed Marissa's sister had fled the palace with no one being the wiser.

When she'd shared the story with Libby, Olivia had learned what had happened after she'd passed out in the bathroom. She'd given herself a couple seconds to regret the loss of her wardrobe and then insisted on telling her story to palace security and the police.

"Her apartment in Milan is being watched," Libby continued, "but she hasn't returned there. From what I gather, she hasn't contacted her friends in six months. But I'm sure Prince Gabriel will not be satisfied until she's caught."

"I'll feel better when that happens," Olivia said, and opened the file sitting on top of the pile. It was a budget proposal for some improvements to a school she sponsored in Kenya.

The mundane work soothed her spirit. Nothing better for the soul than to worry about someone else's problems.

Ariana and Christian visited several times in the next

few days and brought regards from the king and queen as well as flowers. But Gabriel had been absent. She'd sent him away and asked Libby to make certain he understood that she wanted him to maintain his distance. Her grief was still too strong. She wasn't ready to face him. Not until she came to terms with the end of her engagement and her empty future.

"Prince Gabriel is desperately worried about you," Libby said.

As sweet as it was for Libby to say, Olivia doubted her use of the word *desperately*.

"I hope you've told him I'm recovering nicely."

"He might like to see that for himself."

Olivia's throat tightened and she shook her head. The words blurred on the sheet of paper she held in her hand and she blinked to clear her vision.

"He really cares for you. It's obvious." Libby sat forward, her eyes bright and intense. "I don't think I've ever seen a man so distraught as when we thought you might die. He commanded the doctor to do whatever it took to save you."

Joy dispelled Olivia's gloom for a moment as she let herself warm to Libby's interpretation of events. "Of course he cares," she agreed, wishing the situation was as simple as that. "We became…close these last few weeks. But he needs an heir. That's something I can't give him."

"But you love him. Surely that counts for more." Libby spoke quietly as if afraid of how Olivia would react to her audacity.

Olivia starting drawing circles on the notepad. She did love Gabriel, but he must never know. She didn't want to burden him with something like that. He already had enough guilt on his shoulders with Marissa. He didn't need to suffer even more regret because another woman entertained a desperate and impossible love for him.

"I love him, but please do not tell a soul," she rushed on as Libby's face lit up. "Prince Gabriel needs to find someone new to marry. I don't want him thinking of me at all as he goes about courting his future bride."

The thought of Gabriel with another woman made her heart ache, but she fought the pain.

Libby's delight became determination. "I really think he needs to know."

Olivia offered her friend a sad smile. "He can't. Sherdana deserves a queen who can have children."

"What about what you deserve?" Libby pushed. "Don't you deserve to be happy?"

"I will be," she assured her secretary. "My life isn't over. I'm just starting a new chapter. Not the one I expected to be starting, but how often do we get exactly what we expect?"

Eleven

Staring at pictures of women he'd rejected six months ago wasn't stimulating Gabriel's appetite for lunch.

"What do you think of Reinette du Piney?" his mother asked, sliding an eight-by-ten head shot of a very beautiful brunette across the table toward him.

"She's pigeon-toed," he replied, slipping his spoon beneath a carrot and lifting it free of the broth. "What exactly is it I'm eating?"

"Creamy carrot soup with anise. The chef is experimenting again."

"You really must stop him from inflicting his culinary curiosity on us."

"Gabriel, you cannot reject du Piney because she's pigeon-toed."

He wasn't. He was rejecting her because the only woman he wanted to marry had made it clear she was going to do the right thing for Sherdana even if he wouldn't.

In the meantime, his mother had persisted in starting the search for his future wife all over again, despite Gabriel's refusal to contribute anything positive.

"I'm only thinking of our children," he countered, setting his spoon down and tossing his napkin over it. "Imagine how they'd be teased at school if they inherited their mother's unfortunate trait."

"Your children will not be teased at school because

they will be tutored at home the way you and your siblings were." His mother sifted through the pictures and pulled out another. "What about Amelia? You liked her."

"She was pleasant enough. But I think her husband would take umbrage with me for poaching his wife."

"Bother."

Gabriel might have felt like smiling at his mother's equivalent of a curse if he wasn't feeling so damned surly. Olivia had left the hospital a few days ago and was staying at the Royal Caron Hotel until her surgeon cleared her for travel. By bribing the man with an enormous donation toward updating the hospital with digital radiology, Gabriel had succeeded in keeping her in Sherdana longer than necessary. He'd hoped she would let him apologize to her in person, but she adamantly refused to see him.

"Gabriel, are you listening to me?"

"I'm not going to marry any of these women."

His mother sat back and stared at him, her eyes narrowed and searching. "Have you decided on someone else?"

"Yes. The same person I've wanted all along."

"Olivia."

"You don't sound surprised."

"You take after your father. He's a romantic devil, too." Her eyes sparkled at Gabriel's doubtful expression. "Oh, not that anyone other than me would know it, but he wouldn't consider divorcing me when I couldn't get pregnant. Even after I left him and made him think that I'd fallen in love with another man."

"What?" This was a tale he'd never heard. "You fell in love with someone while you were married to Father?"

His mother laughed gaily. "Of course not. But I certainly convinced your father I did." A faraway look entered her eyes. "But he chased after me and discovered there was no other man. I finally admitted that the doctor told me I couldn't get pregnant the old-fashioned way and together we figured out a solution."

That sounded familiar. Except for the part where a solution was found together.

"I'm surprised," Gabriel admitted.

"Because your father counseled you to break your engagement with Olivia even before the hysterectomy? You need to understand how difficult those days were for us. The doubt, the worry. It was hard on us. Hard on our marriage. And we were deeply in love."

Her last words struck a nerve. "And Olivia and I are not." His mother's assumption annoyed him more than it should.

Given that he'd only just begun to get acquainted with the woman he had been planning to marry, it made sense that he couldn't possibly love her.

And if not love, then what emotion was at the root of his miserable existence without Olivia?

"He just wants to spare you." She reached across the table and laid her hand over his. "We both do."

Gabriel captured her gaze. "Would you change anything about the decision you made? Knowing the trials and heartbreak you suffered, would you walk away from the man you love and never look back?"

His mother withdrew her hand and sat back. Her expression was determined and sad at the same time. "No."

"Thank you."

He stood and circled the table to kiss her cheek. Expecting her to ask what he was up to, she surprised him again by staying silent.

Leaving his mother, he headed upstairs to await Olivia's arrival. She'd made arrangements through his mother to visit Bethany and Karina and bring them a special birthday present. Gabriel knew it was cheating to use his daughters to secure time with Olivia, but he was feeling a little desperate. If his daughters had taught him anything it was how to exist in the moment. There was no past or future with them. They lived for hugs, treats, mischief and pony rides. Every second in their company reminded him that wonderful things came out of less than ideal situations.

The twins weren't in the nursery. He'd arranged for them to have a picnic in the garden. In half an hour they would arrive for their nap. He hoped that gave him enough time with Olivia. While he waited, he sat on Bethany's bed and picked up the photo of Marissa on the girls' nightstand. A scrapbook had been among the twins' possessions. Olivia had chosen this particular picture to frame and place between the girls so they would remember their mother.

Marissa was pregnant in the picture. Not full-term, perhaps seven months, yet still huge. Had she known she was carrying twins? He traced her smile with his fingertips. She looked older than he remembered, aged by experience, not years, yet luminescent in motherhood.

Why hadn't she contacted him when she knew she was pregnant? Had she not wished to burden him? Had she feared his rejection yet again? He couldn't have married her. Wouldn't have married her. Even if Sherdana's laws hadn't dictated his bride needed to be a citizen of the country or of noble birth for his offspring to be able to inherit the crown, where Gabriel and Marissa had been most compatible was between the sheets, which was where they'd spent half of their time together.

Out of bed, her passionate nature had revealed itself in turbulent emotions and insecurity. He knew the latter had been his fault. He couldn't offer her a future and she'd deserved better. In the end, he'd let her go and part of him had been relieved.

He'd put Sherdana's needs before hers. He'd done the same with Olivia. Only this time there was no certainty that he'd made the right decision. No sense that a burden had been lifted from his shoulders. His daughters were the only bright spot in his future. His mother wanted him to consider who would become his princess, but he couldn't make that decision until he spoke with Olivia and saw for himself what was in her heart.

Olivia took on the challenge of the palace stairs at a sedate pace, but was uncomfortably short of breath by the time she reached the first landing. Several maids trotted past her, but none of the staff paid her undue attention. Still, she felt like an interloper in the place where she thought she'd spend the rest of her life.

Relaxing her grip on the gaily wrapped packages containing china dolls, Olivia forced herself to keep climbing. As beautiful as the dolls were, giving toddlers such delicate toys was probably a recipe for disaster. But Olivia wanted to share with the girls something special. The dolls were just like the one her mother had bought for her and not lived to present the gift.

In her heart Olivia knew it was selfish of her to want them to remember her. First their mother had died and now they faced the loss of someone else they relied on. It was too much change for ones so young. At least they would still have their father. Olivia was comforted by how much Gabriel loved his daughters.

In two days the twins turned two. The party Olivia had spent weeks planning had stirred the palace into new heights of frantic activity. As much as Olivia wanted to go, attending was out of the question. Even though she knew the twins would want her there, they were undoubtedly the only members of the royal family who would.

Who could blame them? Olivia knew the end of her engagement to Gabriel had driven the media into a frenzy of speculation about whom he might choose for his next bride. Social networks had blown up with news about the top two candidates. As long as Olivia remained in the picture, the news outlets would stir the pot. It was better if she disappeared from Sherdana. But she couldn't go without saying goodbye to Bethany and Karina.

Her slow rise to the second floor gave Olivia lots of time to remember how golden her future had seemed the first time she'd ascended these stairs and to brood about the handsome prince who'd never be hers.

Coming to the palace was a risk. She might run into Gabriel and lose the modicum of peace she'd made with her situation. At the same time, she was foolishly excited at the thought of running into Gabriel again. Even knowing they could never be together didn't stop her from longing to see him one last time.

It was irrational, but she'd been hurt that he'd heeded her desire for no further contact after her surgery. She'd broken things off. While part of her was relieved that he'd honored her wishes, her less rational side had resented Gabriel for taking her at her word.

But what truly upset her was, after everything that had happened, she continued to crave his company. She woke from dreams where he held her close and whispered she was his life, his dearest love, and discovered she was alone. And all along, her heart hung heavy in her chest. Emptiness lingered below the stinging incision in her abdomen. Depression coiled about her thoughts, threatening to smother her. A dozen get-well bouquets brightened her hotel suite but couldn't pierce the fog surrounding her emotions.

Olivia paused at the top step and leaned on the banister to catch her breath before proceeding down the hall to the nursery. She knew the twins would be finishing up lunch and had chosen this time to visit because it limited how long she would stay.

When she got to the nursery, she stopped just inside the

doorway, but didn't see the twins. Instead, Gabriel occupied the space. Her heart gave a giddy leap. He sat on Bethany's bed, a silver frame in his hands, fingertips tenderly resting on the face of the woman in the photo. Marissa.

His expression held such sorrow, his mouth drooping in regret as she'd never seen before. Her heart wept for his obvious grief, but the tears that sprang to her eyes weren't for Gabriel; they were for herself. She'd believed him when he claimed to be over Marissa, but three years later he continued to grieve for what could never be. Was that how she looked in those unguarded moments when she thought about all she'd lost? Was this what it looked like when a heart shattered?

Suddenly this errand didn't seem like a good idea. She should have let Libby bring Bethany and Karina to the hotel instead of returning to the palace. But the media had camped out in front of the hotel in the hope that she'd comment on her broken engagement. During the short walk from lobby door to car, Olivia had worn dark glasses and a wide brimmed hat to prevent the photographers from catching a newsworthy photo of her. Olivia couldn't put the girls in the middle of the chaos.

"Olivia!"

Gabriel's head snapped up at the enthusiastic cries coming from behind her. His gaze crashed into hers. She wobbled beneath the triple impact of the twins wrapping their arms around her hips and the raw emotion in Gabriel's eyes.

The twins' demands for attention offered her no chance to react to what she'd seen, but she was glad. Remaining upright as they pressed against her became that much harder thanks to the bulky, delicate bundles she carried.

Gabriel stepped forward and took the packages from her. "Girls, be gentle with Olivia. She's been sick and is very fragile."

The glow in his eyes warmed her head to toe as he extricated her from the twins' enthusiastic embrace. She had a hard time looking away.

"Don't like sick," Bethany proclaimed, her lower lip slipping forward.

Karina gave her head a vigorous shake.

"I'm much better now, but still a little sore. Like when you skin your knee how it takes a while to stop hurting."

Karina bent down to touch Olivia's unblemished knees. "Hurt?"

Olivia laughed. "No, angel. My knees are okay. My hurt is here." She pointed to her stomach.

"Can we see?" Bethany demanded.

Olivia gestured toward the packages Gabriel had set on their beds. "Why don't you open your birthday presents instead."

"Birthday."

Olivia smiled past her sadness at having to go home to England and never see these girls again. "They are very special. I hope you like them."

While the girls tore into the wrapping, Olivia watched them, but her attention was captured by the tall man who stood so close beside her. It seemed the worst sort of torture not to lean into his strength and forget about the past week. But the twinges in her abdomen kept her grounded in reality.

"That was a lovely gift," Gabriel said as the girls fell to exclaiming over the dolls' hair and wardrobe.

"Something for them to remember me by." Emotion seized her by the throat. "I didn't realize leaving them was going to be so hard."

"You could stay longer."

Olivia flinched at how her heart leaped with hope. "I can't, and it's not fair of you to ask."

Why would he even want her to stay? He knew as well

as she did that having her around would create problems for him both in the media and in his search for a bride.

"A lot of things haven't been fair lately." He brushed her hair off one shoulder, grazing her skin in the process.

To Olivia's immense shock, desire sparked. How was it possible after all she'd been through? She looked up to see if Gabriel had noticed her reaction and to her dismay, he had.

"Olivia." His deep voice rumbled in his chest, creating a matching vibration in her. "We need to talk." He found her hand with his.

The slide of his fingers against hers made her heart race. "I think we've said everything there is to say."

"Maybe you have, but I have a few things you need to hear."

Olivia's gaze shot toward the twins. To her relief, they were oblivious to the charged undercurrents passing between her and Gabriel. The girls had been through enough and didn't deserve to witness them arguing. She turned her back to them and pitched her voice to carry no farther than the foot that separated her from Gabriel.

"Don't do this. There's nothing you have to say that I want to hear. What I need is to leave this country and forget all about you."

"Can you do that?" he murmured, his free hand cupping the side of her face, his tender touch bringing tears to her eyes. "Can you forget me? Forget how it was between us?"

Harsh emotions sandblasted her nerves raw. "Would you want me to do otherwise?"

"Yes. Stay and fight—"

"Fight?" The word gusted out of her on a bitter laugh. "I have nothing left to fight with. It's gone, Gabriel. My ability to bear children. My chance to be a mother. I'm nothing more than a shell." An empty shell without him. "I just want to go home and forget."

Forget how his smile transformed her.

Forget how it felt to fall asleep in his arms.

Forget how much she loved him.

"Can you?" He cupped the back of her neck and pulled her gently against his powerful, muscular body. "Can you forget me?"

Her pulse danced with erotic longing. She tore her gaze away from the sensual light in his eyes that drew her like a candle in the darkness. How was it possible she could want him with such intensity when the parts that made her a whole woman were gone?

He lowered his voice to a husky murmur. "Because I will never be able to forget you."

It wasn't fair of him to tell her that. To tantalize her with longing for what could never be.

Contact with him seared her from breast to thigh. Her incision burned the way it had during those first few days, reminding her that she'd have a permanent mark on her body that would never let her forget.

"Maybe not forget," she told him, keeping her voice soft to hide its unsteadiness. "But you'll move on and be happy."

Before he could respond, they were struck from two sides by the twins. Sandwiched between them, Olivia had no way to escape Gabriel. He saw her predicament and a predatory smile curved his lips before they descended to hers.

Sweet sunshine washed through her body as she surrendered to the delicious drag of his mouth against hers. This was where she belonged. To this man. And these girls. The family she craved.

Her whole world contracted to Gabriel's kiss and the twins' hugs. A great rushing sound filled her ears, drowning out her inner voice and all the reasons why this couldn't be her future. Loving Gabriel had never seemed so easy.

Outside pressure didn't exist. She was free to express herself, to tell him what was truly in her heart.

I love you.

But she never uttered the words because the girls clamored for their own share of Olivia's attention as the kiss fell apart. Her lips tingled in the aftermath as Gabriel held her close a moment longer before letting her step back.

"Tea party. Tea party," Bethany called.

Karina seized her and pulled.

It took her a couple seconds to realize that the girls were referring to the small table set up near the window. She shook her head. "It's your nap time."

"Girls, Olivia is right. Hattie will read to you after you lie down."

While it hurt to kneel and give hugs and kisses to each of the toddlers, Olivia braved the pain for one last goodbye. By the time they had been persuaded to let her go, Olivia's sorrow had rendered her mute.

Gabriel seemed to understand her distress because he waited until they'd descended to the grand hall before speaking. "When are you leaving?"

"My final doctor's appointment is later this week. I expect to be able to travel after that."

"You really should come to the twins' birthday party. You planned everything. It's only right that you be there."

Temptation trembled through her. It would be so easy to agree, to prolong the final parting for another day. But what good would that do? She'd have one more memory to keep her awake at night.

"I think it's better that we said our goodbyes now."

"I don't agree." He took her hand and stopped her from leaving. His gold eyes were somber as he met her gaze. "Bethany and Karina will be sad if you don't come."

His touch made her want to turn back the clock. If she'd not been so rash as to stop taking the pill against her doctor's order, she would be marrying Gabriel in a week. Then again, the burden of producing an heir to the kingdom would still be weighing heavily on her.

"And I'm not ready to say goodbye," he said, interrupting her thoughts.

She delighted at his words, until she recalled how he'd looked at that photo of Marissa. Three years ago he'd turned his back on her and chosen his country instead. Olivia had seen the way he'd been tortured by that choice every time he looked at his daughters. Was he hoping that putting his country's needs second this time would somehow redeem him for failing Marissa?

She eased her hand free. "You already have. The second the story of my fertility issues made it to prime time any chance of us getting married was gone." She touched his arm in sympathy. "People in our positions don't belong to themselves."

"That's true," he murmured, seizing her chin and forcing her to look at him. "You belong to me."

She jerked away and took a step back. "I don't." But her blood sang another tune. She was his, heart and soul. There would be no other.

"Deny it all you want, but I was the first man who made love to you. The first man you loved. That sort of bond may stretch but it will not break."

Her pulse rocked at his use of the word *love*. Did he know the depth of her feelings for him? She'd not been particularly careful to guard her emotions during those long hours in his arms. Had he figured out the truth or was he simply referring to the physical act of loving?

"Why are you saying these things? Do you think leaving is easy for me?" She spied the front door and knew her reprieve was mere steps away, but she had a few hard truths to deliver first. "I was planning on making my life here with you. It hurts more than I can say that I can't marry you. Asking me to stay is completely—"

"Selfish," he interrupted, lifting her palm to his lips. "You're right. I am selfish."

When he released her hand, Olivia clenched her fingers around the kiss. His blunt admission had dimmed her frustration. This impossible situation was of her making. If only she'd told him of her fertility issues. He never would have proposed. She never would have fallen in love with him.

"You have a right to be selfish sometimes." Her smile wobbled, and then steadied. "You are a prince, after all."

"And yet it's not gaining me any ground with you, is it?"

She shook her head. "I'll come to the twins' birthday party."

It wasn't what she'd intended to say, but her heart had a mind of its own. Knowing she would never be able to take it back, Olivia remained silent as Gabriel escorted her to the waiting car and handed her into the backseat.

As the car rolled down the driveway, Olivia knew she'd been a fool to come here today. Obviously she hadn't learned anything these past few weeks. Gabriel held a power over her that was nothing short of dangerous. Thank goodness he would never know how unhappy she was without him because she had a feeling he might do something incredibly foolish.

Twelve

For the next two days leading up to his daughters' birthday party, Gabriel worked tirelessly to bring Christian up to speed on all the things that might come up in the next two weeks. After his last encounter with Olivia, he'd decided to take himself off the grid for a short time. Olivia's stubborn refusal to continue their relationship had forced Gabriel into a difficult position. Sherdana needed a royal heir. He needed Olivia. The opposing forces were tearing him apart.

On the morning of Bethany and Karina's birthday, Gabriel put his signature on the last report requiring his approval and went to have breakfast with his daughters. As usual they were full of energy and he smiled as he listened to their excited conversation.

It pleased him that Karina spoke more often now. Maybe she'd never be as talkative as her sibling, but as her confidence grew, she demonstrated a bright mind and a sly sense of humor. He had Olivia to thank for the transformation. She'd coaxed the younger twin out of her shell with patience and love. As attached as the trio had become, Gabriel was worried that Olivia's leaving would give rise to the girls' feelings of abandonment.

Scooping Karina onto his lap, he tickled her until she whooped with laughter. Could he make Olivia understand that there was more at stake than an heir for Sherdana?

Perhaps today's party would be the perfect opportunity to impress upon her how much she was needed and loved.

The festivities began at three. A large tent had been erected on the expansive lawn just east of the palace. A band played children's songs nearby and a dozen children jumped and twirled to the music in the open space between the stage and the linen-clad tables. Beyond that was a balloon bouncer shaped like a castle. The structure swayed as children burned off energy. On the opposite side of the lawn, their parents enjoyed more sedate entertainment in the form of an overflowing buffet of delicacies and free-flowing alcohol.

The crowd was a mix of wealthy nobility and leading businessmen. Gabriel stayed close to Bethany and Karina as they ate cake and played with the other children, keeping an eye out for Olivia as the afternoon progressed. She didn't arrive until almost five.

Looking pale and very beautiful in a light pink dress with short fluttery sleeves, she moved through the crowd, smiling politely when she encountered someone familiar, but otherwise avoiding eye contact with the guests.

Gabriel snagged a pair of wineglasses off the tray of a passing waiter. It was a chardonnay from one of Sherdana's finest wineries and he remembered how Olivia had wanted to tour the wine country. He added that to the list of things he'd promised and never delivered.

She caught sight of him when she was thirty feet away and very much looked as if she'd like to run away. Besieged by the memory of the kiss they'd shared in the nursery and the longing he'd tasted on her lips, Gabriel knew the only way to circumvent her stubbornness was to demonstrate the power of their passion for each other.

"I'm glad you came," he told her, as he drew close enough to speak. "I was beginning to worry that you wouldn't."

"I almost didn't." Her expression was rueful as she accepted the glass of wine he offered. "But I promised that I would."

"Bethany and Karina will be very glad."

Her gaze moved to where the twins were running with several children close to their age. "They look like they're having fun."

"All thanks to you. The party is fantastic."

"Libby did most of the work."

"But you are the one who came up with the concept and organized everything. You have quite a knack for party planning."

"In London I was on committees for several charities. I've done several large events, including children's parties. And speaking of children, I should probably say hello to Bethany and Karina. I won't be able to stay at the party long."

He inspected her face. Shadows beneath her eyes gave her the appearance of fragility. "Are you in pain?"

"Just tired." Her wan smile held none of her former liveliness. "My strength is not coming back as quickly as I'd like and I'm not sleeping well."

Gabriel tucked her hand into the crook of his arm and led her on a slow, meandering journey toward the twins, extending the amount of his time in her company. The tension in her slim frame troubled him and Gabriel wished he could do something to bring back the happy, vital woman she'd been two weeks earlier. He'd never felt so helpless.

Before he could bring her to where the twins were holding court, his daughters saw them coming and ran over. As they threw their tiny arms around her, Olivia's smile grew radiant. But there was sadness, as well. Sadness Gabriel knew he could banish if only she'd let him.

Hyped up on sweets and attention, the twins didn't linger long. After they'd raced back toward the other children, Olivia sidestepped away from Gabriel.

"I've taken up enough of your time," she said. "You have guests to attend to and I need to go."

He caught her wrist, preventing her from departing. "You're the only one I care about."

"Please don't," she pleaded in a hoarse whisper. "This is already so hard."

"And that's my fault." This wasn't a discussion he wanted to have in the middle of his daughters' birthday party, but he had to try one last time to reason with her. "Let me at least walk you out."

She must have seen his determination because she nodded.

Instead of leading her around the palace, he drew her through the doors leading to the green salon where they could have a little privacy.

"I'm sorry I didn't handle things better between us."

When he stopped in the middle of the room and turned her to face him she sighed. Looking resigned, she met his gaze. "You handled everything the way a future king should. I was the one who was wrong. I should have told you about my past medical issues before you had a chance to propose."

"What if I told you it wouldn't have mattered?" Gabriel lifted her hand and placed her palm over his heart.

"Then I would have to insult the crown prince of Sherdana by telling him he's a fool." She tried to pull her hand free, but he'd trapped it beneath his. Her tone grew more impatient. "You need an heir. That's something I can't give you."

"Unfortunate, yes. But that doesn't change the fact that I chose you and I'd committed to building a life with you. I'm not ready to give that up."

"That's madness," she exclaimed. "You have to. You must marry someone who can give you children."

Gabriel scowled at her response. "That's what the country needs me to do. But I'm not a country. I'm a man. A man who is tired of making everyone else's priorities his own."

"You don't have a choice," she whispered, blinking rapidly. "You are going to be king. You must do what's right. And so must I." With surprising strength, she wrenched her hand free and turned to flee.

"Olivia." He started after her, but realized nothing he could say at that moment would persuade her to change her mind.

Releasing a string of curses, Gabriel pulled out his cell phone and dialed. When the call connected, he said, "She won't budge."

"I'm sorry to hear that, Your Highness. The arrangements you asked for are complete and awaiting your arrival. Are you still planning on traveling the day after tomorrow?"

"Yes."

With the upheaval of the past several weeks, this was probably not the best time for him to leave the country, but he'd let the impossible situation with Olivia go on too long. She'd been right to say he didn't have a choice about his future. Fate had set him on a path and he needed to follow it to the end.

He found his parents together in the garden. They were strolling arm in arm, pausing here and there to greet their guests and enjoying the warm afternoon. He almost hated to spoil their peaceful moment.

"It was lovely of Olivia to come today," his mother said.

"She wanted to wish Bethany and Karina a happy birthday."

"You spent a lot of time with her." The queen's voice held a question.

Gabriel wondered how much his mother knew about his intentions. "It was her first social appearance since our engagement ended. I thought she could use the support."

"Of course. What happened with her was tragic and we cannot be seen turning our backs on her." Although the queen had spoken sympathetically about Olivia's plight, her priorities were her family and the country. "But you must not encourage her."

A bitter laugh escaped him. "She's well aware that I need a wife who can have children. If you think anything different, you don't appreciate her character."

The queen gave Gabriel a hard look. "Of course."

Gabriel shifted his gaze to his daughters. A trio of pre-teen girls were chasing the twins through the gardens. They laughed as they ran and Gabriel's heart lightened at the sound.

"I wanted to let you know," he began, returning his attention to his parents, "that in a couple days, I'm going out of town for a week or so."

"Is this the best time?" his father asked, echoing what Gabriel had been thinking minutes earlier.

"Perhaps not, but I have the future to think about and Sherdana still needs a princess."

The king frowned. "What about the state dinner for the Spanish ambassador?"

"Christian can take over while I'm gone." Gabriel forced his shoulders to relax. "I'm not the only prince in this family, you know. It's about time my brothers remembered that."

"I'm glad to hear you're ready to move forward," his mother said. "Can you give us some hint of your plans?"

"I'd rather wait until everything is finalized before I say anything."

"Very sensible," his father said and Gabriel wondered if the king would feel that way if he had any idea where his son was going and why.

Two days after the twins' birthday party, Olivia sat in an examination room, awaiting the doctor and fighting sadness. She was flying back to London in the morning. Back to her flat and her friends.

Her return would be far from triumphant. She'd been stripped of the ability to have children and because of that lost the man she loved. Thinking about the future only intensified her grief, so she'd spent the past few days finishing up the tasks she'd left undone such as the finalization of the menu for the hospital's children's wing gala taking place the following month and writing to cancel the invitations she'd accepted when she was still Gabriel's fiancée.

After ten minutes of waiting, Dr. Warner entered the room and interrupted her thoughts. Olivia was glad he accepted her assurances that she was getting along just fine in the wake of her hysterectomy and didn't voice the concern hovering in his expression. If he'd encouraged her to talk about her emotional health she might have burst into tears.

"Everything looks good," the doctor announced. "No reason you can't travel whenever you want."

"I'm leaving tomorrow," she said.

"Make sure you check in with your regular doctor within a week or two. He should be able to assist you with any side effects from your procedure and recommend a fertility specialist."

"Fertility specialist?" she echoed. "I don't understand. I can't have children."

"You can't bear children," the doctor agreed. "But your ovaries are intact. It might be possible to harvest your eggs and freeze them in case you decide to pursue motherhood in the future."

"I could be a mother?" Olivia breathed, overcome by the possibility that something she'd longed for with all her heart could still come to pass.

"You'd need to find a surrogate," the doctor said, his eyes twinkling. "And of course, you'd need a father, but it's certainly a possibility."

"I never imagined..." Her voice trailed off.

"Medical science is making miracles happen every day."

The doctor left her alone to dress and Olivia went through the motions in a daze. Her first impulse was to call Gabriel and tell him her news. Then she imagined how that call would go.

Gabriel, I have great news, I might be able to be a mother, after all. It's chancy and it will involve another woman carrying the baby, but it would be my egg.

Could a country as traditional as Sherdana accept a prince conceived in a test tube? And raised by a mother who hadn't actually carried him inside her for nine months?

Could Gabriel?

When Olivia returned to her suite at the hotel, she couldn't stop pacing as her mind spun through her options. Possible scenarios crowded her like desperate beggars in need of coin. Staring out the window at the river, she held her phone against her chest and searched for the courage she needed to dial Gabriel's number and tell him that she loved him and find out if he was willing to take a risk with her.

The sun had set by the time she dialed. With her heart pounding against her ribs, she counted rings, her hope fading as the number grew larger. When his deep voice poured through the receiver, telling her he was unavailable and asking her to leave a message at the tone, she held her breath for five seconds, then disconnected the call. She really didn't want to share her news with his voice mail.

Next, she tried Stewart. This time, she got through.

"I was trying to get ahold of Gabriel," she told his private secretary. "Do you know if he's in the palace?"

"No. He left two hours ago."

"Do you know where he went?" A long pause followed her question. Olivia refused to be put off by Stewart's reluctance. "It's important that I speak with him."

"I'm sorry, Lady Darcy. He has left the country."

"Did he go to Italy?"

Stewart paused before replying. "All he would tell me is that he had something he needed to do that would impact the future generations of Alessandros."

Olivia's stomach plummeted as she pictured Count Verreos and his beautiful daughter from the twins' birthday party and recalled the familiarity between her and Gabriel. Had they reached an understanding already? Was she Olivia's replacement?

"Is there any way to reach him?" she asked, desperation growing as she suspected where Gabriel and gone and why.

"I've left him several messages that he hasn't returned," Stewart answered, sounding unhappy.

"How long was he planning to be gone?"

"A week to ten days. Before departing, he left instructions that you should be given use of the royal family plane. It will be available to take you back to England tomorrow."

"That's kind of him." Although disappointed that Gabriel had at long last accepted their relationship was over, Olivia wasn't deterred. "But when you speak with him, would you tell him I intend to stay in Sherdana until we can speak face-to-face."

She hadn't believed Gabriel when he'd insisted this wasn't over between them. If only she'd known how right he was a couple days earlier.

After hanging up with Stewart, Olivia called her father and gave him the news that she was staying another week, but didn't share the real reason. To her relief, he didn't try to talk her into coming home immediately.

With nothing to do but wait, Olivia had an early dinner and took a walk in the private walled garden behind the hotel. Instead of enjoying the picturesque charm of the boxwood hedges and urns filled with cascades of bright flowers, Olivia grew more anxious with every step. What if Gabriel was proposing to Fabrizia Verreos at this very moment? A painful spasm in her chest forced Olivia to stop. Gasping for air, she sat down on a nearby stone bench and fought to normalize her breathing. She focused on the fat blossoms on the peach rosebush across the path from her. Closing her eyes would have allowed her mind to fill with images of another woman in Gabriel's arms.

A vibration against her upper thigh provided a welcome distraction. Pulling out her cell phone Olivia saw Stewart was calling. Her pulse hitched as hope bloomed.

"Prince Gabriel called me a few minutes ago," Stewart explained. "He is unable to return to Sherdana at the moment, but when I explained you intended to linger until he came home, he asked if you would fly to meet with him tomorrow."

It was what she wanted, but based on her panic attack a moment earlier, she was thinking that perhaps Gabriel intended to tell her in person that he was moving on.

"Of course." Afterward she could fly home.

"The plane will be waiting for you at ten. I'll send a car to pick you up."

"Thank you."

Olivia hung up and continued her walk, plagued by worries.

What if she didn't reach him before he proposed to Fabrizia? What if despite the passionate kiss he'd given her the day of the twins' birthday he wasn't willing to risk the unconventional method needed in order for them to conceive the next generation of Alessandros?

Pushing everything out of her mind that she couldn't control, Olivia concentrated on what she was going to say to Gabriel about the change in her circumstances. By the time Olivia returned to her room, she'd rehearsed and discarded a dozen ways to convince Gabriel they could have children. In the end, she decided the best argument was to tell him she loved him. And she was grateful she only had to wait hours instead of days before she could speak the truth of her heart.

The next morning saw her staring out the window with blurry vision as the royal family's private plane taxied down the runway. Plagued by uncertainty, she hadn't slept but an hour or so. Lulled by the drone of the engines, she shut her eyes and didn't realize she'd drifted off until the change in altitude woke her. Glancing at her watch, she saw that she'd been asleep for nearly two hours.

Stretching, she glanced out the window, expecting to see Italy's lush green landscape, but what greeted her eyes was shimmering blue water. The plane touched down smoothly and rolled toward a series of private hangers.

"Where are we?" she asked the copilot as he lowered the steps that would allow her to disembark into the foreign landscape.

"Cephalonia," the pilot answered, carrying her overnight bag down the steps to a waiting car. He handed her bag to the driver. "Greece."

"Thank you," she murmured to both men as she slid into the car's backseat. Although why she was thanking them, she had no idea. If they were kidnapping her, this was the oddest way to go about it.

"Where are we going?" she questioned the driver as he

navigated along a coastal road cut into the mountainside with a stunning view of the sea.

"Fiskardo."

Which told her absolutely nothing. The only thing she was certain of at this moment was that she was nowhere near Italy and Gabriel. What sort of trick had Stewart played on her? Was this some sort of plot to get her out of the way while Gabriel did his duty and secured himself a new fiancée?

If that was the case, Stewart better be the villain. If Gabriel had orchestrated this stunt, she was going to be even more heartbroken. Pulling out her phone, she dialed first Gabriel, then Stewart when the former still didn't answer. She had no luck getting through.

As soon as she arrived at her destination, she would figure out her next step. If this was Stewart's gambit, she would find another way to get in contact with Gabriel. Perhaps the queen would help.

With nothing to do for the moment, Olivia stared out the window as the car descended from the mountains and drove down into a seaside town. She'd never visited any of the Greek Ionian Islands before and acknowledged the scenery in this area was spectacular. At least Stewart had been kind enough to find a gorgeous place to squirrel her away. As the car navigated through town, she glimpsed the whitewashed houses with their flower-draped balconies and wondered if her final destination was one of the lovely hotels overlooking the harbor. Her spirits sank as they passed each one and came to a stop a short distance from the waterfront.

They were met by a handsome swarthy Greek in his midfifties who flashed blinding white teeth in a mischievous grin. Seeing his good humor restored her own. She followed him along the cement quay, lined with chartered sailboats, believing that there had to be a happy ending to all this adventuring.

"I am Thasos," he said as he helped her onto a luxurious thirty-four-foot cruiser.

"Where are we going, Thasos?" she questioned, accepting the glass of wine offered, glad for it and the tray of Greek food that awaited her.

"Kioni."

Another name that rang no bells. With a sigh, Olivia munched on bread, dolmas, cheese and olives while the boat sped out of the harbor. If she'd thought the water had appeared beautiful from the coast, it was nothing compared to the sparkling blue that surrounded her now. A short distance away, another island loomed, a great green hulk adorned with olive trees and cypress. Few houses dotted the mountainsides. She would have worried about being in such a remote area, but the bustle of the town they'd just left behind told her she hadn't been brought to the ends of the earth.

After polishing off a second glass of wine and taking the edge off her hunger, she stared at the coastline as it passed. Ninety minutes on the water brought them to another harbor, this one shaped like a horseshoe with three windmills on one side of its mouth.

"Kioni," Thasos explained with another wide grin.

Olivia sighed, wondering who was going to meet her here. Could she expect another taxi ride? Perhaps the plan was to keep her moving until she cried uncle. While Thasos maneuvered the boat toward the cement seawall that circled the harbor, Olivia gazed at this town. Smaller and less busy than Fiskardo, it nevertheless had the same charm. A few houses clustered close to the waterfront, but most clung to the side of the mountain that rose above this scenic harbor.

Everywhere she looked vivid purple and magenta bougainvillea vines brightened the whitewashed buildings or arched over the steps that led to the homes perched on the hillside. Silence descended as Thasos killed the motor and the light breeze brought the clank of cowbells to her ears. But she doubted the steep terrain was suitable for cows. More likely the bells she heard belonged to goats.

She stepped off the boat, helped by Thasos and another man, who claimed her bag for the next part of her journey. Olivia followed him for about thirty steps before she spied a tall, familiar figure coming down the street toward her.

Gabriel.

His white pants, pale blue shirt and navy blazer gave him the look of casual elegance. Her heart jumped in her chest as the wind tousled his hair. He slid his sunglasses up on his head as he approached and gave her a gentle smile.

He wasn't in Italy proposing to the daughter of an Italian count. He was here and from the expression on his face, he was very glad to see her.

Thirteen

The unguarded expression on Olivia's face when she spotted him made Gabriel the happiest man on earth. He was her white knight come to rescue her from the dragons. The fact that he was towing a donkey instead of a black charger hadn't made an impact on her yet.

"What are you doing here?" she demanded. "You're supposed to be in Italy."

He shook his head. "Italy? Where did you get that idea?"

"Stewart said you had gone to do something that would impact future generations of Alessandros. I assumed you meant to…propose to the daughter of Count Verreos." She touched the corner of her eye where a trace of moisture had gathered and a ragged exhale escaped her.

"No. I came straight here."

"Does Stewart know where you are?"

"No. I knew he wouldn't approve of what I intended to do."

"That's why I don't understand what are you doing here and why you dragged me all the way to Greece by plane, across an island by car and now here by boat."

"I needed some time to prepare." He grinned. "And I thought you might be less likely to argue with me if you were tired."

"Argue about what?" she demanded, her gaze drawn

toward the small donkey that stood beside him, ears flickering lazily forward and back. "And what are you doing with that?"

Gabriel patted the donkey's neck. "It's traditional for Greek brides to ride donkeys to their weddings."

"Bride? What are you talking about…?" Her voice trailed off as she noticed the donkey came equipped with a riding pad covered with flowers. "You can't be serious."

She sounded aghast, but hope glowed in her blue eyes.

"I'm utterly serious. The church and the priest are waiting for us. All you need to do is hop on." Seeing she wasn't fully on board with his plan, he caught her around the waist and pulled her body flush with his, taking care to treat her gently. "Marry me." He drew his knuckles down her cheek. "Please. I can't live without you."

Tears flooded her eyes. "You love me?"

"I love you. I adore you. You're my world." He peered down at her in surprise. "Haven't you figured that out by now?"

She took his hand and drew it away from her skin. Her grip was tight enough to make him wince.

"What of your parents' wishes? Have you considered the barrage of negative opinions you'll face when we return home?"

"None of that matters. No one matters but us. I have two brothers, both of whom are capable of getting married and having children. There's no reason why I have to be the one who fathers the next generation of Sherdana royalty. It was different when my father became king. He was the only direct male descendant. And besides, I think it's time my brothers took on a little royal responsibility."

A crowd of townspeople and tourists were gathering on the narrow street, drawn by the novelty of a decked out donkey and the argument between Gabriel and Olivia. The late-afternoon sun bathed the town in golden light, softening the scenery. The breeze off the harbor was gentle against Olivia's skin, soothing her anxiety.

"Neither one of them is going to be happy."

"I don't care. It's my turn to be a little selfish. We're getting married. Now. Today. And I'm not taking no for an answer."

That he was ready to marry her despite her inability to give him children thrilled her, and she could no longer wait to share her news.

"There's something I need to tell you."

"That you love me?"

"No."

"You don't?" he teased.

"Of course I do. But that's not what I need to tell you."

"But don't you think it's an appropriate thing to tell your groom on your wedding day?"

"Very well. I love you."

"When you say it like that, I'm not sure I believe you."

She leaned forward and slid her fingers into his hair, drawing him close for a slow, deep kiss. "I love you."

His response was almost a purr. "Much better."

"Now are you ready to hear what I have to say?"

"Yes."

Their impending nuptials had certainly brought out the mischief maker in Gabriel. Or perhaps it was getting away from the palace and all his responsibility. Olivia made a note to kidnap him at least once a year and bring him somewhere with no cell phones and no television so they could get reacquainted.

"When I spoke with the doctor yesterday—" she gathered a deep breath "—he gave me some rather startling news."

The wicked light died in Gabriel's eyes. He grew somber. He caught her fingers in a tight grip. "Is something wrong?"

"No. In fact, I think everything might be okay in time."

"How so?"

"He thinks that a fertility specialist might be able to harvest eggs from my ovaries." She watched Gabriel carefully, hoping he was open to what she had in mind. "It would require finding a woman willing to be a surrogate, but it's possible that you and I could still make babies together."

"This is the most amazing news."

Gabriel caught her around the waist and pulled her against his body. Dipping his head, he captured her lips with his for a long, slow kiss.

By the time he released her mouth they were both breathing heavily. Gabriel's eyes sparkled like the sun on the water behind them. Joy sped through her as she realized she was about to marry the man she adored.

"Come on, let's get you up on the donkey and get to the church."

"Are you sure it's tradition?" she protested, eyeing the creature doubtfully.

"Positive."

Their parade up the steep street to the church was not the formal affair it would have been in Sherdana. There was no gilded carriage pulled by six perfectly matched white horses. No thousands of people lining the streets to wave and throw rose petals at them. But there were smiles and hearty cheers as Gabriel lead the donkey through the heart of the town.

When they reached the church, Gabriel introduced his housekeeper, Elena, who took Olivia aside to help her into the modest knee-length wedding dress with cap sleeves and a large bow at the waist. A note from Noelle accompanied the dress, explaining that Libby had come to her a few days after Olivia went into the hospital because Gabriel was planning on marrying Olivia in a small island wedding and wanted a dress to suit the occasion.

So, despite his lack of contact during her hospital stay, Gabriel hadn't accepted that their engagement was at an end. He'd still wanted her as his wife, even though his family and political advisers would counsel him to move on.

Awash with joy, Olivia clutched the note to her chest and stared at her reflection. Although the design was much simpler than the lace-and-crystal-embellished gown she'd have worn to marry Gabriel in Sherdana, it was perfect. As was the man who awaited her at the front of the beautiful Greek church.

Gabriel's gaze never once wavered as she walked toward him, accompanied by the song of a single violin. There was no doubt, no restraint in his golden eyes, only possessiveness, and she reveled in his love.

He took her hand as she came to stand beside him and she tingled in delight. Elena and her husband were the only witnesses. The intimacy of the empty church allowed them the privacy to focus completely on each other and they exchanged vows in reverent tones. When they returned to Sherdana, there would be celebrations with family and friends. Until then, all they wanted was each other.

After the ceremony, they exited the church and encountered a small crowd. Apparently Gabriel and his brothers were well liked in the coastal town and when word got out that he had come to the island to get married, many had turned out to wish him and Olivia well.

They lingered for several minutes, greeting people and accepting congratulations until Gabriel insisted it was time he took his bride home. Laughing and shaking his head at good-natured invitations to stay in town and celebrate their wedding, Gabriel slipped his arm around her waist and began to edge out of the circle of people.

"My car is this way." He took her hand and began to lead her down the road.

"Oh, thank goodness, I was afraid you'd make me ride the donkey back to your house."

Gabriel laughed heartily. "It would take him too long to carry you that far and I can't wait that long to have you all to myself."

Once he got her settled in the passenger seat and slid behind the wheel, he sat sideways in his seat and regarded her intently.

After several seconds of his attentive silence, Olivia grew restless. "What are you doing?"

"Appreciating our first private moment as husband and wife. The circumstances of the last few weeks haven't given us any time together and when we leave here, there will be public appearances and meetings demanding our time. I intend to spend every possible moment until then showing my beautiful wife how much I adore her."

Being his wife was her dream come true. Olivia smiled. "If I'm beautiful, you have Noelle to thank for that." She gestured to her wedding dress. "Have you really been planning this romantic elopement since before I left the hospital?"

"It was your secretary's idea. She knows how stubborn you can be and came to me with a crazy plan that I should steal you away to someplace exotic and marry you."

"Libby?" Olivia considered her secretary's encouragement anytime Olivia had doubted her future with Gabriel.

"She helped me with the dress and arranged the church and the flowers."

"How were you planning to get me to agree to run off with you?"

"By offering you a ride home in our jet and then bringing you here. You made things a lot easier by asking to see me."

"Did Stewart have any idea what you were planning?"

Gabriel shook his head. "Stewart's loyalty is to Sherdana. Libby's loyalty is to you." He leaned forward and pressed a lingering kiss on her lips. "And so is mine."

Olivia contemplated her new husband during the short drive to his villa, a two-mile journey around the horseshoe-shaped harbor. Never again would she underestimate his determination or his loyalty to her. He'd been willing to go against his family for her. She couldn't ask for a better partner or soul mate.

Because they'd been delayed in town Elena had already arrived and was in the process of arranging a romantic table for them on the terrace high above the harbor. At Olivia's prompting, Gabriel gave her a brief tour of the villa. In the spacious bedroom they would share, Gabriel drew her toward the window and they stared out at Kioni, its lights glowing bright as dusk descended. With his arms wrapped around Olivia's waist and his chin resting on her head, he sighed.

Olivia chuckled. "Was that weariness or contentment?"

"Contentment. You will be hearing many more such sighs in the coming days while we enjoy some much-needed privacy."

"We will have to go back eventually."

His arms tightened around her. "I prefer not to think about that moment until it arrives."

"Won't the media come here looking for us?"

"In the past we've kept a low profile and the people who live on the island respect our privacy." His lips trailed of fire down her neck. "Now, let's go downstairs and enjoy our first dinner as man and wife."

They returned to the first floor and accepted glasses of champagne from Elena. She gestured them out onto the terrace and retreated to fetch the first course.

"This is beautiful," Olivia commented, admiring the simple but elegant scene.

With the sunset long past, the sky had deepened to indigo. A row of white candles stretched along the low terrace wall, pushing back the darkness, their flames protected by glass containers. More candles had been placed in the center of the table, their flickering glow making shadows dance over the fine white tablecloth, beautiful china and colorful flower arrangements.

Gabriel led her to the table and helped her into a linen-clad chair before taking his own seat beside her. The romantic lighting softened his strong bone structure and brought out the sensual curve of his lips as he smiled. "Here's to following our hearts."

Olivia smiled as she clinked her glass to his and marveled at her good fortune. She never would have guessed that she had to lose everything in order to gain the one thing she needed most.

Setting her glass down, Olivia reached for Gabriel's hand.

"A few weeks ago your sister told me to ask you something. I never did."

"Ask now."

"She said we'd met before six months ago. Is that true?"

"Yes."

"But I don't recall meeting you. And I assure you I would. Were we young children? Is that why I don't remember?"

"It was almost seven years ago at a masquerade party. Given the host's reputation I was a little surprised to discover the young woman I rescued was none other than Lady Olivia Darcy."

Gabriel had been her savior. The man whose kiss had set the bar for every other romantic encounter she'd had since. "You knew who I was?"

"Not until after you'd left and Christian informed me who I'd been kissing." Gabriel's fingertips grazed her cheek. "When I kissed you that night, something sparked between us. I wasn't ready to get married and you were far too young, but something told me you were the woman I was destined to marry."

"But that was one kiss seven years ago." She couldn't imagine how a single moment in time could impact him so strongly. And yet hadn't she felt the magic between them? Compared his kiss to those that came after? "And my father approached you about building a plant in Sherdana."

"That's true, but Christian put the idea in his head. My brother is very clever when it comes to business dealings and had an inkling of how much you interested me."

"But you loved Marissa. You would have married her if Sherdanian law had allowed it."

"I never wanted to marry Marissa. She was my way of rebelling against duty and responsibility. I loved being with her, but I know now that I didn't love her. Not the way I love you."

His lips found hers and delivered a kiss that managed to be both incredibly arousing and spiritually satisfying at the same time. Olivia was weak with delight when he set her free.

"I can't quite believe all that has happened today," she murmured as his fingertips worked their way along her shoulder. "When I woke up this morning I was cautiously optimistic. Now I'm happier than I ever imagined I could be."

Gabriel gifted her with a smile of resolute tenderness. "And it's my intention to do whatever it takes to ensure you stay that way."

After disappearing from the radar for a week, and then reappearing with a glowing bride in tow, Gabriel had anticipated a media frenzy, but he hadn't expected the capital's streets to be lined with people.

In the back of the limousine, Olivia waved at the enthusiastic crowd, looking every inch a princess. But by the time the vehicle pulled up in front of the palace, her nerves had begun to show.

"Are we going to be taken to the gallows and shot?" she questioned. "Is that why everyone turned out to see us?"

"A member of Sherdana's royal family hasn't been executed in almost three hundred years."

"That's not as reassuring as you want it to be."

Gabriel squeezed her hand. "Everything is going to be fine."

"Since when are you such an optimist?"

"Since marrying you."

A footman stepped forward to open the limo's door. Olivia nodded toward a glowering Christian, who was striding through the palace's ornate main doors.

"He doesn't look happy."

"I think he's realized the trap has been sprung."

"You sound as if you're enjoying this far too much."

"Do you have any idea how many dossiers I looked through over the years, weighing my future happiness against what was right for the country, while my brothers ran around the United States and Europe following their dreams?"

"A hundred?" she offered.

"Try a thousand."

"Surely there weren't that many girls who wanted to marry you," she teased.

"Oh, there were at least three times that, but only one girl I wanted to marry."

"You really have become a smooth talker. No wonder I fell in love with you."

Christian extended a hand to assist Olivia as she exited the car and kissed her on each cheek before glowering at Gabriel over a perfunctory handshake.

"How are things?" Gabriel asked, overlooking his brother's surly mood. He kept ahold of Olivia's hand as they made their way into the palace.

"Sherdana's been doing just fine," Christian muttered.

"I meant with you. Has Mother come up with a list of potential candidates for your bride yet?"

"You really are a bastard."

"Don't let our mother hear you say that." He thumped his brother on the back. "But what do you have to worry about? Nic is next in line. The burden to produce an heir falls on him first."

"Mother's not taking any chances this time. She thinks both of us should be married."

"I agree with her. Nothing like marrying the woman of your dreams to know complete and perfect happiness."

Gabriel laughed heartily at Christian's look of disgust and followed Olivia up the stairs. As they entered the suite of rooms she and Gabriel would now be sharing, she leaned close and spoke in a low voice. "Why didn't you tell Christian there's a potential we can have children?"

He shut the door to the suite, ensuring their privacy, and took her in his arms. "I think we should keep this development our little secret for the time being."

"Are you sure?" Olivia reached up and threaded her

fingers through Gabriel's dark hair. "If it works, it will let your brothers off the hook."

"There's no reason to say anything until we have something definitive to tell."

"That could take months," she exclaimed, her eyes wide with uncertainty. "They could be engaged or even married by then."

"Making you my wife has been the best thing that could have happened to me. I think my brothers deserve to experience the same."

"You're going to force them into a situation where they have to find wives so that they'll fall in love?"

"Diabolical, isn't it?"

"They'll kill you when they find out the truth."

"I don't think so." Gabriel leaned down and silenced further protests with a deep, soul-stirring kiss. "I think they'll thank me for making them the second and third happiest men on the planet."

"You being the first?" She arched her eyebrows at him.

Gabriel responded with a broad grin. "Absolutely."

* * * * *

LONE STAR BABY
BOMBSHELL

LAUREN CANAN

Special thanks to two brilliant authors who kindly gave their time and expertise. Kathleen Gregory, I could not have done this without you. Angi Morgan, you are my forever hero! Thank you for all you do.

To Jill Marsal of the Marsal-Lyon Literary Agency. You made all the difference. Thank you for believing in me.

To my editor, Charles Griemsman, for your endless patience and encouragement. You are the best.

To Laurel Hamrick for being there when I needed to whine!

And to Terry, my real-life hero, who taught me the true meaning of love and happily-ever-afters.

One

Kelly Michaels slowed the car as she neared the twelve-foot-high black wrought-iron gates banked by native stone walls on either side. A bronze plaque on the left welcomed her to the C Bar Ranch. She stretched to reach the keypad and entered the code Don Honeycutt, the Realtor, had provided.

With a resounding *click*, the gates swung open, separating the giant *C* set in the center. She followed the long winding drive flanked by centuries-old oak trees towering over lush green pastures. She pulled around to the staff entrance. The home was enormous. It was more mansion than typical ranch house. But new construction was generally a breeze to clean. Gathering the implements out of the trunk, she went inside.

Her instructions were to clean two bedrooms and adjoining baths upstairs plus the den, office, foyer and kitchen downstairs. She should be able to wrap this up in time to get ready for the annual music festival and dance that evening. The generous pay she earned occasionally cleaning new homes for the local Realtor was more than worth the effort. It had once been her only income, but even after she landed a job consistent with her field of study, she'd held on to this one and the financial bonus it offered.

She started on the second-floor master suite, working her way downstairs. Some furniture had been delivered. New bedding and pillows lay on the mattresses. Kelly quickly and efficiently put everything in order. An interior designer would probably complete the rooms in accordance with the new owner's preferences.

She loved the smell and freshness of a new home. Holidays in this house would be amazing. A turkey roasting in the oven while pumpkin and coconut pies cooled on the dark granite counters. The aroma of spices and home-baked bread filling the air. She could imagine laughter and teasing banter filling the great space while children played hide-and-seek around a huge tree. She envied the family who would live here. At least, she hoped it was a family. The gossip around town said the old ranch had been purchased by an out-of-state corporation for employee retreats. It would be a shame if no one actually lived in this beautiful home.

A couple hours later, while rinsing the last of the soap from the kitchen sink, she heard the door in the utility room open and close. Must be Don checking on her progress. She smiled, knowing she'd completed the house, just as requested.

"Kelly?"

The breath caught in her throat and all outward motion stopped. The voice did not belong to Don Honeycutt. Her heart slammed against the walls of her chest as denial overwhelmed her mind. *It couldn't be.* Bracing herself against the counter, she turned and stared incredulously at the man standing less than four feet away.

"Jace." His name came out a whisper, a testament to the pure shock pummeling her from every direction. She blinked her eyes, willing her mind to convey it was only an illusion.

But the illusion was very real.

In the year since she'd seen him, he'd changed very little. His rugged good looks hadn't diminished. If anything, he appeared even more handsome than before, something she wouldn't have thought possible. The deep line of his jaw was smooth now, missing the bearded shadow he'd had before. His dark hair was cut several inches shorter. The tiny scar was still visible, the only imperfection of full lips that could widen into a devilish grin showing perfect white teeth, a smile irresistible to most everyone, male or female, young or old.

Kelly swallowed hard. She knew the touch of those lips. A man in his prime, he took extraordinary care to stay in top physical condition. It was, after all, part of his job. Part of who he was. She hadn't known it before, but she certainly knew it now.

"What are you doing here?" His deep, graveled voice mirrored her surprise, sending goose bumps over her skin.

With a wet sponge in one hand and a can of powdered cleanser in the other, she thought the answer should be obvious.

"I might ask you the same question." But she feared she already knew the answer. The giant *C* on the front gate apparently stood for Compton. Suddenly the huge mansion took on the dimensions of a shoe box as the walls came crashing in. "You bought this ranch?" She needed to hear him confirm her worst fears.

"Yeah. I did."

Her heart dropped to her knees. "I…I've just finished. I'll get out of your way."

She grabbed the mop, broom and bucket of cleaning paraphernalia and without another glance in his direction, headed for the door, her mind spinning.

"Kelly, wait. You don't have to—"

She ignored him and all but ran through the side door. Why would Jace Compton, a man with the world at his fingertips, move to this tiny Texas town?

The outside lamp over the side porch provided dim light against the growing darkness. She tossed the cleaning supplies inside the car, not caring where they landed. Her hands shook so severely it took three tries to insert the key into the ignition of the twenty-year-old Buick. It responded in kind, quivering equally as badly as her hands while the engine struggled to engage. After she'd made several attempts and repeated silent pleas to *start*, it became clear the old car wasn't going anywhere.

This couldn't be happening.

Her cell phone lay on the seat next to her, but even if it found a signal there was no one to call. By now her friends were at the music festival along with most of the county. It was the single largest event of the year in their small community, and she would not spoil their evening even though it was a long walk home. If only Mrs. Jenkins, her babysitter, could still drive. She had a nagging fear in the pit of her stomach that this downward spiral had not yet reached rock bottom.

Resting her forehead against the steering wheel, she closed her eyes, giving in to the memories flooding her mind, to the sharp pain once again slicing her heart into tiny pieces. The best and the worst wrapped up in one package. And the name on the label was Jace Compton.

When she'd first tried to reach him at the cell number he'd provided, she got at a voice mail message that Jace Compton—not Jack Campbell, the name he'd given her when they met—was out of the country. And the mailbox was full. Who was Jace Compton? A call out to the ranch where he'd claimed he worked provided the answer. The man to whom she'd given her heart, body and soul, the man who'd said she was so special he never wanted to let her go, was not Jack Campbell, the ranch hand. He was Jace Compton, an award-winning actor and multi-millionaire living in California, having some fun at her expense. The ranch foreman had given her another number to try, but it was disconnected.

As the memories of that day surfaced once again, shame rolled over her in a mind-numbing wave just as it had for months after she'd learned the truth. She'd been so stupid. Her initial awareness that he looked familiar had been easily dismissed with a "Yeah. I get that a lot." No doubt he would have had a pat answer even if she'd asked more pointedly. He'd set out to seduce her and she'd fallen hard. She'd wanted to believe him, to trust him, so any suspicions that he might not be who he claimed were ignored.

Weeks after he'd left, when she finally learned his true identity, it seemed as if his picture was everywhere. Photos and headlines depicting the wild beach parties, shocking affairs with married women and his playboy lifestyle in general headlined the rag sheets at the grocery store checkout lines and the celebrity programs on television.

She'd finally managed to track down his manager, who had been clear and threatening. She meant nothing to Mr. Compton. They'd had a fling. So what? Jace had lots of flings. Unless she was prepared for a court battle over custodial rights, which Jace would assuredly win, she should take the manager's advice and handle the situation herself. Numbly, Kelly had hung up the phone. She hadn't slept that night. Or the next. She'd just sat in the little wooden chair in her bedroom and stared at nothing while her mind bounced between disbelief and utter devastation.

Nine months later, as she lay in the hospital bed praying for her baby to survive the complications of the birth, one of the hospital volunteers brought Kelly a magazine to read. On the front cover, the charismatic, drop-dead gorgeous Jace Compton had again been named Bachelor of the Year. The handsome face seemed to mock her as the tears spilled over and ran down her face.

Why had he come back?

After a year she thought she'd finally put it all behind her. The tears and sleepless nights, the regrets and countless waves of humiliation as time after time her mind relived how easily she'd fallen for his deception. Yet at the same time, despite the lies, the yearning for his touch refused to go away. The memories of his incredible smile fading to a look of serious intent; the knowing glint in his eyes seconds before his lips covered hers, taking her fully, deeply, until she never wanted him to let her go. His powerful arms holding her, his hard body locked to hers, his hot breath and deep voice teasing, whispering sinful things in her ear, tempting her in ways she'd never imagined, always leaving her gloriously satisfied yet wanting more.

Apparently, he hadn't had the same sentiments. If those thoughts ever entered his head, he'd quickly pushed them away. From the minute he'd boarded the plane back to California, she'd become a distant memory. To him it had just been a vacation in the north Texas ranching community with her supplying a few fringe benefits on the side.

Two raps on the car window brought her back to the here and now. Determined to keep her anger at bay, she pushed open the door and Jace took a step back. Standing at a height of well over six feet, he was wearing well-worn jeans that hugged long, muscular legs. His left arm rested on the door frame while his right settled on the roof, effectively trapping her within the boundary of his heavy arms. Getting out of the car brought her within mere inches of the hard wall of his chest. Muscles rippled under the ash-gray T-shirt, the sleeves stretching to accommodate thick biceps.

Kelly didn't want to be this close to him. She didn't want to look into his eyes, but his large stature blocked everything else as if he was purposely giving her no choice. Finally, she looked up, their gazes locked, and for an instant, time stopped. It was still there. In the deep green depths a flicker of the raw passion that once bound them together with such intensity, a passion that slam-dunked any rational thought into nonexistence.

The scent of expensive cologne surrounded her. In spite of the months of heartache, some small part of her still yearned for his touch, which was nothing short of insanity. What she needed was for him to disappear. Again.

"Please step back and let me pass." Her voice, raw with unreleased emotion, held fierce determination. He did as she asked and dropped his arms to his side. "I'll have the car off your property as soon as possible."

Without a backward glance, Kelly took off down the driveway on foot.

"Don't you have a phone? Someone you can call?"

She ignored him and increased her pace.

"You want to use mine?" She heard him mutter a curse.

Her complete focus was to get off this property and away from him as fast as possible. Her mind was still reeling from the fact that he was here. He'd bought land and built a large house, usually an indication of permanency. The thought did nothing to brighten her spirits. Somehow she should have prepared for this even though logic was screaming *how could you have known*? But he had friends in the area. He'd been staying with them when they first met. He'd commented many times that he loved the general region. Why had she never considered the possibility that he would come back? She was an idiot. And now she was going to pay for it.

She didn't hear the truck on the concrete driveway until Jace pulled up next to her.

"Kelly, you can't walk all the way to town. It has to be close to six or seven miles and it's almost dark."

Hearing him so close once again still had the same effect. Her body came to life as irrational hunger for him ran rampant. She clenched her teeth and pulled the evening air deep into her lungs as tears of resentment burned her eyes. She refused to let them fall. He was right about it getting dark. And he'd guessed right about the distance. But she kept walking. She'd be every kind of fool to climb inside that truck.

In spite of her refusal to stop, he continued to roll along next to her.

"Kelly, get in the truck and let me take you home."

"No. Thank you."

The tall gates opened as she reached the end of his property. She went through them and cut to the left onto the white-rock county road. The gravel made it harder to walk, but she refused to slow her pace. The Bar H Ranch was just a couple of miles away. Shea, her husband, Alec, or one of their ranch hands would give her a ride home. In hindsight, she should have called, but her only thought was to get away from Jace. Surely everyone hadn't gone to the festival. But if they had, she would sit on the porch and wait.

Why did Jace have to come back to Calico Springs? It was a small community where everybody knew one another. Eventually someone would tell him about Kelly Michaels and the baby who almost died when he was born four months ago. And Jace would know. He would do the math and figure out the baby was his. Another wave of panic slammed into her. What was she going to do? What *could* she do?

The iron gates clanged shut and she realized he was no longer following her. Apparently, he'd only driven to the end of his driveway and turned back. Good enough. The farther away he stayed the better. Taking a deep breath, she willed her heart to slow its pace.

The consequences of Jace finding out about Henry were beyond comprehension. She had to steel herself against the urge to break into a dead run to more quickly get home to her baby. Regardless of how much money he had and how well he could lie, Jace was not getting custody, no matter what she had to do or where she had to go.

The sun had set, darkening the sky to deep purple. Shadows of the trees and tall grass along the road faded into the overall darkness of the landscape. She wished for a flashlight. Even though the road was still easy to distinguish from the surroundings, the creatures that might slither out to soak up the last of the afternoon warmth were not.

The thought brought her to a heightened sense of awareness. A wrong step might land her in a world of trouble and there was no one in shouting distance if she needed help. If anything happened to her, who would care for Henry?

Right now, her baby should be enjoying his bath before going to sleep thanks to the wonderful woman who kept him while Kelly worked. Because of the festival, no one expected her home early. She swallowed back the touch of alarm. *Think positive.* Once she reached the Bar H Ranch she'd be home free.

As if to dispute that optimistic thought, lightning flashed across the sky followed by deep, rolling thunder. Kelly groaned, not daring to think this night could get any worse.

Jace Compton took in a deep breath of frustration, his jaw muscles working overtime. He couldn't believe Kelly had been in his house. Cleaning it, no less. How bizarre was that? He'd hoped he could find her if he moved to Calico Springs. But he never considered she'd be in the house, and he wasn't prepared for the immediate anger and the glaring gaze shooting beams of blue-green fire in his direction.

Apparently, she'd found out he'd lied about his identity when he was here before. He hoped she would give him a chance to explain. He'd had twenty-five precious days on a neighboring ranch to kick back, relax and be himself, just a guy who'd grown up on the south side of Chicago. The last thing he wanted was someone to discover his identity. Over the years he'd become proficient at staying well under the radar. He'd had no idea when they first met that their relationship would develop into something so much more.

Kelly had accepted that he was a cowhand from a nearby ranch, and there had never been a right time to tell her differently. In hindsight he hadn't wanted to take a chance on putting a wedge between them and that special something they'd found in each other. It was a timeless journey where they were the only two people in the world. It was perfect. When she returned his kisses, he'd known she was kissing *him*, the regular guy, not the wealthy celebrity. It was a damn good feeling. When the time came to leave, he wrestled with his conscience, wanting to tell Kelly the truth. Finally he decided to wait until he returned to Calico Springs. He hadn't expected the four-month interim period he'd planned to expand to over a year.

On the outside, the Kelly he remembered had changed, and those changes immediately had his libido sitting up and taking notice. The curves of her body were decidedly more feminine, more mature, more alluring than those of the model-thin young woman he remembered. She exuded health and considerably more sex appeal than he recalled, making him wonder how he'd ever torn himself away. The long blond locks that used to flow free and silky around the delicate features of her face were pulled to the back of her head in a ponytail, giving her face a different, intensely alluring quality, accenting the almond shape of her eyes. Jace had never seen eyes that color. They were the same brilliance and shade as the turquoise waters of the Mediterranean. Only tonight, instead of containing a welcoming sparkle, they'd reflected more than a small trace of annoyance when she stared at him as if the devil himself had come to life.

While he'd anticipated she would be a bit perturbed if she learned he'd lied about his identity, he didn't expect the high level of animosity she'd shown today. Was she angry because he'd lied or was it because she'd missed an opportunity to gain some of the wealth? Thinking of Kelly in that light didn't sit well. At all.

Some people thought they'd found the proverbial pot of gold when they caught his attention, a fact that galled Jace to his core. People always wanted something, whether it was money or five minutes worth of fame. Making action films was his job. Not who he was. He hated the phony facade he had to maintain, and the ridiculously implausible stories he had to validate all for the sake of keeping his name in the media, all to keep the publicity going. Finding someone who liked him for himself was a rarity. He hoped Kelly would understand. He really hoped she would.

When he'd returned to California, he'd talked nonstop about the young woman he met in Texas. He'd even mentioned buying a place to be close to her until she finished her degree. Two days later, his manager, Bret, handed him a PI report indicating Kelly was a con artist with a rap sheet a mile long, citing numerous jailed offenses. Jace hadn't wanted to believe it then and still had a hard time believing it now.

By the time six months had passed, with the filming of his latest movie hitting one roadblock after another, it no longer mattered if she had a record or not. He probably would never see her again. He'd felt more than a small twinge of loss at the thought. He'd managed to push their time together to the back of his mind until Garret Walker, the friend who had invited him to Texas, called asking if he was still interested in buying some land in the area. Suddenly in his mind's eye, all he saw was Kelly. The memories of holding her in his arms and the pure enjoyment he'd found being with her far outweighed any past crimes she may have committed. He kept Bret's warning in mind. He'd be a fool not to. But Kelly Michaels just didn't fit the mold of a crook. Perhaps she'd had a rough life? They'd never spoken in detail about her past, so all he could do was speculate. But after the way she'd almost run from his house today, it probably didn't matter one way or the other. Apparently she'd made her decision that their relationship would not continue. While he couldn't justify it in his mind, he once again felt a deep loss.

He rubbed the back of his neck. Kelly was out there in the dark, determined to walk all the way to town. He'd returned to the house to give her a chance to calm down and allow him time to get a grip. The instant he'd recognized her, his body had surged to readiness while a vapor of heat surrounded him. It was the same reaction he'd felt the very first time he'd ever seen her in the local feed store when he'd gone with Garret to place an order. The immediate attraction had overwhelmed him then, and today was no different. It was like a giant magnet pulling them together regardless of the circumstances. And when she'd stepped out of her car and her incredible scent of spring rain and nutmeg reached him, he hadn't wanted to move away, his body immediately swelling with need.

But with Kelly, it went beyond physical beauty and sex appeal, although she had plenty of that to turn any man's head. It was the look in her eyes that made him believe he could accomplish anything. Hell, when he'd held her in his arms he could fly. Her soft Southern drawl and impish nature had him bouncing off the walls and loving every second. Had it all been an act? He still didn't know the answer and probably—sadly—never would.

Raindrops began to splatter against the windowpane. He turned toward the door, intent on giving her a ride into town. His glance fell on the thin strap of a pale pink purse hanging over the back of a kitchen chair. As he lifted it from the chair back, the sound of thunder rolled over the house, followed by flashes of lightning.

With purse in hand, he headed back to the truck, ignoring the first heavy raindrops. Whether she was angry with him or not, he wasn't about to leave her outside in the dark and the quickly approaching storm. He'd make sure she got home safely, this time accepting no excuses.

Whether she liked it or not.

Two

Isn't this gonna be a basket full of fun?

Kelly eyed the sky as the thunder rumbled overhead. She didn't dare tempt fate by asking what else might go wrong. Picking up the pace, she topped the next hill just as a bolt of lightning struck a tree straight ahead. Seconds later, the sky opened up and a downpour provided the answer to her unspoken question.

Crossing her arms over her chest, she gritted her teeth and kept walking. The warm temperatures of the afternoon took a nosedive as the chilling rain continued to hammer away, stinging her face, making it hard to see. The strong wind gusts made each step forward a challenge to her determination.

Suddenly the glare of headlights from behind illuminated the road and the white blanket of rain ahead of her. She moved to the right, hoping it wasn't a bunch of liquored-up high school kids out for an evening of fun and harassment. She got her wish, but not in a way she'd wanted.

"Kelly," Jace's voice barked through the darkness as he pulled up beside her. "Get in the truck."

She continued walking.

"You're being a complete idiot," he insisted.

"You're entitled to your opinion." She had to yell to be heard over the downpour.

"You have ten seconds to get your ass inside this truck."

"Or what?"

"Or I'm going to pick you up and put you in here myself."

She turned to face him, her eyes narrowing in a glare.

"Get. In. Now." The darkness concealed his expression, but his angry tone came across loud and clear. She had little doubt he'd do exactly what he threatened.

Just do it and get home to Henry.

She looked from Jace to the dark, seemingly endless road ahead. A blustery gust of rain-filled wind assisted the return of her sanity. Biting her tongue, she walked to the truck and opened the passenger door.

"I'm wet," she unnecessarily disclosed, taking in the truck's beautiful interior.

He muttered a curse. "Everything is wet. I don't care. Get in the damn truck." His demand was accented by a loud crack of lightning directly overhead. She grabbed the hold-bar above the opening and pulled herself up and inside, closing the door behind her. Jace immediately raised the passenger window.

In the warmth of the cab, her teeth began to chatter as uncontrolled shivers assailed her body. Jace quickly adjusted the heat. The new-car smell and the earthy scent of his cologne swirled in the warm air around her. She leaned back against the rich leather and buckled her seat belt. Without another word, Jace hit the gas, sending the truck speeding toward town.

Town. Home. Kelly didn't want him to know where she lived. It took away the small sense of protection, even if it was only an illusion. In Calico Springs, population six thousand, it wasn't hard to find anybody.

"Just take me to the ranch up ahead. The entrance is on the left. I know the owners. They'll drive me the rest of the way home."

No response.

As the big truck ate up the miles, she anxiously searched to the left of the headlights for the big gate to the Bar H Ranch. Finally, the reflection of the stone pillars shone just ahead.

"There," she pointed. "Just pull in…"

The truck didn't slow as it approached, then passed, the driveway.

"You missed it." She looked behind them. "Turn around."

Jace glanced at her, then returned his focus to the road. "No reason to force anyone else out in this weather."

"*Force* anyone else? Like I forced you to be out here?" she challenged, still resenting the fact that he'd coerced her inside the truck to begin with. Never mind that she was grateful to be out of the storm.

"That's not the way I meant it. Of course you didn't." He glanced over as she sat back in the seat, her arms crossed over her chest. "And you didn't leave your handbag in my kitchen on purpose." He held up the small rectangular purse. "And you didn't know it was my house you were cleaning or that I would be arriving around six. Kelly, if you want to see me again…just say so."

Kelly's head snapped around, her jaw dropping. "Stop this truck."

Instead of slowing, he asked, "Shall I take that as a no?" as a grin spread over his handsome features.

"Yes."

"Yes?"

"Yes, I mean no."

Jace pursed his lips as though holding back another grin. "Your sense of humor isn't quite as good as I remember."

"No? Try saying something remotely funny."

He made no further comment. Kelly glared at him for another few seconds before she sat back in the seat, expelled an angry breath and accepted her fate. It was surreal. To not see him for so long, then to suddenly be in the close confines of a pickup cab as they barreled into the darkness. She glanced at him from the corner of her eye. His big hands on the wheel, his sharp jawline and those full lips caused an unwelcome need to stir deep in her belly, a need she hadn't felt for over a year.

She remembered everything: every touch, every erotic whisper, the teasing humor and the arguments over nothing that always ended with his lips on hers. Swallowing hard, Kelly inhaled deeply and turned away, fighting to clear her mind, hoping he couldn't detect her body's traitorous response.

"So," she said, clearing her throat, looking straight ahead, "I can't imagine this tiny spot on the map holding any interest for you. Big celebrity. Small town. Why are you here?"

For a few minutes, she thought he wasn't going to answer her question.

"I needed some downtime," he finally said. "I have a friend who lives in the area, as you know, and this seemed to be as good a place as any."

"You buy an entire ranch to take a break?"

He shrugged.

"And you call me an idiot."

Obviously, he didn't care to share his true intentions with her, which suited her just fine. She should be used to his lies and secrets by now.

"What about you?" he asked.

"What about me?"

"Still in school?"

"No."

So much had happened over the past year his question seemed strange. Her life had changed so radically it felt as though she was answering for someone else. The massive heart attack that had taken her grandfather had been sudden and devastating. Then the bank foreclosed on his farm, leaving Kelly and her younger brother to scramble for another place to live. And just when she thought things couldn't possibly get any worse, she'd discovered she was pregnant by a man who'd hidden his identity, then all but disappeared.

That sobering thought assisted in her return to reality.

"Why did you lie?" It came out a whisper. The question seemed to break free of her mouth, not waiting on her brain to give its permission. "Why did you think it necessary?" He'd wanted someone to share his bed while here visiting friends. She got that. But why lie about who he was? And why promise to call or come back if he'd known all along he wouldn't?

"What does it matter now?"

"The truth always matters."

"I gave you a name. That should have been enough. If you'd known my true identity it would have made a difference in our relationship."

She stared at him in amazement. "Is it tough carrying around all that arrogance?" She shook her head.

"It's not arrogance," he shot back. "If you'd realized who I was you would have—" He inhaled deeply and blew it out.

"What? I would have what? Not thought of you as Jekyll and Hyde? Not known you would rather climb a tree and tell a lie than stand on the ground and tell the truth? Not felt like I was being played? All of the above?"

"You would have treated me differently." Almost under his breath, he muttered, "They all do. And you were not being played. Ever."

"*They all do?* Who is *they*?"

She saw his hand grip the steering wheel in a tight fist. "What I do for a living had nothing to do with us." He glanced at her through the dim glow on the dash lights. "People hear my name and suddenly they can't see *me*. I should have told you the truth, but I wanted you to know *me*, Kelly. I'm just a man. And I enjoy being seen as one instead of all the damned hype. I intended to explain when I got back here. I intended to tell you the truth."

"Really. Why? If, as you say, a name doesn't matter, why bother?"

She heard him expel a deep sigh. "You're purposely twisting this around."

"I am?"

She heard his huff of frustration.

"We were two people who met and enjoyed being together. At least I enjoyed being with you. Why did it need to be more complicated than that? Or am I missing something?"

Her eyes shot toward him. Had he really said that with a straight face? She couldn't hold back a snort. "You do realize you're trying to justify your deception?" The man wouldn't recognize truth if it smacked him in the face. "Unbelievable." She'd gotten her answer. She should have saved herself the trouble of asking. "At least I provided you and your friends with a good laugh."

Heat rolled up her neck at the thought of his wealthy friends laughing about his affair with a stupid country bumpkin. How easily she'd bought into his deception.

"I never laughed." His tone indicated surprise she would think that. He glanced at her, the hard masculine mouth pulled to a taut line, his eyebrows drown into a frown. "Our relationship wasn't a joke. At least not to me. And I had every intention of coming back and talking to you. I'd hoped you would understand."

"I'm sure you did." The anger rolled off her tongue. "But things happen, right?"

"Yeah. I guess they do. For instance, you never told me which correctional center you were in. Apparently I'm not the only one who can be accused of keeping secrets."

Her head snapped around toward him. *What did he just say?* For several seconds she couldn't speak. Had she heard him correctly? "*What?*"

"I said I—"

She raised her hand, palm side toward him. "Does someone write this stuff for you or do you make it up all by yourself?" He expected her to buy the excuse he hadn't come back because he thought she was in *jail*? She shook her head in amazement. "You really need to seek help."

The man she remembered had clearly changed. She

couldn't help but ask herself which one was the real Jace Compton. "Turn left at the light."

"Left?"

"We live in town now." Jace was remembering her grandfather's small farm.

"Kelly, are you saying you don't have a criminal record?"

"Duhhh. Are you saying you honestly thought I *did*?"

"But—"

"You know what, Jack… Jace—whatever your name is today—just don't say anything else." She'd heard more than enough. "Obviously, you're incapable of being honest. I don't care anymore, all right? I don't care why you lied. I don't care why you never came back. I don't give a rat's behind who you are and I don't want to sit here and listen to your wild excuses. I'm sorry I even brought it up."

Jace didn't speak again, but Kelly felt the anger crackling in the air between them.

The route took them south, toward the low-rent side of town where the small forty-year-old houses marred the landscape and even a fresh coat of paint did little to hide the weathered conditions along the rutted streets. Inside the houses lived people like herself, who worked too hard for too little. But she refused to be embarrassed. The house was old and small, but it was clean. It had a new roof and the amount she paid for rent couldn't be beat. "Third street to the right and down a block. On the right. It's the white house with green shutters."

With her hand on the door handle, Kelly made ready her escape. But by the time they pulled up to the curb and she remembered to unfasten the seat belt, Jace held the door for her, seemingly oblivious to the rain.

Her younger brother stood on the front porch leaning on one of the support posts. The glow of the outside light fanned out over the small front yard.

Jace nodded toward the teen. "How ya doing?"

Kelly watched Matt's body language shift as he recognized Jace. It was clear he was having a hard time believing it. He stared at the big man standing next to the truck.

"You're… Are you? You're Jace Compton!" Matt's eyes were as big as dessert plates as his mouth dropped open in sheer astonishment.

"Matt, go inside," Kelly ordered.

"You want to come in?" Her younger brother totally ignored her request. Anger tinged with fear coursed through her, quickening her steps to the house. This was so not happening. What if Matt had picked up Henry from the sitter?

"No," she stated firmly, and turned back to Jace. "I don't think that's a good idea. Thanks for the ride. It was very… enlightening."

Jace made no reply, just stared at her through the soft glow from the porch light. Kelly hurried to the house. "Matt, get inside." When he didn't move, she snapped, "Now."

"But Kelly—" he looked as though she'd just told him to rob a bank "—do you know who that is?"

The question was almost laughable. Almost.

"Have a good night," Jace called from the curb.

Kelly grabbed Matt by the arm and pulled him inside. At fifteen, her brother already stood a couple of inches taller than her own five foot seven and pulling him anywhere was a challenge. This time, with the adrenaline flowing, she managed. She closed the front door and prepared for the onslaught. She didn't have to wait long.

"I can't believe you." Matt glared in her direction. "*The* Jace Compton at our house and you wouldn't let him come inside. What is your deal? Are you like…crazy?"

"Matt…" There was no way to explain.

"Forget all the movies. He still holds the record for completed passes in the entire NFL. The *record*, Kelly. The guy is a football legend."

Matt lived and breathed football, so she understood what he was saying. But her brother didn't know Jace Compton. Unfortunately, she did.

"Come to think of it—" Matt frowned "—what were you doing in his truck? How did you—?"

"He bought the old Miller spread and had a new house built so Don asked me to clean it. When I finished, the car wouldn't start."

"Jace Compton is living here? In Calico Springs? Like *permanently*?" With each question, Matt's voice rose in excitement. His eyes were wide with elation. He hadn't even taken note of the fact that they had no transportation.

"I really don't know." Kelly didn't want to discuss it. Jace had chosen to keep his reasons for being here to himself, so there was really nothing to tell Matt. She just wanted the man to stay as far away from her small family as possible. "I'm gonna walk down to Mrs. Jenkins's and pick up Henry."

"He's here." Matt was clearly still annoyed, his tone full of frustration. "Mrs. J fed him and got him ready for bed. Football practice was canceled because of the rain so I brought him home."

"Thanks, Matt." She smiled and walked toward the small bedroom she shared with her son. Bless the elderly woman down the street who kept Henry while Kelly worked and who refused to accept one penny for her efforts.

The baby slept in his favorite position, on his tummy, his little butt in the air. Kelly pulled off her wet T-shirt and jeans and grabbed her old robe from the closet. Then, unable to resist, she approached the crib and softly caressed the little head. Sensing his mother's touch, Henry stirred. With a smile, Kelly picked up the sleepy bundle, holding him close, loving the sensation of her tiny son against her heart.

Henry had Jace's dark lashes, even his dimples. Kelly shook her head, still in disbelief that he'd moved here. She should have known Jace would come back to stir up the painful memories it had taken months to overcome. He was no different from her father. Love 'em and leave 'em and not give a damn who he hurt in the process. Move on to the next conquest and never look back. Only this time, the man in question had looked back.

Because of her father's lies and cheating, her mom had taken her own life. That was when dear ole dad had disappeared for good. Kelly had made a pledge then and there that she'd never let a man get close to her. And she'd kept up her resolve. Until Jace. She shook her head at the irony. The one man she'd made the mistake of trusting made her father look like a guppy compared to a twenty-foot shark. And look where it had gotten her.

Forcing the negative thoughts from her mind, she kissed Henry's little head and walked toward the kitchen and the aspirin bottle. Her own head was pounding. After the last hour, she might take two. The very idea that Jace actually believed she'd been in jail was…laughable.

But she wasn't laughing. The man apparently believed his own hype. He really did live in a world of make-believe.

She reached for the aspirin bottle and heard Matt talking to someone in the next room. Curious, she rounded the corner just in time to see Jace Compton step inside the small living room.

Immediate and total panic set into every fiber of her being.

"You, ah, left your purse in the truck." He held the small bag out to her, his eyes glinting wickedly. "Practice makes perfect?"

She glared. She stepped forward and snatched the purse from his hand, and then turned toward the bedroom, hoping he'd go out the same way he came in.

"Kelly?"

She stopped. This was so not happening. Jace walked over to where she stood. His gaze focused on the baby in her arms before those green eyes pinned her to the spot.

"Who do we have here?"

Three

It was here. The moment she'd dreaded since the day Henry was born. She looked down at the baby in her arms, hoping Jace wouldn't see the panic that engulfed her.

"This is Henry," she said and swallowed hard.

"Yours?"

She blinked more than once at his question. Apparently his manager hadn't lied when he'd said he wouldn't tell Jace about the pregnancy. He'd never even told Jace she called.

"Yes," she finally answered. "He's all mine."

Jace looked at her, and then glanced back at the baby. Henry kicked his feet, blowing some of his best baby bubbles for the strange man.

"He's cute," Jace murmured. "How old is he?"

No surprise he would ask. She had to give him an answer. To avoid a reply might only increase his curiosity. "Four months."

She saw the wheels turning in Jace's head as he did the math and knew what conclusion he reached: Henry could be his son. He looked at Kelly again, as though searching for a different answer. His full lips were pulled into a straight line of contemplation.

"I'm Kelly's brother, Matt." Her brother grinned from ear to ear, obviously dying to talk to his hero. Kelly welcomed the interruption.

"Nice to meet you, Matt." That killer grin spread across Jace's face. He held out his hand and Matt shook it. Matt was so excited, it was as if he rose two feet above the ground.

"So Kelly says you're living in Calico Springs now?"

Jace nodded, his eyes shifting toward Kelly for an instant and then back to Matt.

"Yeah. I bought an old ranch north of town. Have a friend who has been in horse racing for thirty years. I always wanted to have land and horses. He talked me into trying my hand at raising some thoroughbreds. There's enough room to bring in some cattle later if I decide to expand."

"Oh man, that's cool." Matt's entire body vibrated in excitement. Matt pointed to a chair. "Can you stay a couple of minutes?"

"Sure."

As they sat down, Matt asked, "Do you still throw a ball?"

"Oh, yeah. Any chance I get." Jace's heart-stopping grin reappeared. "I'd still be a wide receiver if the knee hadn't gotten bent the wrong way. Do you play?"

"Yeah. Well, it's just high school."

"Hey, it's where we all started. What position?"

As the football banter between the two continued, Kelly eased out of the room. She put Henry down in the crib, and then collapsed onto the small wooden chair by the door. When would this day finally end? Jace Compton, the lying, two-faced multimillionaire, was sitting in her living room talking with her brother, probably speculating if he'd just been two feet away from his own son. And from the sound of their animated conversation, the two guys shared a common interest. This was going to get worse before it got better.

She wouldn't think it odd of the Jace she'd met last year. A regular guy. One who fit into the world she knew: a guy who loved cheeseburgers, hot rods and practical jokes. He'd been a decent, down-to-earth guy who'd talked of everyday things. No arrogance. No haughtiness. But it seemed unbelievable the suave wealthy superstar who traveled the globe would sit in an old house and enjoy conversing with a fifteen-year-old kid. It was as though Jace was two different people. In spite of everything, deep inside she still wanted to paint him as a good guy. But she knew he was anything but.

Breathe deep. She'd told no one the identity of Henry's father, not even Matt. Infants didn't resemble either parent enough for someone to see a resemblance. Did they? Most babies had dimples. Maybe she'd get through this.

To her brother, Jace was a true hero, a superstar both in his action films and on the football field. The chance to talk to *the great Jace Compton* one-on-one was beyond exciting. She got that. But she would exercise caution. Usually a fair judge of character, apparently she'd misjudged Jace once. She wouldn't make the same mistake again.

The two voices filled the small space as Kelly grabbed dry clothes and headed for a hot shower. When she emerged some twenty minutes later, all was quiet. She saw the glow under her brother's door and heard the faint sound of music coming from inside. She pulled the air deep into her lungs and blew it out as relief loosened the muscles of her neck and shoulders. Like a major storm that dropped down from the sky without warning, Jace had again breezed in and out, this time leaving no damage behind. But more storms would come. Jace wouldn't let this go. She knew in her gut he hadn't been convinced. He would think about it. Remember their time together. And he would be back.

As Jace drove through the small town square headed north toward the ranch, he couldn't get Kelly and her baby out of his mind. His heart had dropped to his knees when he first saw the infant in her arms. The last thing he'd expected was for Kelly to have a child. Then the idea had hit him hard. *Was he the father?* He'd always been so careful. He didn't want to have any kids. He knew all too well what the title of dad meant in his family.

To this day, he could still vividly remember the smell of

burned grease and scorched onions that had filled every corner of the shoddy apartment above the fast-food joint where he and his parents lived when he was around ten or eleven. It was during that time that something had happened. Something had changed. He never knew what. His mother had refused to discuss any of it. But his father had begun drinking and the arguments between them had grown worse. Louder. More intense. Then the abuse had started, his dad taking his fist to the first one he saw when he walked through the door. To try to protect his mom, Jace had endured a lot of it. His mother had been the strong one, taking her son away from the horrific situation. A couple of times after the divorce, his father had found them and it got bad before the cops arrived. Even after all these years, Jace still hadn't completely let go of his hatred of the man. And he would always admire his mom's strength of will.

Finally, in the predawn hours of a Sunday morning, two police officers had stood outside their door. They'd explained that her ex, George Compton, had been killed in an alley behind a bar. Jace's only thought had been that some stranger got to the bastard before he could.

Jace could still feel the sinking sensation he'd experienced when reality hit that night. In that moment, with those two cops standing at the door, he'd had an epiphany. He was George Compton's son.

He'd never put it into perspective before. His primary focus had always been survival. He and his father shared the same face and deep jaw. They had the same green eyes. Same color hair. If they were so much alike on the outside, it had to be true for the inside. When Jace had realized that, the earth seemed to tilt and spin.

Before he turned sixteen, he'd been in and out of juvie a half dozen times for altercations with guys in the neighborhood and at school who had somehow found out about his dad and wanted to see if the son was as worthless. He'd had so many suspensions he never did figure out how they'd let him stay in school. His junior year, he'd tried out for football on a dare. He put himself up against classmates who had been active in the sport since fifth grade and wanted to see Jace Compton go down. They were merciless on the new kid, which suited Jace just fine. He'd poured out all his aggression on the field. It was his saving grace. And, as it turned out, football was something he was good at. After three games, he'd earned the respect of a lot of his teammates. His grades came up, and just before graduation he was offered a college scholarship. His love of the sport carried him almost four years. Then amazingly he'd been picked up by the pros. No one knew that every tackle he made, he was taking down George Compton. Every catch and subsequent dash for the goalpost was a *screw you* to his old man.

After a freak injury ended his football career, Jace began to work with young athletes. He enjoyed teaching them about his favorite sport anytime he got the chance. But any hope that he'd someday have kids and a family of his own had been stomped into the ground a long time ago, beaten out of him by his father's fists.

Still, the idea of Kelly bearing his son was immediately, unbelievably gratifying. His body surged to readiness. Protective instincts rallied to the surface, taking him to a place he'd never been before.

He took a deep breath, pulling the humid night air into his lungs. If the child was his, why hadn't Kelly called? He knew instinctively she wouldn't have kept something so important from him. It wasn't her way. And surely she would want help with the baby, child support…*something*. Most women would beat a path to their attorney as soon as a pregnancy was confirmed. There had been two women who had actually schemed to make Jace think they were pregnant just to get rings on their fingers or obtain a few million dollars in their bank accounts.

But Kelly wasn't like other women. He would be wise to

keep that in mind. It wasn't only her beauty that drew him to her. She was feisty and independent to a fault. She was intelligent and decisively stubborn. Her convictions and beliefs ran deep, and her sense of right and wrong went to the core.

What phone number had he given her before he left? He couldn't remember. The security he had to maintain made it damn near impossible to reach him by phone unless one knew the phrase or identifying password. It changed every few weeks. Had he provided his private cell number? His gut tightened. If she'd tried to call when she realized she was expecting and couldn't get through his security, she would be…furious. Suddenly all the little pieces fell into place with the force and impact of a nuclear implosion.

Dammit to hell.

He slammed on the brakes, bringing the truck to a screeching stop. Jerking it into reverse, he backed into a side street, turned around and headed back to Kelly's house. No wonder she'd wanted to get away from him and been so angry. Not only had he lied to her, but he'd gotten her pregnant and left the country. Then the first time he saw her in over a year he'd called her a crook.

Jace wanted to punch something other than a punching bag. Bret better be glad he was a thousand miles away. Jace had zero doubt his manager had lied to keep Jace from coming back to her. That he'd ever bought into that crap about Kelly having a criminal record caused a giant ball of rage to churn in his gut. His instincts had told him not to believe Bret at the time. Why the hell hadn't he listened to them? Bret probably saw her as a threat to his future income. If Jace quit the films, his manager's gravy-train run would be over.

But while it was easy enough to blame his manager, ultimately, in this, there was no one to blame but himself.

His mind returned to Kelly. A thousand questions hit him with pinpoint accuracy and he couldn't answer even one of them. Did he have a child? A son? Despite using precautionary measures, it was more than possible. When he'd held Kelly in his arms, the passion was intense beyond anything he'd ever experienced. He'd never wanted to let her go. His desire for her was insatiable. Their nights together had turned into days, and then back into nights. It began as hot sexual need. But by the time he had to leave, that white-hot passion had expanded into the blending of two souls. Even now, just thinking about her, those blue-green eyes crazy with need for him, the scent of her shampoo, the feel of her silky skin and the soft cries as her desire crested at the pinnacle of their lovemaking, had parts of him hard and throbbing. Kelly had a way of making him crazy. Apparently some things didn't change.

Kelly sighed with relief knowing she'd skirted one confrontation, but was equally aware there would be more to come. Jace wouldn't give up and just go away. She knew him that well. He went at everything he did with dogged determination. Whether it was training a filly at the ranch where he'd stayed a year ago or hiding his identity from the world. From her. While it had been a shock to learn his real name and profession, it didn't come as a surprise how easily he'd duped her. Jace Compton was proficient at anything he set out to do. It was small wonder he was highly acclaimed as an actor. And according to Matt, Jace had received the same admiration when he played pro football. It was all or nothing. *Defeat* wasn't a word in his vocabulary.

But she qualified the thought: it was possible he hadn't as yet come up against a mother protecting her child. Whatever rules governed his life would fly out the window. There were no offsides or penalties. No interceptions. No retakes. Kelly might not be a match for him on a football field or a movie set, but Jace would encounter significant resistance if he tried to push into her life with intentions of taking her child. Figuratively, he'd be lucky if he came out with only minor scratches and a limp.

She'd just turned off the kitchen light and was headed to her bedroom when a hard knock on the front door stopped her in her tracks. *Surely not.* Surely Jace wouldn't come back here tonight. But intuition told her he was standing on the porch. Squaring her shoulders, she returned to the front room and opened the door.

"We need to talk."

It was neither a demand nor a question, but somewhere in between. She wasn't about to act as though she didn't know what he wanted to discuss. With a glance back at Matt's closed door, she stepped outside, closing the front door behind her. She absently noticed the rain had stopped. A cooling breeze touched her skin. Somewhere in the distance crickets chirped. But her focus was on the big man who stood in front of her, almost a silhouette in the night.

"Is the baby mine?"

Kelly wanted to be anywhere but here. She had often envisioned this moment, but at the same time kidded herself into believing it would never happen. She drew in a deep breath. She couldn't lie to a man about his own child. Regardless of what he'd done to her, he had the right to know the truth. It was what he might try to do with that truth that had her on the brink of panic.

"Yes."

"Kelly, why didn't you tell me? The cell number I gave you should have worked."

He didn't question whether she was telling the truth, a fact that surprised her. But his voice held frustration mixed with anger. She knew only too well what those feelings felt like.

As many times and in as many ways as she'd tried and failed to reach him, his question sounded ridiculous. Part of her wanted to go back inside the house and close the door behind her, refusing to give him a second more of her time. The other part of her wanted to share the wonder of their beautiful son. The little things that made him laugh.

The way he mouthed what would someday be words. The overall amazement of him.

Did Jace deserve to know such things? Did he even care? She'd wasted months of her life alternately wishing he would come back and hoping he never would. In her mind she'd practiced what she would say if she ever saw him again, all sorts of scenarios with a wide variety of outcomes. Now that the moment was here, she didn't have a clue how to proceed or what to say. She crossed her arms over her chest and faced him.

"I did try to reach you. It was a bit of a challenge since I didn't even know your name."

"Kelly—" He raked his hand through his hair.

"The cell number you gave me kicked over to a voice mail box that was full. You really should learn to delete your old messages. Some new ones might be important."

She'd swear he cringed.

"I was able to contact your friend, Garret. The son of the rancher you stayed with last year? He gave me another number and a password, but apparently he had it wrong or it had been disconnected.

"I did speak with your manager. Bret… Gold-something. Goldberg? Goldman? Is that right? It took me about a week to track him down. Another five weeks to get him on the phone. He didn't think it was such a good idea that I talk with you."

She ignored the obscenities that fell from Jace's mouth.

"I tried a couple more times to reach you through your cell, but after a few months, I gave up. So. Now you know. You have a son. Belated congratulations."

Kelly could hear the sarcasm in her own voice but made no effort to conceal it.

"Kelly… I screwed up, okay?"

She shook her head. "No, you didn't. Screwing up is when you do something accidentally. Not when it's done on purpose. And so, no. In this case, it isn't okay. You lied.

You lied to me from the moment we met. Then you disappeared and never looked back."

How many nights had she lain in bed, consumed with the need to hold him, to touch him, to hear his voice again? At times the want had been almost unbearable, her mind elevating it to the level of death. Had he ever thought of her? Did he even remember any part of their time together?

She could sense his aura now, feel the warmth from his body through the darkness, and that same need ran through her like liquid fire. What was it about this man that made her want to forget the past year? Just forget everything and step into his arms and feel his touch once again? The thought made her angry, and she held on to that emotion. She couldn't be weak. She had to think of Henry and be strong.

"I understand why you're mad. You have every right to be."

"Yes. I do. And before you accuse me of getting pregnant on purpose, I didn't. I had a career plan and had envisioned a vastly different future. I have no way to prove it and I don't intend to try. Now, did you want anything else? Or are we finished?"

"I…I don't know. I've only known I had a son for two minutes."

"Give it about nine months. Maybe it will soak in." She hesitated, looking absently at the worn paint on the porch where they stood. "He…he almost died, you know?" Her voice broke; tears burned her eyes. "When he was born? They thought I would lose him. For six days, it was hour to hour, minute to minute. But he's a tough little guy. He may not have been expected or wanted but… Yeah. He's strong. And he's smart." She quickly swiped the tears from her cheeks. "If he gets his strength from his father, I'm grateful to you for that."

"I want to take care of you. Both of you."

Logic demanded she consider if it was fair to Henry to

deny the financial assistance Jace was more than capable of providing. But they were doing okay. Henry wanted for nothing and she didn't want to open Pandora's Box. She shook her head. "We don't need to be *taken care of.* I want nothing from you. And he doesn't need anything from you. There are no shackles here. Contrary to popular belief, I've never tried to con anyone. Or entrap them. I'm not about to start now. So just…you know, carry on with your life. Throw your wild parties. Make your films. It's a little late for regrets, so don't give us a second thought. We'll be fine."

It took a long time before he could swallow the huge wedge of emotion caught in his throat. Jace couldn't let it end this way. In light of this new overwhelming discovery that he had a son, he instantly thought of his own upbringing and the monster it had made of him. For now it lay dormant inside, but eventually it would awaken. He should distance himself from Kelly and the baby. But his heart throbbed with the idea they had a son. They'd created a child. *He was a father.* That, in itself, was enough to mess up any man's mind. And regardless of how hard he fought to hold on, his common sense went down the tubes.

"I want to be in his life." The words fell from his lips as though he was determined to be heard regardless of the consequences.

"Then what?" She shrugged. "Get your attorneys involved? Let them decide on a visitation schedule that meets with your own agenda? See him when you have time or when you happen to be in the country? Introduce him to all your lady friends vying to be his new mommy? Let him grow up seeing his dad's face on TV or the big screen? I'm sure the other kids will someday envy him for that. Wow." Her sarcasm was obvious. "Maybe have your secretary send an expensive gift on his birthday? That's always a nice touch."

"Dammit, Kelly. I don't know how to answer you. I

haven't had a chance to work anything out." He held her gaze as though it was a lifeline while experiencing a rush of emotions he didn't want to feel and had no clue how to deal with.

"Then let me answer the questions for you. No. No to you seeing him once or twice a year. No to long-distance phone calls and the inevitable excuses when you miss his birthday. Or his first spelling bee. Or his first softball game. No to him being a media spectacle. He deserves more, and I won't step aside and let you do that to him. Somehow I'll stop you if you try."

He ran a hand over his face. *Dammit.* He couldn't deny that a lot of what she said was true. She'd pretty much nailed what would happen if his life continued as it had for the past twelve years. He was more than ready for some normal in his crazy life. He wanted a home, a family. But he didn't know how to change, and if he was honest with himself, he didn't know if he wanted to. The work, the travel, the physical aspects of it, the concentration needed…it was the only thing keeping the monster inside at bay.

It was a damned if you do, damned if you don't situation. He should take the out she was offering, make sure Kelly had plenty of money in her bank account and leave them both alone before he caused them to be thrown into the media spotlight, which she would no doubt view as under the bus. Before he became abusive like his old man. It made Jace every kind of selfish for wanting to keep them in his life. But he did. And how convoluted was that?

Despite her show of bravado, he wanted to pull her into his arms, hold her close and promise he would make everything okay. But he couldn't. He didn't know how to make her believe things would work out when he had doubts about it himself. He knew he had to do *something*. But the answer of how to make this right seemed worlds away.

After all she'd been through Kelly had more internal fortitude than anyone he'd ever known, with the single exception of his mom. But while Kelly's resilience and internal strength were admirable, he couldn't leave things as they were regardless of what she said she wanted or, in fact, didn't want.

"He is my son."

"Yes." She nodded. "He is."

"And you want me to just walk away?"

She looked down, as though giving her answer serious thought. "I'm telling you that you have a choice. His life will not revolve around yours. I won't stand by while you break his heart, then try and pick up the pieces after you again disappear."

"Kelly—"

She raised her hand to silence him.

"That said…" She hesitated as if making up her mind about a difficult decision. "I have plans for tomorrow, but if you want to see him while you're here, come by Monday afternoon. I get home around five thirty. He's still too young to form any attachment or be upset when you leave." She again brushed at a spot just below her eye. He heard a soft sniff. "I'm not doing this to be mean, Jace. You have every right to see your son. He's beautiful. You will be so proud. I…I wish you could be in his life always. Every day. But we both know that isn't realistic. And I have to protect Henry, even if it's from his own father."

"We can work this out, Kelly. I know we can."

Her eyes found his through the darkness. "Maybe," she whispered.

Maybe was better than *no*. Jace would take it for the time being. He understood what she was saying. Between the travel his career required and the fear that he might someday become as abusive as his father, he couldn't argue— even though he wanted to.

"I have to be up early in the morning. It's late."

"Okay. Monday. Five thirty. I'll see you then."

Kelly nodded, stepped inside and closed the door.

* * *

Jace blindly turned and walked to his truck. His emotions were all over the place. Even though he didn't like it at all, he had to give merit to Kelly's need to protect the baby. He wanted to be angry with her, his mind playing out the possibilities of what would have happened if he hadn't come back. Would she have waited until the child was grown to introduce them? Or simply raised the boy to believe he had no father? Either way was unacceptable. Yet on the heels of that thought was the fact that she had tried to reach him. He had no doubt she'd tried. It was a vicious circle and it all came back to him. He'd screwed up. Royally.

He climbed inside the truck, slamming the door quite a bit harder than was needed. All the regrets, all the shouldas and couldas, were tripping through his mind. But the big question was: what was he going to do now? It was so overwhelming he wished he had reason to doubt his paternity. But he knew, without any doubt, the baby was his. Kelly just wasn't a person who would make up something like this. Some would. But not Kelly.

Inasmuch as she intended her life to continue as it had so far, Jace knew it wouldn't happen. Her world was about to change and, from her perspective, not necessarily for the better. Sooner or later the media would find out about the ranch. It was only a matter of time. And eventually there was a very good possibility they would discover Kelly and their son. Especially if she'd listed Jace's name on the birth certificate. It would turn her life into a media circus, one she was not equipped to handle. He'd dealt with overzealous fans many times and knew what they were capable of. It wouldn't be safe for Kelly or the baby, and he could not stand back and let that happen.

He pulled away from the curb and headed for the ranch. *He had a son.* Even knowing all the obstacles in front of them, the idea of having a child was enthralling. The more the fact soaked in, the more incredible it became.

How could he go forward and not include Kelly and the baby in his life? Her vulnerability, her innocence about the world and the people in it who would use her for a stepping-stone to further their career, concerned him. The overwhelming desire to take care of her and the baby fought the knowledge that it could never happen because someday he could hurt them. A surge of intense feelings for her made him ache inside. The war that raged was the most intense pain he'd ever experienced. Broken bones had nothing on the anguish tearing his insides to shreds.

If he cared about Kelly, about his son, he needed to walk away. But where would he find the strength to do so?

Four

"Thanks so much for the ride, Gerri," Kelly told her friend as together they walked through the outside glass doors and down the steps of Great West Insurance. "I really do appreciate it."

"Not a problem, ever. You know that."

Kelly still hadn't found anyone to check out her car. With fall roundup in full swing, all the guys she knew had either signed on as ranch hands for the extra wages or had something else going on. The local garage had offered to send someone out, but wanted one hundred and fifty dollars just to make the trip to Jace's ranch. She'd told the mechanic she'd have to get back with him, biting her tongue to keep from calling him a crook.

The car had been on her mind constantly since she'd left Jace's home two days ago. Knowing it still sat on his property was unsettling; it was a tie to him she didn't want.

But as they turned onto her street, Kelly had to blink twice. Her old car sat in the driveway, and parked next to the curb was Jace's dark metallic-blue pickup.

"Hey, Kelly," Gerri said. "Looks like someone decided to help you out after all."

When Gerri pulled up behind the truck, Kelly saw Matt and Jace tossing a football across the expanse of three front yards.

"Yeah. Maybe. I'll see you tomorrow. Thanks again."

Kelly walked toward Mrs. Jenkins's house, hoping Gerri would drive away. Thankfully, she did, sticking her hand out the open window to wave goodbye as the Toyota continued down the street.

Mrs. Jenkins's home was only two houses down and around the corner. She was lucky to have such a kind and loving woman to keep the baby while she worked. Mrs. Jenkins's family had moved to another state the previous year and she longed for her own children and grandchildren. She'd assured Kelly that keeping Henry was a joy. It filled a void in her life. It was a great solution for all concerned.

Returning to her house with Henry, Kelly had just set the baby bag on the sofa and still had Henry in her arms when she saw Jace walking toward the door. Her heart immediately began doing flip-flops. Even the warmth of the baby snuggled against her couldn't make her relax. What she wouldn't give for Jace to be a regular person with a normal job. Maybe then things would have turned out differently. But why waste her time wishing for something that wasn't even in the realm of possibility? She didn't want to keep Jace from his son. But at the same time, his father's world was not a place the baby should be.

As soon as Jace spotted her standing behind the screen door with the baby in her arms, that infamous smile spread across his face. Kelly pushed open the door and bade him to enter. Gingerly, Jace reached out and touched Henry's hand. The baby laughed and grabbed the offered finger, kicking his feet in excitement.

"Hi, buddy." The acceptance was immediate. Apparently on both sides. "He's amazing."

"Would you like to hold him?"

Jace nodded, his eyes switching from Kelly to the baby, then back to Kelly. A twinge of heat surged through her body. Jace was so masculine, so totally male, every hormone she had was screaming to get closer. It was unsettling. His earthy aroma swirled around her, and she swallowed hard.

"Take a seat," she offered, clearing her throat, then placed the little bundle in his father's arms. Henry looked so tiny, and Jace looked so awkward, so out of place, but she couldn't miss the look of pride in his handsome features. As she silently watched father and son interact for the first time, she couldn't help but ask herself how Jace could look even sexier when he held the baby. His tanned arms and dark features were such a contrast to Henry's pale skin and hair. The sheer sexuality rolled off him in waves. So male. So powerful. So compelling. She ran the fingers of one hand through her hair in an effort to regain control of her wayward thoughts.

"He's just starting to respond to voices and smiles. He can almost roll over from his tummy onto his back. One day soon I'll go in the bedroom and find him trying to pull up and stand. His pediatrician said he is exceptional in both his mental and physical development."

Jace nodded, still staring at the baby as if he were in a trance. Kelly knew the feeling. The first time she'd been allowed to hold her son, she'd been captivated. A miniature of his father, complete with dimples, Henry was going to be a heartbreaker someday.

Just like his dad.

While Jace held his son, speaking softly to him and chuckling at his antics, Kelly eased into the kitchen and took her cell phone from her purse. Bringing up the camera, she returned to the living room and clicked away. This was a memorable moment for all three of them.

"If you'll give me your email address, I'll send them to you."

"Thanks, Kelly," Jace said in a tone that indicated he really did appreciate the gesture.

She returned to the chair and sat down.

"Tell me more about him."

She shrugged. Where to begin? "He's a happy baby. He loves the water and bath time. He has a small yellow plastic duck he will try and grab. His efforts send water splashing in every direction and it makes him laugh, so he splashes some more. My coworkers bought him a little swing. You wind it up and it will stay in motion about half an hour. Henry loves that, too."

"How did you choose his name?"

"Henry was my grandfather's name."

Jace nodded.

"His…his middle name is Jason."

Jace's head shot up and that green gaze held hers. "You named him after me?"

Kelly shrugged. "It seemed like the right thing to do." The warmth of a blush touched her cheeks as the glint of surprise and obvious happiness showed in his eyes. "I've started reading to him. Of course he doesn't understand what I'm saying, but he seems to like it."

"He responds to the sound of your voice." Jace looked at her. "Like father, like son."

For an instant their eyes met and held. Kelly swallowed hard, fighting against a sudden overwhelming sense of loss. It felt as though somebody had reached in and ripped out everything inside. Which was crazy. How long would this man have such a compelling effect on her? His voice had always sent shivers across her skin, and now was no different. She remembered lying on the blanket under the shade of a giant oak tree, her head resting on his muscled chest, held close and protected in his heavy arms. She remembered how good just being in his presence had made her feel.

Pushing away those memories, Kelly continued to share small things about Henry's life. She kept her gaze locked on the baby. She didn't need any more remembrances of Jace distracting her. The recollections she'd managed to bury could stay buried. Feeling his arms around her again would never happen. The past was best left in the past.

Eventually their quiet conversation lulled the baby to sleep. Kelly took him from Jace and put him in his crib, covering him with his blue puppy blanket. When she returned Jace was standing at the front door.

"Do I have you to thank for getting my car home?"

He shrugged those broad shoulders. "No big deal."

"I called everyone I knew and no one had time to look at it." She felt the need to assure him she'd tried to get the car out of his way. "How much do I owe you?"

He shook his head and shrugged. "I just turned the key. You must have given it too much gas and flooded the engine. Desperation for a quick getaway sometimes causes that to happen."

She ignored the gibe. "Well, thank you."

"No problem." He hesitated. "I'd like to invite Matt out to the ranch to throw some footballs. Maybe I can give him some pointers."

"He would love that. He is so into football, and as you will soon discover if you haven't already, you're his hero. But Jace, don't do it because you feel in any way obligated. Eventually, Matt would figure it out and—"

"Gotcha. No worries there. He seems like a good kid. My mom will be staying at the ranch but won't be here for a few days, so tossing the ball with Matt will be great. Brings back the good old days." He grinned and pushed open the door as Matt came jogging up to the porch. "It gets dark around nine. I'll have him home about then."

The afternoon visits and the ball practice with Matt at the ranch became everyday events. Over the next two weeks, Kelly's anger and resentment slowly began to wane to a controllable level. It was so odd having Jace back in her life. Every day she expected him to not show up. But he hadn't missed a day yet. Initially she'd had some sleepless nights, her mind trying to answer the big question: What now? Where was this going? What was he eventually going to do? Did his plans include an attempt to take Henry?

Jace was a brief moment in her past. He had no part in her future other than being her son's father. Never again would she be back in his arms. Ever.

Pushing open the heavy glass door of the insurance company where she worked as assistant customer service rep, Kelly headed toward the side of the building and the employee parking lot. It had been a long day. But it helped keep her mind focused, leaving no time to think about Jace.

Most of the time.

Rounding the outside corner of the building, heading toward the parking lot, she immediately spotted the very subject of her thoughts leaning against her car, his arms crossed over his broad chest. Her heart skipped a beat. Her determination to keep their past where it belonged was an ongoing battle, and every time she saw him, it grew more difficult.

Inside she was jumble of nerves, wanting him to stay away yet missing him, then hating herself for it. Every time a dark blue truck passed, she had to look to see if it was him. When told she had an incoming call at work, she anxiously picked up the receiver, prepared to hear his deep voice on the other end. Errands around town had her searching the faces in the crowd for him.

Now the pulse surged through her veins as she took in the sight of him, and her mind rushed to figure out why he was here.

"Do you have a minute?" he asked when she reached the car.

Kelly shrugged.

Jace hesitated, as though looking for the right words. "I received a phone call about an hour ago. A friend in the media owes me a couple of favors. He called to let me know someone found out I'm the primary stockholder in a company that recently bought a ranch in Calico Springs, Texas. The news media will probably be staking out the ranch by this evening or soon after. Reporters can be ruthless. They can dig up facts you thought were long buried."

Why was he telling her this? This didn't concern her. And if the media discovered Henry was Jace's son, she couldn't stop it.

"So, why tell me? It's not any of my business."

"I'm afraid it might be only a matter of time until they find out about Henry."

"Are you asking me to deny Henry is your son if anyone should inquire? Sorry if he's an embarrassment for you." She adjusted the strap of her purse on her shoulder. "Excuse me. You're blocking the door. I need to get home."

Jace didn't move.

"That's not what I'm saying at all. Kelly, other than his middle name, did you put my name on his birth certificate? As the father?"

She nodded.

"If anyone finds out about Henry, this will blow up into a very big deal. You won't be safe, or at the least, you will be surrounded by the press. Night and day. Everywhere you go. They will follow you to work. They will find out who keeps the baby during the day and do what they have to in order to get a picture. They could even go to Matt's school."

Jace had to see the skepticism on her face. "So...I'll just tell them to leave my property," she countered. "And once the school year begins they should be able to keep any stranger, reporter or not, away from Matt. I mean, they can't just—"

"They can and they will."

"No." She gritted her teeth to keep her anger in check. "No. This will not happen. Dammit, Jace. Keep your media mania on your side of the street and leave my side alone. This was exactly what I told you I didn't want to happen to Henry."

"I know. And I'm sorry. I'd change it if I could."

"So what's the answer? Why are you telling me all of this if there is no way to stop it?"

"You and Henry and Matt need to move out to the ranch as soon as possible."

Her eyebrows shot straight up as she looked at him with

open disbelief. "Yeah. Right. That is so not going to happen."

"Kelly, you're not equipped to deal with this on your own. I have a full security staff in place 24/7." Jace glanced toward a black sedan parked across the street and nodded. The man behind the wheel nodded back.

"You've got to be kidding." He had to be. "Jace, you're blowing this way out of proportion. This is Calico Springs, population six thousand and two. It isn't Los Angeles. It's a quiet little ranching community. Things like you're describing just don't happen here. Now if you'll please step aside, I really need to go and pick up Henry."

With a muttered curse, Jace moved toward the front of the car and opened the door for her. Kelly didn't hesitate to throw her purse onto the passenger seat and slip behind the wheel.

"Take this." He handed her a cell phone. "Just punch Call. There are only three people who will answer it—a couple of my security team and me. If you get into trouble, change your mind or need to reach me, use it."

This was taking on the ambiance of a James Bond thriller. "Are you kidding me?"

Jace looked down at her and shook his head. He wasn't smiling. A small trickle of fear ran down her spine. She took the phone and slipped it into the side pouch of her purse. It seemed easier than arguing about it.

"I won't be coming back in the afternoons. There's too much of a risk someone will see me. Kelly, I really do wish you would—"

"We'll be fine." She turned on the ignition and put the car into reverse. "I'll let Matt know you won't be stopping by for a while."

Jace didn't nod. He said nothing more. He stood in the same spot as she backed out of the parking space and turned toward home.

It must be tough to live your life always looking over

your shoulder. In a way she found it sad. To become so successful in your chosen career that you actually become a target of the very people you sought to entertain. But it was a life he'd chosen. Consequently, he had to deal with the repercussions. It didn't mean she had to.

Five

An unfamiliar sound woke Kelly from her sleep. Frowning, she rubbed her eyes and listened more intently. It sounded like people talking outside her house. She threw the covers back and rolled out of bed. It was early morning, still not completely light. She checked on Henry and adjusted his blanket. He'd slept through the night, so he would be ready for his breakfast soon.

Without bothering to turn on a light, she headed toward the living room, literally bumping into Matt in the hallway.

"Do you hear that?" It took a major shakedown every morning to get Matt to even open his eyes. For him to be awake at this hour...

"Yeah. I heard it."

"What is it?"

"I'm not sure." Separating the blinds just enough to see, they both looked out the front windows. In the predawn light, Kelly saw people. About a dozen of them. And cars and vans lining both sides of the street.

"What's going on, Kelly?" Before she could speak, Matt added, "I'm going out and see what's happening."

"No! Matt. Don't go outside."

In the ever-increasing light Kelly now saw the cameras and the white vans with satellite antennas on top. People were talking among themselves, calling out instructions to their crews. Large black power cords lay over the ground. She swallowed hard. Jace had told her the truth. Anger flared that he had brought this madness to their family, but it was temporarily pushed aside by concern for Henry and Matt.

"Matt, go get dressed and ready for school. You can't be late the second day. Find something to eat for breakfast. There are waffles in the freezer. Fresh fruit in the bowl on the table."

"This is wild." His eyes were as wide as saucers. "Those are reporters, right? Is all this because Jace comes here to visit?"

"No. Not exactly." She didn't know how her brother would take the news, but it was time he was told. Before he heard it on television. "This is because Henry is Jace's son."

Matt's jaw hung open; his eyes went ever wider. "*What?* Oh, man. Are you kidding me? You had a thing with Jace and you never told me? When? How? Where? Are you serious?"

Kelly nodded. "Yes. But it's…complicated. And we don't have time to discuss it now."

"Does Jace know?"

Kelly rubbed her temples. "Yes."

"Henry is Jace Compton's *son*?"

Clearly Matt was struggling with this truth.

"So that's why he invited me out to his place to throw the ball."

Wow. Left field. His disappointment was obvious. "No. Absolutely not. You guys share a love of football and the two of you seemed to…click. He thinks the world of you, Matt. I would never lie about that. He's told me so on more than one occasion." The very last thing she wanted to add to this insanity was hurt feelings. She'd told Matt the truth. She just hoped he would believe it.

Matt was silent for a few worrying seconds. "Okay," he nodded. "Okay. Good. That's cool." The side of his mouth drew up in a half grin and he looked squarely at his sister. "I guess I'm not the only one in this family he *clicked* with."

She felt the heated blush cover her neck and face. Her

eyes narrowed into a glare. "Right now, Matthew Douglas Michaels, I would advise you not to go there. Go get dressed."

Matt headed for his bedroom, a wide grin across his face. His body language was decidedly springy with a bit of teenage swagger thrown in. He was on the *ins* with a superstar. And no doubt he thought he had something on her, as well. From the number of people standing outside their house, he would have to get in line.

With Henry changed and dressed, she went into the kitchen to ready his food. Her purse was on the kitchen table and the cell phone Jace had given her began to ring. When she pulled it out of her bag, she saw there had been numerous calls. She'd never heard it.

"Hello?"

"Why in the hell haven't you answered your phone?" Jace bellowed out, his frustration obvious. "I've been trying to reach you for thirty minutes. Are you all right? Is Henry—?"

"Henry is fine. We're all fine. There are some people outside. They have cameras. I guess you were right. It appears the media found us."

She heard him take a deep breath and blow it out. Kelly couldn't remember Jace ever getting angry or upset about anything. Clearly he was experiencing some anxiety now. Did he actually think something was going to happen to them in Calico Springs?

"Stay in the house. Keep the doors locked. Tom Stanton, my head of security, just arrived and is standing by outside your house. Let us know when you're ready and he'll bring you guys to the ranch and we—"

"Jace, no. I'm not coming to your ranch. I thought I made that clear. I've got to go to work and Matt has to be in school—" she switched Henry to her other arm and checked her watch "—in twenty minutes. I need to take the baby to the sitter's, then be on my way."

"Kelly, I don't think that would be—"

"Please don't waste either of our time telling me you don't think it's a good idea. If you want to help us, we need to get Henry safely to the babysitter and Matt to school."

A prolonged silence met her statement. "Kelly, you can't go on expecting your life to stay the way it was. I'm sorry, honey."

She heard the sincerity in his tone. His endearment made her heart beat a bit faster, her breathing become shallow. His rich baritone voice calling her honey caused a memory to flash in her mind. Jace's arms around her, his hand covering hers as she gripped the end of a fishing pole. They'd been on the edge of a clear blue pond located in an area of the ranch where he'd stayed last year. It had felt as if they were the only two people on earth. Jace had removed his shirt and shoes, leaving only the well-worn, slightly ripped jeans. She'd had a two-pound bass on the line, the first fish she'd ever caught. When it broke the surface of the water, bending and flouncing in an effort to get free of the hook, she hadn't been able to contain the screams of excitement. And she couldn't forget Jace's laughter at her animated enthusiasm. Then the fish had fallen back into the water and seconds later the line went slack. She'd lost it. Jace had hugged her close and murmured, "I'm sorry, honey. Let's see if we can catch him again." But as she'd turned into his arms the fish was forgotten. The soft rays of the summer sun had been joined by the hot sparkle of desire in his eyes and the burning of his hungry lips.

Would she ever be immune to him? To his voice? His touch? How much longer until she could stop having to fight her own body in order to maintain some small amount of control? Kelly brushed the hair back from her face, striving for practicality. She didn't need to turn into one of Jace Compton's groupies, and the past had shown her that was the most she could ever be.

"Kelly? Are you there?"

"Uh…yeah. Yeah. Jace, I can't walk away from my life. Apparently, you can't walk away from yours, either. Matt has to go to school and I need to get dressed and go to work." Why couldn't he understand? Had he been living the high life so long he could no longer relate to ordinary people living ordinary lives?

He finally agreed, but she could tell by his tone he didn't like it. "I'll have Tom send two men to the front door. Tell them where you want to go."

Three days later the craziness had not subsided and her cell phone wouldn't stop ringing. There was no sign the media were giving up. Not only had they increased their ranks, they had been joined by some of the town's residents, their own curiosity compelling them to be part of the excitement. There were what appeared to be tailgate parties going on just past her driveway as far down the street as she could see in both directions, with dozens of lawn chairs lining the yards on both sides. Her home had become a freak show. For the first time in her life, Kelly felt claustrophobia stir her anger.

The switchboard at work had been bombarded with calls since that first day, overwhelming the phone lines. Just after lunch today she'd had a rather unpleasant one-on-one with her boss, who'd recommended she take off early, adding she had a week of vacation and suggested she use it until she got her life in some semblance of order. And now, apparently, her cell number had been discovered and passed out, free for the taking.

Every day, Jace's security team picked Matt up and escorted him home. He was having a great time with all the excitement, enjoying the sudden popularity and inspiring the envy of his classmates, which only added to her growing frustration.

Pacing around the small house, her mind was filled with murderous thoughts, and all of them revolved around Jace.

How could he do this? And why wouldn't he stop it? *I want to be in your life*, he'd said. Ha! What a joke. This media mania was exactly what she'd wanted to avoid. How dare he dump this on her front doorstep?

The cell phone Jace had provided began to ring.

"Hello?"

"Ms. Michaels, this is Tom Stanton of Jace's security detail. Would you like your mail?"

"My *mail*?" Why not? What else did she have to do? "Yeah. Sure."

"One of our men will deliver it to your back door in two minutes."

"Thanks." It seemed as if they were going to a lot of trouble. She mostly received advertisements addressed to "resident," which immediately went into the trash.

At the man's knock, Kelly opened the door. With a respectful nod, he brought in her mail. Three large bags of it.

"What…? What is all this?"

"They're all addressed to you. Probably fan letters."

"*Fan letters?*" Was he kidding?

By the time Matt got home, Kelly was just about to open the second bag. Sitting on the living room floor with Henry playing on a thick blanket next to her, she'd spent the past three hours reading pure crazy.

"You know," Matt said as he walked to where she sat, "we should sell popcorn to those people outside. Make some money off this. What are you doing?" Frowning, he dumped his books onto the sofa. "What is all this?"

"Fan letters." She didn't look up, but she could feel Matt's surprise mixed with excitement from four feet away. "Have a seat. I wouldn't want you to miss one second of this *wonderful* experience."

Ignoring her sarcasm, Matt quickly found a place on the floor and pulled a handful of letters out of the newly opened bag.

"Ha!" Matt laughed. "This girl wants to have Jace's baby

but is happy for you in spite of you beating her to it." He picked up another and began reading.

"Kelly?"

She noticed his face narrow into a serious frown. "You'd better take a look at this." He handed the page to her.

The letter was filled with alarming descriptions of what they intended to do to Kelly and the baby. Off-the-wall acts of violence directed at her and Henry. She felt the blood leave her face as she realized the implications. Suddenly a crashing sound from the bedroom made her jump. It sounded as if a vase had shattered. "Matt, stay with Henry."

Kelly scrambled to her feet and hurried in that direction.

"Sorry about your vase." A woman about her age was standing inside the bedroom, looking around.

"Who are you? How did you get inside my house?" Kelly's voice was about three octaves higher than normal.

The woman shrugged and looked toward the bed. "Through the window. Is that where Jace Compton sleeps?" She spoke as though she was in a daze, as if she'd just stumbled into Neverland. The woman walked over to the bed, smoothed her hands over the covers, and then proceeded to crawl on top of the mattress.

"What are you doing? Get off my bed!"

"It's so soft," the woman said, completely ignoring Kelly's angry demand. "Wow."

Kelly ran for kitchen table and the phone Jace had provided. Her call was immediately answered.

"There is someone in my bedroom." She could hear the anger in her own voice. "She said she climbed in through the window. She's *in* my bed and refuses to leave."

The line went dead and within seconds men were coming in every door to her small house, guns drawn, with Tom Stanton leading the charge. The woman was seized and handcuffed. Notification of the break-in was called into the police, all handled in a practiced and flawless manner by the men in Jace's security detail.

Kelly went back to the front room and picked up Henry. Matt stood next to her, not saying a word.

"The police will need a statement, Ms. Michaels. They should be here any minute."

Kelly nodded and sat down on the sofa, holding Henry close.

"I think you need to see this." Matt shoved a letter into Tom's hand.

"Where did you get this, son?" Tom frowned.

"In the mail. We were reading all this mail." He gestured to letters spread over the floor and one of the bags, still partially full, next to the sofa. "Most of them are stupid. But this one..."

Tom took out his phone and punched a number before turning and walking out of the room. Kelly could hear his voice. She couldn't understand what he said or who he was talking to.

But she had a pretty good idea.

Six

It took Jace most of the drive from the ranch to Kelly's house to bring his temper under a small bit of control. Tom's phone call had his heart racing, his fear for their safety mounting. *Someone had gotten into their house.* The lives of both Kelly and his son had been threatened. He blew out an angry sigh. Kelly was going to listen to reason. This time he was not going to accept any damned excuses. If he had to play the role of bad guy, so be it. If pleas didn't work, maybe a bluff would. One way or the other, she was leaving that house.

He knew in time the press's feeding frenzy would die down. News of him having a child was enough of a story to bring the cameras to Texas. But no one wanted to read old news. Eventually, some new story would replace the old. The question was, how long until this was considered old? A call to Bret was necessary to ensure he didn't do anything to prolong this mess. The last thing any of them needed was for the manager to jump into the mayhem and milk it for all it was worth.

Putting his sunglasses in place, Jace got out of the truck with two members of his security team, one behind and one next to him. He ignored the shouts from the reporters and what had to be a quarter of the town's population standing behind the yellow tape. Three police cars, lights flashing, were blocking off the street, the officers trying unsuccessfully to disband the gawkers. With more calm than he felt, Jace opened the front door of the house and stepped inside.

Kelly was sitting on the couch, holding Henry. Matt sat on the floor next to her, reading letters. Tom, two of his men and two police officers stood in the small kitchen, quietly talking among themselves.

When Jace approached Kelly, she glared at him with a force that could hurt if it had any substance. But his concern effectively deflected any anger she might have and replaced it with some of his own. He crouched down next to the sofa, his face only inches from hers.

"Are you guys okay?"

"Physically. Obviously I don't appreciate that woman sneaking into my house and crawling up on my bed. You were supposed to do something. She broke my grandmother's vase."

"I'm about to do something. Kelly, this is finished. Do you understand?" His gaze caught hers and he didn't let go. "You're going to pack some clothes and you and Matt and Henry are moving to the ranch until this blows over."

"I don't want to live in your house."

"That's too damn bad." Jace could feel the tight control he had on his temper slipping. "You'd rather stay here and have someone break into your house again? Next time, it might be someone worse than that mentally disturbed woman. It might be the crazed idiot who wrote that letter. Don't be stupid, Kelly." He could hear the growl in his own voice.

Her quick intake of breath and the flash of surprise in her blue-green eyes told him he'd crossed the line. *Damn.* For the first time in his life, with Kelly of all people, the mother of his child, he was in danger of letting his anger override his common sense, doing exactly what he'd been afraid of for so many years. He clenched his jaw in an effort to maintain control. He had to keep it together. For Kelly. He felt a wave of guilt wash over him for what he'd said.

He reached out and gently took her face in his hands, determined to make her understand. "What if someone took

Henry?" Her eyes widened. Apparently the thought had not occurred to her. "A ransom demand is not that far-fetched."

"Then stop it," she snapped at him, a whispered plea. "You caused all of this. We were fine until you came back. Make them leave us alone."

"I'm trying, but it isn't that simple and you're smart enough to know that. I intend to do everything in my power to give the reporters what they want and see if I can make them leave. But the ranch is the only place I can protect you until that happens."

Jace let his hands drop and she looked down at Henry, who was sleeping peacefully in her arms. Jace could see the resentment in her face, the need for all of this to go away. She was frustrated and angry and probably a little scared all at the same time. He knew Kelly well enough to know she was going to try to bluff him out of their moving to the ranch. And no way was that going to happen.

"We can go to my friend Gerri's apartment and—"

"Do you really think that will make any difference?"

As she thought about his question, she moistened her lower lip with her tongue. He remembered all too well his mouth doing the same thing—tasting those lips, sucking the nectar from them before going deeper, enjoying the sweet taste he'd found in the hidden recesses of her mouth.

"I don't know. But I'm not moving to your house."

Jace ran a hand through his hair and huffed out some of the frustration. "Kelly, I can't legally make any demands of you, but Henry is my son and one way or the other, he is leaving this house. Now. It isn't safe. If I have to, I'll get a court order giving me temporary custody. And don't imagine any judge is going to stand by and let a five-month-old baby live in a threatening environment."

He hated playing the badass, but clearly they were in danger. If something happened to any of them he would never forgive himself. At this point it wasn't beneath him to toss her over his shoulder and carry her out kicking and screaming. If that's what it took, so be it. He *would* to keep them safe.

Pale and distraught, she looked up at him. Apparently just the mention of taking her child was enough to terrify her. Jace knew a surge of guilt for what he'd said, but he had to get her to relocate somewhere safe.

"Kelly? It doesn't have to be forever." He ignored the extra beat of his heart and the odd sinking feeling in his gut when he spoke those words.

She nodded. "You don't have to threaten."

"I apologize. You're making the right decision."

"Don't patronize me, either. You're giving me no choice. Of course I'm concerned for Henry's safety. You have to realize how…uncomfortable this will be for me. And in the meantime I expect you to make all this insanity go away."

She would try the patience of a saint. His eyes held hers for countless seconds, and he became aware that he was almost close enough to kiss her. He wanted to. Even now. Even in the middle of this crazy situation. He remembered holding her, making love to her. His body was hard with expectation and he knew she wouldn't be the only one uncomfortable while she lived under his roof. Only a few steps down the hall from his bedroom.

Kelly watched as Jace stood and walked over to Tom. There was a lot of nodding during their low, quiet discussion. Minutes later, they disappeared out the front door. Kelly listened to the muffled conversations as Jace apparently talked to the press. Ten minutes later, they came back inside.

"Here's what we're going to do," Jace said, returning to where Kelly sat. "It's almost dark. That will work to our advantage. Tom will have a car in front of the house in a few minutes, allowing time for some of the media to disperse. It's the same dark green SUV that's been taking you to work. Go to the car. Don't stop for anything. You know the drill."

Kelly stood and handed Henry to his father. Jace accepted the baby as if it were something he did every day. Which, come to think of it, he did. Or at least, he had for two weeks.

"I need to get some things together, unless you have his formula and plenty of diapers?" Knowing the answer, Kelly turned toward the bedroom. With her heart racing, she grabbed the baby bag and shoved it full of bottles, formula, baby food, clothes, diapers and a couple of stuffed toys. She pulled a small suitcase from the closet and packed jeans, assorted T-shirts, toiletries and a few more baby items.

Thirty minutes later it was time to go.

Matt stood waiting by the door. He wore a backpack, no doubt full of clothes, and held a tote bag with his books.

Jace stepped up behind them, still holding Henry. Kelly watched through the front windows as a green vehicle pulled up in front.

"It's here."

The short walk to the SUV was made without incident, although Kelly could feel the bevy of cameras recording every step. The throng of people standing behind the yellow tape surged forward when Jace emerged with his new baby. That provided a few seconds of apprehension but again, his security team took control. The ride to the grocery store parking lot where a helicopter awaited was made with no problems. Soon they were leaving the ground, quickly ascending into the darkened sky. Kelly watched the baby, afraid the sound would frighten him. But Henry took it in stride and continued to chew on Jace's shirt. Teething. Jace would have a major wet spot by the time they landed. Welcome to fatherhood.

"Cool," Matt muttered in fascination as he looked out the window.

In minutes they descended into the clearing of a pasture behind the stately home, setting down on a large round landing pad. The pilot immediately killed the engine, and they were escorted to waiting vehicles. The ride to the house was made in silence other than Henry's babble. Part of her wanted to be grateful to Jace for stepping in to keep Henry safe. The other part resented the fact that were it not for him, the protection wouldn't be needed in the first place.

The mansion was ablaze with lights. Jace escorted them down a path, his hand on her lower back.

"This is Carmen." Jace introduced a robust Hispanic woman who came forward with a welcoming smile as soon as they entered the house. "I need to speak with Tom. Carmen will take you all upstairs and show you where you'll be staying."

Not for long, Kelly thought, her mind slowly coming back on track. She took the baby from Jace and they followed the housekeeper up the stairs. Kelly remembered the day she'd cleaned the house and thought what a great place it was for a family. Never in a million years would she have guessed it would be her own family, let alone that she'd be living here with Jace. She swallowed hard.

The bedroom she was shown was only slightly smaller than the two rooms she'd cleaned a few weeks ago. The color scheme was green and blue pastel. It presented a relaxing and welcoming feel.

"You are next door, Mr. Matt," Carmen said in a strong accent. "This way. Make yourselves at home." She smiled at the baby in Kelly's arms. "I have four daughters, two sons and five grandbabies. Anything you need for your baby, you let me know, Mrs. Compton. I know what to do."

"Thank you. But I'm not…" Carmen and Matt disappeared around the corner before Kelly could explain she was *not* Mrs. Compton. She never would be. But why bother to correct her? They wouldn't be here long enough for it to make any difference.

Henry had finally wound down and was fast asleep in her arms. She put him in the center of the large bed, his little arms falling out to the side as he slept.

Living under Jace's roof was a bad idea. Every time Jace came close to her, memories jumped to the front of her mind. When he spoke, her eyes automatically focused on his mouth, on those lips that could do amazing things. When those all-knowing green eyes gleamed with passion, a chill went across her skin.

She had to keep this situation in perspective. There was no doubt any number of women who had felt exactly the same way about Jace Compton. She had to be one in a very long list who experienced the same pleasures in his arms. She was not a hormone-driven, nitwitted adolescent. She'd survived Jace once. She could do it again. She was here now only because of Henry. Even though the attraction was still strong, she would do well to remember the months after Jace had left and the fact that he'd never given her a second thought.

After unpacking, Kelly paced, not knowing what to do. She switched on the flat-screen TV and ran through the channel options, but found nothing that would hold her attention and turned it off. Her gaze fell on the door to the large bathroom. Venturing inside she passed through the powder room with its antique mirrors and vases of freshly cut flowers on dark marble countertops. Next was a shower large enough for four or five people and a whirlpool tub of equal size. She hurried back to the bedroom and placed pillows all around the edge of the bed to safeguard Henry while he slept. After covering the baby with his blue blanket and assuring herself he was sleeping peacefully, she headed back into the bathroom.

Pouring her favorite lavender bath salts into the quickly filling tub, she turned on the jets and climbed in. Lying back, she closed her eyes and gave in to the sheer luxury that enveloped her. The streams of the water coursing around her, against her back, her sides and neck, through her legs, soon began to reduce the stress of the past few days.

The memory of another time came unbidden to her mind.

There had been no tub at the ranch where Jace had stayed, but they'd made do with the shower.

For the first time in her life, Kelly saw a perfect example of the human male body. Broad shoulders blocked the water from reaching her as the moisture cascaded down over his corded neck and arms. Jace soaped his large hands and began to rub them slowly over every inch of her body, over her breasts, down her stomach, between her legs.

He was heavy with arousal and the air left her lungs as she stared, unable to tear her eyes away. She realized she'd never seen a man in this way before. There was no hiding under the blanket of modesty. He wanted to see every inch of her and offered her the same.

"See anything you like?"

Her gaze shot upward and met his. She could feel the blush spread over her face and neck. Obviously, Jace had no problem with modesty. He seemed totally unconcerned that she was seeing him naked. And aroused. Or that his size had her eyes bugging out of her head.

Jace had noted the blush. "Have you never seen a man before?" He tilted his head.

She swallowed. "Not...not like this."

He continued to watch her for several seconds. "How old were you? Late teens?"

"Yes."

"Quickie in the backseat?"

She nodded.

She saw a look of understanding cross his face. Instinct said her onetime experiment with teenage sex was not even close to what she was about to experience with the fully mature man who stood before her.

"Makes me curious what else you haven't experienced." His head dipped toward hers and he muttered against her lips, "Let's find out."

Without waiting for an answer, Jace took her lips in a deep, penetrating kiss that rocked her senses. He caught her hands and held them, palms up, as he poured the scented soap into them. Kelly stared at her hands for countless seconds, knowing what he was asking of her. Her heart beat in an accelerated rhythm as she contemplated what she was about to do.

Almost of their own accord, her hands moved to his large body. Slowly she began to rub the slick soap over his smooth skin, covering the hard wall of his chest and arms, loving the feel of the muscles that rippled beneath her hands.

She let them glide up to his massive shoulders and neck, then once again over his chest. She couldn't keep from looking into his eyes. He watched her with the look of a cat playing with a mouse. So intense was his focus, her hands stilled in their journey of discovery.

He took them and slowly pushed them down his body. "Touch me," he whispered, placing her fingers around his sex.

She tore her eyes from his face to look at the hard pound of flesh in her hands. Her gaze returned to his face, blue eyes meeting green, as she stood there, frozen, unable to release him yet unable to move. Her breathing becoming almost nonexistent.

"Let me help you, honey," he whispered. He began to move her hand against the silken flesh covering the underlying steel of his erection. It was an amazing sensation, and she caught on fast.

Jace lowered his head, and his lips again found hers. She opened her mouth and welcomed him in. His arms came around her as the warm water cascaded over their embrace.

His hand squeezed her hip then moved on to rub the sensitive area between her legs, encouraging her to open to him. She moved against his hand in an effort to quench the fire burning deep. Two fingers eased inside, and a shudder ran rampant through her entire body. With a muffled moan, she fell back against the shower wall as the mind-blowing sensations overtook her.

"Kelly," Jace groaned, his voice rough with need. Suddenly, his control seemed to snap. He lifted her, positioned her and pushed deep inside.

She felt a sudden draft of cold air mingle with the warm moisture of the bathroom seconds before his warm lips touched the sensitive curve where her neck and shoulder joined. A soft moan escaped her lips and, eyes closed, she turned into his mouth. Hungry lips covered hers, his tongue searching and finding what he sought. Her wet hands rose to hold his face, the need for him strong, essential. She gripped the back of his hair in a fist.

"Mmmm." He groaned, his deep, husky voice breaking the silence.

The memory ended with a shocking recoil, as if she'd had ice water thrown in her face. Her eyes shot open to find Jace leaning over the tub, his handsome face mere inches from hers. Kelly gasped in shock. She could feel herself flush with embarrassment over the memory she'd been reliving. Apparently, at some point they had merged with the present. She prayed his talents didn't include mind reading.

Jace's intense expression increased the simmering heat the daydream had generated. She held her arms over her breasts as she glared at Jace. He stood to full height, hands on his hips, his eyes moving over her naked body with an undeniable gleam.

"What are you doing in here?" Kelly spat the words, but Jace only pursed his lips as though hiding a grin and made no move to leave.

"I'm about to make love to you."

Seven

"You have no right to walk in here just because you own the house."

"You didn't appear to mind."

"I...I was just..."

He tilted his head, eyebrows raised, waiting for her to squirm out of this one. When she didn't reply, the gleam in those forest-green eyes intensified. "I know exactly what you were doing, Kelly. Instead of relying on memories, why don't you let me give you the real thing?"

Kelly frantically looked for a towel. "I need you to leave."

"Actually, I was headed to my room and heard Henry crying. After repeated knocks, I grew concerned. Would you rather I ignore his cries in the future?"

"He wasn't crying."

"As a matter of fact, he was. I gave him his pacifier and sat with him a few minutes and he went back to sleep."

"Well, you didn't have to come in *here*."

"I thought you might want to know about Henry." He pursed his lips, his green eyes glinting with humor. "There's nothing I haven't seen before, Kelly." His low voice caused shivers to run up her arms.

"That's not the point."

"No?"

"No."

He grabbed an oversize fluffy white towel and held it up for her. Kelly clambered out of the bath and down the few steps, and Jace wrapped the towel around her; his arms remained, holding her close.

"I've missed you." His low voice caused shivers to run over her skin.

"No, you haven't."

"Kelly, I want to work through this. I made mistakes. But they were not done intentionally."

She stepped back and his hands fell to his side.

"You miss the point. I don't care."

"I think you're letting your pride talk for you."

"And I think your libido is dictating to you."

"And that's a bad thing?"

She folded a corner of the towel between her breasts and moved away from him into the dressing area. She refused to argue. Especially when she might not win. Grabbing her comb, she began to work through the tangles, praying he would leave.

He stood in the entrance to the bathroom, leaning casually against the wall, watching her. The mirrored reflection did nothing to diminish his pure male presence, making her want to do all sorts of things she shouldn't. Unbidden, her mind kept reliving moments from before, and Jace was apparently more than willing to repeat every single one of them. She wouldn't go there again. She couldn't. The first time, his leaving, his lying, had almost destroyed her. For her own sake, and Henry's, she would not jump back in that rabbit hole again.

Having finished her task, she returned to the bedroom in search of fresh clothes. A peek toward the bed confirmed Henry was fast asleep, his blue pacifier moving slightly as he sucked on it. Jace stood next to her gazing down at the baby, and then shifted his focus to her. What she saw in his eyes was pride for his son, but more: she saw concern. He honestly cared about his son. He'd heard Henry crying and stopped to check on him. The blue pacifier was proof Jace had been telling the truth. That meant he'd sat next to the baby and given comfort until Henry went back to sleep. For perhaps the first time since they'd met, she saw more than a sexy body and killer smile. She saw a glimpse into the heart of the person Jace was inside. And that was a little bit daunting. She didn't want to like Jace Compton.

"I need to check on Matt." She walked to the bureau, removing a clean shirt and jeans.

Jace nodded, this time taking the hint, and walked out the door.

Matt was happily absorbed in a car racing game on his Xbox. To him, this was a grand adventure. He'd better enjoy it while it lasted.

She returned to her room and pulled on her old cotton gown and slipped into bed next to Henry. She had to leave here. She couldn't stay in this house with Jace. He might want to pick up where they'd left off, and she knew her defenses were sadly lacking. Loving him might not be something she could control. Making love to him was not going to happen.

Regardless of how much she might want it to.

"But I don't understand." Kelly blinked back the tears. "I had a week of vacation and it's only been…five days." *Crap.* She'd just quashed her own defense.

"Are you saying you'll be back on Monday?" Her boss was usually a fair man, but this was a low blow. "I should warn you, the press are still camped out at all the exits here. Frankly, this is becoming a problem."

The voice on the other end of the line was apologetic but firm. The work was piling up and they had to get someone in to deal with it.

The call ended and Kelly sank down onto one of the kitchen chairs, totally devastated. Reluctantly, she'd agreed to give up her job. Her boss had called her work top-notch and said that if there was an opening when she was ready to come back, she would certainly be considered for reemployment. He'd again offered his apologies, and then it was over. The call as well as her hope for the immediate future.

This was a nightmare that kept on giving.

"Hey, Kelly." Matt hurried into the den. "Turn on the TV." Matt found the remote and switched on the set himself. A news conference was in full swing. "Now we know where Jace has been for two days."

"I didn't know we cared."

"Yes, I've always liked Texas." Jace's handsome face filled the screen as he spoke.

"Rumors are rampant that you and a woman, Kelly Michaels, have a child? Can you comment on that?" a reporter asked off camera.

Without hesitation, Jace nodded, that award-winning grin flashing perfect white teeth. "Yes. We have a son. We're both very happy. Very excited."

A bevy of questions followed his statement. Kelly didn't see how he could understand any of them, but he soon responded, "I'll provide some pictures when he's older. I'm sure you can appreciate the safety concerns."

Another round of questions, and then, "I can't say where we will live at this juncture. Currently we are enjoying some solitude in Texas. There's always a chance we'll come back to LA. We haven't made a decision."

"Are you planning to get married?" someone asked.

Kelly's heart stopped in her throat, anticipating what Jace would say to that.

"Right now we haven't made any plans. We just want to enjoy our son and some quiet time together. I hope you can respect our privacy, give us a little room."

The subject changed to his next film role. Did Jace think he would get the lead in the rumored blockbuster due to start filming in three months? Again that smile. "You guys will probably know that before I do." He got the laughing response he no doubt intended. After a few more softballs like that, he called an end to the press conference. "Okay. That's all I have for today. Thanks."

He turned and disappeared into the hotel lobby, security stepping in to prevent the throngs of reporters from following him inside. At least he was keeping his promise to do what he could to make the media leave them alone. She just hoped it worked.

"Awesome." Matt turned off the television. "Tell me you're not excited to be here."

"I'm not excited to be here." Kelly met her brother's eyes with a deadpan expression.

"Kelly—"

"I just lost my job, Matt. Soon we'll have no home to go back to. And before you say it, no. We can't continue to live here." She wasn't about to go into the reasons with her kid brother. How could she even begin to explain the complicated emotional mess between Jace and herself? And where would she find another job? In the small community, jobs weren't plentiful.

"I need a personal assistant."

Kelly swung around to find a petite woman with beautiful auburn hair standing in the open doorway. The intricate lines around her eyes seemed to make them sparkle. Her welcoming smile looked very familiar.

"I'm Mona," she introduced herself. "Jason's mother. And you must be Kelly."

"Yes."

"I'm sorry I wasn't here to greet you when you arrived," she said as she walked toward them. "It took longer than anticipated to take care of some lose ends before leaving California. This must be Matt? Very nice to meet you. Jason has talked nonstop about you both."

She stopped in front of where Kelly sat balancing Henry on her knees. "And who is this handsome little man?" The look that softened her face spoke volumes.

"This is Henry." Kelly looked up and smiled.

A wet sheen glistened in the older woman's eyes. For the longest time, Mona stared, unmoving, at the baby in Kelly's arms, her gaze taking in every inch of her grandson, from his head to his feet. Kelly held him with his back against her chest. He kicked his feet while he tried his best to fit his little fist into his mouth. Jace's mother tried valiantly to hold back the tears of joy. It was all there in her face: overwhelming delight, pride and immediate acceptance.

"Would you care to hold him?" Henry loved people. He'd never been intimidated or shown any fear of strangers, and this was someone he might want to know better. Mona pulled out a chair and sat down. She took a moment to compose herself, wiping away the tears now falling from her face. Then she smiled at Kelly.

"I would love to."

Matt headed for his room and another round on Xbox. Mona took Henry in her arms and for a time seemed to be mesmerized. Kelly sat down, content to watch the first meeting between Henry and his grandmother unfold.

As it turned out, she was serious about the job offer. Mona headed an organization that raised money for several charities. One in particular that helped abused women and children was apparently very special to her. For that one she always held an annual ball and banquet in early October. And she needed assistance.

Kelly wasn't entirely sure how Mona did it, but Kelly soon found herself agreeing to help and worse, agreeing to continue to help until the charity ball, which was over a month away. She was losing it. That's all there was to it. But she would not live under Jace's roof forever. Absolutely not. She might be crazy but she wasn't stupid.

She'd give the big news event another week to blow over. Then no matter what, she was taking Matt and Henry and going home. Remaining in Jace's house was a seriously foolish idea. She liked to think she was strong as far as determination and resolve. But she knew if she had a weak spot,

Jace was it. If she caved, she'd be setting herself up for more heartache. That was something she didn't want or need.

As the helicopter began its descent, Jace again thought about who would be waiting for him at the door when he arrived. Kelly. His son. Matt and his mom. A small family. The kind of family he'd wished for most of his life. Granted, he wasn't exactly returning to a loving family unit who would welcome him with open arms, but he wasn't coming back to an empty house. It was a family. Sort of. And it was his.

Matt already had become a great friend. And Henry…a living miracle. Something Jace had never let himself envision. His son. A little face that would someday resemble his own. A young life with everything ahead of him. And Jace wanted to give him the world.

Kelly was the core. She brought it all together. She was the reason he was here, the driving force that had prompted him to purchase this ranch in Texas. The time spent with her last year had been nothing short of bliss. This community of kind strangers, along with the gently sloping hills and valleys, had brought serenity to his soul. It was the dream of a future he'd never before let himself imagine, but for a brief moment in time, he could pretend. Had it all been his imagination? He intended to find out.

He sighed and pulled a hand over his face. The only thing worse than wanting a real home and family was having one and knowing it couldn't last.

"Where is Kelly?" Jace asked his mother as he entered the large kitchen. His mom sat at the table munching on a slice of Carmen's homemade butternut bread. She didn't answer his question, merely took another sip of her coffee, not meeting his eyes. Jace frowned, his senses going on full alert.

"Mom?"

"I believe she had some things she needed to do."

"Did she leave the ranch?"

"Don't worry, dear. She'll be back as soon as she can."

Dammit to hell. He took the cell from his pocket and punched Tom's number. His head of security answered on the first ring.

"She said she had to get some things and she wanted her car," Tom said, answering Jace's unasked question. "Murphy drove her to town, and when they reached her house she told him to leave. Jace, you know we're limited in what we can do. If she tells us to get lost…"

"Yeah, I know. Was there anyone at her house?"

"Just a few dozen determined gawkers. She'll be fine if she stays under the radar. I don't foresee any problems."

Obviously Tom didn't know Kelly.

"What time did she leave?"

"Ten o'clock."

"Thanks."

Kelly was independent as hell. He just hadn't thought she would push her luck to this extent. She knew what could happen. Apparently, whatever she was up to, in her mind it was worth taking the risk.

Jace glanced at his watch and frowned. Two o'clock. It didn't take half a day to make the drive from town. Jace headed outside and jumped into the truck. Three miles down the road, he spotted her, trudging toward his place, baby in her arms, her ponytail swinging side to side.

"Do I need to guess?" he asked as he pulled up next to her.

She didn't look amused.

He threw the truck into Park and walked around to open the passenger door, helping her and the baby inside, and then tossed the bags, purse and brown paper sack she was carrying onto the backseat. He hoped to hell that wasn't her lunch, but he suspected it was. Miss Independence. He had to wonder how far she'd walked.

He turned the pickup around and headed back to the ranch. "I'm getting you a phone."

"I have a phone. I can't get a signal out here."

"Then I'm getting you a better one."

"No, you're not. The one I have works fine in town."

"What about while you're living out here? It's not smart to have a baby and no way to call for help if you need it."

"You're right. I'll buy a new one eventually."

"And what are you going to do between now and then if something happens?"

"With no transportation, I doubt it will be a problem," she answered dully. "First, I need to get the car fixed."

"That piece of junk isn't worth repairing," Jace muttered under his breath. He glanced her way. She was smiling down at the baby, who cooed and held on to his mother's finger. "Pick out a new car and have it delivered tomorrow."

"No."

Jace gritted his teeth and rubbed his neck. "You have got to be the most stubborn, hardheaded woman I've ever come across in my life."

"*Me?* Look in the mirror. Why do you keep pushing? Why do you keep insisting I take things from you? Frankly, it's getting old."

Goddammit.

"I don't need your help. We've already had this discussion. Maybe you should write it down and tape it to your forehead?"

Kelly was the only woman who came close to bringing him to his knees out of pure frustration. And she didn't have to touch him to do it.

"Why did you go into town?"

"I wanted my car."

He snorted.

She glared.

"You mother kindly offered me a job. Temporarily. I have to have transportation to get to the ranch."

"You're staying at the ranch."

"We can't keep living in your house."

"Why not?"

She presented him with a deadpan stare. The silence was deafening.

Okay, so he knew why not. The attraction between them, the pheromones, so powerful that they pulled him to her like a winch and a steel cable. He would have to be dead not to feel it. But he didn't want her to leave the ranch, and it wasn't only because of the safety issue. And it wasn't solely because he wanted to take her to his bed.

He wanted Kelly to like him again.

"Maybe there's another option."

"Like what?" She frowned.

Jace applied the brakes. Coming to a halt, he threw the truck into Reverse. Backing up some fifty feet he turned into a small, one-lane gravel road that disappeared into the trees. In less than a quarter of a mile the road ended at a small white house. Jace pulled up to the side and killed the motor.

"When I bought the ranch, there were four small houses on the property, originally built for ranch hands. I had them updated along with the main house. The ranch foreman lives in one, my head trainer in the second. The third was redesigned for my security team. This is the fourth. It's empty. It has its own entrance separate from the ranch, three bedrooms, a bath and a small kitchen."

"Are you saying…? I can't move here."

"Why not? The house is just sitting here. I have no plans to use it."

She had to admit it was better than living in his house. Barely. Kelly had been concerned about his close proximity if she worked for his mother. Living in his house was her single biggest worry when she'd agreed to help Mona. But this might be a temporary solution.

Or not.

"I don't know…"

"Kelly, don't be so stubborn about everything. This is a great idea."

She snorted at the absurdity. "No, it's not."

She didn't like it. A sense of unease churned inside. If she moved here, she would be totally reliant on Jace for everything. And it didn't come with an expiration date. There was no until-the-end-of-the-month move-out date. And that wasn't a good feeling.

"At least think about it. It makes sense."

"I like living in town."

"You haven't seen the inside of the cabin."

"I don't care. Why would I move out here just for a few months? Seems like an awful lot of trouble. I'm already indebted to your mother for a job. I'm not going to ask you for a place to live as well."

"I don't recall you asking."

Kelly turned to face him. His vivid emerald eyes made her want to waver, but she held firm. "Jace, I have two people who rely on me. I can't take the chance you won't suddenly decide to sell this place. Then where would we be? No job. No home. And you'd be gone without so much as a backward glance, just like before."

A glint of resentment darkened his eyes to the color of singed leaves; the barely perceptible narrowing of his eyes said he was ready to defend himself against her challenge. His jaw muscles tightened, his mouth straightening to a hard line. Then in an instant it was gone, replaced with a look more closely resembling determination.

"You will *never* have to worry about a job or a place to live or money in your bank account. *Deal with it.*"

Her eyes narrowed. "You might be okay with your ex-lover living on your ranch like some kind of leech. I'm not. I'm sure I've already been branded a gold digger. I *hate* that. Moving here… Word would get out and only make it worse."

"I really don't give a damn what anyone else thinks," Jace responded, slight traces of annoyance in his tone. He looked at her, his olive eyes intense and thoughtful. Then he dropped a bombshell. "But if you're that concerned about public opinion, marry me, Kelly. Problem solved."

Eight

Kelly had to steady herself. "That isn't funny."

"I didn't intend it to be."

"Then you're out of your mind."

"Why?"

She turned away from him, looking out the side window without really seeing. She shook her head, swallowing down the bile that rose in her throat. "Do you honestly expect me to respond to a joke? Having a child together does not a marriage make."

"I can come up with more reasons."

"Being good together in bed is not a valid reason, either." It didn't take the mental aptitude of Einstein to guess where his mind was going.

"At least you admit it." He raised his eyebrows as if daring her to deny it.

Kelly fought to keep him from seeing the hurt churning inside. She'd never expected him to say those words even in jest. A little part of her died at the realization that Jace viewed marriage as a joke. A prank. To him life was a game. That fact above all made his words seem almost cruel.

This was a pie-in-the-face wake-up call about how Jace viewed life. She'd always suspected, but never really let herself believe it.

She'd had a front-row seat during her parents' marital atrocity. She'd seen her father's feelings of obligation turn to disinterest, then disgust and finally hatred. He'd maliciously mocked her mother's love, seemingly taking glee in her anguish.

Her mother may have settled for a man who didn't love her, but Kelly was not interested in starring in the sequel. She wanted someone who loved her and wanted to be with her, not a man who felt trapped by circumstance. Despite the deterioration of her parents' marriage, Kelly still believed in the rightness of marriage. It was an ideal she held close to her heart, harboring a childhood dream that maybe someday she could have a chance to do it better. But it wouldn't be with Jace Compton, Mr. Love-'em-and-Leave-'em.

There was a time she would have jumped at the chance to marry the man she'd met and fallen in love with fifteen months ago. But even then, it had to be because he loved her. Not because he felt obligated.

The only reason Jace was spending time with her now was because of his son and the mess he'd created in their lives. Once his baby revelation died down, he'd be out of here so fast his exit would suck the leaves off the trees. Marry today. Divorce tomorrow. Fodder for the gossips and a publicity boon. No harm done. Life goes on.

How had his life morphed into such a bizarre existence?

She blinked the moisture from her eyes and gritted her teeth to overcome her momentary weakness. Inside, a mature, sensible woman battled an immature fool who was willing to believe anything, go anywhere, do anything, just to be with him. Reach for the stars and the delusion of happily-ever-after.

The single common thread between the two conflicting forces was love. She loved Jace. Behind all the barriers protecting her heart, she'd never stopped. But he must never know. She couldn't bear the shame and the mockery that would undoubtedly follow if Jace and the world ever found out.

"Come on. At least look at the cabin."

"No." Her voice was almost a whisper. She released her death grip on the seat, folding her hands in her lap.

"I would prefer you stay in the main house but I understand your need for some privacy. At least wait until you've seen the house before you decide?"

"Jace…"

Walking around the front of the F250, he opened the passenger-side door.

"Come on. Get out."

"Please. Just let it go."

The humor left his face. It was as though he'd suddenly realized something had changed. He looked at her questioningly.

"I respect your need for independence, Kelly. But you're letting your hatred of me overshadow your common sense. I have no intention of selling this place. Mom needs it as much as I do." His eyes were steady as his gaze held hers. "And we both need you."

His deep voice and those last words shook her to the core. Kelly wanted to reach out and touch the strong, handsome face only inches from her own. She wanted to feel his arms around her again despite how badly he'd hurt her. But she'd already used up her share of idiocy for a lifetime.

"I don't hate you, Jace."

For long seconds, neither moved. Then Jace leaned toward her. Ignoring the warning bells going off inside her head, Kelly didn't back away. His lips touched hers, warm, tentative, as though asking for permission. The subtle fragrance of his natural male scent surrounded her. She felt the slight rasp of his day-old five-o'clock shadow as his tongue entered her mouth, bringing with it the rich taste of coffee and the tantalizing taste of pure male. Her right hand lifted to rest on his powerful shoulder. God help her. It was as if fifteen long months had shriveled down to yesterday, his touch both familiar and new.

With a sudden squeal and a string of happy jabber from

Henry, who chose that moment to awaken from the nap in Kelly's arms, Jace drew back, watching her closely. Frowning, he lifted her face to his, his thumbs gently wiping away her tears.

"Why the tears, Kelly?"

She gave her best impression of a laugh. "Don't know what you're talking about."

He continued to watch her, his look intense. "Kelly—?"

"Just don't say anything else, okay? I'm…I'm just grateful. For the offer of the house. That's all."

She knew that look on his face. He didn't buy the gratitude excuse for a second. Unlike him, she was no actress. He would let it go for now, but he wouldn't drop it completely.

He reached to take Henry from her arms, and then held out his hand to her. Kelly reluctantly accepted his help getting out of the truck. His hand was big and warm, his grip strong and sure around hers. The baby laughed, then began sucking on his forefinger, his feet in a simulated run. They walked to the front of the cabin where Jace unlocked the door.

It was nice. The small kitchen was the same size as the one in her rental. A breakfast bar separated it from the living area, and a high-beamed ceiling gave a spacious feel.

"The bedrooms and bathroom are through there." Jace nodded in a direction behind her. The entire house was fresh and clean. The bathroom fixtures and kitchen appliances appeared new. It was already furnished with a sofa, stools for the breakfast bar and beds.

Jace dangled a key in front of her.

"It isn't bait. This is not a trap. It's yours if you want it. No expectations. No hidden agenda. As you saw, it has its own entrance, its own driveway. You'll have the only key." He tilted his head and waited for her decision.

Chewing her bottom lip, she looked back over the spacious room and then returned her gaze to Jace. "Why are you doing this?"

"Does there have to be a reason other than practicality?" He readjusted his stance as though ready for another battle.

"That doesn't answer my question, does it?"

Her mind said she was about to make another huge mistake. She hated weakness, especially in herself. Being weak caused regrets and all kinds of pain. Why did everything have to be so hard? Why did her world suddenly seem to revolve around this man? It was like being strapped to a merry-go-round as it spun faster and faster out of control until the very breath was sucked from your lungs. By the time you realized you had to get off, you knew doing so was really going to hurt.

"You have to live somewhere, and staying at your house in town right now is not a good option. You don't want to live in the main house with me. This is a sensible, workable alternative. The rent on your house in town has already been paid through the end of the year—so don't feel you're trapped here. And I intend to replace your car—which I refuse to argue about."

Despite what had just happened between them, Kelly reached out and took the key from his hand. Her heartbeat increased as she turned it over and over in her fingers. She nodded her head in reluctant acceptance. It was only a couple of hundred yards farther away from him than she was now. But she'd take what she could get.

Jace stepped outside, still holding Henry. "This path leads to the back door of the house. Follow it in the opposite direction and you'll be at the main barn."

Together they returned to his truck. He helped her inside, handed her the baby and got behind the wheel.

"You had no right to pay my rent."

Jace didn't comment as he started the motor but just pursed his lips, obviously biting back a grin, and shook his head as though he'd expected her to say exactly that. She didn't like charity and she damn sure didn't like being a foregone conclusion.

They headed back to the main road, made the short ride around to Jace's front gate and on to his house in silence. Kelly had to wonder where all this would end. She was increasingly becoming part of his life and it frightened her. Putting up a brave front was hard to do. And getting more difficult every day. A wave of reality washed over her and she swallowed hard. Change was always a scary thing. In her life it had never been for the better.

It's only temporary, she reminded herself. *It isn't forever.*

On Friday afternoon, three of Jace's ranch hands moved the boxes she'd packed from her house in town to the cabin on the ranch. Jace stood next to her while they unloaded the truck. He appeared content to hold Henry, even responded to his gibberish. It surprised Kelly how Jace and the baby seemed to have already formed a bond. While it worried her, she had to resign herself to the fact that it was done. If Henry became upset when it was time for them to leave here, she'd have to handle it then as best she could. Mr. Playboy of the Year was definitely becoming a hands-on father. Who would have thought?

"That's the last of it," the ranch foreman told Kelly as two lanky cowboys walked out of the cabin. "We put the baby bed together for you. Looks like all that's left is for you to unpack and settle in."

"Thanks so much, Sam. Thanks, guys."

"I appreciate it, Sam," Jace added, ambling up to where they stood.

"You bet. Jace, you take care of that baby." Sam grinned and seated himself behind the wheel of the old truck. The cowboys tipped their hats, already walking toward the barn. "Good to have you here at the ranch, Mrs. Compton." Sam gunned the motor and with a wave out the window, took off down the driveway.

"I'm not… Ahhh." Kelly stomped her foot in frustration. "*Why* does everyone keep calling me that?"

Jace's free hand shot up, palm toward her. "I'm not say-ing a word."

With a glare in his direction, Kelly took Henry and went into the house. Standing in the center of the living room, she glanced at the boxes stacked around her. It seemed so… permanent. The anxiety she'd been pushing aside all week came back front and center. She couldn't let go of the feel-ing that this was a bad decision.

She put Henry in his swing and began unpacking and arranging their things. Several hours later everything was done, the beds were made, the empty boxes flattened and placed outside next to the small front porch.

That evening after she fed and bathed Henry and put him to bed for the night, she ventured outside. Two old metal chairs, one yellow, one green, sat on the extended concrete slab that served as a front porch. The weather was unusually cool for this time of year. Slipping into the near-est chair, she leaned back, closed her eyes and savored the beautiful evening.

"Looks like someone is enjoying this fine weather."

Kelly jumped at the sound of the male voice.

"Sorry." The man held his hands up. "Didn't mean to scare you."

"That's okay." Her eyes focused on the tall, lean man standing a few feet in front of her. His shaggy blond hair and welcoming smile immediately put her at ease. "It seemed like a good time to put my feet up and relax."

"I know the feeling." He took off his hat. "I'm Sylvester Decker, one of the trainers here at the ranch. People just call me Decker."

"Oh. Of course. It's nice to meet you. Occasionally I see you guys leading a horse from one area to another. There's a chestnut, almost the color of a new penny, with flaxen mane and tail and three white socks. Beautiful."

"That would be Classy Lady." He put one foot on the concrete slab and leaned toward her, resting his arms on his knee and holding his hat in his hands. "And you're right. She's a nice filly. Great bloodlines, but in the racing game, that's not an absolute guarantee. You should come to the main barn area sometime and see them up close. Do you ride?"

"I used to. One of my best friends lives at the neighboring ranch, the Bar H. When we were in school, she used to invite me out for weekends and we would go riding. It was great."

Decker suddenly straightened and took a step back. "Hey, Jace."

"Decker," Jace responded as he stepped out of the shadows into the muted light from the barn. Jace had obviously followed the path from the house, but neither Kelly nor Decker had heard him approach until he was standing in front of her small cabin.

"I just stopped by to welcome our new neighbor to the ranch."

Jace didn't reply. He watched the man like a predator protecting his territory. His eyes almost glowed in the darkness, giving the impression of a panther returning to its lair to find another male stalking the entrance. The air suddenly became thick with the sizzle of animosity. Kelly couldn't help but wonder if Decker sensed it or if it was just her imagination.

"Well, I'll leave you two to talk. It was nice to meet you, Kelly."

"You, too, Decker."

"Don't forget to come see the fillies."

"Thanks. I'd like that."

The cowboy slipped his hat back in place, his long strides carrying him down the path toward the barn until he disappeared into the night.

Jace motioned to the chair next to Kelly. "Mind if I sit down?" He didn't wait for an answer. He lowered his bulk into the old metal rocker, leaned back and brought one booted foot to rest on his knee. "So how goes it with you and Mom? Everything okay?"

"She's great. I love the work. I was afraid it was… That she offered me the job because…"

"You thought it was charity."

"Yeah." Kelly nodded. "But it's not. There's really a lot to do."

"Mom had two full-time assistants when she lived in Los Angeles." Jace cut her a glance, a smile tugging at the corners of his lips. "Be careful what you asked for."

Kelly had to smile. "We're finishing the invitations and considering a theme for the charity ball in October."

"Ah, yes. Mom usually hosts several events a year for different causes, but this one is her favorite. Over the years, it has taken on a life of its own. Be forewarned."

The soft glow of the lights from the barn in the distance provided the only light. Somewhere deep in the trees, a lone cricket chirped and two owls called to each other. Suddenly the tiny porch seemed very intimate. With only a soft breeze passing through the trees, Jace's heady male scent seemed to surround her. She could feel his heat. Her body automatically gravitated toward him. She couldn't help but wonder if he knew the effect he had on her. But no doubt he had the same effect on most women. It was as natural to him as breathing, and he'd probably stopped paying any attention years ago.

He adjusted his position and his knee touched her leg. The small point of contact became a focal point in her mind. She swallowed convulsively. This close, he was entirely too disturbing. Kelly hadn't realized the chairs were so close. Now she fought the temptation to move hers. But her mind and body were giving mixed signals on which way to move it. Jace didn't seem to notice the contact. He sat back, appearing completely relaxed.

"It's too bad there are so many trees out here," Jace said. "They block the view of the sky."

Her gaze automatically veered upward. All she could see were the leaves on the lower branches, which caught the glow of light from the barn.

"I remember watching Texas sunsets until they faded into night. Suddenly, the sky became full of stars." She felt his eyes on her. "Everywhere."

"Yes," she whispered before she could catch herself. She knew he was referring to the nights they'd spent together, him holding her close while they watched the stars through the window twinkle in the midnight sky. Then Jace would put his lips on hers and make similar stars burst in an explosive grand finale before the free fall back to earth.

"Do you still look at the stars, Kelly?"

That brought her out of the past and slammed her face-first into the present.

"No." She shook her head. "Not anymore." She cleared her throat. "Decker said you have some good bloodlines."

"I like what I see so far."

Kelly chanced a glance in his direction. He was looking directly at her; a wicked light glittered in his eyes. She quickly looked away. "I grew up with the cattle ranches, but never saw anything like you're putting together."

He nodded. "It's a challenge. A lot more involved than I originally thought, and we're just getting started. Every day is a new challenge. It's not easy, but definitely well worth the effort. I'm hoping patience and determination will pay off in the long run."

Kelly swallowed hard. She could swear every word out of his mouth referred to her. To them.

"Kelly…" he said, his voice husky.

She couldn't stop herself from turning toward him. Their gazes met and held. In that instant, she wanted to again feel his lips on hers. She wanted to turn the page and let them start fresh. Allow her the chance to make this superstar believe in love. The forever kind. The kind that wasn't a joke. Unbidden, her gaze lowered to his mouth, so tempting. So close.

Electricity sizzled in the air. Her heartbeat increased as the heat of unwanted arousal bloomed in her lower regions, causing her body temperature to rise. He leaned toward her.

He gripped the back of her neck and gently drew her to him. His tongue moistened her lips, tempting her to open to him. She drew air deep into her lungs, but rather than clearing her head and pulling her out of the spell she seemed to be under, inhaling his essence tempted her to come closer. With a fevered sigh, she tilted her head the slightest bit and opened her lips, and Jace took full advantage, entering her mouth, deepening the embrace.

A filament of sanity threaded its way into her mind, and she clung to that small thread. With all the internal strength she could muster, she turned her head, separating her lips from the smoldering heat of his.

"I should go and check on Henry," she whispered, still fighting to retain some clarity of thought, her voice breathy from his kiss. Jace's gaze held hers for a long moment before he released her. Taking a deep breath, Kelly pushed against the metal arms of the chair and rose to her feet. More than anything, she wanted to kiss him forever. She wanted to relive the passion that detonated the stars. And she was edging ever closer to doing something really stupid. "If you'll excuse me, I'll say good-night."

The gleam in his dark eyes clearly told her he understood more than she wanted him to. "Good night, Kelly."

She hurried inside and closed the door. When she was sure Jace was gone, she stepped back outside and crossed the lawn until she came to a spot where the trees parted and offered an unobstructed view of the sky.

She'd lied to Jace. She'd never stopped looking at the stars. At *their* star. One winked at her and she smiled, peace settling in her heart for the first time in a long while.

Kelly had wondered if he remembered the dinners across

a candlelit table, the days spent together under the warm rays of the sun, the nights in his arms as they watched the night sky. She'd doubted it. Compared to the beautiful women he dated, she was nothing. A piece of wheat toast compared to a fine French pastry.

But she'd been wrong. Jace remembered.

But all things considered, did it really make any difference?

Nine

There was something going on with Kelly. It was barely perceptible, and if it were not for his years of training as an actor, he wouldn't have picked up on it. But there was something infinitesimally different in her voice, in her eyes. She had distanced herself from him, even more so than when he'd first come back to Calico Springs. She'd erected a wall that hadn't been there before. He just couldn't get a handle on what had happened. What had changed?

As he walked back to the house, his mind whirled in quiet speculation. He'd noticed the difference around the time she agreed to move into the cabin. Had moving from the main house upset her? Did she want to stay with him instead? Surely she knew the choice was hers. He replayed their conversation in his mind. He recalled that her only objection had involved wanting to return to her home.

She seemed to like her job. His mother had told him Kelly was a delight to work with. Her attention to detail, her intuitiveness as to the direction his mom wanted to go with the charity event, her suggestions… Everything was great. His mother had a baby bed, a swing and a truckload of toys brought in and they were both enjoying Henry.

But something was off. He had no doubt it was something he'd said or done, but he had no clue what it could be.

Whatever the reason, Kelly was right. He should keep his distance. He needed to stop pursuing her. He couldn't give her the forever she undoubtedly wanted and deserved. And Henry. He knew he needed to stay clear of the baby.

But he was drawn to him just like he was to Kelly. It was crazy. Something inside compelled him to be as close to them as possible while it lasted. Henry had already grown so much during their short stay on the ranch. By the time Jace returned from another film project, his son would be walking. And talking. And if Jace distanced himself the way he needed to, the coming years would pass without him ever knowing his son. Without Henry knowing his father.

All things considered, maybe that wasn't such a bad thing.

Kelly straightened the desk and gathered Henry's things in preparation to leave for the day. Before she could pick up Henry, Jace stepped inside the room.

"Can I borrow your assistant?" He looked first at his mom before switching his gaze to Kelly. "Thought you might like to see the horses. I remember you mentioning it to Decker."

Kelly glanced at Mona and received a nod of encouragement. "Henry will be just fine. And I don't mind a bit. You go ahead."

Jace's hand was warm against her lower back as he guided her down the path to the large structure. It was wrong to enjoy his closeness, his touch. But she did. And she was not about to ask him to stop. When they reached the wide-open double doors of the barn they were greeted with knickers from the stalls on both sides of the aisle. The earthy scent of rich, sweet alfalfa, leather and the horses filled the air. The beautiful chestnut filly she'd seen being led back to the barn one day immediately caught her eye through the bars on the top half of the stalls. As Kelly approached, the filly's ears pricked forward in curiosity as she continued chewing her evening grain.

"She's so beautiful," Kelly murmured. The young mare's coat gleamed like polished copper. "I saw her being led from the round exercise pen once. She's even more magnificent up close."

Jace smiled, reached forward and opened the top half of the stall door, giving Kelly unrestricted access. The filly stepped over and put her head through the opening. Kelly couldn't resist stroking the silky neck.

"Hey, sweetheart." She couldn't contain the full grin from spreading across her face. "Oh Jace, she's amazing."

"Most thoroughbreds are pretty high-strung. This one seems a lot calmer. Don't know how that will play out on the track. But she seems to genuinely like people."

"Does she like carrots? Or apples?"

"I really couldn't tell you." He appeared surprised at the question.

"I'll bet she does. And she'll be fast, won't you, pretty lady? I never knew you liked horses, Jace."

He stepped around to the other side of the filly, giving her a pat. "As a kid, I dreamed about someday having a ranch." He shrugged. "There used to be a small carnival that came to our area once or twice a year and it had pony rides for the kids. That's the first place I headed. Never wanted to get down. Then a few years ago, I had to learn to ride pretty proficiently for a part in a film. Once I was trained, every spare second I wasn't needed on the set, I would spend riding. We were filming in New Mexico on a large ranch near Santa Fe. You could ride for miles."

"I can relate. Your neighbor just down the road at the Bar H is one of my oldest friends. Growing up we spent most of our summers on the back of a horse. We'd pack food and water in the saddlebags and off we'd go. Her dad used to get so mad when we were late getting back. A few times it was well past dark and he was *livid*." Kelly grinned at the memories. "Their land backed up to the national forest and grasslands. We found an old gate and that was it. We headed for that entrance every time."

Kelly glanced from the filly to Jace. He was grinning, the

small laugh lines showing at the corners of his eyes while attractive grooves appeared on either side of his mouth. "What?"

He shook his head. "I just never pictured you for a cowgirl."

"I don't know if that's a compliment or an insult." She smiled up at him. "But I love horses. I think your place might border the grasslands, as well. You might want to have someone check it out. You can ride for days. Shea and I would get so turned around. Oh my gosh. I still don't know how we always managed to make it home. I think the horses were our saving grace."

She saw an amused glitter in his dark eyes. She swallowed nervously, not believing she'd just talked so freely with him. But then, she always had. Between them, conversation had flowed easily as they discovered more and more about each other, their likes and dislikes. They had so many common interests. Food. Music. Gazing at the stars on cloudless nights.

"I did the same thing," he said, closing the stall door. "I would ride out so far from base camp in New Mexico, at times I had no idea which way was up. But the horse always knew where its evening meal would be."

In this environment with the scents and sounds of nature surrounding them, and the easy banter between them, Jace was again the guy she met almost a year and a half ago. Silent alarms began clanging in her head. Needing to put some distance between them, she walked down to the next stall. Inside was a horse with a slightly darker coat than the filly.

"This is Chesapeake Dream," Jace offered as he opened the top of the door.

Like the first filly, she came forward and curiously sniffed the two humans who stood in front of her. "She's the one we think will bring it home. She's not yet three, so Lee is taking her training slow, but she's been on the track a couple of times and has really shown some speed."

Kelly reached out to run her hand down the velvety neck. After a few minutes, Jace closed the stall door and Kelly moved down the aisle. She passed an empty stall and proceeded to the next one. Through the metal bars, she saw a magnificent thoroughbred with a coat as black as polished ebony. This one was a lot bigger than the others.

She opened the top of the stall door as Jace had previously done, but this time the greeting was not sweet. It happened so fast. One second she was peeking over the opening, the next the horse had wheeled around, ears flat against its head, teeth bared, ready to take a chunk out of any part of her he could reach. It lunged for her and only Jace's quick action saved her from a vicious bite. A loud, angry scream from the horse followed the near miss.

For several moments, Kelly stood in Jace's arms, trying to slow her racing heart. She'd never had a close call with something that big and that vicious; she'd never been attacked by any animal. She turned her face into the soft, muscle-hugging T-shirt and deeply inhaled Jace's familiar scent as she fought to overcome the fright.

"Kelly, honey, are you all right?"

All she could do was nod. For a few minutes, Kelly stood in his embrace, feeling his strength and power, not wanting to step away.

"That was my fault." His chin rested on the top of her head while his large hand rubbed her back. "This is a stallion here for breeding. The crew is working on the stud barn, but it isn't ready yet. I should have warned you not to open this door. His…job…keeps him a little testy."

Kelly closed her eyes, letting the deep reverberation of Jace's voice calm her. Then, taking a deep breath, she stepped out of his arms and felt a chill that hadn't been there before.

"I should have realized it wasn't a filly by the sheer size of him." She looked at the gleaming black stallion, still aggressively pawing the ground, nostrils flaring, and couldn't help but shiver. That had been a close call. "He's beautiful, though."

She shifted her gaze to Jace's face. Hot fire blazed in his eyes. Despite knowing better, she wanted to walk into that flame until it singed every part of her. In that moment, she wanted Jace to put his arms back around her and hold her forever, consequences be damned.

His gaze held hers as his hands cupped her face. "Kelly," he whispered, his voice graveled and deep.

Every cell in her body screamed for his touch; her lips ached to say *yes*. But Kelly knew there was no future with Jace. He would go back to making his films. Back to the worldwide party scene that was his life. It was inevitable. The ranch was not his home. He'd even told her he'd bought it for some downtime. How could she walk into a situation knowing firsthand how it would end? She hadn't had that foresight before, but this time there was no excuse. And she was frightened. Of herself. Because she loved him. And her resolve to keep Jace at arm's length was weakening more every day.

She stepped back, out of his arms, and he let her go. She knew he could see the desire in her eyes, but she wouldn't say the words he wanted to hear. The words she longed to say.

One of the ranch hands came around the corner, his gaze taking in the two of them standing next to the stall. "Hey, Jace. Glad I caught you. Evening, ma'am."

Kelly gave a forced smile and nodded.

"Lee got the papers for that last colt you bought and said they didn't look right. He told me if I saw you to ask if you could stop by his place in the morning or give him a call."

While the two men talked, Kelly ambled on toward the back of the massive structure. Off to the right she heard something, a small sound coming out of one of the stalls. Curious, she walked in that direction, and the sound gradually got louder. It was a cat. Kelly opened the empty stall door and peeked inside. In the far corner, encased in shadows, a small gray-striped tabby lay on the straw.

"Hi, little one." It meowed in response and sat up. When it did, Kelly spotted more gray underneath where it had been lying. The cat was a female. And she had babies. Three tiny kittens, two gray, one gold, lay sleeping, cuddled together in the bed of straw. The mother showed no fear as she walked to Kelly and rubbed against her legs. Bending over, she ran her hand over the soft fur. Then felt the ribs. The cat was half starved.

Kelly lit out of the stall at a dead run, no second guessing, no consideration needed when an animal, especially a mother, needed help. She didn't slow when she passed Jace and the cowhand, still talking in the center of the isle.

"Kelly?"

"I'll be right back."

She ran out of the barn and down the path to the main house. Entering the kitchen, she grabbed milk from the fridge, and from the pantry, a tin of potted meat, a can of tuna and a breakfast bowl. Racing to the bathroom, she snatched two towels, deep pile and velvety soft. Dumping the food and bowl into one of the towels, she grabbed the carton of milk and ran back to the barn, again passing Jace and the cowboy. She couldn't help but notice a look of curiosity on their faces.

Kelly carefully lifted the kittens and placed them in the center of one of the towels. She folded the second one in half and spread it over the little indention in the hay before gently placing the babies back in the little nest. Mama cat was watching but voiced no concern, as if she understood the human was trying to help. Soon the little cat was enjoying her meat, milk and then some fresh water, eating as if she hadn't had food in a week. Which she probably hadn't.

Kelly felt exhilarated. To be able to help out such tiny, helpless little things in a place that, to them, must be so big

and scary was a good feeling. It was with that glow of happiness she turned and saw Jace standing behind her.

He didn't speak for a long moment. "I take it we have
guests?"

Kelly quickly shook her head. "Aren't they precious? The
mother was so hungry, you can feel her ribs." The smile on
her face wavered. "You don't mind, do you, Jace?"

He entered the stall and knelt down next to her, shaking
his head. Reaching out, he stroked the cat's back, and then
returned his gaze to Kelly. "So what's her name?"

Kelly was radiant. Her face glowed with the innocence
of a child on Christmas morning. It was the first time since
he'd been back he'd seen that smile and the sparkle in her
eyes.

She chewed her bottom lip and damned if he didn't feel
a surge of hot need in his groin.

"How about Jacemina? Or..."

"How about Cat?"

"No," she scolded in that you-should-be-ashamed mother's tone. "It has to be a real name. She deserves a real name."

"I had an aunt named Martha," Jace offered. Where that
came from he would never know. "Mom's older sister."

"Martha." She said it out loud. He could see the name
rolling around in her head. She looked up at him, grinning
ear to ear. "It's perfect." And before he had time to let the
idea soak in that he now had a cat named Martha who was,
apparently, the proud mother of three, Kelly hurled herself toward him. His arms automatically went around her.
"Thank you, Jace!"

Jace swallowed hard. Kelly was exactly where he wanted
her to be. And she was happy and bubbling. Not because
she was in his arms, but because she'd found a cat. His
male pride took a hit, but hell, he'd take what he could get.

She finished her spontaneous hug and sat back on her
heels. Her eyes moved over his face and a more intense
look came into them.

"You're really a very sweet and kind person." She frowned, tilting her head. "I don't know if I ever realized that about you. It's not the same thing as being nice." Of her own volition, she leaned toward him. "Or sexy," she added, placing her lips against his.

His erection jumped to full attention. One arm pulled her closer while his other hand threaded through the silken strands of her long hair. He deepened the kiss, immediate need surging through his body.

"You taste so good," she murmured and he almost lost it. Right there in front of Martha Cat and her babies. Gently, Jace turned her into his arms, her head resting on his upper arm as he held her, his mouth never leaving hers. The moist heat of the kiss sent a shock wave rolling through him. His heart raced, showing no sign of slowing down anytime soon. Her hands cupped the sides of his face and for long moments he enjoyed the pure delight of her touch, the warmth of her body against his, every breath she took. Finally, reluctantly, he pulled back, knowing where they were headed and realizing it would embarrass her if one of the crew walked by.

As she lay in his arms, with her long hair falling over his sleeve and against his shirt, those blue-green eyes holding him spellbound, she reached up and played at his lower lip with her finger, exploring, bringing him to the edge of madness. With a slight movement, he took her finger inside his mouth, sucking, nipping lightly with his teeth. She was killing him. He wanted her beyond anything he'd ever wanted in his life.

"Who'd have thunk it?" She grinned, popped her finger out of his mouth and tapped him on the nose. "Tough guy Jace Compton is a mush melon inside. A sweet, kind man who rescues little kitties."

"Yeah," Jace muttered, reluctantly rising to his feet, pulling Kelly with him. "Who'd have thunk it?"

Ten

Together they headed back to the main house to get Henry. His mother did a double take when they walked into the den, laughing and clearly happy, Jace's arm around Kelly's shoulder. Henry was in the playpen next to where she sat on the sofa paging through fashion magazines.

"Has someone been playing in the hay?" Her smile of welcome turned into a grin of speculation. Her eyes twinkled.

Jace ran a hand through his hair, dislodging several twigs of straw. He then reached over and pulled some from Kelly's long strands.

"Sorry we're late," Kelly said as she walked over to give Mona a hug. "The horses are incredible. There's one that's the color of a copper penny. Mona, you must come out and see her. And the best part—we found *kittens*." She turned and looked at Jace, excitement lighting up her face. "Tell her, Jace."

"We found kittens."

"A mother and three tiny babies. She is almost starved. But I think she'll be okay. She is so sweet. I owe you and Jace for a can of tuna and milk."

"Not a problem, sweetheart. I love cats."

"So do I." Kelly reached for Henry. "Jace named her Martha."

"Did he?" There was a wicked light in her eyes. "Martha Compton. Who would have ever thought?"

"Aunt Martha hated my father," Jace dutifully explained,

seeing the confusion on Kelly's face. "The names Martha and Compton are not synonymous with any feelings remotely seen as warm and fuzzy. That should be a very strong cat." His mother chuckled and Jace leaned over and gave her a kiss on the cheek. "I'm going to walk Kelly back to the cabin."

"I won't wait up." She stood from the sofa. "You both have a good evening. Kelly, perhaps tomorrow you will take me to see the kittens?"

"Absolutely."

With Jace carrying Henry, they walked through the evening shadows to the small house in the trees. Jace followed her inside.

"Do you have time to hold him while I warm his bottle?"

"Sure." As Kelly headed to the kitchen, Jace wondered at the feel of his tiny son in his arms, the weight of his compact little body. It did strange things to Jace's heart. *His son.* He rubbed his face against the downy hair, loving the smell of baby powder, captivated by the little baby sounds. Henry's fist was again planted in his mouth, the sound of his lips smacking interspersed with words only Henry could understand. His head bobbled as he perched on his father's arm. Too soon he began to squirm and whimper.

"What's a matter, Henry?" No amount of coaxing would calm him down. "Kelly, is something wrong?" Jace asked in a concerned tone. "Is he sick?"

"Just hungry." Kelly came forward with the bottle. "Our little man has a very good appetite. Want to feed him?"

His eyes shot to her. It was an offer he hadn't expected. "Yeah. I'd like that."

"Find a seat."

Kelly found it hard to suppress a grin at Jace's intense expression. He sat down, still holding a fussing baby against his chest.

"You need to lay him back in your arms. Pretend he's a football," she suggested.

Nodding, Jace positioned Henry on his left arm, cuddled against his chest.

"Good." Kelly handed him the bottle.

Seeing Henry in his little blue rompers held so lovingly by his big tough dad caused her throat to constrict with emotion. She'd never let herself envision the picture in front of her. A small twinge of sadness touched her heart at the way fate had set their course adrift in different directions. Over the few weeks Jace had been back in her life and now seeing him like this, she knew he would be a great father. *If onlys* flooded her mind. But there was no going back. And there was no going forward. Not together. Destiny wasn't that kind.

Jace seemed to have fallen into a trance as he stared down at the baby in his arms. Henry took his bottle with gusto, his tiny hand gripping Jace's little finger.

"He's amazing," Jace murmured, and then gazed up at Kelly. "He looks just like you."

"No." She shook her head, quick to disagree. "He looks like *you*. Even has your dimples. I hope he doesn't become as bullheaded."

Jace made a huffing sound. She leaned against the wall, content to watch as Jace fed his son.

"I never intended to have kids," Jace said unexpectedly, his eyes glued on his son. "I never pictured a child in my life. Like you said, I'm gone more than I'm home. And even then, there's always something I have to do, something going on. It never stops. Meetings, overnight trips, PR campaigns… This is the longest I've ever managed to stay put."

She shrugged. He hadn't said anything she hadn't already suspected. "It's your job. It's what you do." *It's your choice.*

"Yeah." His tone was not happy. He glanced over at Kelly. "Do you think about his future? Who he will be? What he'll want to do with his life?"

"Every day."

Jace's gaze returned to the baby in his arms. The look on

Jace's face was intense. It was as though his mind had taken him to another place. And not necessarily a good place.

"He's so amazing. From his fingers to his toes…he's perfect. And so innocent." He watched Henry slurp on his evening feeding. After a few long moments, Jace's gaze returned to Kelly. "I don't understand people who would ever hurt a child," he blurted out.

Kelly's eyes widened in surprise. Where did that come from? Had Jace witnessed abuse at some point in his past? Might that be a reason Jace didn't want a family?

"There are all kinds of people, Jace," she said gently, wanting to take away the misery in his expression. "You above all know that, with the oddball fans you have to deal with. You just have to make sure to keep your child safe and well away from any potential harm. That's just part of the job of being a father."

She saw his jaw muscles clench. He nodded and swallowed hard.

"Yeah." Then he seemed to realize the path his mind was on and changed the subject. "When did your grandfather pass away?"

"Um…about a week after you left."

"Was he sick very long?"

"No. Some developers were after his farm and I think he was really stressed over that. They claimed his title was invalid. I came home from school the week after New Year's and found him. He'd had a massive stroke. By the time the paramedics got there it was too late. A letter of eviction was on the floor next to him."

She couldn't stop the sudden rush of moisture that burned her eyes. She lowered her head, hoping Jace wouldn't notice.

"What happened to your parents, if you don't mind my asking?"

It was Kelly's turn to take a few minutes to formulate her answer. She hadn't expected the question, didn't quite know what to say and wasn't at all sure she wanted to go there. It had been a really great evening, and talking about her parents was jumping off a very high cliff with no possibility of a good outcome at the bottom. Finally, she decided to leave off the sugarcoating and tell him the truth. Let him read into it what he would.

"My father, apparently, wasn't happy at home. Like you, he traveled a lot. But even when he was home, there were other women. Lots of other women. A couple of them were the mothers of my classmates. *That* was fun."

Jace frowned. "How do you mean?"

"My classmates blamed me for breaking up their homes..." It wasn't something she wanted to remember. "Gossip was rampant. The stories grew bigger and bigger. It...it was a tough time for us." Her dad was the playboy of the year if the rumor mill was to be believed. But Kelly didn't say it out loud. What good could come of it? "Mom refused to leave him. She just numbed her pain with liquor and pills. She finally got the right combination when I was sixteen." Tears sprang to Kelly's eyes. She put her hand over her mouth, taking a few seconds to get her emotions under control. She rubbed the tears away and blinked hard. "Sorry. Anyway, Dad came to the funeral, but we never saw him again after that."

"*Damn.* I'm sorry, Kelly."

She shrugged. "He didn't care. He wasn't meant to be married. All he wanted was a good time. Gramps was a kind man and we loved him. I hate to think what might have happened had he not stepped forward and taken us in. I finished high school, got a student loan, started at the university and for a while, life went on. Until he died. Then it was Matt and me against the world." She had to smile. "I think we did pretty good. You couldn't ask for a better brother, but don't you dare tell Matt I said that." *Keep it light. Grit your teeth and get through this.*

She'd lost her parents because her father was a two-faced cheating bastard who was too spineless to end the marriage. Her mother had been too weak to leave him. She'd lost Gramps after a wealthy man and his high-priced attorneys found or fabricated a loophole in the deed and took his farm. And here she sat, smack in the middle of a lion's den, Jace being both a philanderer and as wealthy as they come. She'd given birth to his baby and already experienced the temptation to return to his bed. She was as big a fool as her mother.

The silence that filled the room was deafening. Gone was the lighthearted camaraderie from earlier. It would be so easy to let the rest of the tears fall. But she refused. The very last thing she wanted was Jace's pity. She had to wonder if he saw the similarities between him and her father. At least Jace hadn't gotten married before he'd begun *chasing the skirts*, as Gramps used to call it. He'd never had anything good to say about Kelly's father. She couldn't help but speculate what her grandpa would have thought of Jace.

The loud sound of Henry sucking on an empty bottle suddenly filled the room.

"I think he's finished." She stepped forward and took the bottle, glad for the interruption.

"What's next?"

Kelly placed a cloth over Jace's shoulder. "Hold him upright next to your chest. Be careful to support his head. Put one hand under his butt and gently pat his back with the other. Just pretend your favorite starlet needs consoling."

Jace shot her a warning glance, and then wrestled Henry around until he was against his shoulder. It was a sight to behold. Jace's hand was as big as Henry's entire back. But his touch was gentle, as though Henry were so fragile he might break. In fact, Jace was only patting the folds of Henry's shirt.

"You're gonna need to pat him a little harder if you want to get that bubble out." The look Jace gave her was something close to panic. Some tabloid would pay big bucks for a picture of this. "It's okay, Jace. He won't break."

Jace nodded and tried again. After considerable time had passed, Henry turned his head toward his father and appeared to nuzzle his neck. Seconds later, Kelly heard the burp. It was followed by a small stream of milk. Completely missing the cloth, it trickled down Jace's thick neck and into his shirt.

He looked up at Kelly, and the expression on his face was priceless. She hurried to take the baby.

"He's been a little fussy today. Teething. Sorry about that."

Jace cleared his throat and stood up. "No problem."

"He's ready for his bath and then bed."

"I think I know the feeling." He stood and reached for his shirt, pulling the wet material away from his neck.

Kelly bit her lip to keep from laughing. "Bath time can be fun."

"I couldn't agree more with you there," he said, his eyes glinting wickedly. "Baths and showers can be an amazingly good time."

Heat rushed up her neck. He was not talking about bathing a baby. She knew only too well what Jace could do with a bar of soap and a little warm water.

"But this time I think I'll pass." Jace stopped before he stepped outside, still holding his collar away from his skin. "Thanks for...this, Kelly."

"Sure." She covered her mouth with her hand in an effort to hold back a giggle. From smiles to tears and back to laughter. Such was a day spent in the presence of Jace Compton.

Jace followed the path back to the main house, his mind spinning, his gut churning. He and Kelly had been together only weeks before her grandfather died. At a time when she needed him the most, he was twelve hundred miles away listening to Bret tell him lies about her, insisting Jace not call her as he'd promised. By the day of the funeral, he'd been on his way to South America for a film shoot.

He rubbed the back of his neck, a sinking feeling in his gut. A man couldn't get a whole lot lower. He hadn't known her circumstances, but he should have called her before he ever boarded that plane. It explained so much: why she'd left school, why she worked two jobs, why she had to support Matt and her baby. Why, when he'd come to his senses and tried to call, the phone had been disconnected. No wonder she resented him. Hell. She had every right. It was a miracle she didn't hate him.

Did she think he was just like her father?

The thought sent a sickening surge through his body. His actions toward her so far, combined with the bullshit facade he had to perpetuate for the public... Yeah. He could see how she would. And there was not one damn thing he could do to change it.

He respected Kelly for her strength and tenacity. But he knew firsthand how fast that strength could fly out the window when facing down a cruel, vicious adversary twice your size: an intoxicated man determined to hurt you and your child. That his mother had survived and managed to hide them and keep them safe when his father got out of prison was nothing short of a miracle.

Not for the first time, Jace cursed his fate. Having Kelly and Henry here, seeing them, interacting with them, was everything he'd ever longed for. A perfect family. One he could never have. He'd been serious the day he'd told Kelly if she was concerned about public speculation to marry him. But she'd been right when she called him on it. A marriage between them could never last. But not for the reasons she thought. It had nothing to do with Henry. It was because there was a monster inside him, a monster that could hurt Kelly and the baby. Marriage would work fine on paper. Put the gossips to rest. But a real marriage and family, for him, could never happen.

Kelly was a temptation to which he'd become addicted.

He wanted her until it hurt; it was almost unbearable torment every time she came near.

He had to get a handle on it.

Kelly deserved a man who could give her forever. A guy who would pamper her and protect her, not turn on her someday. Not only had his old man convinced Jace he was worthless and then died before Jace could prove him wrong, he'd ensured, even after he was dead and buried, that his son's life was on a direct downhill course to hell.

Eleven

"I'll be damned," Jace muttered under his breath as he leaned out over the railing. They were grilling something. One of the cowboys had rolled in an outdoor grill from God knows where and they were actually grilling food—maybe hot dogs?—just outside of Kelly's cabin. Jace squinted to get a better look. There were binoculars in the study downstairs, but he refused to stoop to that level. Yet.

From the balcony outside his bedroom, he had a fairly clear view of the front of her little house. He'd first noticed the Friday night gathering three weeks ago. He'd heard laughter coming from that direction and stepped outside, wondering who it was and what could be so damned funny.

At first he'd seen old Sam, the ranch foreman, Decker and another trainer sitting out on the tiny porch with Kelly. The next weekend, he'd given into curiosity and looked again. This time they'd been joined by at least a half dozen cowboys, sitting on crates, laughing the night away. Even Matt later joined the party. The little group had grown until now almost every unmarried hand working on the ranch sat circled around that porch. And in the middle of all those lonesome, lusting, hungry men sat the princess bee herself. Kelly drew them like a budding flower, and every drone in the county wanted to get close in spite of the fact that some nights she bounced the baby on her lap. *His* baby. She'd invited him to stop by but he had no wish to join the crowd while they sat and ogled Kelly. It was none of his concern, but at the same time he fought the overwhelming urge to go down there and beat the living crap out of any one of the bastards who tried to put the moves on her.

Adding to his frustration was the knowledge that he'd been the one who had convinced her to move to the little house. He'd wanted her to be close. He'd never considered he wouldn't be the only one she would be close to.

And now they were cooking for her. *Dammit to hell.*

"Jace?" his mother called from inside his room. He turned and headed in that direction. If she caught a glimpse of the goings-on at the little cottage and him leaning over the balcony railing, she might get the wrong idea.

"What are you doing?"

Why did he suddenly feel like a ten-year-old who'd gotten caught with his hand in the cookie jar? He stepped inside and closed the door behind him. "Just getting some fresh air. What's up? Are you okay?"

"Oh, I'm fine. I was just curious if you'd gone to the party."

He couldn't miss the mischievous light dancing in her eyes. "Party?"

"The one at Kelly's cabin."

Damn. "I didn't know about any party."

"Uh-huh. Well, I'm sure you'd be welcome. Why don't you go down and join them?"

The last thing he wanted to do was be yet another bee blazing a trail to Kelly's sweet nectar. "I'm really kinda busy. Need to read the new script. I don't have time to go to a party."

"Right." Turning, she walked toward the door. "Whatever you say. Just wanted to let you know I'm going out this evening."

"Out? Where? With who?"

"Thomas—Dr. Sullivan—invited me to have dinner. He should be here anytime."

"Oh." Jace felt a twinge of uneasiness mixed with surprise. Granted, Sullivan was the town doctor who commanded a certain amount of respect, but what did they really know about him? Jace couldn't prevent visions of his father's fist slamming into her delicate jaw time after time from flashing through his mind. His instinct to protect her was strong. He supposed he should try to remember his mother was, after all, an adult. And the doctor wasn't his father. Still, Jace gritted his teeth. "I don't suppose you'd consider letting one of the security team—"

"Absolutely not."

He nodded. "Well, then have a good time."

"I intend to." She winked and turned toward the door to his suite. "Oh," she said over her shoulder, "the binoculars are in the desk in your office downstairs if they would help with your...work. Bye-bye."

Jace pulled both hands through his hair. Dammit to hell. He had to get a grip on this Kelly thing. He'd become like a daytime barn owl, practically living in the office in the main stable in an attempt to stay away from the house as much as possible. When he did give it up and return to the house, it was straight to the gym or his office to check emails. The new script had arrived, but it sat unread on his desk; Jace had found neither the concentration nor the motivation to even open the mailing envelope. Something had to change or he could plan on spending the rest of his nights pacing the balcony like some seriously messed-up loser.

It was impossible to treat Kelly as just a friend. He refused to be just another of the drooling, lusting men clustering around her. His body knew she was his and responded accordingly regardless of the time and place.

Kelly was the only one who ever came close to being *the* woman in his life. He'd been with beautiful women. He'd known women with kindness in their hearts. But Kelly had that unique something, that special quality that brought it all together. She was in a league of her own. A treasure that remained out of reach.

Jace suspected part of what had kept him from coming

back sooner was a deep-seated fear he was getting too involved with her. He'd begun picturing them together. Forever. He hadn't been prepared for that. And in light of the monster he might someday become, it had frightened him.

But now, over a year later, things had changed. He had a son. And he was still as infatuated with Kelly as he'd ever been. What would happen if he risked it? Kept her in his life? The idea was making him crazy.

Sleeping with another woman was not appealing. But if he persisted and seduced Kelly, he might hurt her someday. It was a hell of a dilemma.

A wave of laughter from outside drifted into the room. *Dammit to hell.*

"C Bar Ranch," Kelly said into the phone.

On Monday Jace asked her to take on the additional duty of answering his private line. Lee arrived with new horses and everyone was running in high gear. At least that was the excuse. Whether Kelly believed it was still open to speculation. Initially the calls went to his voice mail, but by Monday afternoon, that was full. Now, three days later, the calls were coming in fast and furious and Jace had yet to clear them from his phone. No surprise there.

"Just see if you can help them," he'd instructed. "Take their names and numbers. I'll call them back later. If it sounds urgent, try to page me."

They all sounded urgent. Kelly didn't like it. She didn't want to know who called him, hated talking to the smug-sounding women, but she hadn't come up with an acceptable reason to refuse. Yet.

"I have Joanna Reed calling for Jace Compton." The woman's voice was pleasant and professional. A nice change from most of the other callers.

"I'm sorry. Mr. Compton is not currently available. Perhaps I can help you?"

"No. Thank you. Miss Reed must speak directly with Mr. Compton. It's urgent she reach him as soon as possible."

Of course it was. "One moment, please. I'll try and page him." *Urgent* was the magic word. Kelly placed the call on hold and punched the intercom for the barn office. "Jace, you have a call on line one," she said, using their code for his private phone.

There was no answer. *Surprise. Surprise.*

"Jace, if you're there, please pick up."

"Kelly, this is Lee. Jace headed back to the house an hour ago. Don't know what to tell you past that."

"Okay. Thanks."

She punched the button for the house intercom. "Jace, a Miss Joanna Reed is holding on your private line." After waiting several seconds, Kelly returned to the caller. "I'm sorry. Mr. Compton isn't answering the page. Would you care to leave a message?"

She heard voices in the background, and then another voice came on the line.

"This is Joanna Reed. What is the problem?"

"As I've explained to your secretary, Mr. Compton is not near a phone. I'll be happy to take a—"

Her end of the conversation had caught Mona's attention. The older woman stood and walked toward Kelly's desk. Kelly put the call on speaker. Might as well share the wealth.

"Then find him. This is outrageous."

"I'm sorry, Ms. Reed. I seem to have lost the ability to make someone appear by snapping my fingers or twitching my nose. I'll be sure to get that checked. Again, I'll be glad to take your number."

"Do you honestly think he doesn't have it?"

"I really wouldn't know."

Kelly looked at Mona. This was ridiculous. Mona put her slender hand over her mouth to stifle a laugh as her shoulders began to shake.

"Will there be anything else?"

"Just one thing. I will reach Jace eventually and you might as well start packing up your things. You are gone."

"I appreciate the early notification."

"You can also tell Jace the next time he…needs me… I'll be busy. And the fault will be yours."

"Have a nice day."

Kelly terminated the call. Mona and Jace paid her well, but not nearly enough to take that crap.

"I'm not doing this," she said to Mona with as much calm as she could muster. It was the hundredth such call in the past three days, each one progressively worse than the last. Crazy women. Acting as if they owned Jace Compton.

"You might try the gym," Mona said, an impish twinkle in her eyes.

"Thanks." Kelly stomped out of the room and headed for the first-floor gym.

When she rounded the corner, sure enough, Jace was lying on a bench, his hands gripping a barbell with several weights on either end, straining to push it up and down. Beads of sweat ran down his face and neck, his biceps ballooning to an enormous size. She didn't want to startle him and cause an accident, so she stood next to the wall and waited. The man who usually flew in and trained with him every few days was not here. Should Jace be doing this alone?

Finally, he set the heavy bar on the rack and sat up. Grabbing a towel hanging nearby, he wiped his face and neck.

She cleared her throat. Jace saw her for the first time and tilted his head with a surprised look.

"Kelly?"

"I refuse to answer your phone. I *refuse,*" she repeated, leaning forward, her hands perched at her waist.

His eyebrows rose. "Okay. Mind telling me why?"

"Like you don't know." She couldn't hold back a sarcastic laugh. "Do you have any idea how many lunatics call you in a day? Never mind. Of course you do. That's why you stuck me with the job. Then you refuse to answer my page and I'm the one who gets attacked."

"Attacked?" He stood up from the bench. His ragged cutoffs rode low on his waist and molded to the muscular hips and thighs. That's all he was wearing. The tanned flesh of his muscled chest and flat stomach glistened with perspiration.

Good Lord. Couldn't the man put on some clothes?

"They think I'm lying to them. Cherry Newton has called four times. Today. Do people make up these names? That sounds like a sandwich cookie you'd pull off a tree. She's threatening to have me arrested, insinuating I must have done something to you to keep you from talking to her. Cora Spager—Stagler —has called ten times. *Ten.* The last call, I had to sit and listen to her alternately rage and cry for almost an hour. I just got off the phone with the Wicked Witch of the West, who said I should tell you the next time you *needed* her—" Kelly made a snorting sound "—she wouldn't be available and it was entirely my fault. How exactly is it *my* fault? Oh, she also said that I should be forewarned—this is my last day of employment. Finally, some good news."

Kelly noted the grin he was trying to hide, and her irritation doubled. "This is not funny, Jace. Your idiotic calls are taking my time away from Mona and making me crazy."

"I'm sorry." The wicked glitter in his eyes told her he was not sorry at all. His spicy male scent was strong from his workout, and her body responded to the sight of his sculpted chest, sweaty and gleaming. She tried to swallow but her mouth had gone dry.

"Then hire an agency. Use a call center," she said in a ragged voice, then tried to clear her throat, fighting the response of her traitorous body. "But don't expect me to bite my lip while those ladies, and I use the term loosely, call me every name in the book."

As soon as she said the word *lip*, his eyes focused on that part of her face.

"Say no more." He moved closer. "Because no one is going to bite those lips but me."

"Jace." She began to back out of the room, shaking her head. "I'm serious."

"So am I."

"Don't do this."

"You feel it, too."

The husky timbre of his voice told her he sensed the change in her. She'd made a huge mistake coming to the gym. She fought to maintain her poise, taking calm, steady breaths. *Just get out of here.*

A smile played at the corners of his full lips. "I think you want me…to kiss you again."

Yes. "No." She again cleared her throat. "No, I don't." It was almost a whisper. Another step away from him and she felt the wall against her back. A heady sexual tension mixed with a touch of panic enveloped her.

"I damn sure want to kiss you. Hell, I want to do a lot more than that."

"Jace…"

He looped the small towel around his neck and placed his hands against the wall on either side of her head, his huge biceps bulging. She felt the coolness against her back, a vivid contrast to the smoldering heat radiating from him.

"It's making me crazy having you here, seeing you every day and never touching you."

Bending down, he placed his warm mouth against the very place under her ear he knew caused sweet shivers to run through her. She couldn't repress a little cry as her eyes closed and her skin sizzled. Her hands came up against his granite chest and she felt the strong steady beat of his heart.

"Kelly." His intonation was so deep, so mesmerizing, he held her captive using nothing more than his voice.

"You don't play fair," she murmured against his lips,

which were so tantalizingly close. She sounded breathy to her own ears. "We shouldn't do this."

"Who are you trying to convince? Me or yourself? Admit it, Kelly. Say you want me and let's stop this damned cat-and-mouse game."

"I don't think—"

"Good. I don't want you to think. Just go with your feelings."

With a small whimper, Kelly leaned forward, moving her lips even closer to his, seeking the pleasure she knew was there. Jace didn't wait a full heartbeat before his mouth took hers, fiercely, deeply, his tongue filling every crevice. "Say it, Kelly," he groaned, before kissing her again, intensely, with such passion she couldn't have spoken had she wanted to. She heard him growl, and his mouth opened wider, hungrily, as though he couldn't get enough.

Kelly was lost. She couldn't fight this. No one could. It was as though the power of the mythical god Zeus surged through him, proving that all the stories of his erotic escapades were true. Mere mortal women didn't stand a chance. Jace's arms came around her, pulling her closer to his hard frame. His arousal pressed against her belly, and like a branding iron, it singed her skin through her clothes, making sure she knew she was his. She couldn't stop the small moan forming deep in her throat, but it was swallowed by his hungry mouth.

His big hands slid under her hips, lifting her, pulling her tightly against him, making her feel his body's reaction to her, his heavy thickness leaving no doubt what he wanted. She wanted the same. She needed to feel him against her core with shameless intensity.

"Jace?"

A distant voice broke into the moment.

"Hey man, you in the gym?" The head trainer called out from the den, no doubt heading in their direction.

Jace lifted his head and stared into her eyes. "Someday

very soon, your luck is going to run out." He stepped back and dropped his arms. "Yeah," he called out to Lee, still holding her with his gaze.

"I'll make a deal with you, Kelly. Stop the damn Friday night smorgasbord and I'll take care of the phone calls."

Her mouth dropped open. "*That's* what answering your phone is about?" Jace saw her visiting with some of the ranch hands…and he was *jealous*? Jace Compton? The man wasn't jealous of anyone or anything on the planet. He could have any woman he wanted. But the aroused hunk standing two feet in front of her appeared deadly serious. "They are just a few nice cowboys who—"

"Who would take you to their bed in a heartbeat. You're the mother of *my* child," he snarled as if she didn't know that.

"And your point is?"

Jace's eyes narrowed, his nostrils flaring with emotion. "If you need sex, you come to me."

He did not just say that. "I'll tell you what, Compton. You hold your breath until that happens. See how that works for you."

With a last glare, Kelly turned and stomped to the door, colliding smack into the trainer as she rounded the corner. Only Lee's quick reflexes kept her from falling on her butt.

Her mind was blown. The very idea that Jace could ever be envious of the men on the ranch was just not believable. She was an employee in his house, which made her a convenience. That's all it was. He needed to get out of the house for a few days. He needed to be reminded there was an entire world waiting for him outside the boundaries of this ranch and that world was filled with beautiful, desirable women who would do anything to be with him. To say he was a very potent package was an understatement. And the idea that he could be in any way jealous… It was too much to take in.

It took a good part of the afternoon to push Jace's antics

in the gym out of her mind. With Henry napping and Mona there to watch him, Kelly finally went downstairs, gathered a can of cat food and a couple of apples, and headed for the barn. The need to make love with Jace again, to feel his hands and body work their magic, was eating her up inside. She might as well admit defeat. It didn't matter what she felt for him, be it mere physical attraction or something more: he was dangerous. In every single way that mattered. And that enticing element, in itself, would be her undoing.

Wednesday evening Kelly had just settled Henry for the night when there was a knock on the door. One of the ranch hands stood on the porch, his hat in his hands. Kelly remembered meeting him the day she'd moved in.

"Decker?"

"Evening, Kelly. Are you busy?"

"No." She shook her head. "I just put the baby to bed."

"They're having a barn dance at the Bar H spread to celebrate the birth of their daughter. I was curious if you were going and if you might need a ride."

"No, I mean, I didn't know anything about it. Shea and I haven't talked in months."

"Well, I realize it's late notice. I just found out about it myself. It's only intended for the employees and family, but I remember you saying you and Shea were close. I doubt they will mind if you crash the party."

"Oh, I'd love to go," she said, the idea of seeing her friend again immediately taking root. "But I don't have anyone to keep my son. Unless…" *Would Mona watch him for a couple of hours?* "I can ask Mona if she'll sit with the baby. How long did you plan to stay?"

"That's entirely up to you."

Stepping inside, she grabbed the cell off the kitchen counter and dialed Mona's private line. She answered in two rings. After Kelly explained what she needed, Mona enthusiastically agreed.

"I'll bring Henry to the house in just a few minutes. Thank you, Mona."

Decker grinned when she told him she had a babysitter.

"How about if I pick you up in front of the main house in about ten minutes?"

"Perfect."

It would be so great to see Shea again. They hadn't had a chance to visit in far too long. Between Kelly working two jobs and having a new baby to care for and Shea and Alec spending the summer in Europe, the opportunity just hadn't been there. She grabbed the baby bag, gathered a sleeping Henry in her arms and hurried to the main house, excitement at seeing her old friend quickening her steps.

She didn't see Jace as she climbed the stairs to Mona's suite. In fact, she hadn't seen him that day at all. She didn't know if he had as yet met Shea and her husband but maybe he would like to go. Mona was waiting at the top of the stairs, her arms reaching out to take the baby into her arms.

"Do you know where Jace is?"

"He's in Dallas talking with some people about a new film."

"Oh." So much for that idea. "Okay then. I'll see you later. Thanks so much for doing this, Mona."

Decker was waiting when she came back downstairs and they were on their way to the Bar H.

"Wow," Decker said as he turned his truck into the long, rambling driveway of Shea's ranch. "That's some house."

"Shea's husband, Alec, is an architect and builder. Shea was devastated when her old ranch house burned down. Alec went over and above when he built their new home." The sprawling three-story Victorian-style house with its turret towers and four chimneys peeking over the high roof was the talk of three counties.

"I guess. Man."

They pulled into the designated parking area. Kelly heard the music and laughter as soon as she opened her door. The aroma of mesquite logs burning in the large grill tempted all to come and bring their plate.

"I think I see Shea over there." Decker pointed to a huge oak tree. "Go ahead and say hello and I'll catch up with you later."

"Thanks, Decker." Kelly raced to where Shea sat in a lawn chair.

"Shea?"

"Oh my gosh. Kelly!" Shea rose to her feet and the two friends embraced. "It's so great to see you."

"Same here. You look so good."

"Let's get you a chair. I want to know everything that's been happening. How are Matt and Henry?"

"They're good." Kelly grinned as she pulled a vacant chair next to Shea's. "I'm so happy for you. Congratulations on your new baby."

"Thanks. I want you to see her before you leave."

"I would love to. How is Alec handling being the dad to a little girl?"

Shea rolled her eyes. "She has him rolled around her little finger. You'd think she was the only baby girl ever born." It was wonderful talking with Shea and the time passed much too quickly. Too soon it was time to go. But Shea wouldn't let her leave without seeing her new baby.

"Come meet Alexandra Christine." Shea led the way across the yard and into the house. After a short tour of the magnificent home, they went up the staircase to the nursery where a sitter sat reading. Shea lifted the infant from the crib.

"Oh, Shea. She's beautiful. She looks just like you!"

"That's what Alec says. I've never seen a man go totally off the deep end over a baby. He hired a nurse for the first six weeks, then questioned everything she said or did. After a few days he decided he knew what his daughter needed better than she did. I think her leaving was by mutual agreement."

Kelly smiled but was suddenly struck with the hopelessness of her own situation. To have Jace always around every day to watch his son grow and develop into a fine man was a dream Kelly kept locked away deep inside. She'd long ago accepted it would never happen. But in moments like this, she couldn't stop the hope from breaking free, only to have it wither and die in the chill of reality.

"It's so great we're neighbors now," Shea was saying. "You've gotta come over when you have time. Bring Henry."

Kelly nodded, not trusting her voice. If Shea noticed that she'd suddenly became quiet she said nothing. She just leaned over and gave Kelly a hug.

Outside, Kelly easily spotted Decker. When she approached him, his grin faded and he frowned in concern. She tried to smile but Decker apparently sensed something was wrong and asked if she was ready to leave. Was she that transparent? Not good.

"Thank you so much, Decker," she said as they made their back to his truck.

"No problem. I'm glad you got to see your friend." Decker was a nice guy, and with his blond hair and good looks, he certainly wasn't hard on the eyes. But he wasn't Jace.

She slipped from his truck and entered the house. Walking through the kitchen, she headed for the stairs, not bothering to turn on any lights. There was enough radiant light spilling into the house for her to see where she was going.

Before she reached the room Mona had deemed as a temporary nursery, a dark shadow on the left moved toward her. Kelly barely held in a shriek.

"Did you have a good night?"

"Jace. You scared me." What was he doing standing in a darkened hallway? "Yes. I did, thank you."

She moved forward but Jace stepped in front of her, blocking her way. Through the dim glow of the night-light Mona insisted on having at the top of the stairs, she could see he was dressed in only a pair of old jeans. And he wasn't smiling.

"I wasn't aware you were dating anyone."

Did he really have any right to know if she was or wasn't? How rude would it be to just keep walking?

She shrugged. "I'm not." She gave him that much and tried to step around him, wanting to get Henry and go to her cabin. Jace again blocked her way.

"That's not what it looked like to me."

Oh, here we go. Mr. Macho was back.

"You don't consider going out with Decker a date?" Jace continued.

"He gave me a ride to the Bar H," she explained, forcing her voice to remain calm. "Shea just had her baby a couple of weeks ago. Their ranch crew honored her and her husband with a party. They had a barbecue. It wasn't a date. And you weren't here. I asked Mona, thinking you might like to go. Do you know Shea and her husband, Alec?" No answer. "Do you know their ranch hands?" No answer. She'd take bets he was clenching his teeth.

Again she attempted to step to the side and continue on her way. And again, Jace blocked her path.

"Decker has a reputation, Kelly."

"So do you." She was starting to get angry.

"Did he kiss you?"

She glared at him, refusing to answer.

He rubbed the back of his neck, before meeting her gaze across the short space that separated them. "Do you think about us, Kelly? About those three weeks when we first met?" he asked in a low, husky tone.

Her heart increased in tempo. If only he knew.

Twelve

"Do you ever think about the time we spent together?"

"I... Jace, don't do this." She shook her head. Her emotions were already raw, splintered. After seeing Shea's baby and again facing the reality of her own situation, she felt as if she'd been pulled inside out, every nerve in her body scraped raw. Before her stood the man who had given her the world. Then taken it away.

"I think about it," he said as though needing her to know.

Something inside her snapped. "Then why didn't you call?" The unfairness suddenly overwhelmed her and she almost screamed the words as she blinked back angry tears. "Why didn't you come back? I will not be a convenience, Jace. I'll never again be simply a diversion to relieve some rich man's boredom. Now please let me by."

"You were never just a diversion. Dammit, Kelly."

He pulled her hard against him, his hot mouth coming down over hers. For a few seconds, she fought to be free of his arms, pushing against his wide shoulders, crying on the inside as she fought the overwhelming need to embrace him.

This was Jace. This was the man she loved. His lips, his scent, his voice, the feel of his powerful arms holding her firmly but gently, was what she'd longed for all those many months. This was the never-ending dream that came to her on those nights when she was too weak to push it away.

With a small desperate whimper of defeat, she gave in to her weakness, clutched the front of his shirt and opened her lips, letting him in. She kissed him back with an urgency propelled by the torturous need that had ripped at her soul for so many months. No longer held in check, the bittersweet memories pummeled the last remaining bits of her resolve. She gloried in his kiss once again, warmed by the heat of his body, his hard erection pressing against her stomach. His hungry mouth devoured hers as he pulled her closer. She felt his heart beating as fast as her own as his tongue explored the recesses of her mouth, enticing hers to do the same. His hands moved to cup her face, holding her to his, and she heard him moan.

He swept her into his arms and carried her into his bedroom and kicked the door closed behind them. Not breaking the kiss, Jace set her down next to the bed and made quick work removing her blouse. She absently felt him remove her bra, felt the cool air on her skin as his hands cupped her, squeezing gently, his thumbs playing across the sensitive nubs, making them harden under his touch. Bending down, he took one firm nipple into his mouth, sucking gently. Kelly moaned at the exquisite pleasure. Her back arched, her breasts swelled under his touch. He moved to the other breast, giving it the same attention. She heard the faint sound of a zipper being opened and her jeans were pushed down and over her hips. Then his mouth returned to hers and Kelly became lost in the sensation, in the gut-wrenching need overtaking her. Fisting her hands in his hair, she held on as the room began to spin. She felt a floating sensation, and then absently realized she was in his bed, covers thrown back, her jeans tugged from her legs.

He used his knee to ease her legs apart, and then settled on top of her. His hard erection pushed almost painfully, urgently against her core. His breath was hot against her skin as he kissed her neck, slowly moving to her ear, nipping and kissing her jaw before returning to her mouth.

A white-hot flow of heat coursed through her body, building into an unrelenting fire at the apex of her thighs. Her need reached a frantic level as she twisted, trying to adjust her position and take him inside. He was breathing hard as his lips and tongue continued to feed, the sheer heat of his mouth making her want to embrace him, to give in to what they both wanted.

Kelly was out of her mind. Her hips arched against him, conveying her need. She wanted to feel more of Jace. Inside her. Filling her.

Jace unzipped his jeans and let them fall. He felt a long-forgotten tingle at the base of his spine and knew he had to get inside her, fast. She was so damned hot he was going to lose it. Grabbing some protection from the drawer in his nightstand, he quickly put it in place. With Kelly, it had always been like this: a raw, gripping, almost unquenchable need that made them frantic in their actions to unite as one. With one hand, he tested her, two fingers pressed inside, eliciting a soft moan.

"Are you ready for me, Kelly?" he murmured against her ear.

Her body arched against his hand, silently conveying her need. With the pulse hammering in his veins he covered her, positioned his shaft at her core and experienced that tingle again, this time radiating up his spine, splintering his mind. Any illusions that he could take it slow went up in flames as he pushed his heavy length inside, filling her...

Sweat broke out on Jace's forehead and he knew taking this easy was not going to happen. With a rough growl, he pushed still deeper, unable to completely absorb the almost painful pleasure of the throbbing heat that encased him.

"Are you okay?"

She gave a partial nod and pulled his mouth back to hers.

As he began to move, she moaned, biting his lower lip, her hands gripping his back, attempting to hold him to her, expressing the same intense need that ran through him. His lips covered hers, his tongue filling her, simulating what was happening below.

Faster. Deeper. More intense. Until Jace lost hold on reality. He gripped her hips, raising her to him, and pushed even deeper. He rolled his hips and her head fell back against the pillow, her open mouth sending a clear message needing no words. As he took them to the next plane, he returned to the temptations of her lips and she drew his tongue inside, sucking hard. Jace's control snapped. He began to pummel against her, thrusting deeper and deeper with every stroke. He was going to lose it. Suddenly, Kelly stilled and cried out, all the air leaving her body as she arched up against him, shattering in raw pleasure. Her body clenching around him pushed Jace over the top. He couldn't hold back his own ragged moan as the intensity of his release overtook him, pulsating deep within her, spasm after spasm as if there were no end.

It seemed to take a millennium before the stars began to drift back down and settle in his totally shattered brain. His body lost its grip on whatever strength remained. Overwhelmed with heady weakness, he dropped to his side.

His hands found her face and he kissed her softly, loving the scent, the taste that was only Kelly. He felt her tremble as she kissed him back.

She was his.

"Did I hurt you?" he asked against her lips.

Her answer was a smile against his lips and a soft moan in the key of *no*.

The next morning, Kelly worked on the correspondence, logging the RSVPs for the charity gala and responding to both those who would be coming and, as a courtesy, those who would not.

She felt as though Mona could somehow tell what had happened between her son and Kelly just by looking at her face. Therefore, Kelly made every attempt not to look at Mona, turning a different direction if the older woman came into the doorway of her small office. If Mona noticed anything amiss, she chose to say nothing. But it wasn't Kelly's imagination that Jace's mom was smiling more than normal. But Kelly was, too; hopefully Mona didn't catch on.

The work was steady throughout the day. The detailed to-do list for the charity ball required Kelly's concentration, which kept her from reexperiencing the sensations brought by Jace's hands the night before. At least a little.

"Penny for your thoughts…" said a deep voice in her ear.

Kelly jumped and looked up to find the very subject of her thoughts directly in front of her. Bracing his hands on the edge of the small desk, Jace leaned toward her and raised his eyebrows, a small sexy smile on his full lips. She could feel the blush spread over her face.

Before she could respond, she heard Matt's voice call out, followed by footsteps running up the stairs. He entered the room in a full run.

"Kelly. Oh. Hi, Jace. Mrs. Compton." He was grinning from ear to ear. "Guess what happened today? You're never gonna believe it!" He was barely able to contain his enthusiasm. "Frank Gentry broke his leg during football practice!"

Kelly stared at him as though he'd lost his mind. She glanced at Mona, who had a curious look on her face. Jace straightened and placed his hands on his hips, as if waiting for more.

"This is *not* good news, Matt."

"Wait—his dad told Coach Hager he'll probably be out for the rest of the season. The coach talked to me privately and asked me to take his place. Oh, man. It's the *varsity* team, Kelly. I'll be the only sophomore on it."

"Oh my gosh. That's great, Matt." She jumped up from her chair and gave her brother a hug.

"Absolutely. Congratulations, Matt," Mona said.

"That's great, dude." Jace grinned.

"It's all because of you. All the pointers you gave me and how much you made me practice. Oh, man. Thanks, Jace."

"I didn't really do anything, but you are entirely welcome for whatever you think I did. I'm proud of you, Matt."

"I wish you could come to the game. It's this Friday—" he shrugged his shoulders "—but I know you probably can't." Matt turned to Kelly. "Cory is picking me up in a few minutes. He's the quarterback. We're gonna grab a burger and talk about some plays. I'll be home before ten," he added before bounding from the room.

"Do you have any plans for Friday evening?"

Her gaze shot to Jace in surprise. She shrugged. "Not that I know of."

"Want to go to a football game?" He was grinning from ear to ear.

"Matt's?"

"Yeah."

"I would love to go."

Matt's first varsity game. It would be doubly special to share it with Jace. The thought of being seen in public with him made her a bit nervous, but Matt had mentioned that most everyone in town knew Jace Compton was living among them. After the media reports that had lasted for weeks, the world probably knew. And apparently, Matt hadn't hidden the fact that he and his sister lived on the ranch. And really, why would he? So it was pointless for them to attend the game separately.

"I'll meet you in the kitchen. About six thirty?"

"Jace, what about you going out in public?"

He shrugged those broad shoulders. "I have no intention of living my life in hiding. Tom says it has been quiet for a couple of weeks. The folks of this community seem like good people. I really want to see Matt's game."

Kelly assured herself the inner excitement she felt was the anticipation over seeing Matt play, but she knew part of it was about going with Jace. As his date. It would be the first time they'd gone out together since he'd moved to this ranch.

As she counted down the days Kelly had to wonder what the news media might do if they saw her and Jace out and about together. All she could do was put her trust in Jace and hope that he knew what he was doing.

By six thirty on Friday, Kelly had joined Jace in the kitchen and soon they were on their way to the stadium, followed by two bodyguards in a separate vehicle.

The snare drums of the local band beat out a cadence, adding to the spirit and excitement in the air as the small entourage reached the front of the old wooden bleachers. They climbed the steps, heading to a spot that would give them a better view of the field and hopefully allow Jace some degree of anonymity. He didn't seem worried about it. His small two-person detachment would ensure his safety, handling any situation should it get out of hand. The two men were dressed in jeans and T-shirts with light jackets helping to camouflage the weapons they no doubt carried underneath; one of them led the way while the other brought up the rear.

"Fall is on its way," Kelly said as she sat down next to Jace.

"Are you cold?"

She shook her head. "No. It's a perfect temperature. I'm just glad we're past the worst of the Texas summer heat. You'll learn to appreciate November weather."

He laughed. "Be glad Matt isn't playing football in the northeast. I've been on the field when you couldn't see the yard lines for the snow. Played during a blizzard one year."

"How is that possible? How can anyone play in a blizzard?"

"The best way you can." He grinned.

"You loved it, didn't you?" She could see it in his eyes. Regardless of anything else Jace had accomplished in his life, his true love was football.

He nodded, his gaze on the field. "Yeah. I loved every

second," he said, and then turned to Kelly. The dark glitter of his eyes took her breath away. "It was the second best time of my life."

She smiled, immediately understanding his implication. The urge to lean toward him and taste those wickedly handsome lips was overwhelming.

The band began a rousing school fight song and everyone sprang to their feet, clapping and cheering as the home team broke through the colorful paper barrier and jogged onto the field. The black-and-gold uniforms of the Calico Springs Cougars stood out against the bright green turf. It was high school sports at its best. Jace, Kelly and the security team stood and cheered along with the other three hundred people in attendance.

It was surreal, being at a game in the town where she'd grown up, watching her kid brother among the varsity players, while standing next to Jace. The stadium lights made the colors more vivid; the air was thick with excitement. As they tossed the coin and the kickoff ensued, Kelly watched with pride as Matt took his place in the starting lineup.

As the game progressed, becoming more intense, Jace whistled and shouted his encouragement. When the Cougars made the first touchdown of the night, he pulled Kelly into his strong arms and hugged her in a tight embrace.

During halftime, Kelly noticed people walking below them as they made their way back and forth between the refreshment booth and their seats. They would look up at Jace and wave. If he saw them, Jace waved back, displaying that sparkling smile. Only a few approached, welcoming him to their community, wanting only to shake his hand. Their courtesy made Kelly feel a pride for her hometown she'd never really felt before.

"Would you like anything? Soft drink, coffee, hot dog?"

"No, thanks, I'm fine."

Her gaze wandered over his handsomely cut features, lingering for an instant on the strong line of his mouth. She couldn't stop herself from remembering how his kisses had so easily destroyed her preconceived notions of just how erotic a kiss could be. She'd way underestimated the power of a kiss. At least where Jace was concerned.

More than a little unnerved by the intensity of his glance, she forced her gaze back to the field with a shuddering breath.

By the third quarter, the score was tied. The Vikings had the ball. Their quarterback threw a pass and all eyes were on the ball as it soared through the air. At the last instant, it was intercepted. By Matt. Jace was on his feet, with Kelly close behind him. The crowd roared as Matt darted and circled in and around his opponents, jumping free of hands that would take him down. The spectators were on their feet as Matt ran down the length of the field toward the goal post, making it to the thirty yard line before he was finally tackled. Kelly was ecstatic. She swallowed past a lump in her throat as she clenched her hands together, overwhelmed with pride.

Jace caught her gaze and grinned at her reaction. He clearly shared in the pride she felt for her brother. With his run downfield, Matt had set his team up for an easy touchdown. He was the hero of the night.

When there were only three minutes remaining on the clock, Jace's security encouraged them to leave. With the home team ahead by two touchdowns, Jace hesitantly agreed.

"Do you mind?"

"Not at all. I think it's a good idea. Matt will understand. He's been talking all week about a postgame party at the pizza place. They'll no doubt rehash every second of the game. He's going to be floating on cloud nine for a month."

"He has every right to." Jace offered her his hand as he stood up, and she took it. "He did great. He still has this year plus two more to expand his knowledge and hone his skills before college. And he's a natural. He's got a chance at the pros, barring any injury, if that's what he wants."

"I wish Gramps could be here. But I'm grateful Matt has you. Thank you for all you've done for him, Jace."

He shrugged his shoulders. "It was my pleasure, whatever you think I did. Giving Matt some tips wasn't the reason for his accomplishments tonight. He did that all on his own."

As they walked out to the parking lot, she reflected on how she'd seen another facet of Jace Compton tonight. And she had to admit, she liked what she saw.

The drive back to the ranch was quiet, but it was an easy silence. Jace pulled into the main entrance and walked with Kelly through the trees to her cabin.

"I enjoyed it, Jace. Very much," she said as they went inside.

"So did I."

"I guess I'll see you tomorrow."

"Yeah. Tomorrow." For a few seconds their gazes locked across the darkened room.

Reaching out to her, Jace cupped her face, drawing her closer. Lowering his head, he gently kissed her, loving the softness of her lips, the taste of her. Her purely feminine essence called out to him and his body tensed in readiness.

He was about to pull away when she opened her lips to him. His heartbeat quickened and he deepened the kiss. His arms came around her, pulling her tightly to him; he loved the way her smaller body molded perfectly to his. He cupped the back of her head, his fingers lost in the silky texture of her hair. Raw need surged through his body, demanding he hold her close, ensuring she wouldn't turn away.

She was beyond tempting. The need to feel her underneath him once again, taking the pleasure he gave and giving it back ten times over, was eating him up inside. Kelly was everything he'd ever wanted in a woman. He never wanted to let her go.

But he knew it was wrong. She didn't need an affair. She needed a husband and a permanent home. He couldn't offer her either one.

Kelly moaned softly and Jace struggled to keep his passion under control. As the fragrance of her perfume blended with the scent of her desire and the sweet taste of her lips, he knew he was going to lose this battle.

The sound of the latch on the front door being turned and the door opening helped bring Jace to his senses. With more strength than he thought he possessed, he lifted his lips from hers and glanced toward the door.

Matt and two of his buddies stood in the doorway, grinning as if they'd just found gold.

"Oops. Gosh I'm sorry," Matt ventured, but didn't look sorry at all. "Forgot my wallet." He walked over to the kitchen counter and grabbed the dark leather billfold. Returning to the door, he glanced back at Jace, and then looked directly at his sister. "Click. Click." And with a chuckle, they were gone.

"Click. Click?"

"Don't ask," Kelly returned, shaking her head.

A sexy grin kicked up the corners of his mouth. "Your brother isn't sixteen. He's sixteen going on forty."

He reached out and pushed the sweater from her shoulders, and then removed the band holding back her hair. He grabbed the front of her jeans and pulled her closer, unfastening and unzipping.

"This isn't going to resolve anything," she whispered against his mouth. "But I'm tired of telling you no."

His heart rate tripled. "Then don't."

He was on fire. He didn't know how they were going to contend with the future, but at the moment, it didn't matter. It was enough to know she wanted him. As if to make sure he knew, she kissed him with a hunger he remembered so well, her hands fisting his shirt, leaving no doubt in his mind they were going to make love. He was going to take her. Right here. Right now. He was delirious with need. His blood pounded in his ears and he let out a deep growl.

Kelly was his.

He backed her against the cabin wall and kissed her, over and over, long and deep, his tongue caressing hers, making a silent demand that had her clinging to him.

He grabbed the hem of her T-shirt and quickly pulled it over her head. He took off her bra next, and sucked first one breast, then the other, while his hand alternately massaged and teased.

She began unbuttoning his shirt, but with one hard tug, Jace ripped it open, buttons flying everywhere. Her hands roamed over the smooth skin of his muscular chest, and then he felt her lips and tongue against him as she tasted him. As though she could never get enough.

He lowered one hand to between her legs. Even through her jeans, he felt the intense heat. The dampness. The scent of her desire surrounded him. She pushed against his hand and he heard a small whimper.

Without another word, Jace scooped her into his arms and carried her to the bedroom that wasn't full of sports equipment, closing the door behind him. He placed her on the soft mattress, shrugged out of his shirt and kicked off his boots. He quickly removed her jeans and then dropped his own.

The vision in front of him stole his breath. Her long blond hair draped over the pillow, her perfect breasts full and swollen, the light pink tips now hard nubs. But it was the sleepy, steamy look of want in her eyes that held him transfixed, the awareness and need clearly displayed in those blue-green eyes. Her lips, slightly open, showing brilliant white teeth, enticed him even further.

He placed one knee on the side of the bed, bending over her, his face stopping a breath away from hers. He cupped her chin, his thumb rubbing over her lower lip. Her lips closed around him and she moaned. He felt her teeth as she bit down, teasing him, sucking him deeper inside.

With a moan, he took her in a long, deep kiss. He moved to bite at her jaw, and then trailed kisses along her neck, licking, tasting, loving her down to her breasts. When he drew the hard peak of one breast into his mouth, her body surged toward his and she whimpered. He caressed the other breast in his hand, teasing, molding her. His erection throbbed with need to be inside her.

"Kelly," he growled. He could hear the animal rawness in his own voice. Using one hand, he positioned himself and pushed inside her. He stopped to allow her body time to adjust and accept his girth, and then filled her with one hard thrust. The heat and silkiness of her body was more amazing than he remembered. Hands cupping her hips, he held her up to him and filled her again and again. She called out his name as the pace became faster. Hotter. Frantic. He felt her shatter, her release pushing him over the top and beyond. It seemed to go on forever, yet it was too brief. Gasping for air, Jace dropped to his side, pulling her close, bestowing kisses on her face, her hair.

For long moments Jace held her in the darkness, her head resting on his chest, her spicy fragrance filling the air around him. Kelly was his. Every cell in his body screamed it.

There had to be a way for them to be together. He had to find a way.

He must have fallen asleep, because when he opened his eyes, there was faint sunlight coming in through the window. The sun was barely creeping over the far horizon when he awoke. Kelly was still in his arms, her head on his chest and one arm resting across his abdomen. He kissed the top of her head, his hands playing in the long tendrils of her hair. She stretched, raised her head and opened her eyes. The gleam in those blue-green depths was mesmerizing.

"Good morning," he whispered. "Sleep well?"

"Yes." She smiled up at him. The satisfaction of their night's lovemaking clearly shone on her face. "And you?"

"I'm still dreaming." He cupped her face, pressing a soft kiss on her lips. "What time will Matt be home?"

"Noon."

"Good. Because this was billed as a double feature and I'm pretty sure it's rated triple X."

She grinned before his mouth covered hers, and once again he was lost in the magic that was Kelly.

Thirteen

By the time Kelly made it upstairs to her office on Monday, the phones were already ringing off the hook. Kelly settled the baby in the crib and hurried to her desk. The day turned fast and furious and before she knew it, Mona was calling it to an end.

At the end of this week they would all fly to Los Angeles for Mona's charity gala. Then Jace would stay in town for a series of meetings on his next film project. Kelly and Mona would return to the ranch.

On Tuesday, Jace stopped by Mona's office. Her heart went into double time, but he only asked how her weekend had been and wished both Kelly and his mom a good day. He seemed to be giving Kelly space to sort it all out, to come to grips with their renewed love affair.

He couldn't know she already had.

Downstairs that afternoon she found Jace sitting in the kitchen on one of the bar stools, an inch of printed pages in a thick blue binder open on the counter in front of him.

Jace glanced up. "You leaving for the day?"

"Yep." She switched Henry from one arm to the other. "Is that your script?"

"Yeah." Jace glanced down at the papers. "I need to read the damn thing but I'm having a hard time concentrating. Thought maybe sitting out here would help."

He pushed the script aside and reached out to touch Henry's foot. "He's growing."

"Yes, he is."

"Are you and Mom almost ready for her charity event?" he asked before she could turn away.

"I think we're right on schedule. If as many people come as have responded so far, there'll be over four hundred in attendance. Mona is ecstatic."

Jace grinned. "What about you? Are you looking forward to it?"

"*Me?* I'll enjoy seeing it all come together, but I'm not attending the actual dinner and ball."

Jace frowned. "Why not?"

"Because."

"Can you elaborate just a bit?"

"I'm an employee." Her tone said he was dumb for asking. "Mona will have a full catering staff to assist her with drinks and hors d'oeuvres. The food will be prepared on site, overseen by the chef who has assisted Mona at the ball for the past five years. I'll be there to help set up, make sure everything is going according to plan, but once the guests start arriving I'll stay in the background as a precautionary measure. Basically, by then, my job will be over."

"Does Mom know your plans?"

"We talked." She hoped Jace didn't try to muddy the water. It had taken her quite a while to convince Mona she did not want or need to be there during the actual festivities. The social class of the guests was intimidating… Senators. Congressmen. Award-winning actors and producers. The elite of the elite. Kelly didn't need to be reminded she was about as far away from their inner circles as a person could get. And she had no intention of subjecting herself or Mona to any embarrassment she might cause if she committed a faux pas at the gala.

And there was the expense of a gown. No way was she spending a thousand dollars or more on something she would wear only once. She had a hard enough time making herself buy a brand of green beans that wasn't on sale. Her frugal nature didn't allow for thousand-dollar dresses. Being a guest at Mona's ball was simply not going to happen.

"Your mom and I have it all worked out, Jace," she said with as much happy bravado as she could muster. "No worries."

No worries.

With Kelly, that usually meant there was definitely something to worry about. Jace picked up the script as she walked out of the room, heading for the back door. With a frown, he rolled the document up in his hand and headed to his mother's bedroom.

"Mom?"

"Come in, sweetheart." Mona smiled as she entered the bedroom from the adjacent powder room. "I think I may have forgotten something regarding the ball. I just can't remember what it is." She chuckled. "Do you think that really does mean it isn't important?"

Jace shook his head. "I'm afraid I couldn't help you with that one, Mother. Change of subject. I just talked to Kelly downstairs and she said she's not attending the charity event. I thought you both were going. You both went through the dress fitting."

"Yes, I know." His mother sighed. "And she balked at the idea even then. She says she'd be out of her league around the people we expect to be there. Her words, not mine. She contends she's only an employee and has no business going."

"They're not one damn bit better than she is."

"I know, Jace."

He muttered an angry curse under his breath. "Give it another try, will you, Mom?"

"Tomorrow," she promised.

Jace said good-night and headed to his room, his molars grinding in frustration. Kelly shouldn't be concerned about a bunch of blowhard politicians and a few egotistical actors. He'd counted on her being there. He wasn't sure why, other than that she and Matt had become part of the family. Kelly wasn't an employee. He awoke every morning looking forward to seeing her and the baby. For reasons he didn't understand, Kelly's presence calmed him. As infuriating as she could be at times, Jace would take the frustrating with the good anytime. Her being in his life was…right. He was the one who was wrong for her.

Other than dealing with the constant, overwhelming need to make love to her, his life was good. Clearly he should have said something to her about the charity event and asked if she would be his date. Was he ever going to get it right?

"You know, we must go shopping," Mona stated the next day as she and Kelly ate lunch in the kitchen.

"For what?" She crumbled crackers into her bowl of soup.

"For the charity ball."

Kelly wasn't sure she understood. Everything had been ordered down to the last flower. "Have I missed something?" She put down her spoon, mentally going over the details of the plans for the event. "They called and confirmed they would have the ice sculpture delivered by four on the day of the ball. The chef has said—"

"The preparations are fine. You've done an outstanding job. I was referring to us. Surely you know I expect you to attend the gala."

"Yes. No. I mean yes, I know I'll be going but not as a guest. I'll work behind the scenes, stick to the kitchen area. I'll be at the hotel Saturday afternoon to help oversee everything, but like I said before, I have no business attending the ball."

Mona looked at Kelly as if she'd grown a second head. "And why not?"

The idea was so ridiculous. She didn't want to offend this kind, wonderful woman, but going to an event attended by some of the biggest names in both Hollywood and politics was not going to happen. Talk about feeling like a fish out of water.

Kelly just shook her head, refusing to discuss it further, but Mona wasn't going to let it drop.

"You listen to me, Kelly Michaels. This isn't one of Jace's red carpet extravaganzas. It's my charity ball. And as my personal assistant, you are most certainly expected to attend. And you will need a gown to wear, unless you have one already?"

Kelly closed her eyes in temporary defeat and shook her head.

"No? Then Andre will provide the gowns as I originally intended. I'll call him myself and reconfirm."

What had she gotten herself into? She was not part of their world. It was just wrong to think differently. Of course, she wanted to be there for Mona. No matter how carefully one planned, there were always last-minute details to see to. But to attend the gala dressed as one of the guests was just wrong.

The trip to Los Angeles in Jace's Gulfstream was smooth and filled with laughter as Mona recalled mishaps from her past charity events. Kelly enjoyed listening to the banter but the uneasiness hadn't left her. She should not be attending this elite event. And no amount of winks from Jace or pats on the hand from Mona was going to change that.

Arriving at the hotel the day before the event, they hit the ground running. Kelly quickly realized that when Mona Compton set her mind to do something, anyone not going in her direction had better get out of the way. This fundraiser was her passion.

Kelly did her best to keep up, but lack of experience initially left her feeling completely out of her depth. Thankfully, the hotel staff had been prepped and things were accomplished efficiently and to Mona's liking. Kelly oversaw the setup of the banquet hall. The tables, chairs and decorations were brought through the door as fast as she could place them. Meanwhile Mona met with the chef and culinary artists who would provide the special touches that made this occasion a Mona Compton event.

"I think we're done," Mona said the next day as she looked around at the vast ballroom. "The ice sculpture will be delivered at four. Where should it go?"

"I thought we'd put it in an area near the dessert buffet but with enough space in between to make it accessible on all sides." Kelly walked over to the spot. "Around here. There is even an electrical outlet. We can use fluorescent lighting to make it the focus without melting it too badly."

"Perfect. I need to make a couple of changes to the place cards, only because I know these people." She rolled her eyes. "Sometimes it's better to avoid a potentially unpleasant situation than it is to cross your fingers and hope nothing will happen. You'll learn soon enough." She laughed. "Take this card and switch it for any one on the table over there in the corner." After five additional changes, Mona deemed the seating arrangement done.

"Okay," Mona said, "now it's time for us to get ready." She glanced at her watch. "Your dress should be in your room. Let's head to the salon for hair and make-up first."

"Hair? Make-up?"

"Why, of course, dear."

Of course.

Two hours later, Kelly stepped inside her room. Immediately, she saw a large bouquet on the table next to the windows. Tossing her clipboard onto the bed, she approached the flowers. There were several different varieties and the fragrance was amazing. Kelly opened the card.

> *To my dearest Kelly. I couldn't have done this without you. Mona.*

Kelly sat down on the striped silk-covered chair nearest the small table. With all she had to do, Mona had taken the time and the trouble to send her a beautiful and thoughtful thank-you.

Tears welled in her eyes and she fought to keep them from spilling over. This was all happening because of Jace. It was because of him she was here now. It was because of him she had a great job working for an amazing lady.

She placed a quick call to Mrs. Jenkins to check on Henry, receiving the assurance the baby was fine. Then Kelly turned toward the closet.

She unzipped the black garment bag containing her dress for the gala, refusing to speculate on how much it cost.

Her eyes grew wide. Her mouth dropped open. This couldn't be right. Removing the gown from the closet, she held it up. This wasn't the design she'd expected. Not even close. Someone had made a terrible mistake. The dress was not blue. It wasn't satin. It was exquisite black lace, from top to bottom.

A few minutes later she stood in front of the mirror, her reflection nothing like what she was used to seeing. Not by a mile. The stylist had pulled her long hair to one side, the ends curled into ringlets that fell over her shoulder and down her back. The long-sleeved black lace gown fell to her feet, with a short train at the back. The form-fitting dress highlighted every curve.

It was expensive. It was elegant. It was risqué.

It was so not her.

She couldn't go downstairs in this.

She glanced at the clock. Seven fifteen. The event started at eight. A full panic attack hit her with the velocity of an air bag deployed during an unexpected crash. Placing her hands against her temples, Kelly tried to calm her racing heart enough to think. *What was she going to do?* How could she hurt Mona by not showing up for the festivities? How could she refuse to wear a gown that must have cost thousands of dollars? Yet she couldn't wear this in front of all those people. They would stare. She would die. What had the designer been thinking? He obviously sent the wrong dress. She'd expected something like a blue prom dress and instead received an elegant black spiderweb.

Clearly, she shouldn't have let Mona and the designer make the selection. She'd just blown it off the day the man came to the ranch to take fittings. When asked if she wanted to look at styles, she'd politely refused, thinking she wouldn't be going anyway so it wouldn't matter. She couldn't have imagined that with that small action, she'd pulled the trigger and shot herself in the foot.

Fourteen

"Have you seen Kelly?" Jace asked his mom as he scanned the people entering the ballroom.

"No. I haven't seen her since we had our hair done this afternoon and… Oh dear."

"Oh dear?" Jace eyed his mother. "What?"

His mother suddenly appeared apprehensive. "You may need to go up and encourage her to come down."

"Why? I mean, I'll be glad to, but I thought it was settled that she would attend."

"It is. It was. She, uh…she might not be completely happy with her gown."

Jace frowned. "Why would you say that?"

"Oh dear. Jason, please go up to her room and see if you can talk to her. She left the dress selection up to me and I may have made the wrong decision."

His mother wrung her hands, obvious concern in every feature of her face.

What in the world did his mother consider *the wrong decision*?

He rushed up to Kelly's suite. After two raps on the door, she immediately pulled it open. Quickly she looked past him down the long hall, first one way then the other. Grabbing his arm, she yanked him inside, shutting the door behind them.

There were no words for the vision standing before him. Jace swallowed hard. His body surged to readiness. Kelly was a natural beauty, but in that dress, every man at the ball would beat a fast path straight to her. His protective instinct jumped to the fore.

"You look…incredibly beautiful."

She pushed away from the door and walked past him into the suite, her hands fidgeting at her sides. Apparently, she felt something was terribly wrong. The only thing *he* felt wrong was that a certain part of his anatomy was about to explode.

"I can't do this," she said. "I can't go downstairs."

"Why not?" He frowned.

"You're kidding, right? Wearing *this*?"

"What do you think is wrong with it?"

"There isn't enough material to make a shirt for Henry."

"Kelly, you're way overreacting."

"I am not. Oh God. Jace, you've got to help me. I can't hurt your mother."

"Why can't you go in the dress? It's amazing. You look… ravishing. Good enough to eat."

"I'm serious."

"So am I."

"Look at it."

"Believe me, I am."

"It makes me look as if I'm not wearing anything but a few scanty strips of lace."

"And you think that's a bad thing?"

"Well, it isn't *good*."

Jace ran his hand over the lower part of his face. He didn't know what to say. Kelly was beyond gorgeous and sexy and that dress just confirmed it. She would be the sensation of the ball. How could she not realize how beautiful she looked? Had she looked in a mirror?

"The dress is fine. It's beyond fine. And we need to go. Dinner will be called in about thirty minutes. We'll need to find our seats."

Her hands began to fidget again. "Maybe I'll go down later. Food is the last thing I want right now. Anyway, there's no place card for me at the any of the tables. I made sure of it. I'm only an employee, Jace, playing dress-up for the night. And your date won't appreciate it at all if you show up with me on your arm."

"I'm looking at my date for the evening."

"You… I… No. You can't."

"Why not?"

"You *know*. Anyway, I'm not ready."

"You look more than ready to me. And I assure you, there is a place card at the table, next to me. You're good. Mom's better. You look beautiful. Now get anything you want to take with you and let's go before I lock the door and help you out of the dress you don't like."

"Jace, *please*." She moved farther inside the room. "There will be reporters. It will look bad for Mona if you walk into the room with me. The gold digger from Texas."

"Kelly, tonight you're my date," he stated, stepping toward her. "A very beautiful date. In that dress, every man here will sit up and take notice."

"I feel like a sideshow freak. Did you have a stripper pole put in the ballroom?"

He inhaled deeply and rubbed the back of his neck. He knew women who didn't give full nudity a second thought. Kelly was still an innocent in so many ways. It was part of the charm he found so irresistible. He understood after the media blitz about the baby that she was also trying to protect Mona and the charity. She couldn't be more wrong. But he didn't have time for the argument she would no doubt wage. He looked from Kelly through the open door to the large bed in the room to his left.

"If you really don't want to go downstairs, I can't make you." He'd make damn sure the locks were set.

"Oh," Kelly inhaled a deep sigh of relief. "Thank you, Jace."

He slipped out of his jacket, tossed it onto a chair and

then pulled at the end of his bow tie, pulling it free from its knot.

"What are you doing?"

"If you don't go, I don't go." He walked into the bedroom and pulled back the covers on the bed. "I'll just stay here with you. I'm betting we can find something to do."

"You can't do that to Mona." Then she straightened as the light dawned about what he was doing. "This is blackmail."

He shrugged. "As they say, all's fair. Which is it going to be, Kelly? Are you going to accompany me downstairs or do we get out of these clothes and spend the night together in that bed like we both really want to do?"

"Don't do this, Jace."

"I haven't done anything. Yet."

"Jace."

He walked up to her and cupped her face in his hands. If he didn't get them out of this room fast, neither of them would ever make it to the ballroom. His mother might be a little pissed, but he was past the point of caring.

"Take me very seriously, Kelly." His eyes held her gaze. "There's nothing I want to do right now more than remove that dress, inch by inch, and carry you to the bed." He took her hand and pressed her palm against his throbbing erection. "You need to decide. Now."

As soon as they stepped off the elevators, they were surrounded. People filled every available space, in the corridor, around the elevators, in the ballroom, even filling the elegant hotel lobby. As soon as Jace was spotted, reporters came out of the woodwork. Cameras flashed while reporters stood in line for an interview. Jace held Kelly's hand, refusing to let her fade into the background. He gave interview after interview focusing on the charity. He noted his mom across the room doing the same thing. Kelly stood quietly at his side until some of the questions were directed at her.

"Ms. Michaels, are you excited about this charity ball tonight?"

"Of course." She looked into the camera, a beautiful smile on her lips. "We're all excited to be a part of this very worthy cause."

"What about the man standing next to you? Any wedding bells in the near future?"

Before Jace could open his mouth, Kelly responded to the question. "We're here tonight to raise money to help women who are abused and desperate to find a better life for themselves and their children. It's a serious concern and I would expect the media to respect that and focus on the women who so desperately need our help."

"So you're refusing to comment on any personal relationship between yourself and Jace Compton?"

"Yes. As a matter of fact, I am. This is neither the time nor the place for questions of that nature. Now, if you're willing to hand me a check for a million dollars made out to the NCAW, I might be tempted to answer."

Jace was stunned by just how easily Kelly shut the man down. It was as though she had years of experience in front of the reporters' cameras. The poor guy never had a chance. He mumbled something about not having quite that much in his pocket, the others laughed, and further questions along those lines were dropped. Jace had never been prouder of anyone in his life. Though her body trembled the entire time, she'd handled it like a pro.

After dinner, the orchestra began playing. Couples rose from their seats and headed for the dance floor. Jace stood, placed his linen napkin on the table, and held out his hand to Kelly. She gracefully accepted.

He pulled her close, taking advantage of the opportunity to have her next to him. It felt so right.

"Remember when we danced in that little hotel lounge in Calico Springs?" he murmured near her ear. "It was dark. The only light was from the candles on the tables. I could have held you like that forever. And we still fit together perfectly."

"Only because you're a great dancer."

"Dancing has nothing to do with how impeccably you fit in my arms. If you like, I can demonstrate other ways we fit together."

"Be nice."

"I'm trying. But all I seem to want to do is be naughty. Very, very naughty."

"I don't know whether to laugh or take you seriously and issue a reprimand."

"Serious works for me." He leaned down and whispered in her ear, "You can even spank me if you want."

"Jace!" He loved the delicate blush that covered her fine features.

"What?" He intentionally assumed a look of pure innocence. Then couldn't hold back the grin at the expression of reproach on her face.

"You are bad."

"Mmmm. That's not what you said a week ago."

"May I cut in?" asked a man standing next to Jace, his eyes all over Kelly.

Jace nodded and pulled a gulp of air through his nose, aware he couldn't say no.

He watched helplessly as the man stepped up and put his arms around Kelly. She gave Jace a strained smile before they disappeared into the crowd.

"Well, hello there, handsome."

Jace turned to find Lena Maxwell, her dark auburn hair soft and wispy around her bare shoulders.

"Lena. How are you?" His eyes darted from Lena to the crowd on the dance floor as he tried to keep Kelly in sight. "Thanks for coming tonight."

"The pleasure is all mine." The sultry actress gave a deep-throated laugh. "Now dance with me before I have to take another breath without your arms around me."

With a tight smile, Jace complied.

"I heard you bought a ranch. Surely you're not retiring from pictures?"

"Haven't decided. Just knew I needed a break. What about you? Still fending off the offers with a stick?"

She laughed again. Jace searched the room for Kelly.

"She got to you big-time, didn't she?"

"Who?"

"The little blonde on your arm tonight. Congratulations on fatherhood, by the way."

"Thanks." Lena was trying to dig for gossip. She loved the spotlight, and knowing something no one else knew kept her right where she wanted to be.

"Brilliant idea to bring her here tonight. It will be all over the front page by in the morning. Good for the charity. Great for your career at the same time. Rumors are going to fly. Your name will be bandied about for weeks." She gave a sultry laugh. "Now I understand why we haven't seen you for a while."

Jace clenched his teeth in an effort to keep his temper at bay. Lena was the perfect example of why Kelly had been so concerned about attending tonight. He only hoped she wouldn't see this as a setup and think he was using her exactly as Lena described.

"May I cut in?" Another woman was waiting patiently by their side.

"So much for keeping you all to myself," Lena muttered, but politely stepped away. With a quick wink at Jace she disappeared toward the refreshment bar.

"Still have to stand in line to get to the great Jace Compton." The pretty brunette stepped into his arms. "Some things will never change."

"How've you been, Audrey?"

Jace absently moved to the music, only partially listening to the woman's ongoing chatter. He'd attended dozens of these affairs but tonight, for the first time, he saw nothing even remotely enjoyable in the experience. He didn't want to make small talk. He didn't want to be on center stage. Suddenly all the phony flirting and keeping up a front turned his stomach.

He wanted the quiet of the ranch and the privacy it offered.

And right or wrong, he wanted Kelly beside him.

The next man who stepped on her foot was going to regret it, Kelly decided as yet another intoxicated, overbearing fool asked her to dance. What was with the hands? This was an upscale event to raise money for a very worthy cause, not some grab-'n'-go on the shady side of town—even if she was half-naked. The cowhands had better manners.

Mona had called it right. There had to be at least four hundred people crowded into the ballroom. More than half were men, and she speculated that the majority of those were either blitzed or well on their way.

She'd spotted Jace a couple of times, each time trying to sidestep a different woman. They flirted shamelessly with him. He smiled politely but didn't appear to encourage them. He looked extraordinarily handsome in a tuxedo. At one point, their eyes met. He didn't smile, but the look that flared in his eyes warmed her down to her toes.

When the song ended, Kelly took the opportunity to excuse herself and leave the dance floor. She made her way to the ladies' room, hoping the evening would soon end. While it wasn't as bad as she'd first imagined, her feet were aching and her facial muscles actually hurt from continuously smiling, something she'd never before experienced. Perhaps it wasn't too late to call Mrs. Jenkins and again check on Henry.

She entered the elegant powder room, passing through to get to the bathroom facilities. As she was getting ready to exit, she heard the voices of several women in the first room.

"So…what did you think of Jace's new *friend*?"

Several giggles were the reply.

"I think she's nice," one of the women said.

"Oh, honey. She is going to be his downfall. I can't believe she managed to get pregnant. My husband said Jace was not enthusiastic at all about the new film. I guarantee it's because he feels responsible for that woman and her baby."

"Surely he won't turn down the role?" another woman asked. "I heard he is going to be offered the lead."

"She will probably *let* him do it. As long as it puts more money in her bank account."

What? Grabbing the handle, Kelly wrenched open the restroom door and turned toward the women in the powder room. She'd put up with that gossipy bullshit in school. All the talk about her father. Accusing *her* of breaking up marriages. She'd be damned if she would quietly take the hits again or hide like some thief in the night and say nothing as she had before.

"Frankly, I doubt she cares one way or the other. Would you? I mean, she's got her hooks in the most eligible bachelor on this continent. But she'd better ask herself how long she can keep him toeing the line."

"Maybe we should ask her for some pointers."

"Yeah. Maybe you should," Kelly interjected, staring at the speaker and wishing her gaze could do serious damage. "It certainly couldn't hurt." She let her gaze slide from the woman's face down to her feet and back, keeping a look of disgust on her face. "But it absolutely won't help. Excuse me."

Kelly pushed her way through the little group and looked into the large floor-to-ceiling mirror. Puckering her lips, she pretended to check her lipstick and then turned her head from side to side, her hand brushing down the side of her face and neck as if looking for flaws before shrugging her shoulders as though not finding any. Turning to look at herself in profile, she sucked in her stomach, arched her back and stuck out her boobs. What little she had.

"Mmm." She muttered in a disgruntled moan. She ran her hand over her stomach then across her breasts. "There's just too much material to this dress. Don't you think?"

The three women stared, each presenting a different level of shock, resentment and indignation.

"Oh well. I guess I'll leave that up to Jacie. Maybe he likes taking it off better." *Fake smile.* "You girls know what I mean." *Fade to frown.* "Oh. Or maybe you don't." *Uncaring shrug.* "Pity."

"Don't you live on a *farm*?"

One of the women, the oldest, apparently decided she had what it took to bring Kelly down a peg or two. *Bring it on, bitch.* These women were nothing compared to the kids at Calico Springs High.

Pointing finger. Surprised tone. "You're Celesta Mason!" *Aha look.* "I *thought* I recognized you." *Big smile.* "*Your* husband is the one who was caught humping one of the cooks in the kitchen two years ago. Naughty, naughty boy. But then…" *Conspiratorial tone.* "…can anyone really blame him?"

The gasps from all three could have sucked the plaster off the walls. Thank God for Mona's idle chitchat while they were placing the name cards earlier today. With a last glare in Kelly's direction, Celesta stomped toward the door, her face getting redder with each step. Her friends followed close behind.

"Bye-bye," Kelly called in her sweetest voice before the heavy door closed. *And good riddance.* She was gaining a much clearer picture of the way this game was played. Take away the million-dollar entitlements and these people were no different from the wannabes in Calico Springs.

She walked out of the ladies' room intending to check in with Mona and return to her suite. Her feet were killing her. Four hours in five-inch heels was not her thing. Before she could take three steps, she felt an arm slip around her shoulders.

"I was afraid I'd missed you, sweetheart." A man she didn't know smiled down at her. "I've waited long enough. Let's dance."

Oh, brother. He took her hand and pulled her into the ballroom, holding her far too close. He reeked of alcohol. His eyes looked cloudy; his pupils were dilated, making her wonder if he was high on booze or drugs. Probably both. He leaned forward, placing a kiss on her shoulder.

"Don't." Kelly was beyond disgusted. She'd had enough.

"You staying here at the hotel?"

She ignored his question, trying to think of a way out of this situation without making a scene.

"Come on, baby," he persisted, "what say you and me get out of here? I can think of a lot better things to do."

"I don't think so." She tried to push away, but he held her firmly in his arms.

"Don't be a fool." His voice suddenly sounded malicious. "If you think you and your kid are enough to make Jace leave the industry, you're sadly mistaken." He laughed harshly. "Yeah, I saw the way you looked at him across the room. But he's too into Lena Maxwell to care about anyone else. It's been that way for years. If you're smart, you'll let it go."

"You seem to know an awful lot about Jace Compton."

"We go way back. Sorry babe, maybe I should have introduced myself. Most people know me on sight. I'm Bret Goldman."

Bret Goldman. The man she'd spoken to when she'd called to tell Jace about the baby. So this was the jackass in person.

"It's okay, sweetheart. You're new. You'll learn."

"What will I learn?" She pushed back from him enough to look at his face. He was handsome enough, but his arrogance overshadowed any attraction someone might feel. Plus, he had some serious graying at the temples, and he carried the general look of one who overindulged. In everything, apparently.

"Who to be nice to and who doesn't matter. I matter."

"Really? To whom?"

His eyes narrowed. She needed to get away from this guy. Making a scene was becoming less and less important. Elite gala or not, he was about to be on the receiving end of an easily understood no.

He laughed contemptuously. "Be very careful, honey. Some people you don't say no to. I'm one of them."

Kelly could only gape at his arrogance. She tried her best to stifle a laugh, but the giggle broke free in an uncontainable snort. Suffice it to say it did not go over well with Mr. Full-of-Himself.

The man glared and seized her wrist. "Let's see if I can give you a better understanding upstairs." He began to pull her out of the room toward the elevators. The conceited jerk was serious. This had gone too far.

"Remove your hand. Now."

"A little wildcat. I love it."

"I don't think Ms. Michaels wants to party, Bret."

Bret stopped and Kelly looked behind her into Jace's strong face. He was clearly holding his anger in check. To someone passing it would appear they were all just having a nice conversation. But Jace had a deadly look in his beautiful green eyes. Anyone with any common sense at all would know to back off. Immediately.

"She's a little tease. We'll get past that upstairs."

Kelly struggled to remember…was she stronger with her left knee or her right?

"Let her go, Bret."

"Or what?" the man challenged.

There were no more words as Jace's fist shot out, landing squarely against the man's nose with a force that would have made Rocky Balboa proud. Bret released her arm as he crashed to the floor, taking out a waiter carrying a tray full of dirty plates in the process.

With a few muttered curses, Bret got to his feet. He

brushed at the trickle of blood running from his nose and the sight of it seemed to set him off. He lunged at Jace and grabbed his arm and swung him around, his fist flying toward Jace's face. With a quick, easy move, Jace avoided any contact and sent the man flying across the room and crashing into the wall with a roundhouse kick. Jace made it look easy. Bret attempted to keep his balance and actually came at Jace again.

This time Jace let go with a right uppercut to the head that once again sent the man flying from one side of the room to the other. When his body made contact with the opposite wall he slid to the floor like a sack of rotten potatoes.

The sight was unreal. Camera flashes filled the room. Jace's face was wrought with rage, his nostrils flaring, his mind and body not yet receiving the message it was over as he walked over to Bret, his fists clenched in anger. Jace was still in fight mode as two men stepped between him and his now unconscious—and no doubt soon to be former—manager. Their voices were low as they talked Jace down, assuring him it was over.

There was a moan and Bret struggled to sit up. Someone handed him a handkerchief and he held the cloth against his nose, not yet realizing that blood had soaked the front of his shirt.

Jace's eyes cut to Kelly. In that moment, he seemed to visibly calm down before a look of remorse and dismay flooded his features. He shrugged out of the men's hold and glanced at Bret, still lying on the floor, and then back at Kelly.

A moment passed between them before Jace turned and walked out of the room.

Fifteen

Jace entered his suite, letting the door close behind him. Shrugging out of his jacket, he tossed it onto a nearby chair, pulled off the tie and ripped open the dress shirt, sending the buttons flying. At the en suite bar he poured a triple and threw it down his throat. Bracing his arms against the countertop he stared at the image in the mirror. The contorted face that stared back, partially concealed by shadows, was not Jace Compton. It was a man with deadly eyes and a cold, menacing stare. The mouth was a thin straight line with deep grooves of leftover rage on either side. The white shirt hung open, bearing traces of Goldman's blood. Jace clenched his jaw as he stared at the face of George Compton in the mirror. His father had rematerialized and displayed all the trademark brutality and cruelty of Jace's childhood.

The beast had come out. Right in front of Kelly.

Jace poured another shot, downed it the same way and headed for the bathroom. Turning on the shower, he shucked the remaining clothes and stepped under the warm spray. He was still angry. He knew Bret was a pompous ass, knew he screwed around on his wife, knew his reputation in Hollywood circles was that of a ruthless, pushy, conniving, hard-nosed son of a bitch. But Jace had never witnessed him in full assault mode before tonight. It made it a thousand times worse that he'd set his sights on Kelly. She'd been so hesitant to attend the ball, and then to be accosted by a degenerate like Bret had Jace wishing he'd pounded the guy harder than he did.

But what churned in his gut was the knowledge that Kelly had witnessed everything. The shocked look on her face when he'd met her gaze before he turned and walked from the room would haunt him forever. Her eyes had been as wide as saucers, her hands clenched tightly in front of her as if in fright. She'd looked away from him to stare at the man lying on the floor, his face blotchy, his white dress shirt covered in blood. Jace couldn't be sure if it was shock or disbelief that froze her delicate features and made her skin lose some of its healthy color.

If there had ever been any hope he could keep Kelly in his life, hope that he wouldn't turn into his old man, he now knew with absolute certainty he could toss that dream into the trash. Someday it might be Kelly on the floor, her face bruised and bloodied. Just the thought made him physically sick.

Trudging out of the shower, he wrapped a towel around his waist, walked toward the en suite bar and poured himself another.

"Hi, baby." The sultry voice came from the general location of the bedroom. "We meet again so soon."

Jace froze. Flipping on the lights, he walked to the doorway of the bedroom and glared at the partially clothed woman in his bed, her long red hair covering her bare shoulders.

"Lena. *Goddammit.* What in the hell are you doing in here? Who let you in?" But Jace knew it wasn't the first time Lena had charmed her way into his private space, convincing an innocent employee it was her room. She and Bret, the two schemers, should get together. Or maybe they already had.

"Ah...come on, baby, don't be mad." The sound of her voice made him cold inside.

"This is not happening. You need to leave."

He grabbed her clothes from the chair and tossed them in

her direction. A contrived pout formed on her full lips as her brown eyes beseeched him to let her stay. Quite the actress.

"I can't believe you're going to throw me out. Why spend the night all by yourself?"

"Whether I do or don't is none of your goddamn business. What happened to Jack? Weren't you all into him?"

"Jack didn't work out." She sat up, not bothering to cover her bare chest. "I made a mistake, Jace. Can't you forgive one little mistake?"

"I don't care one way or the other, Lena." He settled his hands on his waist. "Whatever we had, if anything, ended a long time ago. I told you two years ago when you came up with that insane idea of pretending to be married, that was it for me. No more. Get dressed. Now. Then get out."

The pout still on her face, she grabbed her clothes and began to get dressed.

There was a persistent knocking at his door. *What now?* He glared at Lena. "If that's the press, Lena, so help me…"

She shook her head, her hands palms up. "No. At least it's nothing I had anything to do with." Standing, she pulled on her gown and began to fasten the buttons that ran the full length of the sparkling black evening dress and headed into the bathroom.

Jace took in a deep breath and clenched his hands into fists, wanting badly to reshape a wall.

Looking through the peephole in the door, he all but cringed. It wasn't reporters standing outside. It was Kelly. Running his hand over his face, he hesitated. He knew what she would think when she saw Lena. But after what she'd witnessed downstairs did it really make any difference? Swinging open the door, he stood back and she stepped inside the room.

"I just wanted to make sure you were okay."

"Yeah. I'm good." It was a sheer miracle he wasn't sitting in a jail cell. Again. "Kelly, there's something I need to tell you—"

"Jace, give me a call the next time you're—"

He heard Kelly's intake of breath as Lena walked back into the room, still buttoning her dress as she rounded the corner. The two women stared at each other.

"I'm…I'm sorry." Kelly bolted for the door. Luckily, Jace got there first.

"No. This is not what you think."

Lena smiled, her eyes sparkling in humorless amusement as she glided slowly toward the pair. "It never is." She leaned over casually and picked up her clutch, and then tossed her hair back over her shoulders in a practiced manner.

"This must be Kelly." She looked at Jace. "She is beautiful." She turned to Kelly. "Don't look so shocked, honey. Remember who you're with. This is Jace Compton's world. Better get used to it."

Firmly holding Kelly's wrist, he opened the door and Lena walked through it without a backward glance.

"Kelly, I did not invite her into this room. In fact, I'm not sure how the hell she got in."

"It's not really my business although you both being undressed was…convenient. Her timing is very good."

She glanced around the room, as though looking for a secret portal that would transport her magically far away from this place.

"Kelly?"

She tilted her head and her eyes found his. "I believe you, Jace. But Lena was right. I appreciate the glimpse into Hollywood's inner circles, but if it's all the same, I think I'd better stick with the small-town country bumpkins. Your ranch hands have better manners than most of the people here tonight." She shook her head as if in sad defeat. "There's so much more to life than…this." She attempted a small laugh that fell flat. "Is this usually the way your parties end? A few drinks, slugging it out, then a little bed-hopping with…whoever?"

Jace felt as if his heart had been hit by a meteorite. He'd

probably frightened her so badly that even coming to his room had taken every grain of intestinal fortitude she possessed. But what brought him to his knees was the knowledge almost everything she said was true.

"No, not always. Sometimes the police get involved and jail cells are added to the mix. I'm sorry you had to see what happened downstairs."

Jace didn't know what else to say. There was nothing he *could* say.

And only one thing would make this right with Kelly.

He had to end this. Now. Before he hurt her.

Bile rose in the back of his throat and his entire body tightened. He closed his eyes, dropped his head and grimaced in pure self-disgust.

What an idiot he'd been to even think of a future with Kelly. She wouldn't travel the globe with a newborn son. And she wasn't one to stay at home for months at a time waiting for him to return. And even if she was willing, he wouldn't ask that of her.

It would be an understatement to say she wouldn't be comfortable with the droves of media that would surround and follow her. Kelly would not sit back and ignore the ridiculous headlines claiming he'd had yet another affair. It would cause her to relive what her own father had done and the consequences they'd all suffered.

But all that aside, even if he walked away from films, all she would have was the beast inside him and no way of knowing what would set it off. Or when. The same monster she'd gotten only a small glimpse of tonight. It was a no-win scenario.

The very last thing she needed was mistreatment by an abusive man. God, he wanted to be part of her life, to make her, Henry and Matt part of his. He wanted Kelly until his mind and heart threatened to explode and sparks of desperation lit the darkness. But he knew, in this moment, it could never happen. He had no right to pursue her with his father's DNA running rampant through his veins.

"You were right. This is no life for you. It's no life for Henry."

He watched her. It was past time she knew the truth.

He caught her gaze and held it. His nostrils flared with the pain of what he was about to say. "What you saw tonight is who I am."

She stood in the doorway, the overhead lights making her an ethereal vision. He stepped back to the bar and poured another drink. It wouldn't be his last before the sun rose tomorrow.

"Jace? I don't understand."

"I'm trying to tell you I can't stop living this way because of who I am inside. I can't change it." He threw the amber liquid down his throat and turned to face her. "What I do for a living and all that goes with it provides an outlet. An escape from my own sick reality. It lets me drink myself into oblivion—" he held up the glass "—and the media just report a party. It lets me pound somebody—usually a professional but not always, like tonight—and release some of the rage. Makes for good headlines." He gave a false laugh at the ridiculousness of it. "Hell, they even pay me to do it. The travel, the new film locations, memorizing scripts, it keeps me from thinking. From remembering what I am inside. It helps prevent me from doing what you saw me do tonight. It's the only way I have to get through another day.

"I can't offer you the man you want, Kelly. I can't give you forever. I can't provide the home and the life you and Henry need. I can't be the husband you deserve. Ever." He clenched his jaw, determined to make her leave while she could. "I'm not even sure I can love you."

He watched her flinch as though she'd been shot. He stood helplessly as shock, then anguish, played across her fine features. Kelly bravely blinked back the tears that filled her eyes. He'd hurt her deeply, but she would be better off in the long run. Better off without him.

"After spending time with you, getting to really know you, any fool could see…" He clenched his jaw with a force that should have cracked teeth.

"See what, Jace?" Her voice was unsteady, barely a whisper. Her face had lost all of its color.

"That you don't belong here. You don't belong with me."

Kelly was a person who lived life from the heart. She was a woman who would fight to the death to protect her son, who got back on her feet every time life knocked her down, who made a home for her brother when there was no one else and kept his dreams of a future alive even at the cost of her own. A stubborn, tenacious woman who scorned pity and would rather chop off her nose than accept what she though was charity. A beautiful woman who needed to be loved and cherished—not abused. "You were right that first night, Kelly. The night we talked outside your house. I should have left then. I just didn't want to accept the inevitable."

Kelly nodded. She miraculously managed a smile without allowing even one tear to fall even though they filled her eyes, a tribute to her strength.

A brittle stillness filled the space around them, so rigid and taut with emotion the slightest movement would cause it to crack and bring the walls surrounding them tumbling down.

She turned to leave and paused when he said, "I wish things could have been different."

Without turning to face him she opened the door and walked out.

A rage filled Jace. A rage beyond anything he'd ever felt before and all directed inward, at himself. All hope turned to hopelessness. The monster had won. With a silent scream, he hurled the glass across the room into the mirror, shattering it into a million pieces. Like his heart.

* * *

A week later Jace sat in the meeting, wishing he were a thousand miles away. Anywhere would do. He absently twirled a pen in his fingers as producer Doug Hamrick went over the plans for filming his next big-budget blockbuster. Around the expansive conference table sat the director, assistant directors, five other actors, scriptwriters, technical advisers, and the attorneys and agents representing them all. Only Bret Goldman was noticeably absent. Jace had made sure of that, firing him before he'd ever left the ballroom.

Filming would last six to seven months with postproduction another four. The locations were some of the most exotic in the world. Hard as hell to reach, a challenge to film, but the ambiance couldn't be beat.

In front of Jace on the shiny mahogany table was the contract awarding him the leading role. It would afford him the opportunity for another best actor nomination along with the possibility of best picture of the year.

The mood in the room was jovial, the excitement and anticipation obvious in the faces of everyone who sat around the table. But as Jace idly listened to the questions and answers, his thoughts were of Kelly. Seven months was a long time to be away. It had never seemed so long before. But what in the hell else did he have to do? Kelly and his mom had flown back to Texas the day after the ball. He'd stayed over in LA for this meeting, hiding out at his house in Malibu, wondering how long Kelly would stay at the ranch.

The rolling surf that used to calm him couldn't touch the panic and utter devastation that festered inside. His mind scrambled to find a solution—*any* solution—that could keep Kelly in his life. But the same scenario bumped along, around and around, like a flat tire on a car going downhill, preventing him from catching a glimpse of hope.

He remembered the first time he ever saw Kelly, arguing with the guy in the feed store over the cost of a bag of oats. She'd won. No surprise there. Jace had carried the horse feed out to her truck, determined to find out her name and get a phone number before she disappeared. He remembered how her face radiated tenderness and natural beauty in the glow of the little candle on the table in the café later that evening.

Days later, when he'd taken her to the small motel, he'd immediately realized her inexperience. He'd been determined to show her what making love was really about, and that night would go down in the history books. She'd stripped him of every ounce of control he could find and made him wish for a lot more. She was so damn sexy yet so innocent in the ways of the world, so trusting of him, so eager to please. He was left speechless, shaken to his core and totally and completely enthralled.

And by the next morning, using a condom never entered his mind.

He'd asked her to dinner the following night. Partly to ensure she was okay and partly because she was so damned amazing he had to prove to himself she was for real. She accepted. And that night, after they'd eaten, he had taken her straight home to her grandfather's ranch even though it was the last thing he wanted to do.

Later that night, he'd been awakened by a light tapping on his guest cabin door. He'd opened it to find Kelly standing on the other side. Neither said a word. Both knew why she was there. The attraction worked both ways; one was not whole without the other. He pulled her into his arms and they didn't leave the hotel room for the next three days.

Later he'd secured the loan of two horses and together they roamed the hills and valleys of north Texas. They'd talked and laughed the day away, her naturally golden curls falling loose from the old brown hat she'd plopped on her head. They'd splashed in a pond surrounded by grass and cattails, fed each other olives they'd found tucked in one of the saddle bags, and made love under the shade of a willow tree on an old red blanket cushioned by thick native grasses. The memories were permanently etched in his mind.

It was in those moments when time hung suspended and his crazy world faded to nothing that he'd fallen in love with Kelly Michaels.

Kelly's charm went beyond physical beauty. It was the sparkle in her eyes when she laughed. It was in the way she held their son with such love and tenderness. It was the praise she heaped on her brother, always keeping alive the promise of a bright future. It was the soft, melodic sound of her voice and her inner strength and fortitude. It was the sparks that shot from her eyes when she was angry. Her intelligence and quick wit that kept Jace on his toes. She made him glad to be alive. No one else had ever done that.

His entire life had been built around the fear that he would become like his father. Despite his lifelong determination to remain detached, Kelly had found a way into his heart. She'd given him a child. A son. And he was still totally and completely in love with the mother of that child. But the reason they were not together—and never could be together—hadn't changed.

The vibration of his cell phone jerked him out of his reflections. Looking at the screen, he saw it was his mother. His mom knew he had this meeting. She wouldn't call unless it was important.

Jace excused himself from the conference room and stepped outside into the hall.

"Mom?"

"Jason." He could hear the quiet anguish in that one word. He had his answer. "Kelly's gone."

It was dark by the time Jace walked into the house. His mom was sitting at the kitchen bar, a cup of coffee in one hand, a well-used tissue in the other. Her eyes red-rimmed, her nose pink from crying.

"When did she leave?"

"Around three." His mother's voice was hoarse from the many tears she'd shed.

"Do you know where she went?"

"She went back to her house." Mona shook her head. "She promised she would stay in touch."

Jace could only nod. He'd pursued her. He'd taken advantage of her feelings for him and taken her to his bed all the while knowing he could give her no promises. Then he'd figuratively slapped her in the face, possibly broken her heart and stood three feet away, presenting the appearance of a cold unfeeling bastard, while she crumbled and bravely tried to hold on to her emotions, her self-respect. It was because of him and the son of a bitch who fathered him that she was gone now. He'd wanted her to walk away, to hate him if it helped her, and never look back.

He'd done his job well.

He walked to the bar, grabbed a bottle of whiskey, then proceeded to his office where he closed and locked the door. He'd drink a toast to the old man. Hell, why not?

He'd become just like him.

Sixteen

Jace entered the house, needing more coffee. His mother joined him in the kitchen. He knew she was worried. About him. About Kelly. About the situation. He looked like something dredged up from the pits of hell. Bloodshot eyes. Beard stubble. Maybe a little weight loss as well, but he didn't give a damn.

"Jason, talk to me."

He shrugged. "About what?"

"It's been over a month since Kelly left. Maybe it's time you talked to her."

"Let it go, Mom." He poured the fresh coffee into his mug.

She shook her head in frustration. "Jason—"

"Just drop it, okay? It's over. It's done. It's too late to go back. And I don't want to talk about it."

Jace had done what he'd had to do when he made Kelly leave. Out of respect he'd eventually have to give his mom some kind of explanation, but it wasn't going to happen today.

"Nothing is ever too late, Jason," she said softly. "Not as long as your heart is still beating."

With a polite nod, Jace stepped around her and headed back to the barn. The anguish of losing Kelly never let up. The pain had become a permanent extension of his body and mind. And always, with every breath, he questioned if he'd done the right thing. He'd finally stopped telling himself to let it go. He couldn't. He knew he never would.

The what-ifs plagued him. Night and day. What if his

love for her was enough to quiet the beast? In normal circumstances Kelly made happiness swell inside him. Even when those turquoise eyes shot bolts of fire in his direction because of something stupid he'd said, he felt the love for her that went to the marrow.

What if he'd done the wrong thing? What if they *could* have a life together? What if ten years from now it became apparent he'd thrown away something special for no good reason, something he would never find again? It was making him crazy.

Dammit to hell. During the day he barked at every hand on the ranch, throwing out threats that had them scrambling, the frustration and internal anger refusing to be contained. Two men had already quit. There would be more if he didn't get a handle on this. But he couldn't make himself give a damn. At night, he lay staring into the darkness. Only then did he let himself imagine going to her, holding her. Only then in the obscurity of a dream did he feel alive.

Shouts broke the silence. Glancing ahead, just outside the corral, his ranch hands circled two of their fellow cowboys who appeared determined to take each other out one punch at a time. Their faces were red, their anger obvious. These were not stuntmen rehearsing a future scene. These were men he employed, and he would not tolerate this kind of behavior.

Gritting his teeth, Jace hurried forward. The foreman stood steps away from the brawling men. "Somebody grab Decker. I'll get Colby."

Jace never slowed his stride. Before anyone moved forward per Sam's orders, Jace walked between the two men, grabbing one by the arm, slinging him to the ground. The other suffered a similar fate.

Jace continued to stand between them. "What in the hell is going on?" This was all he needed. The whole damn world was falling apart. "You have less than two seconds to explain or you're both out of here." His gaze shot from one to the other. The cowboys not involved in the fight stood quietly, waiting to see what Jace would do.

One of the men rubbed at the trickle of blood under his nose with the back of his hand. "He's been making passes at my wife."

Jace could hear the fury, the pain in the man's voice. "Is that true, Decker?"

Decker glared. "So what if I have? It wasn't like she gave me the cold shoulder."

"You son of a bitch," Colby growled and went for Decker again. Jace quickly halted his forward motion.

"That's it, Decker. Get your stuff and get off my property. Sam will tag along just to make sure you find your way." Jace turned his attention back to Colby, who still struggled to get free of Jace's hold. "Colby, let it go." He called to a couple of the cowboys. "Take him and stay with him until he cools off."

As the men hurried to follow his orders, Jace rubbed the back of his neck. Had everyone gone crazy? He had to sympathize. He knew exactly what Colby was feeling. Maybe his wife egged him on. Maybe she didn't. But Colby had a right to defend what was his. Normally a decent, hardworking man, he'd let his love for his wife blind him to everything but the need to protect her.

The breath died in Jace's throat. Is that what he'd been doing when he took out Bret? The epiphany almost blinded him. Why in the hell hadn't he seen it before? He hadn't lost himself in a mindless fit of rage. He'd done what he needed to do to stop Bret from hurting Kelly. To protect the woman he loved. There was a difference. A big difference.

Stunned from the belated realization, Jace was equally elated and afraid.

Had the realization come too late?

The television blared with the intended purpose of ensuring Kelly didn't have a chance to think. It wasn't working.

Regardless of what she did to try to keep her mind from dwelling on Jace, nothing worked. She grabbed the remote and switched it off.

Returning to the kitchen, she turned on the oven and finished stirring the homemade dressing. It was her offering to Gerri's family for her mother's birthday.

The last thing Kelly wanted was to be around people but Gerri insisted she was part of the family and refused to take no for an answer. Kelly had finally given in to her friend since second grade. It seemed the least she could do to repay Gerri for her many kindnesses and concern since Kelly left the ranch.

Gerri had asked if she could take the baby, reminding her how much her mother wanted to see him. When Gerri's brother stopped to pick her up, Kelly agreed, saying she would finish the dressing and follow in Gerri's car. At least that was the plan.

She spooned the mix into the baking pan, shoved it into the oven and set the timer. After washing the bowl and utensils, she ventured into the small living room and plopped down on a chair. Tomorrow she would call Mona. She wanted to hear her voice. She needed to hear Jace's voice, too, and feel his arms around her, but that was not going to happen. Ever.

Picking up a magazine, she idly paged through it. If she dwelled one more second on Jace she would go crazy. She didn't want to go to Gerri's mother's birthday party with her eyes red and puffy. Since that night at the hotel in LA, she couldn't seem to stop crying. Trying to make sense out of what had happened left her even more confused. The pain never ended.

The timer on the oven began to ding. She pushed herself out of the chair and walked to the kitchen and removed the dressing from the oven before turning it off. What had made Jace go from a person who had worked to rebuild her trust and made her think he loved her to suddenly assuring her she didn't belong in his life? Apparently she was good enough while they were isolated at the ranch but not good enough to fit into his life in Hollywood. She'd known she didn't belong, but he'd insisted she was wrong. Why? Why had he even bothered? She had so many questions that would never be answered.

A knock on the apartment door broke into her thoughts. Frowning, she walked back to the living room. She opened the door and the shock that hit her was like the blow of a baseball bat to the solar plexus.

Jace stood on the doorstep. He wasn't smiling. His green eyes carried a haunted look, as though he wasn't sure he should be here. But his clenched jaw established his determination; he wasn't going anywhere. "Can we talk?"

Her mind tried to grasp the realization he was here. "I think you've already said everything there is to say."

"No, I haven't. Will you invite me in? Or are we going to argue out on the sidewalk?"

"*I'm* not going to argue at all."

"That might be a first." His attempt at humor fell flat. He forced a smile that didn't reach his eyes.

Glaring, she turned away but left the door open. If he wanted to come in she wouldn't try to stop him, but she wasn't going to invite him. Her heart pounded so hard it was difficult to breathe.

Why is he here?

Kelly moved to the center of the room, wrapping her arms tightly around herself in an effort to control the storm of emotions raging through her. She wanted him to go. She wanted to put her arms around him and never let him go. His presence caused the blood to race through her veins while her mouth went dry and tears stung the back of her eyes. She'd been an emotional wreck for weeks. She couldn't sleep. She didn't want food. She only wanted to scream and pound on his chest and demand that he explain *why*. Now was her chance and she couldn't look at him. She was down two strikes and already out. She couldn't survive a third.

Jace stood in front of her as though waiting for something. Finally she glanced at him. He held her gaze and didn't let go. He bore the same haunted look she saw when she looked in the mirror.

"I just have one question."

"Really? I have about a hundred."

"Do you love me, Kelly?"

"What?" By her reaction, he clearly knew she thought he was crazy.

"If I had a regular job, say…as a ranch hand. Would you give me a second chance?"

She struggled to hold back the tears. She loved him with all of her heart. But what was the point of these questions? "You're not a ranch hand. I think we've sufficiently cleared up that little misunderstanding."

He stepped up to her. "Are you in love with me?" He repeated the question, his voice a rough demand. "After what I did…is it even possible?"

It was hard to answer a pointless question.

"Kelly?"

"What's the reason for this, Jace? Did you come all this way, go to all this trouble just to catch me off guard and knock me down again?" She was furious. She hated him. She loved him. "I don't get it. I really don't. Is this what you do? You just play with people? Play with their emotions?"

"I guess I'll take that as a no."

"What in the hell do you expect me to say? You…you made it clear you couldn't love me. You said I didn't belong in your life. I'm not good enough and I never will be. At least for once you were honest."

"That's not what I meant," he bellowed. He was getting angry. *Well, bring it on, babycakes.* He had a long way to go to equal what she was feeling.

"Then a month later you show up here, asking if I love

you? You're a jackass, Compton. Worse, you're…you're… deranged."

"I guess that really is a no." He nodded his acceptance and turned to leave.

"Most of the attendees at Mona's ball would say the answer to your question is a resounding no. I don't love you. Apparently, I got my hooks in deep enough to haul in some big bucks without letting my heart get involved."

He spun around and gripped her shoulders. "Kelly, do you love me?"

She could sense he wanted to shake her, but he merely held her instead.

"Are you in love with me?" This time his voice was soft, almost a plea.

"Yes." It was only a whisper, the best she could do, but he heard her. "Are you happy now? What…did this win some kind of bet? Do I get an award for the biggest fool of the year?"

At her confession, he closed his eyes and seemed to relax. "Thank God."

"Why?"

"Because I'm in love with you."

"Oh, please."

"You're the only woman I've ever said that to. I've never been in love before, Kelly."

"Jace…" She shook her head. "You're not in love now. I appreciate the sentiments, I guess. But this is not love. Let me clue you in. Treating someone like you treated me in LA is not love. Not even close."

He took a deep breath and blew it out, his hand wiping the lower portion of his face.

"I said some really stupid things, but for a good reason. I was trying to protect you that night at the hotel."

"Do I honestly have to tell you how ridiculous you sound?"

"My own father was bad news, Kelly. He was in and out of prison most of my life. And he was a mean son of a bitch.

He beat Mom. She left him so many times, she had him arrested, tried to find a place we could hide. But he found us. And it was bad. She fought back, but he was so much bigger than she was. When I tried to stop it, he turned on me. I was twelve when he broke my jaw. Thirteen when he busted six ribs. He didn't give a damn. He just wanted those around him to hurt as much as he did. To pay for his mistakes. He screwed up his life and he wasn't man enough to admit it."

Jace let out a breath. "I've lived with the very real possibility that someday I'll become just like him. It's in my genes. I didn't want you or Henry anywhere around when that day came. I was afraid if you loved me, if I didn't make you leave, you'd stay."

She frowned. He was serious. "You will never be like that, Jace."

"In the past month, I finally realized it came down to a choice. Beg you to stay in my life and run the risk I might someday become...abusive. Or go on with my life as it has been—empty, lonely, wanting the things most men take for granted. I'm a selfish bastard, Kelly. I need you. I can't live the rest of my life knowing I gave up the best thing that ever came into it. And if you'll give me a chance, I'll fight with every breath I take each and every day to keep the monster at bay. I will not hurt you, Kelly. Ever."

His eyes beseeched her. "Come back to the ranch with me. Marry me. Marry me for no reason other than I want you to be my wife. Because I love you."

Kelly didn't know how to take all this in. Was he telling her the truth? Did he actually believe he would hurt her?

"I've quit acting, Kelly," he said. "I never signed the contract for the new film. I walked out. It took me a while to get it through my thick head and understand what you were saying. You and Henry are so much more important than making films."

She looked up into his eyes and the tears brimmed in hers. She clamped her hand over her mouth. *What had she done?* "Jace, no. No. I didn't have the right to demand you change your life if you wanted to be part of Henry's. Oh God. That was wrong. You're leaving your career, what you love, for the wrong reason. Eventually you'll hate me for it. Don't you see? Don't do it, Jace. You can see your son whenever you want. Please don't pity me and think giving up your career will make anything right."

A look of dark humor settled into his handsome features. "*Pity?* You are the most stubborn, hardheaded female I have ever run across in my life. Where in the hell do you get these crazy ideas? I don't pity you, Kelly. I respect the hell out of you. What...you think I would pity you for making a home for Matt and Henry by working your ass off when you had no one else? You think I pity you for coming to the ranch even though you hated me, because it was a safer place for Henry? Take pity out of your vocabulary because there is no pity. Not for you. But there is respect. A lot of respect.

"I gave up the film career because I'm tired of it." Jace watched her closely, as though she might bolt and run. "I'm tired of the travel, the media circus, keeping up appearances, the lies...all of it. You were right when you said there was so much more to life. If I had any doubts I needed to get out, those were wiped clean the night of Mom's charity event. I saw everything, the people, the bullshit, all of it through your eyes. When Bret attacked you... When you walked into my room and saw Lena. I never want to relive any of that again."

"I knew you were telling the truth about Lena. I told you I believed you. As far as that creep, that wasn't cruelty, Jace. It wasn't a monster inside you. You were protecting me." She reached out to him. "I've never had anyone... No one has ever done that for me."

"Kelly, I want a home and a family." He pulled her closer. "I want to raise horses. And all of it has to include you. It's the reason I bought that ranch."

"What?"

"I could have purchased land anywhere. But you were here." Jace reached out and touched her face. "Be my wife, Kelly. Be the mother of my children. You showed me how good life could be. Don't take that dream away. Please give us another chance."

He was an award-winning actor. But she knew he spoke from his heart. She closed her eyes, the reality almost too much to take in. The only man she'd ever loved was offering her more than she'd ever dared to dream.

"If you love me, we can make this work. I haven't been with another woman since Henry was conceived. I just... there was no one... I don't *want* anyone else, Kelly, and I've had a year to think about that. I can't change what your father did, but I'm not him. I can never undo all you've been through because of me. All I can do is promise, if you'll have me, I'll spend the rest of my life making the rest of your life as good as I possibly can."

His hand went under her chin, gently raising her lips to his. In that moment, she gave him her heart, her trust, her love, returning his kiss with everything she had.

"I love you, Jace." She fell into his arms and the tears of joy fell down her face. He kissed her deeply, passionately, letting his hunger for her free, holding her tightly as though he would never let her go, as though he couldn't get close enough. And Kelly kissed him back with every ounce of love she had for this incredible, amazing, complex man. Her hands slipped up his chest.

"You're still a moron," she whispered against his lips.

"What?"

"What in the hell took you so long?"

He laughed. "Woman, you make me crazy." Then all humor left his voice and was replaced with earnest desperation. "Marry me. Now. Today. As soon as we can arrange it. Say yes. I need to wake up next to you every morning. Make love to you every night. I want a family. I want kids. I hope you do."

She chewed her lower lip as she enthusiastically nodded in agreement. He cupped her face in his hands. "There is nothing I want more than to make you pregnant again." His deep voice made her shiver. "But this time I want to look into those amazing blue eyes when we conceive our next child. I want to know the instant it happens. I want to know you see the love in my face. But you're going to have a ring on your finger when I do."

"Jace... Yes. I love y—"

Jace's mouth covered hers, with a passion she hoped would last forever. No longer would she have to gaze up at the night sky. She had found her star, and in his arms was exactly where she needed to be.

* * * * *

NEWBORN ON
HER DOORSTEP

ELLIE DARKINS

For Rosie and Lucy

CHAPTER ONE

LILY TUCKED HER pencil behind her ear as she headed for the door. She almost had this website design finished, with a whole day to go before the client's deadline. She was privately amazed that she'd managed to get the thing done on time, given the chaos in her house. Even now she could hear chisels and hammers and God knew what else in her kitchen, as the builders ripped out the old units ready for work on the extension to start.

The ring of the doorbell had been welcome, actually. When she'd glanced at her watch she'd realised that she'd not taken a break since settling down in her home office at six. She was overdue a cup of coffee—and no doubt the builders would appreciate one, too.

A glance through the hallway window afforded a glimpse of a taxi heading up the road, but she couldn't see anyone waiting behind the frosted glass of the front door. Strange… she thought as she turned the key and pulled the door open.

No one there.

Kids? she wondered, but she'd lived in this house almost all of her life, and she couldn't remember a single case of knock-door-run.

She was just about to shut the door and head back inside when a kitten-like mewl caught her attention and she glanced down.

Not a kitten.

A Moses basket was tucked into the corner of the porch, out of the spring breeze. Wrapped tight inside, with just eyes and the tip of a soft pink nose showing from the yellow blanket... A baby.

Lily dropped to her knees out of instinct, and scooped the baby up from the floor, nestling her against her shoulder. Making sure the blanket was tucked tight, she walked down to the front gate, looking left and right for any sign of someone who might have just left a baby on her doorstep.

Nothing.

She moved the baby into the crook of her arm as she tried to think, her brain struggling to catch up with this sudden appearance. And as she moved the baby she heard a papery crackle. When she pulled the corner of the blanket aside she found a scribbled note on a page torn from a notebook. The writing was as familiar as her own, and unmistakable.

Please look after her.

Which left all the questions she already had unanswered and asked a million more.

She walked again to the gate, wondering if she could still catch sight of that taxi—if she had time to run and stop her half-sister before she did something irreversible. But as much as she strained her eyes, the car was gone.

She stood paralysed with shock for a moment on

the front path, unsure whether to run for help or to take the baby inside. What sort of trouble would her half-sister have to be in to do this? Was she leaving her here forever? Or was she going to turn up in a few minutes and explain?

For the first time Lily took a deep breath, looked down into the clear blue eyes of her little niece—and fell instantly in love.

His feet pounded the footpath hard, driving out thought, emotion, reason. All he knew was the rhythm of his shoes on the ground, the steady in-out of his breath as he let his legs and his lungs settle in to their pace.

The sun was drying the dew on the grassy verges by the road, and the last few commuters were making their way into the tube station. The morning commute was a small price to pay to live in this quiet, leafy part of London, he guessed.

He noted these things objectively, as he did the admiring looks from a couple of women he passed. But none of it mattered to him. This was the one time of the day when he could just concentrate on something he was completely in control of. So, no music, no stopping for admiring glances—just him and the road. Nothing could spoil the hour he spent shutting out the horrors of the world—great and small—that he had encountered in his work over the years.

Tomorrow he'd be able to find a solitary path through the Richmond Park, but this morning he was dodging café tables and pedestrians as he watched the street names, looking out for the address his sister had texted to him. She'd been taking furniture deliveries for him before he flew home, and had left the keys to his new place with a friend of hers who worked from home.

He turned the corner into a quiet side street, and suddenly the fierce cry of a newborn baby ahead skewed his consciousness and he stumbled, his toe somehow finding a crack in the footpath.

He tried to keep running for a few strides, to ignore the sound, but found it was impossible. Instead he concentrated on counting the house numbers—anything to keep his mind off the wailing infant. But as the numbers climbed he felt a sense of growing inevitability. The closer he drew to the sound of the baby, the more he wished that he could get away—and the more certain he became that he wouldn't be able to.

The rhythm and focus that had always come as easily as breathing when he pulled on his running shoes was gone. His body fought him, sending awareness of the baby to his ears. Another side street loomed on his left, and for a moment he willed himself to turn away, to *run* away, but his feet wouldn't obey. Instead they picked up their pace and carried straight on, towards a dazed-looking woman and the wailing baby standing in the porch of one of the houses ahead.

He glanced at the house number and knew that he'd been right. His sister had sent him to a house with a baby—without a word of warning.

'Hi,' he said to the woman, approaching and speaking with caution. Lily, he thought her name was. 'Is everything okay?' He couldn't help but ask—not when she was standing there with a distressed baby and looking as if she'd just been thunderstruck.

Her blonde hair was pulled back into a loose ponytail so shiny that he could almost feel the warmth of the sunlight reflecting off it. Her eyes were blue, clear and wide—but filled with a shock and a panic that stopped him short.

She stared at him blankly and he held out his hands in a show of innocence. 'I'm Nic,' he said, realising she had no idea who he was. 'Dominic—Kate's brother. She said to drop by and pick up my keys?'

'Oh, God,' she said. 'I'd completely forgotten.'

But still she didn't move. Her eyes did, though, dropping to his vest and running shorts, moving as far down as his ankles before her eyes met his again. There was interest there, he could see, even behind her confusion and distress.

'Is everything all right?' he asked again, though everything about her—her posture, her expression—told him that it wasn't.

'Oh, fine,' she said.

He could see the effort it took to pull the muscles of her face into a brave smile, but it wasn't enough to cover the undercurrents of worry that lay beneath. There was something about that contrast that made him curious—more than curious—to know the layers of this woman.

'*My* sister...' she said, boldly attempting nonchalance. 'She never gives me much notice when she needs a babysitter.'

Which was about five per cent of the truth, if he had to guess. He found himself looking deep into her eyes, trying to see her truths, all the things that she wasn't saying. Was there some sort of trick here? Was this something Kate had set up? Surely she'd never be so cruel, never willingly expose him to so much pain?

But he wanted to know more about this woman, he acknowledged. Wanted to untangle her mysteries.

Then he could ignore the screams of the baby no longer, and knew that he mustn't even think it. He should turn and walk away from her and the little bundle of trouble now. Before he got drawn in, before wounds that had taken a decade to become numb were reopened.

But he couldn't, *wouldn't* walk away from someone so obviously in trouble. Couldn't abandon a child, however much it might hurt him. He'd discovered that on his first trip to India, when he'd seen children used as slave labour, making clothes to be sold on British high streets. He'd not been able to leave without doing *something*, without working to improve the shattered lives that he'd witnessed.

Now, ten years later, the charity he'd founded had helped hundreds, thousands of children from exploitation or worse. But that didn't make him any more able to ignore this single child's cries.

Distressed children needed help—whoever they were, wherever they were living. He finally forced himself to look at the crying baby—and felt the bottom fall out of all his worries. He was in serious trouble, and any thoughts of walking away became an impossibility. That was a newborn baby…as in hours-old new. Completely helpless, completely vulnerable and—by the look on Lily's face—a complete surprise.

The baby's crying picked up another notch and Lily bounced it optimistically. But, if he had to guess, she didn't have what that baby needed.

'Did your sister leave some milk? Or some formula?'

She looked up and held his gaze, her eyes still a complicated screen of half-truths. There was something dangerously attractive in that expression, something drawing him in against his better judgement. There was a bond growing between himself and Lily—he could feel it. And some connection with this baby's story was at the heart of it. It was dangerous, and he wanted nothing to do with it, but still he didn't walk away.

'She asked me to pick some up,' she replied, obviously thinking on her feet. 'Thanks for stopping, but I have to get to the shop.'

He chose his next words carefully, knowing that he mustn't scare her off, but seeing by the shocked look on her face that she hadn't quite grasped yet the trouble that this newborn baby might be in. Who left an hours-old baby with a relative who clearly wasn't expecting her? There was more, much more, to this story, and he suspected that there were layers of complications that neither of them yet understood.

'That's quite a noise she's making. How about to be on the safe side we get her checked by a doctor? I saw that the hospital round the corner has a walk-in clinic.'

At that, Lily physically shook herself, pulled her shoulders back and grabbed the baby a little tighter. There was something about seeing the obvious concern and turmoil in her expression that made him want to wrap his arms around her and promise her that everything would be okay. But he was the last person on earth who could promise her that, who could even believe that it might be true.

'Maybe you're right,' she said, walking away from the open front door and through the garden gate.

'Kate's keys are in the top drawer in the hall. Can you pull the door closed on your way out?'

And then she was speed-walking down the street, the baby still clutched tightly to her, still wailing. He glanced at the house and hesitated. He needed his keys, but he could hardly leave Lily's house with the door wide open—the woman hadn't even picked up her handbag. Did she have her own keys? Her wallet? So he had no choice but to grab her bag and his keys and jog in the direction of those newborn wails.

He just wanted to be sure that the baby was going to be okay, he told himself.

'I'll walk with you,' he said as he caught Lily up.

The words were out of his mouth before he had a chance to stop them. However much he might wish he hadn't stumbled on this little family drama, he had. He might be wrong, but gut instinct and not a little circumstantial evidence told him that this child had just been abandoned—which meant, of course, that both mother and baby could be in danger.

He tried to focus on practicalities, tried to put thoughts of what might have been had he and Lily met on any other sunny day out of his mind. He should call Kate. And maybe the police—they were the best people to ensure that the baby's mother was safe and well. But he couldn't ignore the fascination that he felt about Lily. There was an energy that seemed to pull him towards her and push him away at the same time—it had him curious, had him interested.

CHAPTER TWO

LILY EYED NIC, where he leaned against the wall by the door—a position he'd adopted almost as soon as they'd been shown into this room. He looked at the door often, as if reminding himself that it was there. That he could use it any time. So why was he still here?

Under normal circumstances she'd say that an attractive man, background-checked by her BFF, somewhat scantily clad, could involve himself in her life at any time he chose—as long as she had the option of checking out those long, lean thighs. But he really had killer timing.

She didn't have time to ogle; she didn't have time for his prying questions. All she could think about was her sister, Helen, and the baby, and what she needed to do to take care of both of them.

She paced the room, glancing over at the baby and wondering what on earth they were doing to her. Had they found something wrong? If everything was okay, surely someone would have told her by now. She hadn't wanted to hand her over to the doctors, but she'd had no choice.

It was becoming a pattern, this letting go, this watching from afar. She'd lost her father before she was born, to nothing more dramatic than disinterest and a lost phone number. Her mother had died the year that Lily had turned thirteen, and it seemed her sister had been drifting further and further from her since that day. All she wanted was a family to take care of, to take care of her, and yet that seemed too much to ask from the universe.

And now someone had called the police, and her sister was going to be in more trouble than ever, pushed further from her. She tried not to think of the alternative. Of Helen out there needing help and not getting it. If it took the authorities getting involved to get her safe and well, then Lily was all for it.

She started pacing again, craning her neck each time she passed the baby to try and get a glimpse of what was happening.

'Just a couple of tests,' the doctor had said. How could that possibly take this long?

She glanced across at Nic, and then quickly away. How had she never met Kate's brother before? Surely there should be some sort of declaration when you became best friends with someone about any seriously attractive siblings. He'd been abroad, she remembered Kate saying. He ran a charity that tried to improve conditions for child workers in factories in the developing world. He'd recently been headhunted by one of the big retailers that he'd campaigned against, and would be sitting on their board, in charge of cleaning up their supply chain. So attractive, humanitarian, and with a job in retail. There should definitely be a disclaimer for this sort of thing.

But there was something about him that made her nervous—some tension in his body and his voice that told her this man had secrets too: secrets that she couldn't understand. It was telling her to stay away. That he was off-limits. A warning she didn't need.

Nic came to stand beside her. 'Try not to worry. I'm sure that everything is fine—they're just being thorough.'

Lily bit her lip and nodded. She knew that he was right. He gestured her back to a seat and cleared his throat, giving her a rare direct look.

She continued pacing the room, waiting for news—until she heard a shriek, and then she was by the bed, her arms out, already reaching for the baby.

The doctor barely looked up from where he was pricking the little one's heel with a needle.

'I'm sorry, we're not quite done.'

'You're hurting her!'

Lily scooped the baby into her arms as she wiped away the spot of blood from her foot and cooed soothing noises, gently rocking her. Back in Lily's embrace, the baby stopped crying and nuzzled closer. Lily leaned over, instinctively shielding the baby from the doctor who had hurt her, until she felt the little body relax. She kissed the baby's forehead, leaving her own face close for a moment, breathing in her baby smell. Once she was satisfied that she was calmed she looked up at the doctor, and instantly stiffened her resolve at the look of disapproval on his face.

'I'm her aunt,' she stated, as if that were explanation enough for everything. 'Have you finished with the tests? It looks as if she's had enough for now.'

She stared him down until he conceded that they had everything they needed. That was when she spotted Nic, looking grey and decidedly ill by the door.

'When she cried out…' he said. 'I thought…'

Whatever he had thought had scared him witless, she realised, instinctively taking a step towards him.

'She's fine. We're fine,' she told him, in the same soothing tone she'd used with the baby. She turned her towards him. 'Look, she's settled now.'

He breathed a sigh of relief and Lily could almost see the adrenaline leaching from his body, leaving him limp and drawn. She met his eyes, looking for answers there, but instead saw only pain. An old pain, she guessed, one that had been lived with a long time and had become so familiar it was hardly noticed. Until something happened—a baby screamed—and it felt like new again.

For a moment she wished that she could soothe him as easily as she had the baby—smooth those creases from his face and the pain from his body. But something told her that taking this man in her arms would bring him anything but peace. She pressed herself back against the wall, trying to put whatever space she could between them.

'Is everything okay?' she asked.

'Fine.'

Nic's reply was terse, sharper than she'd expected, and she saw the fear and hurt in his expression being carefully shut down, stowed away.

'I need to grab a cup of coffee. Do you want to find the canteen? We've been here for hours.'

And leave the baby alone with strangers? 'I'm fine, thanks. I don't want to leave her.'

He gave her a shrewd look. 'I'll go, then,' he said, pushing himself away from the wall.

He looked better now, as he had in her front garden, all bronzed skin and taut muscles. No sign now of the man who had looked as if he might slide down the wall from fear.

When he returned with coffee and cake his manner was brisk and his eyes guarded. *Good,* Lily thought. *Guarded is good. If we're both being careful, both backing away slowly from whatever this energy between us is, then we're safe.*

'I've got to go,' he said. 'I promised that I'd meet Kate and she's not answering her phone so I can't cancel. I don't want to leave her stranded.'

And then he was off—out of their lives, and no doubt relieved to be so. She held in her heavy sigh until he'd slipped out of the door with her polite words of thanks.

CHAPTER THREE

KATE BURST THROUGH the door of the treatment room, wearing her air of drama queen as if it was this season's must-have.

Lily smiled at the arrival of her best friend. If anyone was going to help her make sense of this situation it would be Kate, with her remarkable ability to see through half-truths and get straight to the point.

'So I get back from court and pop in to see my brother in his new flat, and he's got this crazy story about your dear sister and a baby and a hospital. I didn't have a clue what was going on, so I thought I'd better get down here and find out just what he's talking about. Explain, Lily! Where's this flippin' baby come from? What are you doing here? And why does my brother look so cagey whenever I mention your name?'

Lily couldn't help but laugh—trust Kate to boil this down to the bare essentials.

'She's Helen's baby. Helen left her on my doorstep with a note. Your brother was passing by to pick up his keys and…and kept us company while we were waiting here.'

It was rare that she saw Kate lost for words, but she dropped into a chair now, silent, and Lily could practically see the thoughts being processed behind her eyes. Her barrister's brain was reading all the evidence, everything that Lily was saying, and everything she wasn't.

'Okay, give it to me again. And this time with details.'

Lily sighed and took a breath, wondering how many times she would have to repeat everything that had happened. But when she came to talking about Nic her words stumbled and faltered.

'Nic turned up to collect his keys just as I'd been left literally holding the baby and was freaking out. He suggested we walk over here and have her checked out.'

'And then he waited with you? How long for?'

Lily glanced at her watch. 'A couple of hours, I guess.'

Kate blew out a deliberate breath, and Lily raised her eyebrows.

'What?'

'Nothing...nothing,' Kate said, but Lily had known her long enough to know that she was hiding something.

'Not nothing,' she told her best friend. 'Definitely *something*.'

Kate looked at her for a long time before she replied.

'Something,' she agreed, nodding, her eyes sad. 'But not my something to tell. Can we leave it at that?'

Lily nodded. Though she was intrigued, her friend's rare sombre tone had pulled her up short and warned her to stop digging.

'So you and my brother, then...?'

'It's not like that.' The denial came to Lily's lips as soon as she realised what Kate was getting at. 'I don't think he wanted to be here at all. He looked like he was going to bolt the whole time.'

'So why didn't he?'

True to form, Kate had hit on the one question that Lily had been searching for an answer to—to no avail.

'I've no idea.'

'I've got one or two,' Kate said with a sly grin. 'So what happens with the baby now?'

Another question Lily had no answer to.

No doubt between the hospital staff and the police someone would be arranging for a social worker to visit her. But she had no intention of letting her niece be looked after by anyone but herself. She knew that she could look after her—she already ran a business from home, and had flexibility in her hours and her work. It was one of the things that she enjoyed most about her job as a freelance web designer—the chance to balance work and home life. She'd manage her work commitments around caring for the baby—whatever it took to keep the little girl safe and with her family.

'She's coming home with me.'

Lily gulped at the baldness of that statement, and backtracked.

'Until we can find Helen.'

'Right. And then you're going to hand her over to a woman who's been living God-knows-where and doing God-knows-what for years?'

'Helen's her mother—'

'And she seems pretty clear about who she wants taking care of her daughter. I'm not saying that taking her home is a bad thing—she's family. Of course you want to look after her. I'm just saying it looks like it might be slightly more commitment than a regular babysitting gig. Are you ready for that?'

Ready for a family? It was what she'd wanted for as long as she could remember. She'd been lucky after her mother had died. She'd been placed with a wonderful foster family who had slowly and gently helped her to come to terms with her grief. She'd certainly been luckier than her sister, who, at sixteen, had decided that she was old enough to look after herself.

They'd exchanged letters and emails, but over the years they'd become less and less frequent, until now she couldn't even rely on a card at Christmas. All she wanted was a family of her own. To recapture something of what the three of them—herself, her mum and Helen—had had before the accident.

She'd even looked into ways to build that family. After her own experience of foster care she'd thought of offering her house to children who might need it.

The old family home had seemed echoey and empty when she'd moved back in when she was eighteen. Her mother's will had protected it in a trust for her and her sister, but it had been lonely with no one to share it with. But she'd never considered she'd ever be handed a newborn baby and asked if she was ready to be a parent.

'We have to find Helen,' Lily said. 'That's as far as I can think right now.'

'There is one slight flaw in that plan,' Kate said.

'Only one?' Lily asked, only half joking.

'Your house. It's currently a building site, and— unless I'm much mistaken—not exactly ready for a newborn…whether she's going to be there permanently or not.'

Lily's face fell. In all the drama she'd somehow managed to forget the chaotic state of her house. There was no way that she could take a baby back there. And if she couldn't take care of her niece that left only one option. Letting social services place her with strangers. Her gut recoiled at the thought of losing another member of her family, of her and Helen and their past being fractured even further.

'Don't look like that,' Kate said. 'This is not insurmountable. We can sort this out—'

'That's really kind,' Lily said, her mind still racing, 'but your place barely has enough room for me to pull out the sofa bed. I'm not sure that—'

'Not *me*!' Kate exclaimed. 'Good God, no. We'd lose the baby under a stack of briefs or something. Nic's place—it's perfect.'

Lily gave a little choke.

'Nic's place? I couldn't possibly impose…'

She couldn't share a flat with that man—not when she felt drawn to him and afraid of that attraction in equal measure. When her skin tingled just from being in the same room as him.

'Honestly, you should see his place. It's ridiculous. A penthouse—overlooking the river, naturally. He told me it was something to do with investing his golden handshake money, and London property prices, and being able to do so much more with the money once he sold up. Personally, I think it might have something to do with sleeping in hostels for the best part of a decade. It's huge, and he's barely ever there.'

Even the thought of a Thameside penthouse couldn't convince her that spending more time with a man who had her wanting him and wanting to run from him was a good idea. But what choice did she have? If she wanted to take care of her niece she couldn't afford to be picky about what help she accepted. And, anyway, what she thought was probably irrelevant...

'Nic would never—'

'Nic will be travelling on and off for the next few months. He's due to fly out again tomorrow, I think. You won't see each other much. And if the man who's preached charity and child welfare at me for the past ten years can't see it in his heart to give an abandoned baby a home for a few months, then I'll disown him.'

Somehow Lily didn't think that was a threat that would carry much weight for Nic.

'*And* trash his lovely new apartment,' she added.

'Okay, ask him,' Lily said eventually. What choice did she have?

An awkward silence fell for a few moments, until Kate obviously couldn't stand the quiet any longer.

'So, does this little one have a name, or what?'

Lily shook her head. 'Helen didn't exactly say.'

'Well, that's just not right, is it? She's had a rough enough start in life already, without ending up being named just Baby Girl. So what are we going to go for: naming her after a pop star or a soap star. Or we could go big and Hollywood?'

Lily raised an eyebrow.

'Okay, so I'm guessing that's a no. What do *you* suggest?'

Lily looked closely at the baby, trying to work out who she was. 'Look at her,' Lily said. 'All pretty and pink and fresh and soft…like a flower. A rose. What about Rosie?'

'I think it's perfect,' Kate agreed. 'Little Rosie—welcome to the world.'

Nic's feet pounded on the pavement as he tried to get thoughts of Lily Baker out of his head—with zero success. Since the moment he'd met her she'd invaded all of his thoughts, forcing him to keep busy, keep working, keep running. But even two days on his body still wouldn't co-operate, refusing to find the quiet place in his mind where he could retreat from the world.

His sister wasn't exactly helping, with her pointed remarks and regular updates on how baby and aunt were faring. Did she think he couldn't see what she was doing? That the strings of her puppeteering were somehow invisible? But he *did* wonder how the baby was. Kate had said that she was doing well, and the doctors hadn't seemed worried when he'd left the hospital, but he knew better than most how precarious a new life was, how quickly it might be lost.

Turning for home, he tried to find his usual rhythm, but his feet carried him faster than he wanted, rushing him.

His mobile rang as he reached his flat, and Kate's latest unsubtle update gave him all he needed to know. No news on the missing sister. Baby apparently doing well in hospital. But somehow it wasn't enough. What did that mean anyway? 'Doing well in hospital.' Surely if the baby was 'doing well' then she wouldn't be in hospital at all. She'd be home, tucked into a cot, safe. And this time Kate had not said anything about Lily.

He hadn't been able to think of a way to ask about

her without raising suspicious eyebrows. He could hardly say, *And how about the aunt? The one with the glowing skin and the complicated expressions and the fierce independence? How's she getting on?*

But he was desperate to know. Lily Baker seemed to have soaked into his mind until his every thought was coloured by her. It was no good. The only way he was going to get this woman and her niece out of his mind was to get some answers, some closure.

He saw her as soon as he walked onto the ward. He should have known that she would have been there all night. Had been there for two nights, he guessed. Her hair was mussed, rubbing up against the side of the chair she'd curled into, but her face was relaxed, looking so different from when she'd worn that troubled, burdened expression before.

He knocked on the door, aware that he didn't want to answer the questions that being caught watching her sleep would give rise to. Lily sat bolt upright at the sound, her hand instinctively reaching for the cot, eyes flying towards the baby. Only once she was satisfied that she was sleeping soundly did she turn towards the door. Her eyes widened in surprise, and he realised how unguarded she was in the moment after waking—how her expression shifted as her eyes skimmed over him appreciatively.

There was no mistaking the interest there, and his stomach tightened in response as he fought down his instinctive reaction. Eventually her eyes reached his, and he saw her barriers start to build as she emerged properly from sleep. Her back straightened and her face grew composed.

The rational, sensible, *thinking* part of his brain

breathed a sigh of relief. He was glad that she was as wary as he was of this energy he felt flowing and sparking between them, the pull that he felt between their bodies. Much as he might find her attractive, he would never act on that. He wasn't the kind of man she needed in her life. When she found someone she'd need a partner—a father for this child and the ones that would come in the future. She would need someone she could rely on, and he knew that he wasn't capable of being that man.

But the part of his brain less removed from his primal ancestors groaned, trying to persuade him to get that dreamy look back on her face, to seduce her into softness.

'Morning,' he said, rather more briskly than he'd intended. 'I brought coffee. I know the stuff here's awful.'

'Morning. Thanks…'

Her voice was as wary as her expression, and he guessed that he wasn't the only one who'd thought that they would never see each other again after he'd left the hospital. He wondered if she'd found it as impossible not to think of him as he had of her. Of course not, he reasoned. She had the baby to think about—there was probably no room in her life right now for anything other than feeding, nappies and sleep.

At the sound of her voice the baby had started to stir, and Lily automatically reached out a hand to stroke her cheek.

'How is she?'

'She's fine…good. They've said that I can take her home today.'

Home. So that settled it, then. Kate had been right

the other day—Lily was going to look after the baby
as her sister had asked. And that meant he'd been right
to fight off this attraction. Because if there was one
thing he was certain of it was that he could never get
involved with someone who had a child. He could never
again open himself up to that sort of hurt.

Even if Lily's sister returned, he couldn't imagine
that Lily saw a future without children. He'd seen the
melting look in her eye as she'd gazed down at her
niece—there was no hiding her maternal instincts.

'That's good. I'm glad she's okay.' Now that he had
his answer he felt awkward, not sure why he had come.
No doubt Lily was wondering what he was doing there,
too. Or perhaps not. Perhaps his real interest was as
transparent to her as it had been opaque to him.

Perhaps he had imagined this energy and attraction—imagined the way her eyes widened whenever
her skin brushed against his, the way she flushed in
those rare moments when they both risked eye contact.
Maybe she saw him as nothing other than the Good
Samaritan who had happened to be there when she'd
needed someone. If only she knew that when someone
else had really needed him, when they'd relied on him
to be there for them, he'd let them down.

He glanced up at the name plate above the crib and
realised that the little girl was no longer Baby Baker.

'Rosie?' he asked, surprise in his voice. Kate hadn't
mentioned that.

'It seemed to suit her,' Lily said with a shrug. 'It's
not official yet. If Helen doesn't like it…'

'It's pretty.'

'Look, I hate to ask this when you're already doing
so much for us…'

Lily glanced at the door and Nic guessed what was coming. Instantly he wished himself anywhere in the world but here. But Lily was still speaking, and he knew that it was too late.

'…just for fifteen minutes or so, while I grab a shower. I know the nurses are listening out for her, but I hate the thought of her being alone. I know I can trust you with her.'

A lump blocked his throat and he couldn't force the word *no* out past it. He'd not been responsible for a child since the morning he'd found his son, cold and still in his crib. But the look on Lily's face—the trust that he saw there—touched his heart in a way he hadn't realised was even still possible. And more than anything he wanted to know that the baby— little Rosie—was going to be okay. That was why he'd dragged himself down here, after all. Fifteen minutes alone with a sleeping baby—surely he could manage that, could ensure that she was safe while Lily was away?

He nodded. 'Sure, go ahead. You look like you could do with a break.'

Her smile held for a moment before her face fell. Oh, God, that wasn't what he'd meant at all. He'd all but said, *You look awful,* hadn't he? What was it about this woman that made it so impossible for him to function anything like normal?

He started back-pedalling fast. 'Sorry, I didn't mean it like that at all. You look fine. I mean—I just meant you've slept in that chair two nights in a row, and I bet you're tired. You look great.'

This wasn't getting any better. But Lily grinned at him, probably enjoying his discomfort, and the fact that he didn't seem at all able to remove his foot from his mouth.

A disconcerting noise and a very bad smell halted Nic's apology in its tracks, and as he caught Lily's eyes they both laughed.

'Well, perhaps if you change her I might find it in my heart to forgive you.'

Before he had a chance to argue she was out of the room, leaving him alone with the baby. This was not at all what he'd expected when he'd reluctantly agreed to watch a sleeping baby for fifteen minutes, but he reached for the nappies and the cotton wool, acting on instinct.

He narrowed his eyes, trying not to see Rosie's little pink cheeks or her tiny fingers. He just had to concentrate on the task in hand, and he could do that without really looking at her, without thinking about the fact that this little body was a whole new life—maybe a hundred years of potential all contained in seven pounds of toes and belly and new baby smell. Without thinking about his son.

He had nearly finished the nappy when Rosie began to fuss. As he fastened the poppers on her Babygro and washed his hands, he silently pleaded with her not to start crying. But her face screwed up and the tears started, and her banshee-like wail was impossible to ignore. He shut his eyes as he scooped a hand under her head and another under her bottom and lifted her to his shoulder, making soothing noises that he hoped would quiet her. He tried not to think at all as he bounced her gently, waiting for her tears to stop, tried not to think of the first time he had held his son, Max.

Or the last time.

The memory made him clutch Rosie a little tighter, hold her a little safer, knowing how precarious a young life could be. Eventually her cries slowed to sniffles as she snuggled closer to his shoulder and started looking for a source of food. He looked around the room, wondering where he'd lay his hands on formula and a bottle. He could ask the nurses, he supposed.

He transferred Rosie to the crook of one arm, only flinching momentarily at the remembered familiarity of the movement, and headed for the door. As it opened he was greeted by the sight of Lily, fresh from the shower, with no make-up and her hair pulled back, and it took his breath away.

Any chance of kidding himself that his interest was only in Rosie's welfare was lost. It was more than that. It was...*her*. He just couldn't stop thinking about her. But that was the problem. If he'd met Lily just one day earlier, before her sister had turned up with a baby, he wouldn't have hesitated to explore this connection between them, to imagine Lily looking as she did now—all fresh and pink and polished from the shower. But the shower would have been in his flat, and she'd have just left his bed.

Everything about her fascinated him. But she'd taken in her sister's child without a thought. And because of that he knew that they could never be happy together. He could see from her every look at Rosie that Lily was born to be a mother. She wanted a family, and he could never give her that—nor could he ask her to sacrifice it for him. There was no point considering a brief fling, either: a taste of her would never be enough—and if he started to fall for her then how would he make himself stop? And all that was even without the added complication of his sister's unspoken threats to hurt him in a *very* sensitive place if he messed with her best friend.

'I was just going to try and find her a bottle.'

Lily waved the bottle of formula she was carrying. 'No need. I see you couldn't resist a cuddle? I don't blame you—she's very squeezable.'

'It's not like that,' he replied instinctively. 'She was crying, that's all. Here—take her.' He almost shoved the baby at her, alarmed at how quickly he'd adapted, how natural it had felt to hold her.

'What's wrong?' Lily asked, her eyes wary. 'I don't mind you holding her.'

'I know.' Nic breathed slowly, trying to fight the urge to run from the room, knowing that he should explain his harsh words to Lily. Hating the wary, guarded look that had just entered her eyes. 'I'm just not good around babies.'

She glanced down at Rosie, who looked happy and content. 'Seems like you're pretty good to me.'

An awkward silence fell between them, and Lily looked as if she was trying to find the right words to say something. Suddenly he wanted out of the room. Her face was serious, and he wondered if she had guessed about his past, or if Kate had told her about it. His heart started racing as he remembered all the times he had failed at that in the past. All the broken conversations, the broken relationships that had followed.

'Nic, I don't know how to thank you for being there for us the other day. And Kate told me—'

Before he knew it he was reaching for her, wanting to stem the flow of her words. He didn't want to know what Kate had told her of his failings as a father and a partner.

He'd do anything to stop her speaking.

His lips pressed against hers as his fingers cradled her jaw, and for just a second he wondered what would happen if she opened her mouth to him, if her body softened and relaxed against him. If this kiss changed from a desperate plea for mercy to something softer, something more passionate. But he pulled away before it had the chance.

'I'm sorry,' he said, shutting his eyes against the confusion on her face and heading towards the door. 'I shouldn't have done that.'

Lily stood shell-shocked in the middle of the hospital room, the baby in one arm and the bottle held loosely in her other hand. What on earth had just happened? She'd been about to thank him for letting them stay with him—just until the work on her house was finished. But the cornered look in his eyes had stopped her words, and the kiss he'd pressed against her lips had stopped her thoughts.

It had been difficult enough to see herself living in his apartment. How was she meant to do it now, with this kiss between them, dragging up every fantasy she'd been forcing herself to bury? If she'd had any other option she'd have jumped at it. But Kate had been right. This was her only choice—kiss or no kiss.

She wondered at the expression on Nic's face, at the way he had cradled Rosie in one arm as if it was the most natural thing in the world. He'd obviously been around babies before. Had he been a father once? Was that what was behind the fear and the pain she saw in him? She couldn't imagine that anything but the loss of a child could draw such a picture of grief on someone's face. He carried a pain that was still raw and devastating—so why on earth had he agreed to let her live with him?

She spun at the sound of a knock to the door, wondering for an instant if it was Nic, back to rescind his invitation, to tell her she wasn't welcome anywhere near him. But instead of Nic it was her social worker standing in the doorway, case file in hand and a smile on her face.

CHAPTER FOUR

LILY LEANT AGAINST the wall of the lift as it climbed to the top of the building and snuck another look at Rosie, sleeping in her pram, not quite believing that she was really going to do this. But Kate had promised her that Nic was okay with it. He would be away on a business trip for the next week at least, so she'd have plenty of time to settle in and find her feet before she had to think about him. Or that kiss.

What had he been thinking? Perhaps the same as her—nothing. Perhaps the touch of their lips had banished all rational thought and left him as confused as she was.

At least all the paperwork and everything in officialdom was ticking along nicely. It was just a case of getting the right legal papers in order, and making sure that Helen had the medical help—both physical and mental—that she needed to get and stay well. There had been no talk of prosecution for abandonment—only concern for Helen and Rosie's welfare.

A stack of half-opened parcels littered the hallway, making the apartment look less bachelor sophisticated and more like a second hand sale. Kate must have beaten her here and picked up all the internet shopping that Lily had done while she was in the hospital with Rosie. They had some work ahead of them to get the apartment baby-ready—that was clear.

She peeked into the living room and was tempted to shiver at the abundance of black leather, smoked glass and chrome. Everything in the room shone, and Lily wondered if Nic was quite mad for letting them stay here. One thing was for sure: even with Rosie on her best behaviour it wasn't going to be easy keeping the place looking this show-home perfect.

'Kate?' Lily called out as she stood in the living room with Rosie in her arms, her eyes drawn to the glass walls with a view out over the river. 'Are you here?'

A voice sounded from the end of the hallway.

'In here!' she shouted. 'I'm just doing battle with the cot.'

Lily followed the sound of Kate's swearing and found herself in a luxurious bedroom. Between the doorway and the enormous pillow-topped bed Kate's curly head was just visible between the bars of a half-built cot.

'Are you winning?' Lily asked with a laugh.

'Depends on who's keeping score,' came the reply, along with another string of expletives.

Lily covered Rosie's ears and tutted.

'Sorry, Rosie,' Kate said, finally dropping the screwdriver and climbing out from the pile of flat-packed pieces. 'How are we doing?' she asked as she crossed the room to give Rosie a squeeze and Lily a kiss on the cheek.

'She's fine,' Lily told her. 'Clean bill of health. Thanks so much for getting started with this.' She waved a hand towards the cot.

'Don't be daft. It's nothing. Now, are you going to put the baby down and give me a hand?'

'Let me just grab her carrycot and I'll see if she'll go down.'

As Lily walked back into the hallway she jumped against the wall at the sight of a man's dark shadow up ahead of her.

'Nic...?' she said, holding Rosie a little tighter to her.

As Nic took a step forward his face came into the light and she could see the shock and surprise written across his features.

'Lily, what the hell—?'

'Kate!'

She wasn't sure which of them shouted first, but as it became apparent that Nic had had no idea she was going to be there Lily felt flames of embarrassment lick up her cheeks, colouring her skin. Oh, Kate had some explaining to do.

Kate at least had the good grace to look sheepish when she emerged into the hallway.

'What the hell is *she* doing here?'

Lily's gaze snapped back to Nic at the anger in his voice and she felt herself physically recoil. She was as surprised to see him there as he was to find them both in the flat—Kate had promised her he would be out of town for at least a week yet—but the venom in his voice was unexpected and more than a little offensive.

'Nic!' Kate admonished. 'Don't talk about Lily like that. I promise you, I can explain. You're not meant to *be* here.'

'It's my home, Kate. Where else would I be?'

'Well, India, for a start. And then Bangladesh. And Rome. And...'

'And I decided to spend a few weeks in the office before I go abroad again. I pushed some of my trips back. Not that I need to explain myself—*I'm* not the one who's in the wrong here.'

He threw a look at Lily that was impossible to misinterpret.

'Look...' Kate was using her best lawyer voice, and Lily suddenly felt a pang of sympathy for Nic. When she took that tone there was little doubt that she was going to get her own way.

But it didn't matter how Kate was planning on sweet-talking her way out of 'stretching the truth', as she was bound to call it. There was no way she could stay here—not with the looks of pure anger that Nic was sending their way.

'This is how I see things: Lily needs somewhere to stay. Rosie can't go back to Lily's as it has no kitchen, no back wall, isn't warm or even watertight. You have a big, ridiculous apartment that was *meant* to be empty for at least the next week, and which even when you're here has more available square footage than most detached family homes.'

Nic opened his mouth to argue, but Kate held up a hand, cutting him off.

'You, Mr Humanitarian, having spent the last decade saving the world one child factory worker at a time, have the opportunity to practise what you preach here. Charity begins at home, you know.'

Lily rolled her eyes at the cliché, and from the corner of her eye caught just the hint of a smirk starting at the corner of Nic's lips. When she built up the courage to look at him straight she saw that the tension had dropped from his face and he was smiling openly at his sister.

'Oh, you're good,' he said. '*Very* good. I hope they're paying you well.'

'And I'm worth every penny,' she confirmed. 'Now, seeing as you're home, I don't want to step on any toes.' She thrust the screwdriver into his hand and Nic had no choice but to take it. 'I'll leave you two to work out the details.'

And before Lily could pick up her jaw from the floor Kate had disappeared out of the front door, leaving her holding the baby and Nic staring at the screwdriver.

'I'm *so* sorry,' she said, rushing to put Rosie down in her pram and take the screwdriver from Nic's hand. 'She told me that you'd okayed it, but I should have guessed…I'll pack our stuff up and order a cab and we'll be out of your hair.'

Nic gave her a long look, and she watched, fascinated, as emotions chased over his face, first creasing his forehead and his eyes, then smoothing across his cheeks with something like resignation.

'Where will you go?'

'Oh…' Lily flapped a hand, hoping that the distraction would cover the fact that she didn't have a clue what her next move was. 'Back to mine, of course. It's not that bad. I'm sure I can come up with another plan.'

Nic rubbed his hand across his forehead.

'What plan?'

'A hotel,' Lily said, improvising wildly. 'Maybe a temporary rental.'

He let out a long sigh and shook his head slowly.

'Stay here.'

'Nic, I couldn't—'

Lily started to speak, but Nic's raised hand stopped her.

'Kate's right. You need a place to stay. I have loads of room here.'

A warm flood of relief passed through Lily. For a moment she'd thought that she might be out on the streets—worse, that she wouldn't be able to provide Rosie with the home she so desperately needed. And it was the thought that Rosie needed somewhere safe to stay that had her swallowing her pride and nodding to agree with what was almost certainly a terrible idea.

'Thank you. I promise we'll keep out of your way.'

Lily stood in the kitchen, coffee cup in hand, surveying the vast array of knobs and buttons on the espresso machine built into the kitchen wall. She'd already boiled the kettle, intimidated by the levers and chrome of the machine, but in the absence of a jar of good old instant coffee she was going to have to do battle with this beast. She tried the sleek-looking knob on the left—and jumped back from the torrent of steam that leapt from the nozzle hidden beneath. Thank God she'd left Rosie safely sleeping in their room.

A lightly haired forearm appeared over her shoulder and turned off the knob, shutting down the steam and leaving her red-faced and perspiring.

'Here,' Nic said, taking the cup from her hand. 'Let me.'

'Thanks.' Lily handed over coffee responsibility gratefully, and leaned back against the kitchen counter.

Embarrassment sat in the air between them, and Lily's mind couldn't help but fly back to that kiss in the hospital. The way that Nic's lips had pressed so firmly against hers, as if he was fighting himself even as he was kissing her. He'd known that it was a bad idea at the time—she was sure of that. And yet he'd done it anyway. Now they were living together—and apparently they were just going to ignore that it had happened. But even with them saying nothing, it was there, in the atmosphere between them, making them awkward with each other.

She wondered whether she should say something, try and clear the air, but then she heard a cry from the bedroom.

'You go and get Rosie. I'll sort the coffee.'

Was that an invitation? Were they going to sit down and drink a cup of coffee like civilised adults? And if they did would he bring up the kiss? Would she? Surely they couldn't just carry on as if nothing had happened. It was making her clumsy around him, and she could never feel relaxed or at home unless they both loosened up. Maybe that was what he was hoping for. That he'd be able to make things awkward enough that she'd have no choice but to leave. Then he'd get his apartment back without having to be the big bad wolf in the story.

Lily had returned to the kitchen with the baby in one arm, and set about making up a bottle for her. Nic watched them carefully, knowing that a gentleman would offer to help, but finding himself not quite able to live up to that ideal.

'It's good we've got a chance to sit down and talk,' he said as he carried their coffees over to the kitchen island. 'I wanted to apologise for the other day. The…

the kiss. And the way I left things. I know I was a bit abrupt.'

'It's fine—' Lily started, but he held up a hand to stop her.

The memory of the confusion on her face had been haunting him, and he knew that if they were to live together, even if it was only temporarily, he had to make sure she knew exactly why that kiss had been such a mistake. Why she shouldn't hope for or expect another.

They had only known each other for a few days, but after that parting shot at the hospital he wouldn't be able to blame her if she'd misinterpreted things—if she'd read more into that kiss than he'd ever wanted to give. She deserved better than that...better than a man with his limitations. And with Rosie in her life she was going to have to demand more. Demand someone who would support her family life whatever happened. He'd already been tested on that front and found wanting. It was only fair that Lily knew where they both stood.

'Please,' he continued, 'I want to explain.'

A line appeared between her brows, as if she had suddenly realised that this was a conversation neither of them would enjoy. The suggestion that she was hurt pained him physically, but he forced himself to continue—for both their sakes.

'There's no need to explain anything, but I'll listen if you want me to.'

She glanced over at the counter, her edginess showing in the way she was fidgeting with her coffee cup. The anxious expression on her face told him so much. She'd guessed something of his history. Guessed, at least, how hard it was for him to be around Rosie. Had

she seen how impossible it would be for them even to
be friends?

Not that *friends* would ever have really worked, he
mused, when the sight of her running a hand through
her hair made him desperate to reach across and see if
it felt as silky as it looked. When he'd lain awake every
night since they'd last met remembering the feel of her
lips under his, imagining the softness of her skin and
the suppleness of her body.

He kept his eyes on Lily, never dropping them to the
little girl in her arms, not risking the pain that would
assault him if he even glanced at Rosie or acknowledged that she was there. The way Lily looked at him,
her clear blue gaze, gave him no room to lie or evade.
He knew that faced with that open, honest look he'd
be able to speak nothing but the truth.

'There's something I need to tell you...' he started.

His voice held the hint of a croak, and he felt the
cold climbing his chest, wondered how on earth he
was meant to get these words out. How he was meant
to relive the darkest days of his life with this woman
who a week ago had been a stranger.

'I know there's something between us—at least I
know that I've started to feel something for you. But I
need you to know that I won't act again on what I feel.'

He kept his voice deliberately flat, forcing the emotion from it as he'd had to do when faced with people
living and working in inhuman conditions. And he
looked down at the table, unable to bear her sympathetic scrutiny. Or what if he had read this wrong—
what if there was nothing between them at all? What
if he'd imagined the chemistry that kept drawing them
together even as it hurt him? It wasn't as if he'd even

given her a chance to return his kiss. He risked a glance up at her. Her lip was caught between her teeth and the line had reappeared on her forehead. But he wasn't sure what he was seeing on her face. Not clear disappointment. Definitely not surprise.

'It's fine, Nic. You don't need to say any more.'

'I do.'

He wanted her to know, wanted to acknowledge his feelings even if just this once. Wanted her to understand that it was nothing about *her* that was holding him back. And he wanted her to understand him in a way that he'd never wanted before. He'd never opened up and talked about what had happened. But now he had been faced with the consequences of the choices he'd made so many years ago he wanted to acknowledge what he had felt, what he felt now.

'I want to explain. For you to understand. Look, it's not you, Lily.' He cringed when he heard for himself how clichéd that sounded. 'It's…it's Rosie. It's the way that you look at her. I won't ever have children, Lily. And I know that I cannot be in a relationship—any relationship—because of that.'

'Nic, we barely know each other. Don't you think that you're being—?'

He was thinking too far ahead. Of course he was. But if he didn't put an end to this now he wasn't sure how or if he ever could. What he had to say needed to be said out loud. He needed to hear it to make sure that he could never go back, never find himself getting closer to Lily and unable to get away.

'Maybe. Maybe I'm jumping to a million different conclusions here, and maybe I've got this all wrong. But the thing is, Lily, I'm never going to want to have children. Ever. And I don't think it would be right for me to leave you in any doubt about that, given your current situation.'

He allowed himself a quick look down at Rosie, and the painful clench of his heart at the sight of her round cheeks and intense concentration reminded him that he was doing the right thing. It was easier to say that it was because of the baby. Of course that was a big part of it. But there was more—there were things that he couldn't say. Things that he had been ashamed of for so long that he wasn't sure he could even bear to think of them properly, never mind share them with someone else.

'Well, thanks for telling me.'

She was fiddling with her coffee cup again, stirring it rapidly, sloshing some of the rich dark liquid over the side. He'd offended her—and what else did he expect, just telling half the story? All he'd basically done so far was break up with a woman he wasn't even dating.

'Lily, I'm sorry I'm not making much sense. It's just hard for me to talk about… The reason I don't want children…I was a father once. I lost my son, and it broke my heart, and I know that I can never put myself at risk of going through that again.'

And if she was going to take this gamble, raise her sister's child with no idea of what the future held, then she needed someone in her life she could rely on. Someone who would support her with whatever she needed. Who wouldn't let her down. He hadn't been able to do that when Max had died, hadn't been the man his partner had needed, and he'd lost his girlfriend as well as his son.

A hush fell between them and Nic realised he

had raised his voice until it was almost a shout. Lily dropped the bottle and Rosie gave a mew of discontent. But Nic's eyes were all on Lily, watching her face as she realised what he had said, as the significance of his words sank in.

She reached out and touched his hand. He should have flinched away. It was the reason he had told her everything, after all. But he couldn't. He turned his hand and grabbed hold of hers, anchoring himself to the present, saving himself from drowning in memories.

Now that he had told her, surely the danger was over. Now she would be as wary of these feelings as he was. He just wanted to finish this conversation—make sure that she knew that this wasn't personal, it wasn't about her. If Rosie had never turned up...if he'd never had a son... But there was no point thinking that way. No point in what-ifs and maybes.

'Nic, I'm so sorry. I don't know what to say, but I'd like to hear more about your son. If you want to talk about it.'

He breathed out a long sigh, his forehead pressed into the heels of his hands, but then he looked up to meet her gaze and she could see the pain, the loss, the confusion in his eyes.

'It won't change anything.'

She reached for his hand again, offering comfort, nothing more—however much she might want to.

'I know, but if you want to talk then I'd like to listen.'

He stared at the counter a little longer, until eventually, with a slight shake of his head, he started to speak.

'I was nineteen and naïve when I met this girl—

Clare—at a university party. We hit it off, and soon we were living in each other's pockets, spending all our time together. We were both in our first year, neither of us thinking about the future. We were having fun, and I thought I was falling in love with her.'

Lily was shocked at the strength of her jealousy over something that had happened a decade ago, and fought down the hint of nausea that his tale had provoked.

'Well, we were young and silly and in love, and we took risks that we shouldn't have.'

It didn't take a genius to see where this was going but, knowing that the story had a tragic end, Lily felt a pall of dread as she waited for Nic's next words.

'When Clare told me she was pregnant I was shocked. I mean, a few months beforehand we'd been living with our parents, and now we were going to be parents ourselves... But as the shock wore off we got more and more excited—'

His voice finally broke, and Lily couldn't help squeezing his hand. There was nothing sexual in it. Nothing romantic. All she wanted was to offer comfort, hope.

'By the time the baby was due we'd moved in together, even started to talk about getting married. So there I was: nineteen, as good as engaged, and with a baby on the way.'

His eyes widened and his jaw slackened, as if he couldn't understand how he had got from there to here—how the life that still lit up his face when he described it had disintegrated.

'The day Max was born was the best of my life. As soon as I held him in my arms I knew that I loved him. Everyone tells you that happens, but you never believe them until you experience it. He was so perfect, this tiny human being. For three weeks we were the perfect little family. I washed him, changed his nappies, fed him, just sat there and breathed in his smell and watched him sleep. I've never been so intoxicated by another person. Never held anything so precious in my arms.'

His face should have glowed at that. He should have radiated happiness, talking about the very happiest time of his life. But already the demons were incoming, cracking his voice and lining his face, and Lily held her breath, bracing herself.

'When he was three weeks old we woke one day to sunlight streaming into the bedroom and instantly knew that something was wrong. He'd not woken for his early feed. And when I went to his crib...'

He didn't have to say it. All of a sudden Lily wished that he wouldn't, that he would spare her this. But *he* hadn't been spared; *he* hadn't been shown mercy. He'd had his heart broken, his life torn apart in the most painful way imaginable. She couldn't make herself want to share that pain with him, but she wanted to help ease it if she could. She'd do just about anything to lift that blanket of despair from his face.

'He was gone. Already cold. I picked him up and shouted for Clare, held him in my arms until the ambulance arrived, but it was no good. Nothing I could have done would have helped him. They all told me that. They told me that for days and weeks afterwards. Until they started to forget. Or maybe they thought that *I* was forgetting. But I haven't, Lily.'

For the first time since he'd started speaking he

looked up and met her gaze head-on. There was solid determination there.

'I can never forget. And when I see Rosie...'

It all became clear: the way he turned away from the baby, the way he flinched if he had to interact with her, the stricken look on his face the one time he'd had to hold her. Seeing Rosie—seeing any baby—brought him unimaginable pain. There could be no children in his future, no family. And so she completely understood why it was he was fighting this attraction. Why he pushed away from their chemistry, trying to protect himself. Knowing that there could never be anything between them didn't make it easier, though. The finality of it hurt.

But there was one part of the story he hadn't finished.

'And...Clare?'

He dropped his head back into his hands and she knew that he was hiding tears. It was a couple of minutes before he could speak again.

'We were broken,' he said simply. 'We tried for a while. But whatever it was that had brought us together—it died with our baby. She needed... I couldn't...I saw her a couple of years ago, actually, in the supermarket, of all places, by the baked beans. We exchanged polite hellos, because what else could we say: *Remember when we lost our son and our world fell apart and could never be put back together? Remember when you needed me to be there for you, to help you through your grief, and I couldn't do it?*'

Lily choked back a sob. She couldn't imagine, never *wanted* to imagine, what this man had been through. She wanted to reach out and comfort him, to do anything she could to take his pain away, but she knew there was nothing to be done. Nothing that could undo what had happened, undo his pain. All she could do was be there for him, if that was what he wanted.

But it wasn't.

'So now you know why getting close to Rosie scares me—why getting close to you both can never happen. I can't go through that pain again, Lily. Just the idea of it terrifies me. How could I cope with another loss like that?'

Lily didn't have the answer to any of it. Of course she could say that the chances of it happening again were slim, but she couldn't promise it. No one could. And how could she blame him for wanting to spare himself that?

She didn't say anything when Nic stood from the table, only reached out a hand and rested it gently on his arm.

'Thank you,' she said. 'For everything. And I wish you all the best, Nic, I really do. I hope you can be happy again some day.'

CHAPTER FIVE

THREE WEEKS AFTER her sister had dropped her little surprise off on her doorstep Lily still hadn't heard anything from her. Social services seemed happy that Lily was being well cared for by her aunt, and were trawling through the appropriate paperwork. To begin with she'd thought it must be temporary, that one of these days Helen would call and ask for her daughter back. But so far—nothing.

And barely a word from Nic, either. Not that she had expected much after the way things had been left, but it was strange living with someone who could barely say more than good morning to her. A part of her had hoped, she supposed, that he might rethink things. That he might think that she—they—were worth taking a risk on. And then she remembered the look on his face when he told her about losing his son and knew that it couldn't happen. Knew that he wouldn't risk feeling like that again.

She lifted her head from the pillow and looked over at Rosie, still tucked in her crib, fast asleep again after her six o'clock feed. Lily listened to her breaths, to the steady whoosh of air moving in and out of her lungs. Rosie was the same age now as Nic's son had been when he died. After three weeks together, Lily could no longer imagine life without Rosie—couldn't imagine the pain of being torn from her.

So what would happen if Helen wanted her back? How could she keep mother and daughter apart, knowing how much it hurt to want a family and have them disappear from your life?

She collapsed back into her pillows and threw her arms over her face, blocking out the world, fed up with the circles her mind was spinning her in. She wanted to make sure that Helen was well and happy, but would that mean handing Rosie over? Accepting the fact that Helen might take off again, leaving her missing Rosie as she missed the rest of her family?

Much as she had tried to remember that she wasn't Rosie's mother, somewhere the line had become blurred. Because Helen hadn't just nipped to the shops, and Lily wasn't just being a helpful aunt: she was almost her legal guardian. It was Helen who had blurred this line, and Lily wasn't sure how she would cope if she suddenly turned everything on its head.

Thoughts still racing around her mind, she swung her legs out of bed and reached for her dressing gown. She'd learnt that if Rosie was sleeping she'd better shut her eyes, too, but this morning that was a luxury she couldn't afford. She had managed to put off a couple of her deadlines when she'd told her clients what had happened—sparing them most of the details—but she couldn't put them off for ever.

She had beta designs for two sites to finish, and while Rosie was sleeping she couldn't justify not working. Then there was the fact that she'd not bothered with the dishes last night, the fridge was looking decidedly bare, and when Rosie woke up she'd want milk, clean clothes and a clean nappy. The round of chores was endless, even with Nic's generosity, and she sometimes felt she'd been walking through fog since Rosie had arrived. A joyful fog, obviously, but an endlessly draining one, too.

She padded into the kitchen and hit the button on the kettle—still too foggy to attempt espresso—knowing that she needed coffee this morning, and wondering how breastfeeding mums coped with the newborn stage without caffeine. She felt as if she was flailing, barely keeping her head above water, and she wasn't even recovering from giving birth.

Over the rumbling of the kettle coming to the boil she heard her mobile ringing in the bedroom and ran to get it, hoping that she could reach it and hit 'silence' before it woke the baby.

When she got to it Rosie was already mewling quietly, and Lily scooped her up quickly before swiping to answer her phone.

'Hello?' she said, as quietly as possible, rocking Rosie in the vain hope that she'd decide to go back to sleep.

When her social worker told her the news she couldn't think of an answer. *Why* couldn't she think of an answer? So many times these past weeks she'd wondered how her sister was, whether she'd ever be ready to be part of a family again, and now here was the proof that she might want that one day. She wanted to see Lily—and her daughter—that morning.

'Okay,' she told the social worker eventually. 'I'll bring Rosie to her.'

As soon as she ended the call tears were threatening behind her eyes. Irrational tears? she wondered. Through the sleep deprivation she was finding it hard to remember what was reasonable and what wasn't. She needed Kate and her no-nonsense way of seeing the world, her way of cutting through the mess and making the world simple.

She dialled her number and waited, rocking slightly on the bed. 'Come on, pick up…pick up…' She walked back through to the kitchen as the ringing continued on the other end of the phone. 'Come on, Kate. *Please* pick up…'

'Everything okay?'

Not Kate. At the sound of Nic's voice she spun around and the tears started in earnest, though she couldn't rationalise why. Too much family drama. Too little sleep.

'Any idea where your sister is?'

'Not sure,' he told her, and she could hear concern for her in his voice. 'But I know that the Jackson case is coming to trial this week. My guess would be chambers or court. Is everything okay? Rosie?'

'She's fine,' Lily told him, though she couldn't stop the tears.

She still clutched Rosie tight against her, her every instinct telling her that she must protect the baby at all costs. But protecting her didn't mean keeping her from her own mother, if seeing her was what she wanted.

'Look, I've got to go out, but please can you find Kate and tell her to meet me at the Sanctuary Clinic as soon as possible?'

He paced the corridor of the clinic, asking himself for the thousandth time what he was doing there. The sense of déjà vu was almost overwhelming. It had been only a couple of weeks ago that he'd paced a similar corridor, asking himself a similar question.

Lily.

She had been the reason then, and she was the reason now. Her voice, so quiet and shocked, but filled with a fierce protectiveness for Rosie. *Find Kate*, she'd said.

But he hadn't been able to. When Kate was embroiled in a case there was no telling when she might emerge for sunlight and fresh air. All she could see was her duty to her client. Just as impossible as getting his sister on the phone was the thought of leaving Lily alone. She'd been so stoic, but he had heard the vulnerability in her voice and been unable to ignore it. The way she'd sounded—those intriguing layers of vulnerability and strength—had made him want to be here for her, *with* her. She could do this on her own, he had no doubt of that, but that didn't mean he wanted her to have to.

He was just relieved for now that Lily's sister was safe and well—he knew how much Lily had worried about her, how much she'd hoped to have her back in her life.

Lily emerged from the bathroom with Rosie smelling fresh, but there was a fearful look on her face. When they were halfway down the corridor, without thinking, he wrapped an arm around her. Holding her close to him, he could feel her body trembling.

'Here—' he gestured to some seats set against the wall '—do you want to sit for a minute? Get your breath? Helen's not going anywhere, and nor is Rosie.'

She sat in a chair and he pulled his arm back, suddenly self-conscious, aware of the line that he had crossed.

'Do you want to talk about it?'

Lily shook her head, but spoke anyway.

'Helen's been staying here since she left Rosie with me. She's not wanted to see us before now, but she's decided she's ready.'

'And you and Rosie—are *you* ready?'

She sat silent for a long moment. 'She's my sister. She's Rosie's mum. She's family. I don't want to lose her.'

'But you're the one making decisions for Rosie. Helen asked you to do that. If you're not ready…'

'*I'm* ready,' she said, with sudden steely determination. 'But I want to see Helen alone first, before I decide whether I'm ready for her to meet Rosie. I can't get hold of Kate and there's no one else. I know that I shouldn't ask. That after everything we've spoken about—'

'It's fine.' The words surprised him. He'd been all too ready to agree that she shouldn't ask, that it *was* too much, that he couldn't… But he'd looked down at Rosie, and he'd looked up at her aunt, and he'd known that this family had touched him. That Lily had touched him. And that much as he wanted to pretend he had never met them, that was impossible now.

It had been impossible from the moment he'd found Lily on her doorstep, babe in arms and already with a fierce determination to protect. It had been impossible when he'd laid out the hardest and most painful parts of his past, hoping that it would scare her off, hoping that the pain the conversation dredged up would be enough to scare *him* off. But it hadn't. He'd spent all that time questioning what he'd done. Wondering how he was going to live life full of the regret that he felt when he thought of Lily. Wondering if he could be brave enough to try and live another way.

And when he had reached out just now and taken her in his arms he'd had his answer. He didn't have a choice. The feelings he had for Lily weren't going to go away. Trying to convince her—convince himself—that they shouldn't do this hadn't made the pain less. It had made it worse. Walking away from Lily would leave another hole in a life that was already too empty.

'I'll watch her for you.'

'Are you sure?'

Her disbelief was written plainly on her face, and when he nodded he thought he saw a flash of hope there, of anticipation. He smiled in response—they had a lot to talk about later.

'We'll be fine. Your sister needs you now.'

Lily hesitated outside the door. She'd waited patiently for her sister to be ready, hoping every day that she would come back into their lives, but feeling terrified at the same time that she might ask for Rosie back, take her away. And then Lily would have lost a niece—almost a daughter—as well as her sister.

She took a deep breath and pushed open the door.

At the sight of her sister in the bed, pale and skinny, all her fears left her. As long as they were all safe and well, the rest of it didn't matter. She'd hoped so many times that she'd have a chance to reconnect with Helen. She couldn't be anything but pleased that she had somehow found her way back again.

'Lily?'

Lily hadn't realised that Helen was awake, but she reached out a hand to her with tears in her eyes.

'I'm so happy to see you,' she told her.

Helen sniffed, her expression cautious. 'I thought you might be angry.'

'I'm not angry—I've been so worried. I'm just glad that you're okay.'

'But what I did…'

'We don't need to talk about that now. The most important thing is to get you well again. Everything else we can talk about later.'

A tear slipped from the corner of Helen's eye and Lily wiped it away with a gentle swipe of her thumb.

'I knew that I couldn't look after her,' Helen went on, her tears picking up pace.

And even though Lily hushed her, told her that they didn't have to talk about it now, she carried on as if the words were backed up behind a failing dam and nothing could stop them surging forward.

'The house that I was living in—it wasn't safe. Not for me or her. And I couldn't think of another way, Lily. I knew that she'd be better off with you.'

'You did the right thing,' Lily reassured her. 'And your daughter's fine. She's doing really well.'

At that the dam finally broke, and Helen's face was drowned in tears.

'I…was…so…scared.' She choked the words out between sobs. 'After I left her with you I realised I couldn't go back to where I had been living, but I couldn't come home to you, either.'

'That's not true, Helen. You can come home any time. The house is yours just as much as it is mine. And I know that we both want what's best for Rosie.'

'Rosie?'

Lily gulped. She hadn't meant to use her name, knowing that she'd taken something of a liberty by choosing one in the first place. But there had been no one else to do it.

'If you don't like it…'

'No, it's perfect. I love it.' Helen's tears slowed. 'It just goes to show that I was right. You're the right person to look after her, Lily. I know that the way I did it wasn't right—just dumping her and running—but I didn't make a mistake. I can't be the one to raise her.'

Lily took a deep breath, feeling the thinness of the ice beneath her feet, knowing that one misstep could ruin her relationship with her sister for ever, could lose her Rosie.

'You've not been well,' she said gently. 'And you don't need to make big decisions right now or all at once. There'll be plenty of time to talk about this.'

Helen nodded, her features peaceful for the first time since Lily had arrived. 'I want to be part of her life—and yours, too, if you'll still have me. But I'm not going to change my mind. You're the best person to look after Rosie. I'm not ready to be a mother, Lily. I might never be. I'm not going to change my mind about this.'

Lily just squeezed her hand, lost for words.

'And maybe I will want to come home one day—but not yet, Lily. I can't do that until I'm really properly well, and that's going to take me some time.'

'I could—'

'I know you want to do everything for us, Lily. But you're already doing so much. I have to get better on my own, and I need space to do that.'

Space? How much space did she need? She'd given her nothing *but* space for years, and where had that got her? Living somewhere she didn't feel safe with a baby she couldn't care for.

'Will you do it? Will you take care of Rosie.'

There had never been any question about that.

'Of course I will. She's here, you know. If you'd like to see her.'

Pain crossed Helen's features for a moment. 'I thought I was ready, but…I'm not, Lily. It would hurt too much to see her. So what do you say? I'm not talking about a few weeks or months, Lily. I need to know that she'll be safe for *ever*. That I can concentrate on getting well without the pressure of… I know it's selfish.'

It wasn't. It might have been the most self*less* thing Lily had ever heard. Because the yearning and the love in Helen's face was clear. She hadn't abandoned Rosie because she was an inconvenience, or too much hard work, or because she cried too much. She'd done it because she loved her. She'd broken her own heart in order to give her child the best start in life, and Lily couldn't judge her for that.

'It's not selfish. And of course I'll take care of Rosie.' Her voice was choked as she said the words. 'I love her, Helen. You don't have to worry. I'll keep her safe.'

Some of the tension left Helen's body, and Lily could tell that she needed some of that space she'd been talking about.

She gave her hand another squeeze. 'I'll come back and visit again when you're ready. Rest now.'

'Thanks, sis,' Helen said, drifting off. 'You were always going to be an amazing mum.'

Back in the corridor, Lily leaned her forehead against the wall and took a couple of deep breaths, wanting to compose herself before she saw Rosie, not wanting her to sense that she had been upset.

She glanced down the corridor and saw that she was no longer in her car seat but on Nic's knee, being fed from a bottle. Lily couldn't help but smile. While she had been talking to her sister she'd almost forgotten that Nic had stayed, and the look on his face when she'd asked him to watch Rosie even though she'd known that she shouldn't. But the fear and the panic that she'd been expecting to see there hadn't emerged. Instead there had been something different, something new, and it had given her hope.

Now, seeing him holding the baby, she wondered what this meant. After everything that he'd said to her back at his flat, the harrowing story of his loss, she'd thought they'd said all that needed to be said about their feelings, their future. But here he was.

'Thank you so much for this,' she said as she reached the chairs and sat beside him. 'I can take her if you want.'

'She's fine. Let her finish her bottle.'

His words suggested that he was comfortable, but his body language was telling a different story. He was sitting bolt upright on the plastic chair, his shoulders and arms completely stiff. Rosie was more perched on him than snuggled against him, but that hadn't stopped her staring up at him with her big blue gaze locked onto his face as she fed.

I wish I could look at him like that, Lily thought. *With no need to hide what I feel, no need to look away when I realise that he's seen me.* How simple life must seem to Rosie, with no idea of the impact her birth had had on her whole family.

'How was it?' Nic asked her at last.

Lily blew out a breath. 'I don't really know—it's not like I have a lot to compare it to. But okay, I think.'

'That's good…'

'It's good that she wants to get better. But I wish she'd come home, that she'd let me take care of her. It's what I've been hoping for for years. But…'

'But you're worried about what will happen to Rosie if she gets well?'

She nodded, the lump in her throat preventing the words from coming.

'You know I can't tell you for definite what will happen.' The tone of his voice was soft and measured. 'But everyone involved will want what's best for Rosie.'

She nodded, still not trusting herself to speak.

At the beginning she had genuinely believed, when she'd said she would look after Rosie, that she was only taking care of her temporarily, until Helen was back and better. Now she couldn't imagine watching someone else sing her to sleep, someone else comfort her when she was upset. She was a little jealous just watching Nic giving her a bottle.

'So, are you heading home?' he asked when Rosie had finished.

'I thought I might walk through the park first, as the sun's out. I think me and Rosie need some fresh air. The smell of hospitals…'

'I'll walk with you, if that's okay?'

CHAPTER SIX

WALKING THROUGH THE PARK, just the three of them, Nic couldn't shake the feeling that he had wandered into someone else's life. To anyone else they would look like a family—a loving husband and wife, perhaps—taking a stroll with their baby, talking together, making plans for the future. This had been his life once, and it had left him so scarred that he had sworn he would never let himself come close to it again.

Until he had met Lily and been unable to forget her. And now was the moment he had to decide. It wasn't fair on Lily to keep pushing her away and then changing his mind. If he was going to take this chance, he had to commit to it.

'So...' he started as they exited the park. 'Have you got plans for dinner?'

She looked a little panic-stricken for a second.

'There're a few bits and pieces in the fridge. I was just going to rustle up something simple. Or maybe order something in...'

He could see the doubt in her eyes as she finally looked up at him, and he cursed himself for the confusion he must have caused her over the past days. He was more aware than anyone of how hot and cold he had blown. He wanted to reach out and smooth the lines of concern from her face. Instead he offered an encouraging smile, urging her to take a risk—as he had—and invite him in.

'We could order something together?' she suggested at last.

'I'd love to,' he agreed, opening the gate for her.

Back in the apartment, Nic reached across for another slice of pizza and asked the question that had been nagging at him since they had left the hospital.

'So, did your sister say anything about what her plans are…with Rosie?'

'It's still early days. I don't think she's really in a position to decide anything yet.' Lily took a long drink of her cola. 'But…'

'But?'

'She said that she wants me to take care of Rosie permanently. If I don't want to, or can't, I don't know what will happen. She'll go into care, I suppose.'

'And how do you feel about that?'

'About Rosie going into care?' She fought off a wave of panic and nausea, reminding herself that the social worker had told her that they tried their hardest to keep families together. That Rosie being taken away completely would be a last resort. 'Honestly, the thought of it makes it hard to breathe.'

Nic looked at her closely and she dropped her eyes, not enjoying the depth of his scrutiny, feeling as if he was seeing all too much of her.

'There must be a lot of fantastic foster parents out there. And couples waiting to adopt. All you ever hear on the news is the horror stories, but every type of family has those. I'm sure that Rosie would find a happy home if that's what you and Helen decide is best.'

Lily shook her head, not trusting herself to speak for a moment. After a long breath, she chose her words carefully. 'But she should be with her family. I *have* to look after her.'

'Why do I feel there's more to this story?' Nic asked.

'What do you mean? I just want to take care of my family.'

'It's not all your responsibility.'

He was using his careful voice again, and she read the implication in that loud and clear. He thought she was being irrational, that she needed talking down like some drunk about to lose her temper. Well, if he carried on like this…

'It's okay to admit that maybe sometimes you need help.'

'I don't need help to look after my niece, thank you very much. I'm sorry if that's not what you want to hear. If you were hoping that maybe I'd wake up one day soon unencumbered by a baby. It's not exactly what I had in mind for the next few years, but she's my responsibility and I'm not handing her over to strangers.'

He held his hands palms up and sat back on his stool, surprise showing in his raised eyebrows and baffled expression. 'Whoa! I'm sorry, Lily. That's not what I meant at all. I'm not going to lie and say that Rosie doesn't make things complicated, but I'd never expect you to give her up. I'd never want that.'

'Then what *do* you want? Because I've got to tell you I'm struggling to keep up. The last time we talked you were very clear that I was nothing more to you than a temporary lodger—and not even a very welcome one at that. But now here we are, strolling through the park and sharing dinner. Why?'

She hadn't meant to get mad at him, but he'd already squashed her every romantic and X-rated fantasy, when she'd only just started to realise the feelings she was developing, and it was suddenly all too much. She'd held back before—keeping her feelings at the back of her mind, not questioning his—and she'd had enough. They were both grown-ups. If he was man enough to have these feelings then he'd damn well better be man enough to talk about them.

'Because I can't make myself *not* want this. And I've tried, Lily. I've tried for both of us. Because I'm not the right guy for you. I've tried to keep my distance because I know that this isn't good for either of us—I can't be the person you need me to be. But something keeps throwing us back together and I don't know if I can fight it any more.'

Man enough, then.

Lily froze with a slice of pizza halfway to her mouth. Complete and utter honesty was what she had been hoping for, but really the last thing she'd been expecting. The raw power of his words made her want to move closer and pull away at the same time. He'd just told her that he wasn't sure he was ready. He was taking a big gamble with her feelings and with his, and she wasn't sure that was a game she wanted to play. Had he really thought this through?

'I'm not sure, Nic. I barely have the time or the brain capacity to think beyond the next bottle and nappy-change. I'm not sure that I can even *think* about a relationship. And you know me and Rosie come as a package deal, right? I don't know what's going to happen with Helen in the future. I don't know whether I'll be Rosie's caregiver for the next week, the next month, or the rest of her life. There are no guarantees either way.'

She let out a long, slow breath.

'I'm sorry, but I don't think I can even consider a relationship right now. If you want to be friends, I'd like that.'

He gave her a long, searching look, before sighing. 'Of course. You're right. But friends sounds good. I'd like that.'

'That's exactly what I need.' She offered him a small, tentative smile, feeling her hackles gradually smooth.

'I guess I could take that as a compliment. But how about we leave off over-analysing getting to know each other and change the subject? If we're going to be friends, then talking over pizza and a glass of wine seems like something we should master.'

'Agreed. So, Dominic Johnson, in the spirit of getting to know each other, tell me something about you I don't already know. Please, let's talk about something completely normal for a change.'

She took a bite of her pizza while she waited for him to reply, trying to make her body relax. Instead all it was interested in was Nic—his smell, his nearness, the fact that he was tearing down barriers she'd been counting on for weeks.

'There's not really much to tell.'

His words snapped her attention back, and she listened intently, trying to school her resistant body.

'I grew up with Mum and Dad and Kate in the suburbs of Manchester. Completely unremarkable childhood. Kate and I still get dragged back there regularly for family Sunday lunches.'

'Sounds lovely,' Lily said. She *knew* it was lovely, actually, and had been up there with Kate more than once. 'You're lucky,' she told Nic.

He nodded in agreement. 'How about you?'

Lily took a deep breath, realising too late that of course her question had been bound to lead to this. In wanting to hear something completely unremarkable about his life she'd led them to talking about the most painful parts of hers.

'Uh-uh.' She shook her head as she reached for the last dough ball, wondering how best to deflect his question. 'I'm not done grilling you.'

She thought around for a topic of conversation that wouldn't lead back to her family, and her failure to hold things together at the heart of it.

'How did you start your charity? Why did you decide that you wanted to spend your life improving the conditions of child factory workers? It seems like a bit of a leap the suburbs.'

He smiled softly, obviously resigned to being the subject of her questioning for now.

'It never really seemed like a choice. I travelled after…after Max, and I was horrified by some of the things that I saw. I had nothing to come home to—or that's what it felt like at the time—so I stayed and tried to do something about it.'

'And was it what you expected?'

'It was worse—and better,' he replied. 'I saw things that I wish I could forget, and I saw people's lives saved because of my work. But what I loved most was that it was so all-consuming. It exhausted me physically and mentally. It didn't leave room for me to think about anything else. It was exactly what I needed.'

'And now? Is it still all-consuming?' Because there wasn't room for anyone else in what he'd just described.

'It can be on the days I want it to be,' he said, thoughtfully and with a direct look. 'There've been a few of those lately… But usually, no, it doesn't have to be. That's part of the reason I took the job in London. I knew that I couldn't carry on the way I had been. And I knew that my parents wanted me to be closer to home. I've spent the last ten years trying to change these companies from the outside—I thought trying from the inside might work better.'

She watched him closely, wondering whether she had been part of the reason he'd needed a distraction lately. Or was it just his grief he didn't want to face?

She sat back on her stool and rubbed her belly as Nic eyed the last slice of pizza speculatively. 'I'm done,' she declared. 'It's all yours.'

They fell into an easy silence as Nic ate, and Lily smiled up at him, feeling suddenly shy, and also shattered. Rosie's feeds through the night and her early starts were catching up with her, and much as she was loath to admit it suddenly all she could think about was her duvet, her pillow, and the fact that Rosie would be awake and hungry almost before she managed to get to them.

For half a second she thought about Nic being under that duvet with her, about seeing his head on the pillow when she woke in the morning.

Something of her thoughts must have shown on her face, because Nic raised an eyebrow.

'What?' he asked. 'What did I miss?'

'Nothing!' Lily declared, far too earnestly. 'Nothing…'

'Something,' Nic stated, watching her carefully. 'But if you don't want to share that's fine.'

'Good. Because your reverse psychology doesn't work on me.'

Nic laughed. 'Busted. I want to know what you were thinking!'

'And I'm not going to tell.'

He looked triumphant at that. 'Well, then, I'll choose to interpret that look however I want to, and there's nothing you can do about it.'

Lily shook her head, laughing. 'Right, that's enough.' She stood good-naturedly, clearing away the pizza box and their glasses. 'I'm going to bed.'

He walked through to the hall with her, and she hesitated outside her door.

'This was nice,' she said eventually, feeling suddenly nervous, unable to articulate anything more than that blatant understatement.

He grinned, though, his smile lighting his whole face. Maybe he'd heard all the things she hadn't said.

'I'm glad we talked.'

So he could do understatement too. On purpose? Or was he feeling awkward as well?

Lily reached for the door handle, but as her hand touched cold metal warm skin brushed her cheek, and she drew in a breath of surprise. Nic nudged her to look up at him as he took a step closer. The heat of his body seemed to jump the space between them, urging her closer, flushing her skin. She looked up and met his gaze. His eyes swam with a myriad of emotions.

Desire, need, relief, hope… All were reflected in her own heart. But they couldn't have timed this worse. She'd meant what she said earlier. Friendship was all she had space for in her life.

She closed her eyes as she stretched up on tiptoe and let her lips brush against his cheek. Soft skin rasped against sharp stubble and for a moment she rested her cheek against his, breathing in his smell, reminding herself that even if she did drag him inside to her bed she'd be snoring before he even got his shirt off.

Nic's other hand found the small of her back and pressed her gently to him, appreciative rather than demanding. She let out a long sigh as she dropped her forehead to his shoulder, and then finally turned the door handle.

'Goodnight…?'

There was still the hint of a question in Nic's farewell, and she smiled.

'Goodnight.'

CHAPTER SEVEN

HE BARELY HAD a foot through the front door when Lily flew past him. Shirtless and running.

'Everything okay?' he called to her retreating back, knowing that he should drag his eyes away from the curve of her waist and the smoothness of her skin, but finding that his moral compass wasn't as refined as he'd always hoped. There was something about the way the light played on her skin, the way it seemed to glow, to luminesce…

'I'm sorry,' she called over her shoulder as she ran into her bedroom. 'Spectacular timing. I'll be right out.'

Rosie was in a bouncy chair in the kitchen, wearing most of her last bottle, he guessed, and had clearly been hastily and inadequately mopped up by the kitchen roll on the counter. Lily turned suddenly and he threw his gaze away—anywhere but at her. His mind was filled by the image of her bare skin, the sweep of her shoulder, the curve of her…

No. To ogle a shoulder was one thing, but there were lines he shouldn't cross.

Instead he went into the kitchen and looked at Rosie and at the dribble of milk trickling down her chin. With mock exasperation he grabbed a muslin square and started mopping. He kept it objective, detached. There was no need to pick her up, but it wasn't really fair to leave her damp and uncomfortable, either. If he was going to be spending more time with Lily, he couldn't ignore Rosie completely.

Lily emerged a moment later, pulling down a T-shirt to cover that last inch of pale flesh above her jeans.

'Thanks for doing that. I started, but I seemed to be getting messier from trying to clean her up. Seemed one of us should be clean, at least.'

'It's no problem,' he said, holding out the muslin, handing back responsibility. His eyes were fixed just above her T-shirt, where shoulder met collarbone and collarbone met the soft skin of her neck.

And then it was hidden behind Rosie's soft-haired head and he was forced to look away again. He wondered how he could pinch Rosie's spot, how he could get his lips behind Lily's ear, breathe in her smell as Rosie was doing.

For another whole week, while he'd been putting in fourteen-hour days at the office, all he'd had to remember was that brief kiss on the cheek, the press of her soft warm skin against his, the fruity scent of her shampoo and the heat that had travelled from her body to his without them even touching. The long nights had been filled with plans he knew would never be fulfilled: for picking up where that kiss had left off, for having her cheek against his again, but this time turning her, finding her mouth with his, scooping her up in his arms and heading straight for her bedroom, or the couch, or the kitchen table...

'I'm so sorry. I know I said I'd cook tonight, but

I haven't got started on dinner yet,' she said, bouncing Rosie and trying to snatch up tissues and muslins from the kitchen counter and shuffling dirty pots from the breakfast bar. 'I just don't know what happens to the hours.'

Rosie was showing no sign of settling, so he grabbed ingredients from the fridge and tried to fire his imagination.

'You don't have to do that,' she told him, still bouncing and rocking. 'I'll be on it in just a minute.'

'Don't worry—let me,' he insisted. 'I like to cook.'

She looked up at him in surprise. 'Hidden depths?'

He took a few steps closer to her, pulled the muslin from her hand and stopped her rocking for just a minute. For the first time since that too-brief kiss on the cheek she met his eyes, and he relaxed into her gaze.

'There's a lot you don't know.'

She wanted to find out, she realised. She wanted his secrets.

'I'm pretty sure that you'd rather not arrive home to a strange woman in your apartment, baby spit-up, no sign of dinner, and—'

'It's not so bad,' he said with a grin.

It was true, he realised as he spoke. And he wanted her any way she came—baby spit-up and all. Because for this scene to be any different, *she* would have to be different. *Not* the sort of woman who took in a vulnerable child. *Not* the sort of woman who put feeding that child before her own appearance. He wanted her just as she was.

He looked down at the top of Rosie's head, at the way she was nuzzling against Lily's shoulder, the way she'd started to snuffle again since he'd stopped

Lily moving. If he wanted her to be that woman, if he wanted to be *with* that woman, then he was going to have to learn to be patient. If these few weeks had taught him anything, it was how to wait for Lily.

'She needs you,' he said. 'I'll look after dinner. And then, when she's sleeping, we can…'

She looked up again, this time with a blush and a smile.

'We can eat. And talk.'

The smile spread into a grin—and a knowing one at that.

He started chopping an onion, and had to bat away Lily's one-handed attempts to help. Ten minutes later he had a sauce bubbling on the stove, and had to snatch the wooden spoon from Lily's hand as she attempted to stir it.

'Did you never hear the one about too many cooks? Out.' He threatened her clean T-shirt with the sauce-covered spoon until he could close the door behind her.

Finally, after she'd popped her head around the door twice, just to 'check' there was nothing she could do, they had Rosie asleep in her Moses basket and dinner on the table. Conversation flowed easily between them as he shared stories of his client meetings, and told her about his plans for the new product lines he'd like to stock. They talked about what she'd been up to, but she managed to deflect most of his questions.

He wondered how much of it was her trying to protect him, shielding him from Rosie because she knew the baby caused him pain.

He couldn't remember which of them had suggested watching a movie, but now, in the dark, sharing a couch with her, he wanted to curse whoever it had been.

He felt like a teenager again. Even their choice of a comedy, hoping to steer clear of the romantic, seemed hopelessly naïve. And, like the awkward fifteen-year-old he vaguely remembered being once, he was thinking tactics. How to break their silence and separation? Trying to guess whether she was watching the film or if—like his—her line of thought was on something rather different.

They had agreed to be just friends, but his week of long days in the office—giving her the space she needed—had proved to him that keeping his feelings friendly was going to be anything but easy. Especially knowing that she was attracted to him too. She hadn't denied that before, after all. Only said that the timing wasn't right. Well, when was it *ever* right? Had she missed him, too, this week? Rethought their very grown-up and very gruelling decision to keep things platonic?

As he glanced across at her Lily turned to him, lips parted and words clearly on the tip of her tongue.

'I was just going to…to get a drink. Do you want anything from the kitchen?'

Her cheeks were rosy again, and he wondered if that was really what she had planned on saying. But most importantly she'd hit 'pause' on the movie, broken the stalemate. He watched her retreat to the kitchen and relaxed back into the cushions of the sofa. How was he meant to make it through the rest of this movie? It was torture. Pure torture. She *must* be feeling this tension as much as he was. Was she as intrigued by the attraction between them as he?

She emerged from the kitchen with a couple of glasses, balancing a plate of cakes. She'd pulled her hair back, exposing even more of the soft skin of her neck, and it took every ounce of his self-control not to sneak his arm along the back of the sofa until his hand found it, touched it. He knew that if he did his whole experience of the world would be reduced to the very tips of his fingers, and he'd be able to think about nothing other than how much he wanted her.

Her face was turned up to his, and when he breathed in it was all *her*, fruity and fresh. She smiled, and the sight of it filled him with resolve. She didn't want more than this. He would never be everything she needed in a partner, a husband. They were doing the right thing.

But when he closed his eyes he imagined her hand on his jaw, pulling him close, her tongue teasing, him opening his mouth to her and taking control. One hand would wind in her hair, tilting her head and caressing her jaw. He could practically hear her gasp as he pulled her into his lap. He knew the sound would reach his bones.

But even in his fantasy there was something else: a hesitancy, a caution that he couldn't overcome. He opened his eyes to find her watching him from the other end of the couch. He knew that his fantasy was written on his face, and other parts of his body.

'Nic…'

'Don't,' he said, holding up a hand to stop her. 'Nothing's changed since last time we talked about this. Apart from the fact that I've not been able to stop thinking about you… But it doesn't matter. We're doing the right thing. I know that. One of these days Rosie's going to need a dad—or a father figure, at least. You'll meet someone amazing who can give you the family life you deserve.'

He could never be that man.

'It's been a long week,' he told her, faking a yawn. 'I think I'm going to hit the sack.'

And with that he left her, staring after him as he practically ran from the room.

CHAPTER EIGHT

'RIGHT THEN, MISS. Are you going to tell me what's going on? Because Nic is being annoyingly discreet. I don't know what's got into him.'

'And I have no idea what you're talking about.'

'Oh, like hell you don't. The pair of you have been making doe eyes at each other since the day he pitched up on your doorstep. I can forgive *him* not telling me what's going on: he's my brother, and a bloke, and he has been irritating me for as long as I can remember. It's like a vocation for him. But you're my best friend and you have a new man in your life and you're telling me *nothing*. That's just not acceptable by anyone's standards of friendship.'

Lily groaned as she tipped the pram back and lifted it onto the pavement. 'A nice walk in the park,' Kate had said. 'Fresh air and a catch-up,' Kate had said. Since Rosie had landed they'd barely had the chance for more than a hello. It was her own fault for not realising that what she'd actually meant was *I will be grilling you for details about my brother*.

Well, if that was what she wanted…

'Okay, if it's details about the wild, sweaty sex I've been having with your brother you want you should have said. I hope you've got all afternoon free, though. Because that boy has stamina—and imagination.'

Kate's squeal had an elderly couple by the pond swivelling to stare at them and pigeons taking off from the path.

'That is all kinds of disgusting. I don't want details. But the fact that you've been doing the dirty with my brother and not telling me...*that* we need to talk about.'

Lily laughed at the look of horror on Kate's face. 'Calm it down, Kate. There has been no dirty. I'm winding you up.'

'You're— Oh, I'm going to kill you. *And* him. I've not decided yet which I'm going to enjoy more. So there's nothing going on?'

'Nothing.'

It was absolutely the truth. The fact that they were both *thinking* about what might be going on was beside the point.

'Then why are you blushing?'

Damn her pale skin—always getting her into trouble.

'I know that he likes you.'

Lily took a deep breath. 'I know he does too. But it's more complicated than that.'

'You don't like *him*?'

'Of course I like him. You've met your brother, right? Tall, good-looking, kind—all "I have a brilliant business brain but I choose to use it saving the world"?'

'Then what's the problem?'

What was the problem? There was the fact that she'd just become solely responsible for raising a brand-new human without even the usual nine-month notice period. There was the fact that Nic was still so scarred from losing his own son that he couldn't look at Rosie without flinching. There was the fact that she fell asleep any time she sat down for more than six minutes at a time, and the fact that her life was threatening to overwhelm her. It was hard to imagine how anything more complicated with Nic *wouldn't* push her over the edge.

And there was more that he hadn't told her. It wasn't just Rosie he was fighting. When he looked at Lily she saw something else—doubt. He'd told her that he wasn't the right man for her, but she failed to see why. Not wanting a life with a baby in it was one thing, but there was more to it than that. He warned her away whenever they got close, as if he couldn't trust himself.

What really tipped the situation over from difficult to impossible was the fact that she didn't want to care about any of that. That all the time she was walking around sleep-deprived and zombified her thoughts went in one direction only—straight to Nic.

'We're just friends—it's all we can handle right now. Honestly, Kate, if there was more to tell you I would. But we're still trying to work it out ourselves.'

Kate gave her a long look, but then her face softened and Lily knew that she was backing down and the grilling was over—for now, at least.

'And how are things with Rosie. Any word from Helen?'

'Nothing more yet—only that she's still at the clinic and doing well. Social services are happy with how things are going with Rosie, so it looks like this is it. Once they've decided Helen's well enough to make a final decision I guess we'll have more paperwork to do.'

'And you're still sure you're making the right decision?'

'I can't see what other decision I could make. She's my family. We should be together.'

Kate gave her a long look. 'I know you miss your mum, and your sister, but that doesn't mean—'

Lily stopped walking and held up a hand to stop Kate. 'Please—don't. I promise you I've thought about this. I've asked myself again and again if I'm doing the right thing and I honestly believe that I am. I *want* to do this. I love Rosie, and we're having a great time.'

'Well, she *is* completely adorable. I can't blame you—totally worth turning your life upside down for.'

Lily looked down at the pram, where Rosie had been sleeping soundly for over an hour. When she was like this, how could she disagree?

She'd just got the baby fed, changed and sleeping when the front door opened. She backed out of the bedroom on tiptoes, holding her breath to avoid waking Rosie. Nic was standing in the hall, bearing a bunch of flowers and a grin.

'Hi.'

He bent forward to kiss her on the cheek—strictly friendly—and she sneakily soaked up the smell of his aftershave and the warmth of his body.

'Hi, yourself. You look good. Did you do something different with your hair?'

She knew for a fact that there was milk in her hair, and that she'd pulled on this T-shirt from where she'd tossed it by the side of the bed last night. What a gentleman.

'How was it?' Lily asked as they walked through

to the kitchen. 'Did you manage to clear your desk for rest of the weekend?'

He'd been working and travelling non-stop since he'd arrived back in London, and had declared last night that he was ready for a break. He'd suggested a touristy day, sightseeing, and had volunteered *her* as tour guide.

'All sorted. I'm free till Monday morning. Are you still on for today?' He thrust the flowers at her. 'I'm banking on you saying yes, and these are a thank-you in advance.'

Lily thought about it—a few hours in the sunshine in one of the parks, perhaps the Tower of London or the London Eye to really up the cheesy tourist factor.

'Of course we're still on. Do I have time to change?'

'An hour before the car arrives. Is that enough? I can always call and delay.'

'An hour's perfect.'

She left Nic in the kitchen while she dived into the shower and grabbed jeans and a clean shirt. Rosie didn't stir in her crib, and Lily kept an eye on the clock, wondering when she'd wake for her next feed. She'd been sleeping for an hour already, which meant that she'd be waking up…just as the car reached them. *Not* perfect, then—far from it.

Maybe she should just tell Nic that they needed to leave a little later—but he'd seen too much of her struggling already, and she didn't want to admit that an hour wasn't enough time to get two people ready and out of the house. She'd just have to wake Rosie early from her sleep and feed her before they set off. Hopefully she'd pop straight off back to sleep afterwards.

Clean from the shower, Lily headed back out to the

kitchen, to find Nic immersed in stacking the dish-washer.

'Nic! You shouldn't! Leave those and I'll do them when we get back.'

'It's no problem,' he insisted as Lily gathered up sterilised bottles and cartons of ready-mixed formula, trying to work out how many bottles they would need to get them through the day.

Nic finished the washing up, despite her contin-ued protests, and with twenty minutes to go until the car arrived the kitchen was looking more like a home than a bomb site.

'Right, then—anything else I can do to help?' Nic asked.

'Absolutely not. I just need to give Rosie a quick feed and then we're all good.'

She cracked open the curtains in the bedroom slightly—just enough so that it wouldn't feel like night to Rosie—and then lifted her from the crib, tickling her fingers up and down her spine and over the soles of her feet. When her eyes started to open Lily moved her face closer and smiled at her, holding eye contact.

'Morning, sleepyhead,' she crooned. 'Time for some-thing to eat, and then we're going on an adventure!'

She swiped a bottle from the kitchen on her way, and then settled into a big comfy chair in the living room, where Nic had turned on some music.

'So, am I allowed to know what's in store for us today?' Lily asked once Rosie had started to feed.

'I can tell you if you really want to know, but I thought a surprise…'

Lily grinned. She couldn't remember the last time someone had organised a surprise for her, and after

weeks of being enslaved to a demanding newborn, the
thought of being spoilt for the day was irresistible.

'A surprise sounds divine. Though I'm not sure how
I'm meant to play tour guide if I don't know where
we're going.'

'Without giving too much away, let's just say that
you don't have to worry too much about that. You're
doing enough, indulging my need to see the tourist
hotspots. I don't expect you to sing for your supper,
too.'

Lily was distracted by Rosie spitting out the bottle,
but managed to rearrange the muslin square before
she got a direct hit on her clean shirt. She tried to get
her to take the bottle again, but she turned her head
and pursed her lips. Lily gave a small sigh. Perhaps
choosing this morning to try waking her for a feed for
the first time wasn't the best idea she'd ever had—it
seemed Rosie wasn't a big fan of spontaneity.

She sat her up and rubbed between her shoulder-
blades, hoping that she just had some wind and could
be persuaded to take the rest of her bottle.

'Everything okay?' Nic asked, when she gave a
small huff of exasperation.

'Just fussing,' Lily told him, not wanting to admit
that her mistake was probably to blame.

'There's no hurry, you know. We can move the car
back.'

'It's fine—honestly.' The damage had been done
now, after all.

She offered Rosie the bottle again, but she absolutely
refused it, and Lily knew that she was being unfair
on her when all she wanted to do was sleep. Cursing
whatever instinct it was that had kept her quiet when

she could so easily have asked Nic to change their plans, she rocked the baby back to sleep and wondered when she'd wake next—when she'd be hungry next. She couldn't shake the feeling that she'd just played Russian roulette with their day.

The doorbell rang just as Rosie dropped off and Lily held her breath for a moment, wondering if the sound would wake her, but it seemed they'd got away with it. She lowered her gently into her car seat and hefted her to the hallway—for a tiny bundle she was certainly starting to feel like a heck of a weight to carry around.

Nic answered the door to a driver in a smart-looking uniform, and for a second Lily was surprised. She'd heard 'car' and thought local minicab, but it seemed Nic's idea of a day's sightseeing might be somewhat different to her own. She glanced down at the plimsolls she'd been about to pull on and wondered whether she ought to go for something smarter.

'Should I change?' she asked Nic. 'I'm in the dark about what we're doing, but if I need to be…'

'You look perfect as you are,' he told her, and she smiled, but still wasn't entirely at ease.

Lily watched out of the window as they headed down towards the river, trying to work out where they were going. They zoomed past a couple of parks, which ruled those out, and by the time they pulled up at a wharf Lily had to admit defeat. She had no idea where they were going.

'We're here?' she asked Nic, and he grinned by way of an answer. 'What are we doing?'

'Wait and see,' he told her with child-like enthusiasm. 'But it should be amazing.'

She pulled Rosie's car seat out and looked up at

Nic, hoping for some guidance. He nodded towards the water, where a sleek white and silver yacht was moored.

'Are we going aboard?' she asked.

'We are indeed.'

He was practically bouncing now—and no wonder. The yacht was magnificent—all flowing lines and shiny chrome, and decks scrubbed to within an inch of their lives. She could see through the expanse of glass that a dining room had been set with sparkling crystal and polished silverware. It looked as if they were in for a treat.

'Would you like the pram, madam?' the driver asked as he opened the boot of the car.

She glanced at the gangplank and the yacht's decks, and for a shivery moment had visions of a runaway pram rolling towards the railings that edged the decks.

'I think I'll take the sling instead.'

Nic grabbed the changing bag from the boot and hefted it to his shoulder. Climbing up onto the gangplank, he held out a hand to her. As his fingers closed around her palm warmth spread through her hand, and she had to remind herself sternly of the very sensible decision that they'd both taken to remain just friends. But with the fancy dining room and the glamorous yacht this was starting to look more like a date than temporary flatmates hanging out for the afternoon.

'Welcome, sir, madam—and to the little one. You're very welcome on board. Luncheon will be served in thirty minutes. In the meantime feel free to explore the decks or take a drink in the champagne bar on the upper deck.'

Lily smiled at the man as he discreetly retreated

from them, though she couldn't help a little twist of anxiety. Luncheon, champagne bar... She'd had takeaway sandwiches in mind when Nic had first mentioned something to eat and sightseeing, and she wondered if he had higher expectations of the day than he'd let on. This was looking less and less like a casual day out and more like a seduction.

She looked up at Nic, wondering whether she'd glean any clue from his expression. But his beaming smile didn't give much away.

'Nic, this is amazing,' she said. 'If a little unexpected...'

'I know...I know. It's a bit over the top. But I wanted to see London from the water, and my new assistant said the food on board was not to be missed. There's nothing wrong with treating ourselves, is there?'

She searched for double meanings, but found none in his words or in his eyes. She was worrying about nothing. It was no surprise, really. After he'd ended up cooking for them both these last few weeks, he wanted a slightly more refined dining experience.

'So, what will it be?' he asked. 'Exploring or the champagne bar?'

Lily thought about it for a second, measuring the rocking of the boat under her feet and the weight of the baby in her arms. 'Exploring, I think,' she said with a smile.

They walked the decks, gasping over the unrivalled luxury of the vessel, the attention to detail and the devotion to function and aesthetics in every line. Polished chrome and barely there glass provided a barrier between them and the water, but as they climbed step after step Lily's head grew dizzier and her feet a little less steady.

When she had to pause for a moment, at the top of the highest step, Nic gave her a concerned look. 'You okay?' he asked, with a gentle arm around her shoulder.

'Fine,' she told him, shrugging off his arm.

It was making it too hard to think, and she needed to focus all her energy on keeping herself on her feet at the moment.

Nic's face fell—just for a second, before he caught it—and she knew that she had hurt his feelings. She'd opened her mouth, without being entirely sure what she would say, when a liveried steward came up the steps behind them and asked that they take their seats in the dining room. With just a quick glance at Nic, Lily shot down the stairs, glad of the moment to clear her head.

It wasn't that she hadn't wanted Nic's support. God knew it had felt good to have his arm around her. But there was the problem. It was *too* good. It would be too easy to forget all the very sensible, grown-up reasons that they were staying friends and friends only. And it wasn't as if Nic had meant anything by it; he'd just been trying to help when he'd seen that she needed it. It was her overactive libido that was complicating things—having her jumping like a cat every time he came near her.

There were about a dozen tables in the dining room, each set for two with a shining silver candelabra and fresh-cut roses in crystal.

'Wow,' Nic said behind her. 'This is…'

She turned round to look at him, not sure how to interpret the wavering in his voice.

Go on, she urged him silently. Because this dining room had 'romance' written all over it, and right now she was struggling. Struggling to see how they were meant to stay friends if Nic was going to spring romance on her with no warning. Struggling to know what he wanted from her if this was where he thought they were in their 'friendship'.

'This is…unexpected,' he said.

The candlelight made it hard to tell, but she was sure there was a little more colour in his cheeks than normal. She let out a sigh of relief. Okay, so she was worrying over nothing. This wasn't some grand seduction—just a lunch that was turning out to be a little more romantic than either of them had been expecting.

Lily watched the other diners taking their seats as they were shown to a table by the window, tucked into a corner of the room. Light flooded in through the floor-to-ceiling windows, throwing patterns and shapes from the crystal and the flatware.

Nic tucked the changing bag under the table as they sat, and Lily reached down to adjust Rosie in her carrier. She'd slept through their tour of the vessel and Lily glanced at her watch, not sure what time she would wake.

Nic looked determinedly out of the window, Lily noticed, and was careful to make sure that his eyes never landed on Rosie.

'Come on, then,' he said, gesturing at the window. 'What are we looking at? I can't waste the fact that I'm out here with a genuine Londoner.'

'How have you never been sightseeing in London?' she asked with wonder. 'Never mind the fact that your sister has lived here for years, you've been to —what?—six different cities in the past couple of months alone. You don't honestly need me to point out the OXO Tower, do you?'

'And in not one of those other cities did I have a tour guide. Or time off for lunch, for that matter. What can I say? Maybe I've packed in too much work and not enough fun.'

'Well, we'll make today all about fun, then. What else have you got planned for us?'

'Nope—still not telling.'

She laughed, and then looked down as she felt Rosie rubbing her head against her chest, a sure sign that she was about to wake up and demand a bottle. She was just going to suggest that they find a way to heat up some formula when the maître d' appeared.

Seemed everybody was ready to eat.

As a team of waiting staff paraded into the dining room, carrying their starters, Lily dug through her bags and found a bottle and a carton of ready-mixed formula.

'Excuse me,' she said to their waitress, once she'd placed their starters in front of them, 'could I have some hot water to heat a bottle?'

The girl shot Rosie a look that was fifty per cent fear of the baby and fifty per cent disdain. It turned out that diners under one weren't exactly flavour of the month on luxury restaurant cruises.

'Is she okay?' Nic asked, as Rosie started to mewl like a mildly discontented kitten.

'Just hungry, I think,' Lily said, rubbing her back and trying to get her to settle.

If only her fusspot of a niece would take a cold bottle—but she had tried that before, with no success. She tried again now anyway, hoping that maybe she'd be hungry enough not to care, but after screwing up her face she spat out a mouthful of milk and Lily knew they had no choice but to wait for the hot water. She really ought to get one of those portable bottle warmers...

The doors to the dining room swung open, and Lily looked up, hoping to see a steaming pot of water heading her way. Instead the waitress was carrying bottles of wine, topping up the glasses on the table nearest the kitchen. Rosie chose that moment to let out a scream, and every head in the room turned towards her—Nic's included.

'I think maybe I should take her out... Just for a few minutes...until she settles.'

'If you think that's best,' Nic replied, his expression hovering somewhere around concerned. 'Is there anything I can do?'

'If you could get that bottle warm, that would be amazing. Sure you don't mind?'

She'd have done it herself—marched into the kitchen and found a kettle—but from the looks she was getting a hasty retreat seemed like the safer option.

'Course. I'll grab someone. Want me to bring it out to you? Or will you come back in?'

She should have an answer to that. But all she could think was, What was he asking *her* for? *He* was the one who'd done this before—*he* was the one with experience of being a parent, having had months to prepare for it and classes to learn about it.

But she couldn't ask him about any of that.

She pushed through the heavy door and went out onto the deck, taking in a deep lungful of breeze and spray. She let the breath out slowly, her eyes closed, focussing on calming thoughts, knowing that it would help Rosie settle.

Could everyone still hear her? She risked a glance at the windows. Whether they could hear her or not, she was still providing the entertainment, it seemed, as more than one pair of eyes was still fixed on her. It was hard to tell, though, what normal volume was with her eardrums about to rupture.

She rolled her eyes in the face of their disapproval. As if none of *them* had ever had to deal with a hungry baby. Smiling, she looked down at Rosie, determined to stay cheerful in the face of her cries. She was still cooing at her when she realised that Nic had left their table, and she only had a moment to wonder where he was before he emerged through the double doors with a steaming jug of water and the bottle.

What a hero. She could kiss him.

Well, actually, that pretty much felt like her default setting these days. But she was more grateful than ever to have him in her life right at that second. She watched him walk towards her as if he were carrying the Holy Grail.

'One bottle,' he declared as he closed the door to the deck behind him and passed it over to her.

She'd expected him to be sprinting back through the doors as soon as he'd offloaded his cargo, but instead he dropped down onto a bench, spreading his arms across the back. Lily sat beside him as Rosie started sucking on the bottle, quiet at last.

'Why don't you go in and eat?' she said to him. 'It seems a shame for us both to be missing out on lunch.'

'I don't mind—'

'Honestly—go and eat. She's perfectly happy now, so I'll be back in soon.'

He hesitated for a second, but then stood and headed for the door. Lily leaned back against the bench and closed her eyes for a moment, letting herself drift with the rhythmic rocking of the boat. At the sound of the deck doors opening her eyes flew open—to see Nic juggling glasses and plates as he fought to shut the door behind him.

'If Rosie's picnicking out here, seems only fair that we get to as well,' he said with a grin.

Lily risked a glance into the dining room and could see that more than one set of eyes was disapprovingly set in their direction.

'Open up.'

A forkful of delicate tartlet appeared in front of her nose and Lily hesitated, meeting Nic's eyes as he offered the food to her. *Definitely* too intimate for friends. But Rosie's weight in her arms reminded her that this wasn't romance, it was practicality, and she opened her mouth, let her lips close around the cold tines of the fork.

Closing her eyes seemed too decadent, too sensuous. But holding Nic's gaze as he fed her so intimately seemed like a greater danger. As balsamic vinegar hit her palate she smiled. With food this good, why let herself be distracted by anything else?

She sat looking out across the water, enjoying seeing the city that was so familiar to her with the unfamiliar smells and sounds of the boat. Nic's arm was still stretched across the back of the bench, but she didn't move away. It was too easy, too comfortable to sit like this, enjoying the moments of quiet and savouring their lunch.

Eventually, when both plates were cleared and Rosie had finished her formula, Nic nodded towards the dining room.

'Think we can risk human company again?'

CHAPTER NINE

N<small>IC LOOKED DOWN</small> at Rosie, milk-drunk and sleepy again.

'I think we should be safe,' Lily said, setting the bottle down beside them, lifting Rosie to her shoulder and starting to rub her back.

'Let me do that,' Nic offered, already reaching for Rosie.

He hadn't meant to: he'd been clear with himself that the only way he could let himself explore this connection with Lily was if he remembered to keep his distance with Rosie. But he could hardly invite them out for the day and not expect to help. It was what any friend would do, he told himself. Friendship wasn't just offering the parts of yourself that were easy. Taking the parts of the other person that fitted with your life. It meant taking the hard bits too, exposing yourself to hurt, trusting that the other person was looking out for you.

They'd agreed that a relationship was too much to take on, but if they were going to be friends he was going to be a *good* friend.

He nestled the baby on his shoulder as they walked back inside, and for a moment he was caught by her new baby smell—a scent that threw him back ten years, to the happiest and hardest moments of his life. His eyes closed and his steps faltered for a second, but he forced himself forward, pushing through the pain of his past and reminding himself that Rosie wasn't Max, and Lily wasn't Clare.

As they reached the table their main courses arrived, and he slid into his seat with Rosie still happy on his shoulder.

'This looks amazing,' declared Lily, looking down at the plates of perfectly pink lamb and buttery potatoes. She reached for her knife and fork, but then hesitated. 'Are you sure you don't want me to take her?'

'You can if you want,' Nic told her, wary of overstepping some line. 'But I don't mind.'

Lily's eyes dropped to Rosie again as she thought for a minute.

'No, you're right. It would be silly to disturb her when she's settled.'

He picked up his fork, wondering how he was meant to tackle a rack of lamb one-handed.

'Here,' Lily said, with a smile and a sparkle in her eye. She pinned the meat with a fork while he cut it, and when she caught the maître d's shocked expression, she laughed out loud. 'I don't think I've ever caused such a scandal before,' she whispered to him.

He laughed in return, relieved to feel the tension leaching from the air.

'I feel like we're doing him a service. His life must have been very sheltered if we're so shocking to him. Maybe we should up the ante? Give him something to really disapprove of...?'

Oh, did he like the sound of *that*. His skin prickled,

his grin widened and he leaned closer across the table. 'What exactly did you have in mind?'

Lily blushed.

God, it was such a turn-on when she did that—when the evidence of her desire chased across her skin like watercolours on a damp page.

'I...I...I don't think I really thought that sentence through,' she said at last with a coy smile.

He laughed again, feeling his shoulders relax, leaning back in his chair as they seemed to find common ground again...as he started to feel the subtle pull and heat between them that had brought them together in the first place.

'Maybe I'll ask you again another time,' he suggested, unable to resist this spark between them. 'When we've a little more privacy and a little less company.'

She looked up at him from under her lashes—a look, he suspected, not entirely uncalculated.

'Maybe I'll give it a little thought this afternoon.'

For a moment the silence spanned warm and comfortable between them, and he held her gaze as gently and sensuously as if he was reaching out and touching her.

A little choking sound from the baby he'd almost forgotten was in his arms drew his attention and he smiled down at her, so exposed from the conversation with Lily that he didn't have a moment to try and defend himself, had no chance of raising any sort of resistance to those adorably round cheeks or her big blue eyes.

'Sorry, little Rosie,' he told her, mopping her up automatically and shifting her to his other shoulder. 'I guess we weren't paying you enough attention.'

Lily gave him a complicated smile, but then with one more bite of potato she dropped her knife and fork.

'That was incredible—truly,' she told him. 'The closest thing to heaven I've ever eaten.'

'Agreed,' he said, looking a little longingly at the lamb still on his plate.

'I'll take her back,' Lily told him, her tone brooking no argument this time. 'Seriously—you'll kick yourself if you don't eat every bite.'

CHAPTER TEN

THE BOAT SLOWED as they approached the wharf and Lily could practically feel the collective sigh of relief from everyone on board. Not that she cared. The three of them had enjoyed another picnic out on deck, when Rosie had been testy again during dessert, and she couldn't help but think that it had been nicer, anyway, to be out in the fresh air than in that dining room, with its candles that spoke of a romance they were definitely *not* going to be pursuing.

Part of her had wanted to explain to the other diners —to confess that she'd thought more than once that maybe if she was Rosie's real mum she might be better at this. She might be flailing a little less at the prospect of a baby whose needs were really pretty simple if only she could work out the code that everyone else seemed to understand. She couldn't really blame them for being annoyed. No doubt they'd paid handsomely for their lunch, and hadn't expected to encounter a crying baby while they enjoyed it. But their silent judgement was cutting nonetheless.

At least she'd had a partner in crime.

Nic had actually taken the baby today. Offered to help and then cooed at her and rocked her until she was calm. Though the ghost of pain and doubt etched into his every feature was enough to show her that, romantic as the setting was, his thoughts were anything but. There was nothing more likely to put him off, she thought, than being reminded of the realities of parenting.

'You okay there?' Nic asked, breaking into her reverie. 'You look a million miles away.'

The car had met them as they'd disembarked and they were crawling through London traffic again, on their way to sightseeing event number two.

The car stopped outside the Tower of London, and she sent Nic a questioning glance. She couldn't hide her deep breath of apprehension. The last time she'd been to the Tower had been years ago, and she'd had to fight her way through crowds, elbow her way into a picnic spot and strain her ears to hear the commentary from the obligatory Beefeater. She couldn't imagine it being any more relaxing with Rosie strapped to her chest.

'We're here,' Nic announced with a smile.

He reached for her hand to help her out of the car, and then reached in after her to take Rosie from her seat. He handed the baby straight over, but she couldn't help seeing a tiny bit of progress.

They were met at the gate by a uniformed Beefeater, and as she passed through the entrance she realised how different it felt from the last time she'd been there. Looking around her, she realised why. The place was deserted. How on earth had he pulled *this* off?

The Beefeater puffed up his chest as he turned round and launched into a clearly well-practised speech, welcoming them to Her Majesty's Royal Palace and Fortress, The Tower of London. 'There's a thousand years of history here, sir, madam: more than you could discover in a week. So what would you like to see? The armouries? The torture display? The Crown Jewels?'

Lily gave an involuntary gasp at the mention of the jewels. The day of her teenaged visit the Jewel House had been packed and sweaty. She'd managed to get stuck behind someone with a huge backpack on the moving conveyor, and had passed through without getting one decent look at a crown.

She looked up at Nic, who laughed. 'Looks like the Crown Jewels it is,' he declared to their Yeoman Guard.

'You're sure you don't mind? I'd understand if diamonds weren't your thing.'

'That look on your face is exactly my thing,' he told her quietly as their guide discreetly moved away. 'And if it's a diamond that gets it there…'

His sentence trailed into silence, but his gaze never faltered from hers. He *was* talking about diamonds? Had he realised what he'd said? Of course he didn't mean a *diamond* diamond—the type that led you up the aisle and towards happy-ever-after. But if he'd meant nothing by it, why wasn't he looking away. Why was he reaching out and touching her face, as if trying to see something, touch something, that wasn't quite there?

His hand dropped gently to cup the back of Rosie's head, then lower still to Lily's waist, pulling her towards him. She closed her eyes as he leaned in for a kiss, and felt the lightest, gentlest brush of lips over hers. For a moment she couldn't move. Not even to kiss him back or push him away. In that moment she didn't know which she wanted more—which she was more scared of. Because this kiss was something different.

It wasn't the desperate press of his lips on hers at the hospital, or that regretfully friendly kiss on the cheek. This kiss was the start of something new. Something more than they'd had before…something more serious…something more frightening.

Rosie let out a squawk, clearly less than impressed at being trapped between the two of them, and Nic backed off a little, his smile more of a slow-burning candle than a full-beam sun.

He called over to their guide and let him know that they were ready.

Rosie started to whimper a little as they headed over to the Jewel House, and their guide slowed a little.

'Aw, is she out of sorts? She looks just the same age as my granddaughter—and that girl has a pair of lungs on her, I can tell you. Do you want to sit somewhere quiet with her for a while?'

'Thank you, but she's just tired. I think if we keep walking she'll send herself off.'

'Of course. Mum knows best,' he told her with a wink. 'Though if you ask me…' he gave her a careful look '…it's probably Dad's turn.'

He carried on speaking, but Lily couldn't make out what he was saying. Her focus was pinned entirely on Nic as his face fell, then paled, and then as he slowly put himself back together. His eyes refocused, and his jaw returned to its usual position.

'Here,' he said, just as Lily caught something about Colonel Blood in 1671 from their guide. 'He's right. My turn.'

He held his hands out for her, and Lily sent him the clearest *Are you sure?* look she could manage without speaking out loud. He took Rosie in his arms and lifted her to his chin, then leaned down and pressed a kiss to the top of her head. He closed his eyes for a moment and Lily knew that he was remembering. But then he looked up at her with a brave smile, grabbed her hand and squeezed.

They followed the guard, and she tried to listen to his stories, tried to take in the information, but really she just wanted to look. And not at the diamonds or the gold or the ancient artefacts. She wanted to watch Nic with Rosie. Wanted to witness the way he was resisting his hurt and his past and trying to endure, trying to move on. And he was doing it for her.

When they emerged from the Jewel House the evening was starting to draw in. Car headlights were lighting up Tower Bridge, and the banks of the river were bustling with tourists calling it a day mixed with commuters heading home.

'A walk along the river before we head home?' Nic asked. 'I had thought maybe dinner, but…'

Lily burst out laughing, remembering how they'd spent barely half an hour of their lunch actually in the dining room. With a few hours' distance suddenly the whole cruise seemed like a farce. For dinner she wanted nothing more than a sofa and a cheese sandwich. Michelin-starred cuisine was all well and good, but you couldn't exactly eat it in your pyjamas. Or with a baby nearby, apparently.

'I think we'd better quit while we're ahead,' she said. 'Lunch was spectacular, in so many ways, but I think Rosie needs her bed. Enough excitement for her for one day.'

'I understand. We should probably head back.'

Lily nodded, suddenly feeling sombre. The prospect

of an evening together in the apartment was suddenly overwhelming. That kiss—there'd be nowhere to hide from it once they got home.

In the privacy and seclusion of the car, nipping through London traffic, Lily's thoughts were heading in one direction and one direction only—behind the so far firmly shut door of her bedroom. She risked a glance up at Nic, wondering whether her feelings were showing on her face. Were they going to talk about this again? Put aside all their good intentions to do the sensible thing? That kiss had promised so much that couldn't be unsaid.

But she stayed silent—as did Nic. Silent in the car, silent in the lift, silent until Rosie was settled in her cot and they were alone in the living room—with nothing and no one standing between them and the conversation they were avoiding.

Nic let out a long, slow breath, rubbing his hand across the back of his neck, and for a minute Lily wondered if she'd completely misread what had been going on between them—maybe he was happy with things as they were? Maybe he was only interested in being friends?

She risked a glance up at him and all her doubts fled. The heat in his eyes told her everything she needed to know about how he felt—and it was a lot more than friendly. She felt that heat travel to the depths of her belly, warming her from the inside until it reached her face as a smile. He pulled gently on her hand, bringing her close to him, and planted his other hand on her hip.

'Is this a good idea?' she asked, knowing the answer…knowing just as well that it wasn't going to stop them.

'Terrible,' Nic answered, dropping her hand and finding her cheek with his palm. 'Want to stop?'

It took considerable effort not to laugh in his face. Stop? How *could* they stop? They'd tried to avoid this. They'd talked about exactly why this was a bad idea. Looking deep into Nic's eyes, she could see that he still had reservations, that he still didn't fully believe this was the right thing to do. But stop...?

'No.'

'Everything we said, Lily—it still stands. I've not changed who I am, what happened...'

'I know. But what are we meant to do—just ignore this? I can't, Nic. It feels too...big. Too important. So let's see where it goes. No guarantees. No promises. Let's just stop fight—'

His lips captured hers before the word was even out, and she knew that they were lost. They'd been crazy to think that they could live here, together, and pretend that this wasn't happening—that their bodies hadn't been dragging them towards each other, however unwillingly, since the moment that they'd met.

With her spine wedged against a console table and her feet barely on the floor, Lily thought how easy it would be to surrender completely. To let Nic literally sweep her off her feet, caveman-style if he wanted, and really see where they could take this.

But as his hands found the sensitive skin at the back of her knees, lifting her until her legs wrapped around his waist, she knew that the easy road wasn't the right one.

'Nic...' she gasped into his ear, not able to articulate more than that one syllable.

But he'd perched her gently on the table and now, al-

though his breathing was still ragged, he pulled back—
just an inch…just enough to give her the space she
needed to clear her head. His expression held all his
questions without him having to say a word.

'Slower,' Lily said eventually, when she'd regained
the power of speech. 'That was…I want to see where
this will go, but…slower. Slower than that.'

She could barely believe that she'd managed to get
the words out, and even as she was saying them she
was already half regretting that she wasn't more fear-
less. But she couldn't be. Just because they had decided
to stop fighting, it didn't mean that she had decided
to be stupid. There was no happy ending in sight—no
easy way to set aside everything they'd convinced each
other was good reason to stay apart.

They'd still have to work through it…whatever it
was that made Nic's eyes dim at the most unexpected
times. It wasn't all going to disappear because they
wanted things to be easy. And until they were more
sure of each other there was only so far she could take
this.

CHAPTER ELEVEN

SUNDAY MORNING, LILY WOKE to sunshine at the curtains and Rosie gurgling happily in her crib. She stared at the wall opposite, trying to picture Nic just on the other side of it, sprawled across the king-size bed she'd seen when she'd sneaked a look at his room. And she could be in there with him now, she thought, rather than be trying to conjure the feeling of his arms around her waist, the warmth of his chest warming her back as she turned on the pillow and drifted back to sleep…

If only she hadn't been so darned sensible last night.

Much as she was cursing herself, she was glad, really, that she'd made the decision she had. Sure, daybreak wrapped in Nic sounded like perfection—but then what about breakfast? Lunch? All the conversations they hadn't had yet? The things that needed to be said before they decided if whatever it was between them could turn from 'let's see where this goes' into something more real, more lasting?

Footsteps padded down the hallway, and as they approached her room she held her breath, wondering whether they would stop—whether Nic wanted to pick up where they'd left that kiss last night. But they faded

again, towards the front door, until she heard a key turn
in the lock and then silence.

He'd just gone! Without a word! A cold shiver traced
her spine. But she forced herself out of bed and into
the kitchen, determined not to read too much into it.
He often went for a run at this time of day, before the
streets were busy. But it was a Sunday—and, more
than that, it was the morning after *that* kiss, when she
had a million things to say and no idea where to start.
Was that what he was avoiding?

She shook her head as she boiled the kettle and
scooped formula. Who said he was avoiding anything?

When he strolled into the apartment at half past ten,
still in his running gear, she'd just got Rosie down for
a sleep and was thinking of following her back to bed.
But the sight of Nic's legs in his scantily cut running
shorts gave her second thoughts.

'Good run?' she asked, having still not entirely
shaken the worry that he'd left early that morning to
avoid her. But he was smiling—beaming, actually—
as he fiddled with the coffee machine.

'Brilliant—really good. What about you? Good
morning?'

'Milk, nappies, sleep. Pretty much standard.' She
said it with a smile, and she could hear the dreamy
edge in her voice. It might be hard work, but she would
be hard pressed to think of another job that was more
worth it.

'I stopped by the office,' Nic said as he placed a
cup of coffee in front of her. 'Had a bit of a brainwave
when I was running…'

Lily's eyebrows drew together.

'What sort of idea?'

'What have you got planned this week?'

She gave it a moment's thought. One tiny design job that she had to finish and email to her client, and other than that more milk, more nappies, more sleep.

'Just the usual.'

'Then come to Rome with me.'

He was still talking, but a crash of thoughts drowned out his words as she tried to process what he'd just said. A trip to Rome with the man she knew she was rapidly falling for? How could she say no? *Why* would she say no?

Nic squeezed her hand.

'Lily? Still with me?'

'I am—sorry. I think that's an incredible idea, but…'

Even as she was saying the words the real world began to intrude.

'But you're worried about the practicalities and about Rosie? I know—of course you are. But she'll have everything she needs. The logistics might not be easy, but they're not impossible.'

'She doesn't even have a passport.'

'No, but she does have an appointment at the passport office tomorrow. *If* you decide it's what you want,' he hastened to add. 'There'd be a skycot on the flight, and a cot in your room at the hotel. Formula, nappies… I've organised a pram and a car seat—the same ones as you have here—to use while we're there. I think I've thought of everything—if not the hotel's concierge is on standby for anything baby-related. We can even organise a nanny, if you want one.'

Lily slumped back in her chair, her mouth agape.

'I don't know what to say.'

'Say *yes*,' Nic said with a boyish eagerness. 'Have you been to Italy before?'

'No, I've never been to Italy...' she said, her words coming out slowly as her brain fought to catch up. 'But I'm not sure that really comes into my decision. I've got to think practically.'

'You can think practically if you want, but I swear it's all taken care of. Instead you could think about Rome: sipping coffee in a quiet *piazza*, genuine Italian cuisine, the shopping...'

'You're a great salesman—very persuasive. No wonder you were head-hunted.'

'What can I say? I'm only human. Now, stop changing the subject. If you need time to think about it, that's fine.'

Would she use the time to think about it? Or would she use it to talk herself out of it? *Rome*. It was hardly the sort of opportunity that came along every day. And the opportunity to take a spur-of-the-moment trip to a romantic city with Nic seemed like a once-in-a-lifetime sort of thing. She'd be mad to say no.

'Okay, yes. I'd love to.' She could feel the smile spreading across her cheeks, feel the warmth in the pit of her stomach rising to glow in her chest and her heart. '*Rome*, Nic. I don't know where to start being excited about that!'

Nic simply sat and watched as Lily enthused about Rome, so pleased that he'd been able to convince her to come with him. He'd had a flash of inspiration this morning and not been able to rest until he'd got the details in place. His trip had been booked for a while—a meeting with a fabric supplier he'd been in contact with several times over the years. And now that he and Lily had decided to see where this chemistry between them might go, Rome seemed like too good an opportunity to miss.

For a brief moment—just a split second—he'd been tempted to call his sister and ask if she'd babysit Rosie for a night. But he'd stopped himself. He wanted Lily and everything that came with her. He couldn't pretend—didn't want to pretend—that Rosie wasn't going to be a part of their life together. He'd made a few calls, pulled in a few favours, and had plans for the trip underway before he'd even got to the office.

'You know, you don't talk about your family much,' he remarked, once they'd exhausted all possible Roman topics of conversation.

'There's not a lot to tell,' Lily said with a shrug, but the shadow that darkened her eyes told him a different story.

'I know how sad it makes you that you and your sister aren't close...'

He wasn't sure why he was pushing the issue. Maybe it was because he wanted to be close to her, to *really* know her. He'd laid bare the darkest parts of his own history, but he knew so little about her. How could they try and be something more than friends to one another if he didn't really know her?

'It does,' she admitted. 'But maybe now... Maybe things will be better.'

'Was there a big falling-out?'

Lily shook her head as she drank her coffee. A drop caught on her lower lip and he watched, entranced, as her tongue sneaked out to rescue it.

'Nothing dramatic.'

'How do your parents feel about it?'

She caught her breath in a gasp, and though she tried to cover it he knew that he'd just stumbled into dangerous waters.

'Actually, my parents aren't around. My dad never was, and my mum died when I was twelve.'

He felt a gut-wrenching stab of pain on her behalf, and at the same time wanted to kick himself for causing her distress. What an idiot he was to go stumbling around in her past. If she'd wanted to talk about her family she would have brought it up. But then he was sure he'd heard Kate say something about her visiting her family. If not her sister or her parents, then who?

'I'm sorry, Lily. I didn't mean to pry. We don't have to—'

'It's fine,' she told him, settling her mug on the table. 'I don't mind talking about her. It's nice, actually, to have a reminder occasionally.'

'What was she like?'

'She was lovely—and amazing. That doesn't seem like enough, but I'm not sure how else...' Her voice trailed off and she rested her chin on her hand, leaning on the table. 'It was all rather wonderful when I was growing up—which, knowing what I do now about what it is to bring up a child on your own...'

She still had no idea how her mother had done it. Every day she spent battling to keep her head above water with Rosie was another day when her respect for her mother grew exponentially. And when she found herself looking at her own efforts and wondering why she found it so hard...

'And I had a big sister to look out for me. But then Mum was in a car accident and everything changed.'

'I'm so sorry.'

He couldn't believe that he hadn't known this about her before now. That she'd let him talk about his loss and his grief while never hinting that there were people she loved missing from her own life.

'It's not as bad as all that,' she said, catching his eye and giving a little smile. 'At the time, obviously, it was horrendous. But I was placed with a wonderful foster family who helped me come to terms with losing my mother. Helped me so that I could remember her with love, remember the wonderful family that we were. I was lucky to find a second set of people to love me and take care of me.'

He marvelled at her composure, but sensed that her sister's story was somewhat different.

'And Helen?'

'Helen's older,' she said. 'She was sixteen when we lost Mum—too old for foster care. Not that that was what she wanted anyway. After Mum was gone it was like she wanted to prove that she didn't need her. She wanted to do her own thing, take care of herself. She was always welcome with my foster family, and we all tried hard to make her feel included, but it wasn't what she wanted. With our mum gone, the "half" part of being her half-sister suddenly seemed to matter more than ever.'

There were only so many times that he could say he was sorry before it started to sound trite. He couldn't fathom the way Lily had dealt with these blows—how she had come out the other side able to smile fondly when she thought about the family she'd once belonged to but which had since fallen apart. When he'd lost his son and then his fiancée, it had been as if the world had changed overnight. As if the warmth of the sun had stopped reaching him. He'd stopped living. Whereas Lily had grieved and then moved on.

'You didn't stay in touch?'

'We tried. *I* tried. I'd write to her—letters at first, then emails. Sometimes she'd reply and sometimes not. Eventually my letters started coming back to me and the emails started bouncing. She'd drop me a line occasionally, but the message was pretty clear. She was happier without me in her life—I think I was a reminder of what she'd lost.'

'But when she was really in trouble it was you she came to. She must trust you—love you—a lot.'

'I've thought about that. A lot, actually. And done a little bit of reading. I'm not sure that was why she left Rosie with me. Perhaps it was just because we're related. Maybe she didn't want Rosie in the care system. Hadn't completely decided what she wanted for her. Perhaps she thought that if she left her with me and changed her mind she could get her back. It didn't matter *who* I was—it only mattered that we had the same mother.'

'Oh, Lily.' He reached for her hand, turned it under his and threaded their fingers together. 'I can't believe that's true. I think she knows just what a special person you are—that you'll take care of her daughter without even questioning it. That you'll give her the happy childhood Helen remembers having.'

'Perhaps…'

Lily smiled, though he could see that there were tears gathering in her eyes.

'So, what's happening with…?' He wasn't sure what to call it. The Rosie Situation? 'With your guardianship? Have you had any update from the social worker?'

Lily explained the situation—that it was looking more and more likely that she would become Rosie's permanent guardian—and he tried hard to pin down how he felt. Tried to judge the proportions of fear, trepidation, excitement and affection that seemed constantly to battle for supremacy in his heart.

He wasn't sure that he could admit it to Lily, but maybe he could admit it to himself. In those early days, when he'd first been getting to know her, despite her fierce protection of Rosie, he'd managed to convince himself that her guardianship would only be temporary. That he could let himself fantasise because one day Rosie's mother would return, Lily would be a simple aunt again, and the baby's presence in her life would fade to the background. Then there would be nothing to come between him and Lily.

Now he knew that wasn't going to be the case. And it was too late—way too late—to stop falling for her. But what would happen when he hit the ground? He tried to imagine that life and it still filled him with a cold dread. He wanted to embrace all the possibilities that a relationship with Lily might bring, but when he allowed himself to think about the certainties of it he was filled with fear.

He watched her across the table and saw how she became shy under his gaze, dipping her eyes and concentrating far more than she needed to on sipping her coffee. She still wasn't sure of him—and with good reason. She deserved a lover who had no reservations, who was ready for a commitment to her, and he wasn't sure that was him—not yet.

For the first time he questioned whether he'd done the right thing in inviting her to Rome, whether that was leading her on—but, no. Rome was different. It was a way for them to get to know each other better, not a promise.

Three days to plan and she was just thinking about waxing her legs *now*? She glanced at her watch. Not a hope. Nic would be back from work in half an hour, her hair was still wet, and dinner was at least an hour off going in the oven. In fact most of it was still in the supermarket. Rosie was overdue a bath and it was veering dangerously close to being past her bedtime.

Where had three days gone? And how was it that she found it so impossible to do something as simple as cook dinner? Since the moment Rosie had turned up all she'd wanted to do was be a good mum…aunt… sister. To make a family for Rosie and for herself. But it seemed as if every time she thought she had it sorted she found herself in the middle of a disaster of her own making. They sneaked up on her and were suddenly right in front of her eyes.

She heard his key in the lock just as she had Rosie stripped off and ready for her bath. Cursing his bad timing, she wrapped the baby in a towel and carried her with her as she went to the door. Her plan had been to have an uninterrupted bedtime routine for Rosie this evening—to have her down and sleeping before Nic got home, so they could enjoy dinner together before heading off on their trip first thing tomorrow. But Rosie had slept late this afternoon. So she'd fed late and played late. And now—almost—she was being bathed late.

And then Nic was there, and in a moment her stress fell away. The width of his smile created fine lines of pleasure around his eyes as he leaned in to kiss her without hesitation.

'Hi,' she breathed, letting her eyes shut and enjoying that simple pleasure.

When she opened them she realised that the man was not only absurdly good-looking and radiating charm, he was also brandishing carrier bags and a bottle of red wine. It was almost enough to have her crying into Rosie's towel.

'I've interrupted bathtime,' he said, pointing out the obvious. 'I thought I'd leave a bit early and make a start on dinner. Couldn't wait to get home to you, actually, kick off our holiday tonight instead of in the morning.'

There were no games, no subtexts.

'You ladies get back to it, and I'll have dinner ready when you're done.'

Lily opened her mouth to argue: she'd promised him dinner and wine on the table when he got home—a small way of thanking him for the holiday.

'You're a hero,' she told him, meeting his honesty with her own. 'A genuine, real-life hero. Are you sure you don't mind?'

'My pleasure,' he said, already opening drawers and cupboards and emptying the carrier bags onto the worktop.

She shut the bathroom door behind her and checked the temperature of the water, smiling to herself when she found it was still warm enough—no time wasted there. She slid Rosie into the bath and soaped her, distracting her with bubbles as she washed her hair and ran a flannel over her face, rubbing away the last few remnants of milk.

And as she went through their bathtime routine her mind strayed to the man in the kitchen, wondering what his expectations were for this evening…wondering how well prepared he had come. Had he replayed their conversations as often as she had? Had he wondered when would be the right time to take their relationship further? When 'slow' would become impossible?

And what would that next step mean?

Of course she was hoping that they would make love, but doing something like that didn't come without strings attached for Lily. For her it would be a commitment—but did Nic feel the same?

She left the bathroom with Rosie all clean and fresh and tucked into her pyjamas, wishing that she looked half as good herself. Unfortunately she knew that she looked little less than crazed. And, while she couldn't *see* any stains on her T-shirt, the laws of parenting probability meant that there had to be one there somewhere.

When she reached the kitchen Nic was cooking up a storm, but everything seemed to be perfectly under control. What did *that* feel like? She tried to remember a time when her life had felt like her own, when she had been confident that she knew exactly what she was doing and that she was doing a good job. Some time in the haze her pre-Rosie life had become, she assumed.

The paradox plagued her. It was the time when she most wanted to pull her family together, to prove that she could be mother and sister and aunt with the best of them, and it all seemed entirely out of her hands. The more she fought to show that she could do this—

be the matriarch, hold it all together—the faster things spun around her.

Nic stopped stirring the sauce on the hob for long enough to steal a quick kiss, and Lily plonked herself on a stool at the breakfast bar, watching him for a moment.

The kettle clicked and she noticed the bottle and tin of formula standing next to it, ready to be made up.

'I figured if the grown-ups are hungry then Rosie might well be too,' he said.

He'd dropped the wooden spoon and now stood leaning against the counter, hands in pockets. Lily looked at him closely, observing the slight change in his posture, the tension that had sneaked into his body and was holding him a little stiffer. Still trying, still struggling, she deduced. But he kept coming back for more. Not only that, he'd come carrying dinner and was helping to make bottles. She couldn't judge him for still finding things hard: he had earned her respect for trying despite that.

'So, what's for dinner?' Lily asked, placing Rosie in her bouncy chair and making up the bottle.

'Not very exciting, I'm afraid. Gnocchi, pancetta, cream sauce, a bit of salad—I've brought a little of Italy home with me.'

'You are the consummate domestic goddess,' she told him with a smile, hoping that it would cover the twinge of—what? Resentment that that had been *her* role, *her* talent, until she was faced with her first real challenge?

He must see how much she was struggling. Must have guessed that she wouldn't be able to put dinner on the table for him. Not that she was even *trying* for

Stepford-wife-style Cordon Bleu cuisine. She'd have settled for managing to get oven chips ready.

Something of her fears must have shown on her face, because Nic pushed himself up from the counter, hands no longer in his pockets. Instead they were reaching for her waist and pulling her into him. Suddenly emotional, Lily kept her eyes lowered, not wanting to look up and show him how upset she was that she was *still* not getting this right.

'I'm sorry if I did the wrong thing,' he said. 'I only wanted us to have a nice relaxed night. I've been looking forward to this, and the last thing I wanted was to cause you more work, more stress.'

He palmed her cheek and she turned into the warmth of his skin instinctively, and then slowly looked up.

'It wasn't a criticism, or a judgement.' He leaned in further, and pressed a quick kiss to her lips. 'You're doing an amazing job with Rosie, and I just wanted to do my bit.'

Another kiss and her limbs started to feel loose and languid, her body like a gel that wanted to mould to him.

Nic pulled away slightly and rested his forehead on hers. 'I've been thinking about that all day. *Every* day, actually,' he admitted. 'The least you can do after keeping me awake three nights in a row is let me make you dinner.'

She smiled. He was good—she'd give him that.

'Thank you,' she said. 'It's a lovely thought. And, for the record, I *might* have thought about you too. Just once or twice.'

He broke into a grin at that, and swooped a kiss onto her cheek.

True to his word, once Rosie was in bed Nic set two places at the dining table, lit the candles, served Lily an enormous portion of gnocchi and filled up their wine glasses.

'This is incredible,' Lily said as she sat down.

'I wouldn't get carried away,' Nic told her with a self-effacing smile. 'It's just gnocchi and sauce.'

'It's gnocchi, sauce, good wine and better company. It's like being in an alien land, and it's divine.'

'Well, I can drink to that,' Nic said, raising his glass in a toast and clinking it against hers. 'So, what have I missed?'

He'd been in the office until late the last couple of nights, making sure that everything was in place for his trip.

'Well, I have two big pieces of news—Rosie lifted her head for the first time today, and then I thought she smiled at me…but it turned out to be gas. It's been hectic!' She laughed, wondering what he'd make of her day.

'I'm sure it *was* a smile,' Nic said. 'Most likely because she's got such a wonderful aunt to take care of her.'

Lily smiled, bashful, acknowledging his praise with a blush, if not his knowledge of development milestones.

'And did you get the work done that you needed to?' Nic asked.

'Only just,' Lily admitted. 'But it's done now. I've not got anything else lined up for the next few weeks so I can concentrate on Rosie. I'm sure I'll miss it soon enough, and want something to challenge me. A *different* sort of challenge,' she clarified, just in case he'd missed the point that Rosie was an Olympic-sized challenge in herself. 'I'm only going to take on small commissions for now, but it's good to keep my eye in… keep my skills ticking over.'

'I'm impressed,' Nic told her.

Lily shrugged off the compliment.

'No, seriously.' He reached out for her hand as she tried again to brush off his words. 'I'm actually in awe—I can't even think how you find time in the day for it all.'

Lily laughed. 'Oh, it's easy. You just forget the laundry, and mopping the floor, and filing your nails, and…'

'And focus on what's important. Like I said, you're incredible.'

Lily held her hands up and shook her head. 'Okay, that's officially as much as I can take. We're going to have to change the subject or I'll become unbearable. What about you? Did you get everything sorted that you needed to?'

'Everything's taken care of. All we have to do tomorrow is get in the car when it shows up.'

And then make some pretty huge decisions about their future.

That bit didn't need saying, but after the careful way they'd spent the last few days she thought they both knew that that was what Rome was really going to be about. About finding out what they wanted to be to each other. What risks they were prepared to take and what hopes they were going to nurture.

They lingered over their coffee, neither of them making a move to go to bed—alone or otherwise.

But as Lily stifled a yawn Nic stood and cleared

away the last few dishes. 'You look done in,' he said over his shoulder. 'And I'm ready to turn in. I guess we should call it a night.'

So he wasn't going to suggest it. Well, she shouldn't be surprised. She was the one who had insisted on 'slower' the last time things had got out of hand. The ball was really in her court now.

'If you're sure...' Lily said, aiming the lilt in her voice at pure temptation.

But he didn't look as if he was wavering.

'We've an early start tomorrow,' he said, but the tense lines of his forehead told her he was struggling to do the noble thing. 'It's probably best if we call it a night.'

'Of course.' Lily stood up, but the slight shake of her legs revealed her hidden emotions.

Nic stood too, and rested his hands lightly on her waist. 'It's not just that...' he told her.

He surprised her with his sudden honesty. But she supposed they *were* trying to see if they had any hope of a future together. If they couldn't talk to each other, be honest with each other now, at the outset, then what hope did they have?

'Don't think for a second that it's because I don't want to take you to bed—that I haven't been imagining it every day.' He was rewarded with a flash of colour in her cheeks, and he traced the colour with his fingertips and then his lips. 'But once we take that step I'm yours, Lily. Everything I am will belong to you. We both have a lot to think about...a lot to decide... Let's not rush. We have as much time as we want and as we need.'

She nodded, the smile on her lips now genuine, if a little wary.

He walked her to her bedroom door and grabbed her hands as she reached for the handle. 'Still time to say a proper goodnight,' he said, pulling her close and running the backs of his fingers down the soft skin of her arm. From there he rested his hands on her waist, until there was nothing between them but their heavy breaths.

He dipped his head and brushed his lips gently against hers, testing. But she smiled against him, yielding to him for a moment and then drawing back, yielding and drawing back—until one of his hands was at the nape of her neck, the other was clamped at her waist, and he was backing her slowly against the hard wood of the door. He was desperate for more, to feel her giving herself wholly to him. For her to stop her teasing and give him everything she was…to demand all of him in return.

When she opened her mouth to him and touched his tongue with hers he let out a low groan, his hand fisting behind her back. He leaned back and smiled at her flushed face, laughed a little breathily.

'Oh, you're good,' he said. 'Really, *really* good. But I'll see you in the morning.'

She nodded, biting her lip.

'If you're sure…' she said, with a minxy little smile. 'I guess I'll see you then.'

'I've never been less sure about anything in my life,' he said, and his voice had a little gravel in it as he tried to pull her closer again.

But her hands had found his chest and were pushing

gently. 'No, I won't take advantage,' she said. Then, more seriously, 'You're right. I want us to be sure.'

He nodded, reason starting to return to him as the blood returned to his brain. 'So I'll see you in the morning?'

'I'll be waiting.'

CHAPTER TWELVE

LILY LIFTED THE delicate espresso cup to her lips and savoured the full, rich flavour as it touched her lips. Nic hadn't made it up to the hotel suite yet, but the smell had been so tempting she'd not been able to wait. There was a lot of that going on at the moment, she realised, still not sure what to make of Nic's decision last night to go to his own bed—alone.

It was gentlemanly of him, and deep down of course she knew that it had been the right decision. There was too much at stake, too many ways they could get hurt, for them to rush a decision like that. But... But nothing. The fact that she'd been desperate for him since the moment he'd left her last night shouldn't be a part of their decision-making process.

Well, if you were going to try and temper a girl's disappointment a suite in a five-star hotel in the Piazza di Spagna was a good start. She wandered around the living area of the suite now, stopping to admire the artwork adorning the walls and the artfully placed side tables. It was exquisite—unlike anywhere she'd seen before, never mind stayed. Rosie was still fast asleep in her carrycot, as she had been since they had left the airport. True to his word, Nic had arranged everything they needed, and they had been whisked from house to car to airport to hotel with barely a whimper from Rosie and barely any intervention from her.

There were two doors leading off the living area and she crossed to the one on her left, still a little awe-struck by her surroundings. She tried the handle to the door and found it unlocked. She nudged the door open, feeling as if she was about to be caught snooping. An enormous bed—king-size? Emperor? Bigger?—dominated the room, draped with rich silky curtains and topped with crisp white sheets. Her room? she wondered. Or Nic's? Then she spotted the cot in the corner and her question was answered. Her room. And Rosie's. For a moment she wished she'd wake, so that she could share her excitement with her, waltz her around the suite and wow her with all the fincry she couldn't yet understand.

But she'd woken her early once before, and that hadn't exactly gone well. She took another sip of her coffee, wondering where Nic had got to. He'd wanted a quick word with the concierge—that was all he'd told her as he'd encouraged her to go straight up to the room. The coffee had been awaiting them, along with fruit and pastries. She'd intended to wait for Nic to arrive before she indulged further, but now she questioned that decision. Well, if he was going to leave her here, he had only himself to blame.

She'd just selected the lightest pastry from the platter when the door opened and she was caught red-handed.

'Glad to see you're settling in,' Nic said, tossing his carry-on bag onto the couch and crossing to the table to grab a pastry for himself. 'These are incredible,' he said, devouring the morsel in a few quick bites. 'Worth flying out for these alone.'

'The coffee's not bad,' Lily said, with a smile to show she was joking. 'And the room's just about adequate.'

He surprised her with a quick kiss to the lips.

'I'm glad you like it,' he said. 'I've not stayed here before, but I've heard great things.'

'Not your usual haunt?'

'No, I normally stay somewhere a little more…rustic. But I promised you girls an adventure in Rome, and I don't think that Nonna Lucia's *pensione* really fits the bill.'

'Nonna Lucia?'

'She looks after me when I'm here—seems to rather like having someone to fuss over.'

'Won't she be offended that we're not staying with her?'

'Actually, I already ran it by her. I knew she'd be offended if she found out somehow. I explained that I was bringing a friend with me, and that we'd need some more space, and she nodded in a very knowing way and said, "Of course." I think maybe I've given her the wrong idea…'

Lily laughed, delighted with this description. 'Will I get to meet her?'

'If you'd like to. I know that we'd be welcome any time. I was just speaking to the concierge about dinner, and he was making some enquiries, but if you'd rather—?'

She thought back to how well a fancy meal had gone last time and didn't hesitate. 'I'd love to. I'd like to see what your life is like when you're travelling,' she said. 'If it's not all five-star suites and divine coffee.'

'Oh, Nonna's coffee is second to none,' he reassured her. 'I'll call her to arrange tonight—if you're sure you don't want to go somewhere more…?'

'I'm sure,' she told him.

'Well, that's dinner sorted, then. What do you fancy doing in the meantime? Settle in here a little longer? Or head out for some sightseeing?'

She glanced around the room, caught sight of the bed in the other room, and suddenly lost her nerve. 'Let's go out,' she said. 'I don't want to waste a minute of this trip.'

'Brilliant,' Nic replied. 'What about Rosie? I don't want to wake her if she's not ready, but Rome's not known for being pushchair-friendly. There should be a baby carrier around here somewhere, though.'

Torn, Lily tried to decide what to do. She didn't want to wake the baby, and risk her grumping through the afternoon, but the whole of Rome was waiting for them and she couldn't wait to see it. She glanced at her watch, wondering how much longer she would sleep. Perhaps another half an hour…

'What about this?' Nic said. 'We head up to the roof terrace—I can carry the carrycot. We take in Rome from above, and once she wakes we hit the town.'

'Perfect.'

An hour later Rosie was awake, looking from Nic to Lily, wondering who was most likely to give her attention and a cuddle. Lily got to her first, reaching down to the carrycot, which Nic had tucked into a shady corner, and scooping Lily into her arms.

'What do you think she makes of it so far?' Nic asked.

Lily laughed. 'She's been asleep since we left the airport! But I'm sure she'll love it as much as I will.'

'Shall we dig out that baby carrier and find out?'

They wandered out from the hotel with Rosie strapped to Lily's front, and the heat of the summer afternoon hit them hard. The roof terrace had been shaded, with creeping plants over gazebos, but out on the street there was nothing more than her wide-brimmed hat to protect her and Rosie's pale skin from the burn of the sun.

'You okay?' Nic asked.

'I didn't realise how hot it is,' she told him, fanning her face. 'The terrace was so shady.'

'Let's keep off the main streets, then,' Nic said, taking her hand and leading her down one of the winding side streets that led off the main drag.

She breathed out a sigh of relief as they walked along in the shadow of the buildings, the blare of car horns and buzzing mopeds fading behind them.

'Better?' he asked.

'This is lovely.' She squeezed his hand as they passed a sleepy-looking restaurant, its owners still at their siesta, perhaps.

'So, what do you want to see? The Colosseum? The Vatican? Trevi Fountain? We can start wherever you like.'

'They all sound nice...' Lily started.

'But...?'

'But this is nice too,' she finished, smiling up at him as he pulled her to a stop.

The lane had meandered past delicious-smelling

bakeries and traditional-looking *trattorie* until it had become no more than a sun-dappled alleyway, with apartments on either side, their balconies spilling colour and texture as flowers hung down from the walls.

'Seeing Rome like this…it's something I never really imagined. But what I'm most looking forward to about this trip—' She bit her lip, looking for the confidence she needed to make this confession. Then she remembered his honesty the night before, and knew that she owed him nothing less than the truth. 'I want to spend it with *you*. Whether we do that at the Colosseum or here—and frankly this is the prettiest little street I've ever seen—doesn't seem that important.'

She watched him carefully, wondering what he had made of her words. The expression on his face left her none the wiser. Then, instead of speaking, he dropped his head and his lips landed on hers, soft and gentle. Their warmth, his taste, was becoming deliciously familiar. With each time they kissed she felt more comfortable, and that heat in her belly grew, leaving her wanting more and more. The backs of his fingers brushed the skin of her neck, her collarbone, and it was only as she instinctively moved closer that she remembered that Rosie was there between them—physically as well as emotionally.

With a smile, she pulled away. Nic met her gaze and held it for a few seconds, then, with his eyes on hers until the last minute, he dropped his head slowly and kissed Rosie on the top of her head.

He straightened, meeting Lily's eyes with an intense look. 'I want to make you promises, Lily. I want to tell you that I'll be everything you deserve. But I can't.'

Lily froze, not wanting to break the intensity of the moment, knowing that Nic had more to say.

'I've been here before, Lily. I've tried to be the family man, tried to support a partner and a family, and it didn't end well.'

'Nic, you can't blame yourself for what happened to Max.'

'If that was all I had to feel guilty about…' His voice was filled with anguish and his eyes were faraway, lost in the past. 'It wasn't just Max I let down, Lily. It was Clare. After what happened she needed me. Needed her fiancé to be there for her, to talk to her about what had just happened. To try and find a way to get past it. I couldn't do it.'

'Nic, everyone copes in different ways.'

'That's no excuse. She needed something from me—something very simple—and I couldn't give it to her. It was *my* fault that our relationship broke down after Max died. *My* fault that we fell apart when she thought she was already at rock bottom. You need to know this, Lily, before you decide where you want this to go. You need to know that if—God forbid—it all goes wrong, and you lose Rosie, I can't promise to be there for you. You deserve someone who can.'

Lily stood and stared at him for a moment, and shivered even in the thirty-degree heat. This was what he'd been hiding, then—this was the shadow she'd glimpsed and never understood.

'Nic, I can't believe that it was all your responsibility. I'm sure you tried your hardest.'

'You're right—I did,' he said, his voice steadier now. 'I tried my hardest and it wasn't enough. I like you—a hell of a lot. I don't want to keep fighting it. But if we're doing this you deserve to know what you're getting into.'

Lily placed her hands either side of his face and reached up on tiptoes to press a kiss to his lips. 'Nic, I trust you. You've done more for me these past few weeks than just about anyone else I can think of. You can say what you like, but if there's a crisis heading my way I know I want you there with me. Nothing you tell me about your past is going to change that.'

His face softened slightly, and she let herself hope for a moment that she'd got through to him.

'I want to do this,' she went on. 'I want us to take these feelings seriously. I'm not talking about sitting back and seeing what happens. I'm talking about working hard to make each other happy.'

He closed his eyes for a brief moment, and then leaned forward and kissed her quickly, sweetly.

'Can we walk?' he asked, keeping hold of her hand as he started moving again, towards the arch of sunlight at the end of the lane.

She said nothing, knowing that he was still working through his feelings.

'I don't know how I thought I could stop myself,' he said at last.

Lily bit her lip, wondering whether she was supposed to understand that enigmatic sentence.

'Falling for you, I mean.'

She risked a glance up at him and saw that it wasn't only tears that had made his eyes bright. There was a light there—something bright and shining. A smile that hadn't quite reached his lips yet but was lighting his face in a way that she recognised.

'You're sure that you don't want to get out now? Because I'd understand.'

'I'm going nowhere, Nic. But are *you* sure you're ready for his? Because I come as a package deal, remember?'

'I know that. I don't know how I thought I could fall for you without falling for Rosie as well, but I tried—and I failed. I want you for everything you are. And that includes the way you care for Rosie.'

'And you're okay with that?'

By his own admission he'd been fighting it, and fighting it hard. How could he be so sure now?

'I'm not going to lie and say that it doesn't hurt. Sometimes when I look at Rosie, growing all bonny and fat and healthy, it does make me think of my son and everything that he and I missed. But it's too late, Lily. She's a part of you, and I feel like she's becoming a part of me too.'

She was falling for him too—she knew that. The feelings that had been growing these past few weeks had only one possible end point. She smiled up at him and saw relief wash over his features as she reached up to kiss him, pressing her lips hard against his, trying to show with her body what she couldn't find the words to express.

They wandered the city hand in hand for another hour or two, with Rosie alternately snoozing or cooing from her baby carrier. The Trevi Fountain was magical, even packed with tourists, and the coffee in a little *piazza* café was hot and strong—but it was the light in Nic's eyes that made the afternoon perfect…the way he sneaked touches and kisses when they found themselves alone, the promise in his eyes and his body and the feelings for her that he had already declared.

When Rosie began to grumble, a little tired, they headed back to the hotel. Once she was tucked into her carrycot, all ready to be clipped into her pram when they went out for dinner, Lily headed out into the living room, a little nervous to be alone in a hotel room with Nic after all that had been said, all that had been resolved between them. She found Nic by the sofa, pouring glasses of something deliciously cold and sparkling.

'Something to start our evening off with a bit of a pop,' he said as she approached. 'Nonna's expecting us in about an hour, but if you need a bit more time…?'

Lily glanced at her watch. 'I think Rosie will sleep for another two hours at least, so as long as we don't have to disturb her that should be perfect. Just enough time to shower and change.'

Nic raised an eyebrow. 'You know you look perfect as you are.'

Lily had to laugh. He must have it bad, she thought, knowing full well that there was formula on her T-shirt and that she'd perspired more than was strictly ladylike during their walk.

'Don't give me that look,' Nic admonished. 'You could go out without doing a thing and be the envy of every woman in Rome.'

'Flattery will get you everywhere.'

She said the words without thinking, with a chuckle and a sip of her wine. But when she lowered her glass and met Nic's eyes it was to find them full of the passion they'd barely been suppressing all afternoon.

'An hour?' she asked, thinking of everything they could do in that time—all the possibilities open to them now they had admitted what they were feeling for one another.

'An hour's not nearly enough time for everything I've been thinking of,' Nic said, his face full of promise. 'And I think I might want a good meal first...'

Now, *that* sounded encouraging: the sort of evening one needed to carbo-load for.

Nic crossed the room until he was by her side and took the glass of Prosecco from her hands, placing it carefully on a side table before taking her in his arms. One hand sneaked up her spine and rested at the nape of her neck, the other settled in the small of her back, pulling her close against his hard body.

She let out a breathless sigh, wondering how they were meant to make it out of this hotel room without things getting out of hand. Reaching up, she cupped Nic's face in her palm, enjoying the rasp of his stubble against the smooth pads of her fingers, the hardness of his jaw and the softness of his cheeks. When her fingertips found his mouth, he kissed first one finger then the next.

With her thumb she explored the fullness of his bottom lip and the cleft of his chin. When she felt she knew every inch of his face she stretched up on tiptoes and traced the path of her fingers with her lips. Butterfly kisses that teased and promised more, but she wanted to savour every moment. They had all night to explore one another. And while there were parts of him she was desperate to know better, she was determined to make the most of every minute with him. Not to rush a single second of the experience.

For so many years she had waited, wondering when it would be her turn to have a family of her own. Now that she had found it she wanted to remember every moment, appreciate every sensation. Finally her lips found his, and she brushed a gentle kiss across his top lip, and then the bottom. Nic's fingers flexed behind her head, twisting strands of hair but not pressing her closer, not taking what she wasn't ready to give.

His body was strung like a bow, and with every caress she felt more tension in his muscles, more possession in his hold at the small of her back. When her thumb brushed the sensitive skin behind his ear his mouth opened in a groan, and she could resist temptation no longer.

She explored the warmth of his mouth, tested the limits of his restraint, measuring the desperation in his hold. The man was determined—she had to give him that. He'd said they should wait, and it seemed that wait they would. But she had only just started exploring, and at a guess they still had a good forty minutes before they had to leave.

When her tongue touched his, the fire she'd banked in his veins burst free. With the passion she'd seen in him earlier he possessed her mouth, his hands roaming now, rather than settling her against him. One dropped to the curve of her buttock, alternately caressing, exploring and pressing her against him. The other moved from nape to collarbone, and then lower. When his thumb brushed against her breast she moaned into his mouth, sure that at last she was going to get everything she had been fantasising about for the past month.

But he broke off their kiss, moved fractionally backwards until there was a good inch of space between them.

'You…are an absolute…siren.'

She gave him her most minxy smile as he struggled to speak, his voice ragged and breathless.

'And I am going to make you pay for that later. But for now a shower—a cold one, I suggest—and then let's go to dinner.'

'Spoilsport.'

But she couldn't be disappointed really—not when she'd seen the effect she'd had on him, and now knew better than ever what she had in store when they got home. Waiting had done nothing to temper their passion before now, and another couple of hours could only make them more ardent.

She hadn't known what to expect of Nonna's *pensione*, and at times when they'd passed by the brightly lit windows of the Trastevere area she'd feared that they would find themselves in either a fine dining restaurant, where she would feel awkward and out of place, or one of the *trattorie* designed to trap tourists—all plastic vegetables and fake bonhomie. But when she walked through the door of Nonna's her fears instantly vanished.

This was neither pretentious nor tacky. It was—almost instantly—*home*. The moment they walked through the door she found herself enfolded in a generous matronly bosom and kissed on both her cheeks. Nic had pushed the pram across the challenging Roman cobbles and was now wrestling it up the front steps, leaving Lily undefended against this friendly onslaught.

'*Bella*, you are the friend of Nico. You are so very welcome tonight,' she said, kissing her again on both cheeks.

'Signora Lucia, it's a pleasure to meet you.'

'*Tsch*, you must call me Nonna—like my Nico.'

At that, Nic finally made it up the steps with the carrycot, and Nonna's attention was lost completely as she peered into the carrycot and spoke in a loud whisper.

'And your *bambina*. She is a beauty. Nico told me this and now I see. *Bella*—like her *mamma*.'

Lily blushed, both from the compliment and the mix-up. But she was distracted from correcting her by the sensation of Nic's arm settling across her shoulders. The gesture was comforting, possessive, natural, and she turned into the warmth of his body.

Nonna bent over the pram again and Lily held her breath, hoping that the baby wouldn't wake up and fret through their dinner, but Nonna only stroked her cheek and muttered a string of Italian babytalk.

'Come—I have lovely table for this lovely family,' she said, and she stood and led them to a table set for two, tucked in a private corner. A candle flickered on the crisply ironed cloth and Nonna pulled up a bench for them to set the carrycot on.

'When she wakes up you call me and I come see her, okay?'

Lily was filled with such a sense of warmth and welcome that she felt tears welling behind her eyes.

'You didn't correct her,' Nic said, his voice carefully casual, and Lily knew he was referring to Nonna's use of the word *'mamma'*.

'I didn't really know what to say…how to explain… Anyway, you distracted me.'

'Me? What did I do?'

'That casual arm around the shoulder. I couldn't think for a minute.'

'An *arm*? After what you tried earlier, you couldn't think because of an arm?'

She laughed. 'Well, maybe the arm brought back a memory or two,' she clarified. 'What must she think of me? A mum with a new baby, out for dinner with a man who's not the father. Wait—she knows you're not Rosie's dad, right?'

Nic took a sip of the Prosecco that Nonna had poured when she'd shown them to their table. 'She knows. And I think it's as clear to you as it is to me that she already adores you both. She doesn't care about the details of how Rosie came into our life any more than I do. She can see that you love her like a mother.'

'But I'm not, am I? Rosie and I have spent all this time getting to know each other, trying to see how our lives can fit together, and it could all have been for nothing. We could get back to London and find that everything's changed. I could lose Rosie—and then what?'

'First,' Nic said, pressing her hand into his, 'I'm sure that whatever happens with Helen you're never going to lose Rosie completely. I think that your sister loves you, and loves Rosie, and she knows that you're both better off with each other in your lives. If Helen was to turn up tomorrow and take Rosie away—we'd try and cope…together.'

She took a deep breath, forcing her body to relax. She wasn't sure where the sudden surge of fear and apprehension had come from. Perhaps it was inevitable, she thought. With things going so well in one part of her life now that she and Nic seemed to be finally finding their way towards happiness, some other aspect of it had to fall apart. Surely this was too good to be true—

a kind, handsome man, a romantic getaway in Rome, a beautiful niece whom she thought of as a daughter...

'Are you okay?' Nic asked, concern creasing his forehead.

Lily nodded, determined to throw off this sense that it was all going too well. It would be unforgivable to ruin this evening just because of some strange sense of foreboding. There was no such thing as karma. The universe wasn't going to punish her for being happy with Nic by taking Rosie away.

'Better than okay,' she said, and after glancing around to check that no one was looking she sneaked a quick kiss. 'Sorry—just a wobble. I guess I'm still not quite sure what I am to Rosie—mum or aunty. It's going to take a little time to get used to what other people might think.'

'It doesn't matter what anyone else thinks. What matters is that you and Rosie are happy.'

'Well, we are. Blissfully,' she replied honestly. 'This has been just a perfect day, Nic. I don't know how to thank you.'

'Oh, well, I can think of an idea or two,' he replied with a cheeky grin. 'But there's no need to thank me. The pleasure of your company for today is thanks enough.'

She smiled back, and then turned her head as Rosie stirred in her cot.

'Will she wake soon?' Nic asked.

'Maybe just for a feed, but she normally goes back to sleep after a bit of a cuddle.'

'She's changing so quickly,' Nic said, watching her as she wriggled awake.

Lily reached out and touched his arm, knowing that

he was thinking of Max. But he wasn't frowning when she looked up at him. Instead he had the same soppy, dopey expression that she normally wore when she was talking about Rosie.

'It's amazing to watch her, you know. I feel very lucky to be a part of it.'

'We feel pretty lucky too,' Lily told him. 'I know how hard you've found it, but having you here for me these past few weeks…I'm not sure what I would have done without you.'

'You'd have done fine,' he told her. 'But you're right. Some things are better when you can share them with someone.'

'I'm glad you said that,' Lily said, trying to lighten the mood. 'Because I have to nip to the bathroom. Are you okay with her for a minute?'

Before today she'd have watched him carefully, trying to judge his reaction to the thought of being left alone with Rosie. But now she trusted him to tell her what he was feeling. To tell her if she was asking too much.

'Of course.'

He pulled her down for a brief kiss as she passed him, and she was filled with a sense of warmth and well-being.

When she returned from the bathroom it was to find Nonna seated at their table with the baby on her lap drinking from her bottle and lapping up the attention. She moved to stand beside Nic, but when she arrived Nonna stood, offering her her seat back.

'I cannot resist such a beautiful baby,' she told Lily. 'Nico tells me she's hungry and I find myself sitting like this. I think I'll never put her down. She is so wonderful I keep her for ever.'

'I hope she wasn't causing trouble?' Lily replied.

'Not at all,' Nic reassured her. 'Nonna just couldn't resist. I hope that's okay?'

She told him that of course it was, and when a shout emerged from the kitchen both Nic and Lily held out their hands to take the baby.

Lily could almost feel the weight of her in her hands, but Nonna passed her to Nic instead, and Lily was left watching as Rosie settled happily into his arms.

'Ah… Daddy's girl, I think you say. I must go back to the kitchen now, but if she cries I will come straight away and take her. You two need a quiet dinner. Lots of talking,' Nonna commented sagely, before bustling in the direction of the kitchen.

Lily watched as Nonna walked away, her mouth slightly open in surprise.

'What can I say?' Nick commented with a laugh. 'She's quite a force. I'm always too terrified to argue with her. I think she's crazy about you, though.'

'Crazy, perhaps,' Lily agreed. 'You didn't even flinch,' she said, 'when she said Daddy.'

He took a deep breath, and Lily knew that he was working up to something.

'You know that I've never thought about having any more children, but when Nonna said that my initial reaction wasn't horror or fear. Instead I thought about how much I liked being a dad. How I might like that again one day.'

Lily couldn't speak. She'd paused with her glass halfway to her lips and now found that she couldn't move. Was he talking about starting a family? With *her*? For a fleeting second she could see it—the three of them, the four of them…God, maybe even more—but then a gentle panic started to nag. Things were moving too quickly, surely, to be talking about this now.

'I didn't mean right away,' he said, interpreting her expression. 'I just meant that one day I think I might want it again. And I've never thought that before.'

Lily finally took the sip of her wine, buying herself a few more moments to calm herself.

'I'm glad if me and Rosie have helped.'

The words sounded trite, even to her, and she wondered how she had wandered into this politeness—wondered at the distance that seemed to have sprung from nowhere.

She *wanted* Nic to want a family. Deep down, she wanted Nic to be part of *her* family. Surely that was what it was all about? Getting to know someone, exploring a relationship. She'd always envisaged marriage, a husband. Equal partners. But now she wondered if she'd really thought about what that would mean. She'd never considered that her family growing meant that she was a smaller constituent part. Since Rosie had landed on her doorstep she'd been everything to her, and it was going to take some getting used to if she wanted Rosie to share her affections with someone else.

She wanted to show that she could do it herself. Wanted to build a family and keep it close. What did it say about her if she couldn't do it? If one day she wasn't the person Rosie turned to?

Their starters arrived and she ate, watching Nic and Rosie, despising the curl of jealousy she couldn't deny, despite the fact that she knew it was ridiculous. She pasted on a smile, not wanting Nic to guess that her thoughts were still dwelling on Rosie's willingness to go to him. It was just one bottle, she reminded herself. Not a competition, or anything.

Rosie finished her bottle with an enthusiastic gurgle, and the familiar sound broke Lily's tense mood.

'Do you want to take her?' Nic asked, looking a little hesitant.

Well, maybe she hadn't hidden her worries as well as she had hoped.

'You cuddle a little longer if you want to,' Lily said—and meant it. How could she begrudge these two some time together? Rosie deserved this full-on attention—deserved the full force of Nic's smile and the warmth and comfort of his arms. There was a connection between the two of them, Lily acknowledged, and she was glad of it.

'So, did you tell your sister about this little excursion?' Lily asked, finding it a little strange that Kate hadn't called for a run-down of the latest developments.

'Well, it all happened so fast...' Nic said with an expression of insincere innocence. 'I only just managed to tell her that I had to go away. There simply wasn't time to tell her that you two were coming as well.'

'By which I take it to mean you were too scared to confess?'

He laughed. 'The woman's capacity for inappropriate questions knows no bounds,' he said, holding up his hands in defeat. 'It takes a stronger man than I am to volunteer for that sort of grilling.'

'Oh, gee, thanks—so you leave me to handle the fall-out when we get back?'

'Is there a chance that she might just conveniently never find out?' Nic asked, looking hopeful.

'Not any chance, I'm afraid. You're right—she sniffs these things out, and if she ever discovered that I'd kept it from her there'd be hell to pay. *So* not worth it. She has to forgive *you*—you're her brother. If I held back on her I'm not sure that she'd ever take me back.'

Nic laughed. 'I'm not so sure about that. Some of the lectures I've endured—I think she's rather more concerned with you than with me.'

Lily could imagine. Kate was protective of her friends at the best of times, but since Rosie had come on the scene, and Lily's life had become at least twenty-seven thousand times more complicated, she'd stepped things up a level. Lily had tried telling her that she didn't need to worry so much, but Kate seemed determined to be the gatekeeper to Lily's life.

Conversation flowed like wine through the rest of their dinner, and by the time Nonna was cooing over Rosie as she brought over their coffees the earlier tension had disappeared completely. Well, not *disappeared*, exactly. It had morphed into a different sort of tension.

The sort that drew her close to Nic's side as he manoeuvred the pram back to the hotel. The sort that had her up on her tiptoes and stealing a quick, hard kiss in the hotel lift. And the sort that made her draw away from him, a little shy, once they'd reached the privacy of their suite.

But her kiss in the lift had clearly fired something in Nic, and the moment they were through the door his arms were around her, lifting her and moulding her, until his lean body was perfectly fitted to her soft curves and his lips had found hers in a kiss that stole her breath.

All thoughts of shyness fled under the onslaught of sensation: hips and lips on hers, his hands in her hair, the cold wood of the door behind her back contrasting with the heat of his body. She tore her lips away and tilted her head, inviting him to kiss the soft skin of her neck. He responded greedily, nuzzling at her collarbone, sipping kisses from behind her ear, biting gently on her shoulder.

She let out a groan as she let her body loosen, her weight held entirely by door and man, and instead focussed her energy on Nic, on kissing and exploring and reaching bare skin.

Until a snuffle from the pram behind him drew her up short.

Her body froze instantly and Nic backed away, a question in his eyes.

'Sorry…' she gasped, fighting for reason as much as she was for breath. 'I nearly forgot…' How could she have forgotten that Rosie was right there? That she was responsible for a little human life before giving in to her own needs and desires?

But Nic didn't look concerned, or even shocked that she had put her own passions above her responsibility to Rosie.

'Don't worry about it,' he said, kissing her again on the lips, but gently this time. 'She was fast asleep and perfectly safe. You didn't do anything wrong.'

She let out a long breath, thankful to have this understanding, intelligent man in her life. Someone who saw her worst fears even more clearly than she saw them herself.

'Why don't you get her settled? Take your time,' he added, with an expression full of dark, seductive promise. 'I'm not going anywhere.'

Take your time. Why had he said that? It seemed as if she'd been in her bedroom for an age, and he paced the living room, waiting for her to return. He could hear Rosie, grizzling slightly—disturbed, he guessed, by the move from warm pram to cold cot. *Settle quickly*, he pleaded with her silently, desperate to pick up where he and Lily had left off.

He poured wine, for the sake of something to do, though he knew that they wouldn't touch it. He'd sipped one glass all night and Lily had barely started hers.

Finally the door to Lily's room opened, and he turned on the spot to see her closing it softly, peeking through at the last minute to make sure that Rosie was okay. With barely a whisper the latch closed, and they were alone at last.

He forced himself to stay where he was—not to rush over and hold her against the wall as he had earlier. He'd moved quickly—too quickly—when they'd first arrived back, and she'd ended up looking uncertain and concerned. He couldn't risk that again. Instead he'd wait for her to come to him, as she had before they'd gone out for dinner, teasing him with her kisses and caresses.

She crossed the room to stand in front of him, but kept her body from him still. He stood firm, determined that she must reach for him and not the other way around. She'd dropped her eyes. He loved to see bashfulness warring with passion in her posture and in her features. Was she having second thoughts? God knew *he'd* had enough over the past few weeks. But none tonight. He wouldn't ever again, he suspected, after his revelation this afternoon of what she'd come to mean to him.

Caving at last, unable to keep himself from touching her, he brushed his lips gently across her cheek. 'Everything okay?' he asked gently.

'Fine,' Lily said, finally looking up.

Her smile was brave, but not entirely genuine. There was still something troubling her, he knew.

'What is it?' he asked, pulling on her hand until she dropped down next to him on the sofa.

'Nothing's wrong,' she said, but then paused. 'It's just hard…trying to do what's right for Rosie and what I want for me.'

'Those two things aren't mutually exclusive, you know,' he told her gently.

'I know. But when we came in just now I just wasn't thinking. I mean *at all*. Anything could have happened and I'd have been completely oblivious.'

The smug smile was halfway to his lips before he got it under control.

'That's not true, Lily,' he reminded her. 'As soon as she made a peep you were right there. You can do a good job of taking care of her *and* have a life of your own as well. Trust me,' he said, wrapping an arm around her shoulder. 'You're doing an amazing job. But if you want to turn in now, cuddle up just the two of you in your room, then I would understand.'

She thought about it for a long minute.

'It's not what I want,' she told him, her voice carrying a slight waver. 'I know what I want—you.'

He breathed a long sigh of relief. He'd meant what

he'd said—he would have kissed her gently goodnight and watched her shut her bedroom door behind her—but, God, was he glad that he didn't have to.

He'd wrapped his arm around her shoulder to comfort her, but as his fingers brushed across the soft skin of her upper arm the caress turned from soothing to sensual, and his fingertips crackled with the electricity that surged between them.

Lily turned to him, but he knew the next move had to come from her. If she'd had doubts—if she *still* had doubts—he'd understand, and he wouldn't rush her.

Slowly, quietly, she moved closer to him, until her lips were just an inch from his, the lower one caught between her teeth. He could bite it for her, he thought, imagining the warmth and moistness of her mouth. She looked from his eyes to his lips and reached out her hand. Her thumb caught his lower lip, as it had earlier, caressing gently. He opened his mouth to her, inviting her in, and finally, excruciatingly, she leaned forward and pressed her lips to his. But it wasn't surrender on her part—it was triumph as she kissed and tasted and explored.

He ran his hands down to her hips, pulling her closer to him, and swallowed the satisfied groan that emerged from her mouth. Now, with no distractions, no limits on their time, no reason not to do everything he had ever imagined…it was intoxicating. He pulled her closer still, until she was nestled onto his lap, her arms around his neck. When he could hold back no longer he stood, lifting her as if she weighed no more than a feather, and started towards his bedroom.

She pulled back for a moment and gazed into his

eyes. 'Yes?' he asked, hoping with every part of his being that he had judged this right.

'Oh, God, yes,' Lily replied, her voice barely more than a husky murmur. *'Yes.'*

CHAPTER THIRTEEN

LILY CRACKED AN eyelid and glanced at the clock on the bedside table—it was nearly six. Rosie would be up again soon, and Lily didn't want her to wake up alone in a strange place. She eased herself out from under Nic's arm, careful not to wake him, and threw on what she could find of her clothes. She sneaked out of the room, closing the door softly behind her.

Rosie was awake when she went into their room, happily gurgling in her cot. 'Morning, sunshine,' she whispered as she got closer. 'Did you remember we're on holiday?'

She picked up the phone and arranged for hot water to be brought up, then started digging in Rosie's bag for formula and a bottle.

Once she'd answered the discreet knock at the door and made up Rosie's breakfast she wasn't sure what to do next. In the night she'd fed Rosie in bed, and then crept back to Nic and initiated round two, and three... What if Nic woke this time and found her gone? It didn't seem like the right way to start their day. But bringing Rosie into their bed—it screamed *family*, and she wasn't sure if they were ready for that.

I'll go back to him, she decided eventually. It might

not be the right thing to do—there was no way to know until she did it—but getting back into her cold bed alone didn't seem like the right thing, either.

She tiptoed back into Nic's room, trying not to wake him as she eased herself under the blankets without dropping either baby or bottle.

She settled into the pillows and looked around her. This was it, she thought. Beautiful baby…beautiful man. This was how she had always imagined Sunday mornings would be. Admittedly, their path to here had been a little unconventional, and, yes, it was a Thursday, but now she was here it seemed pretty perfect to her.

It was almost impossible not to reach out and touch Nic. She wondered whether it was possible to wake him just by staring at him. Apparently not. But Rosie didn't have the same scruples as Lily and was more than happy to wake Nic up, practising a raspberry noise with a mouthful of milk. Lily tried to mop up without waking him, but the stirring hand beneath the sheet gave him away and she knew that Rosie had managed what she hadn't dared.

She watched his face as he swam up from sleep. A lazy smile lifted his lips as he realised she was there: he'd forgotten, perhaps. Though how he couldn't remember last night, when it was seared on her memory, she had no idea. His face fell when he spotted Rosie and he pulled himself up on the pillows, blinking rapidly and wiping sleep from his eyes with the heels of his hands.

'Morning.'

His voice was gruff, and not entirely friendly. She instinctively pulled the blankets a little tighter around them, feeling suddenly vulnerable under his scornful gaze. Was it her presence or Rosie's that was the problem? She knew the answer to that—he'd been more than happy to see *her*, it had only been when he'd spotted the baby that his face had turned to stone. And when his face had dropped, so had Lily's.

'Sorry, we didn't mean to wake you.'

She *was* sorry for waking him, but she didn't see that she really had anything else to apologise for. Nic was the one who had told her he was ready for this. That he'd struggled in the past but wanted her and Rosie to be a part of his life. He couldn't have expected her to sneak back to her own bed this morning as if nothing had happened, could he? Or to leave Rosie where she was and pretend that this wasn't the reality of her life?

Nic tried pasting a smile back on to his face but it was too late: the damage was done. The cracks were showing anyway, and Lily knew that however much he might say otherwise he wasn't as ready for this as he'd said he was. He would have been happier not to find them both there this morning, and that cracked Lily's heart more than just a little.

'No, it's fine—just a surprise, that's all.'

A surprise? It shouldn't have been. If he really understood her life—and how could he decide if he wanted to be a part of it if he didn't understand it?—then surely he should have expected this.

She hadn't known when she'd woken in the dawn light what to expect of this morning—whether they would be awkward, or whether the natural-as-breathing intimacy of last night would carry through to today.

The last thing she'd expected was this: the sight of Nic climbing from the bed and pulling running shorts from a drawer.

'I think I might make the most of the early-morning temperature,' he said, not meeting her eye. 'Fit in a quick jog before it hits thirty degrees. You don't mind, do you?'

Did it matter what she thought? It was pretty obvious that he was going, either way.

As the door to the bathroom shut she looked down at Rosie and breathed out a long sigh. Last night everything had seemed so perfect, so right. She had known even then that it was too good to be true.

Nic counted his breaths in and out as his feet struck the unfamiliar cobbles, trying to pace himself around the irregular maze of streets and alleyways. That was maybe the most cowardly thing he'd ever done, and no number of heel-strikes was going to make him any less ashamed of it. The look on Lily's face had been heartbreaking. A mixture of confusion and sorrow.

He pushed himself harder and checked his watch: he'd been gone forty-five minutes. The guilt was more than a twinge—it was closer to a knife in his gut. He really should go back. But what to say to her?

He'd seen her face. How could he make her see that he'd meant everything he'd said to her yesterday? When he'd told her he was falling for her, that he wanted both her *and* Rosie in his life, he'd meant it—and he'd thought he'd known what he was taking on.

But nothing had quite prepared him for the sight

of them both when he was barely awake, barely conscious. There had been a split second when he'd seen a different baby, when he'd been in a different bed. And the thought of what had happened, of the different reality that he was waking up to, had crushed his heart for a moment.

This was harder than he'd expected, but that didn't mean he was giving up. Anything worth having was worth fighting for. Hard. But how could Lily know that he felt that way? He'd already told her that he didn't know if she could rely on him, and now he'd gone and proved it—he'd bailed at the first opportunity. As far as she was concerned he'd got what he'd been looking for and then left her alone in his bed while he pulled on clothes and headed out through the door.

He turned back to the hotel, wondering what he'd find when he got there. Her bags packed, perhaps. Or the suite empty, her clothes gone from the wardrobe and her lotions missing from the bathroom.

He let himself into the suite and was relieved to hear her singing in her bedroom, Rosie gurgling along. There was clearly something about the combination of nursery rhymes and power ballads that was irresistible to that girl.

Obviously encouraged, Lily turned up the volume and sang even louder. The door was open and he crossed the living room, resting his shoulder against the frame as he watched her dancing around, pulling faces to try and make Rosie smile. Despite his serious mood, he found himself smiling too.

But he knew that he was intruding on something personal, so he cleared his throat, drawing her attention. Colour rose on her cheeks as she turned towards him, and she stopped singing instantly.

'You're back.'

'Yes. And I'm sorry for leaving like that.'

She dropped her gaze, but not before he could see the hurt in her eyes. He had a lot of explaining to do—and a lot of making up. For weeks they'd been moving so slowly, feeling their way towards trusting each other, and then with one rash move—running instead of staying and explaining—he'd destroyed something of the bond they'd built. Had he learnt nothing from the way things had ended with Clare?

'Are you hungry?' he asked. 'I thought we could call down for some breakfast and eat up here. I know that I've upset you, and I think it would be good to talk.'

She didn't answer for a moment; instead she picked up Rosie from the bed and held her against her chest. Her arms were firm around her, and Nic knew that the cuddle was more for Lily's comfort than for Rosie's.

'Sure,' she said eventually. 'I'll order something while you take a shower.'

He washed quickly. Part of him wanted to delay this conversation—delay the moment when he had to look at Lily and know how much his selfishness had hurt her. But it wasn't fair on her to make her wait longer than she already had for his apology and his explanation. So he grabbed a towel and dragged it over his limbs.

The softness of the cotton reminded him of her tender caresses last night—the way that every sensation had been heightened until even the brush of the sheet against his back had driven him to heights he hadn't recognised.

He glanced at the clock as he walked towards his wardrobe. He had meetings today—it was why he was here, after all—but the thought that he'd have to leave in an hour, whether things were settled or not, twisted that knife in his gut.

When he arrived back in the living room a waiter was laying a breakfast of pastries, cold meat and absurdly good-smelling coffee on the table by the window. Lily was standing, looking out over the city, Rosie still in her arms. She had grabbed a handful of Lily's hair, and Lily was gently teasing her as she eased it out of her grasp.

She turned—must have heard his footsteps—and the smile dropped from her face at the sight of him. She looked guarded, wary, as if about to do battle.

'This looks nice,' he told her, and could have kicked himself for hiding behind pleasantries.

She just nodded—didn't even answer as she settled Rosie into the bouncy chair by the table and then sat herself.

'Lily, I'm sorry,' he said as soon as the waiter had left the room. 'I shouldn't have just taken off like that. You have every right to be angry with me.'

She nodded—which didn't do much to help the guilt in his belly.

'I should have stayed to talk to you, to explain what I was feeling.'

She met his gaze head-on and nodded. It was everything he'd feared. Everything he'd warned her of. He'd let her down.

'Right. You should.'

Good. She wasn't going to make this easy on him. He didn't deserve *easy*. He deserved to see how his actions had affected her. This was what he wanted. To be Lily's lover and partner. Maybe—if he could fix this unholy mess he'd made—more. He couldn't expect all that without giving everything of himself in return.

'Why did you go?' she asked.

He tried to find the right words to express what he had felt, to tell her that he'd been hurt but it hadn't been her fault.

'It was seeing you and Rosie like that, when I was barely awake. It just brought back…memories.'

Her face softened and relief swept through him like a wave. She understood. He'd known deep down that she would. She wouldn't be the woman he thought she was if she wasn't able to sympathise with another person's pain. But that didn't make what he'd done right. He should have spoken to her, explained what he was feeling, rather than running from the pain and from her. That was what he'd done at the start, when he'd first met her. If he couldn't show her that things had changed, if he *hadn't* changed, then what chance would he have of showing her that they could be happy together.

She nodded. 'I understand,' she said.

And maybe she did. But that didn't mean she'd forgiven him. She picked at her pastry, and he knew that hurt was still simmering under the surface.

'But you could have asked for my help, my support.' She gave him a long look before she spoke again. 'What are we to each other if we can't do that?'

What are we to each other? Genuinely, he didn't know. Had he been naïve, thinking that they could make a relationship out of good intentions? Maybe there was too much history, too much pain. After all, he'd been tested once and hadn't come out of it well. But the only way to know was by trying, and so far things weren't looking great.

'This is why me and Clare…' he started. 'I couldn't talk. She needed me to. I tried. I couldn't.'

She let out an exasperated sigh. 'I don't want to hear again that you let Clare down because you wouldn't talk to her about how you were feeling. It wasn't fair of her to expect you to grieve the way she wanted you to. I wasn't planning on making you do anything you weren't comfortable with this morning. But instead of finding that out you decided to bail. You don't have to talk to me about your feelings for your son, but if we can't find a way to communicate with each other then we're lost before we've even really started.'

Her words made him stop his pacing. He'd never considered that maybe there was another side to what had happened in his last relationship. That perhaps he wasn't entirely to blame. If only the same could be said about this morning.

From the corner of his eye he caught sight of the clock on the wall and cursed under his breath.

Lily followed his eyeline. 'Your meeting,' she said, remembering.

'I don't have to leave just yet.'

'But you'll be late if you leave it much longer. It wouldn't exactly give the right impression. If you don't get this contract signed then what was the point of us coming here? You should go.'

What was the point of them coming here? Could she not see that the whole thing had been his—clearly misjudged—way of contriving to find some time for them to get to know each other? The whole point of this trip was *them*, not the business.

But she was already heading back to her room, and he didn't have to ask to know that he wasn't invited to follow her.

CHAPTER FOURTEEN

THE HOTEL DOOR closed behind Nic and she breathed out a long sigh—disappointment? Relief? She wasn't sure. Her heart had started hurting the moment he'd left the suite earlier that morning and hadn't stopped since. His brief return and apology hadn't helped. It wasn't that she didn't forgive him—he'd clearly been in pain, and she could understand and sympathise with that. But instead of asking her to face that pain *with* him, trying to find a way to get past those feelings *together*, he had turned from her. Literally run from her.

Twenty-four hours in Rome. Well, their time was nearly up. By the time Nic got back from his meeting she'd need her bags packed and ready to go, and they'd have to go straight to the airport. There was no time to fix this before they had to leave, and her shoulders slumped with sadness that a day as sweet and as perfect as yesterday could be tarnished so soon.

Rosie had gone back to sleep, so she moved around the room quietly, tucking her belongings into bags and cases, checking under the bed and in the bathroom drawers.

Rosie gave a whimpering little cry in her sleep, a sound Lily didn't recognise, and she stopped her packing and crossed to the cot. Whatever had upset her hadn't been enough to wake her properly, and she'd settled herself back to sleep, but Lily watched her a little longer, feeling a swell of trepidation. It was just the remnants of her disagreement with Nic, she reasoned. Making her see trouble where there was none.

Rosie gave another sniffle, and this time Lily reached into her cot to check that she wasn't too hot. The air-con was on, and the thermostat was showing a perfect eighteen degrees, but her skin was just a little clammy and warm. Lily pulled the blanket back, so that Rosie was left under just a sheet, and then dug the thermometer out of the first aid kit she had brought with her.

Rosie's temperature was on the high side of normal. Maybe she'd picked up a cold, Lily thought, trying not to let her mind race ahead. She had some infant paracetamol in her case, and she woke the baby to feed her some. She barely opened her eyes, but swallowed down the medicine, and Lily told herself just to keep an eye on things and not to panic as she rocked her gently.

Nic arrived back from his meeting and she could see from his face that it had gone according to plan. That was something, at least. And the paracetamol had seemed to do the trick with Rosie. Her temperature had returned to normal, and she seemed to be sleeping easier.

A maid had turned up to pack Nic's things, so by the time he was back they were all but ready to go. They stood in the living room, their cases at their feet as they waited for a porter, and Lily wondered if they would ever rediscover the intimacy they had felt yesterday. Perhaps she had overreacted when Nic had left this morning, but it wasn't just her sadness and disappointment that was between them. It was more than that. At the first instance of something hard in their relationship Nic had decided to leave rather than work at it.

Yesterday they had been full of optimism about the future—aware of the challenges they might face, but ready to tackle them together. This morning had shattered that illusion.

Nic wanted to face his demons alone, and so must she.

She'd worked so hard to be a good mother to Rosie that she knew she could do it alone, that she didn't need Nic by her side to be a good parent, to hold her and Rosie together in their little family. She just needed to remember that. Remember that the most important thing in all of this was to be a good mother. Everything else came second. If that meant protecting Rosie from someone who wasn't ready to be in her life then she would have to do that, however much it hurt.

The flight had been short and uneventful, their way smoothed by Nic's charm and first-class tickets. Again his preparations had been thorough, and the onboard staff had responded to everything Rosie had needed, though she had slept for most of the flight. Lily had kept thermometer and paracetamol in her handbag, and kept a careful eye on her, looking out for any signs that this might be more than a cold.

Nic had asked her more than once if she was okay, if Rosie was okay, if there was anything that he could do. She'd smiled and said no thanks, needing to focus on Rosie. With her baby still grizzly and unhappy there was no time or space in her head to tackle this frosty wasteland that was expanding between them.

Now, in the luggage hall, Rosie started crying feebly, and it didn't seem to matter what Lily did—she paced, she rocked, she bounced—she wouldn't stop. She took her temperature again, and as soon as she saw the number on the little digital display—nearly two degrees higher than when she'd last taken it—she was reaching for the phone.

She dialled the NHS urgent helpline and bit her lip with nerves as she waited for her call to be taken. Nic guided her through the airport and out to their car as she answered the operator's questions, telling her what Rosie's temperature was and how sleepy she'd been.

The car pulled away from the airport and she barely even noticed. She had no time or energy to mark the end of their trip. Her ear was glued to her phone, and her eyes flitted between Rosie and the thermometer. She cast Nic the occasional glance and noted that he looked grey, drawn. No wonder, she thought, given everything he had been through.

But she had to focus on Rosie. She had to funnel out Nic's pain and concentrate on her girl.

Finally, after running through a seemingly endless list of questions, the operator spoke in a calming, measured voice that made Lily instantly terrified.

'Now, I know that you're in the car, so what I'm going to suggest is that you go to the nearest hospital with an Accident and Emergency department. If you can give me your location I'll be able to let you know where that is. Or if you want to pull over I'll arrange for an ambulance to come to you.'

Lily had never believed that a person could feel their

own heart stop, but in that moment she could have sworn her every bodily function ceased. She didn't breathe, blood stopped flowing in her veins, she stilled completely.

'Lily, love, are you still there?'

She nodded, before finding her voice and asking the driver for their exact location, then relaying it to the operator on the phone.

Lily thanked her for her help and hung up. She turned back to Rosie, who was sleepy, but still grizzling in her car seat.

'Lily?'

She could barely bring herself to look at Nic, because she needed to focus with everything that she had on Rosie. She had to give her her full attention. She couldn't bear to lose another member of her family—and this time she knew if it happened she would be the only one to blame. She was solely responsible for taking care of Rosie, and she had to make sure that she got better. If she didn't…it wouldn't just be Rosie she was losing. How could she ever face her sister again if she let anything happen to her?

'Lily, what's going on?' Nic asked.

She turned towards him but couldn't meet his eye. Instead she kept her gaze around his jaw, noted the tension there, and the pallor of his skin, but couldn't let herself worry about that now. Couldn't let herself think of anything but Rosie.

'We have to go straight to a hospital,' she told him. 'They didn't say what they thought might be wrong, but they want her checked out asap.'

'Three minutes,' their driver called from the front seat. 'Hospital's just up ahead and there's no traffic.'

Lily couldn't allow herself an ounce of relief. She had to stay alert, stay ready, make sure that she was focussed only on her little girl.

Nic reached for her hand and squeezed it gently. 'Lily, I'm sure they're just being cautious. Rosie's going to be fine.'

She opened her mouth to answer, but her voice wasn't there. Instead tears were welling in her eyes and threatening a flood. She couldn't do this. Not with him here. Not with his fear of the worst-case scenario written so plainly on his features. Her only responsibility was taking care of her family, and Nic had told her and then proved this morning that when things were tough he wasn't going to be there for her.

Lily unbuckled her seatbelt and put her hands on the straps of Rosie's car seat, ready to have her out of there as soon as the car pulled up outside A&E.

The click of Nic's seatbelt being unbuckled drew her attention, and she glanced over at him. 'You don't need to come in.'

'It's okay,' he said, though the dread and fear in his face told a different story.

'No.' Lily took a deep breath, knowing that she had to do this—for her niece, for her family, for herself. 'I can do this on my own,' she said firmly.

Nic stared at her, clearly shocked. Was there relief there too? she wondered. There must be. He'd never wanted to get involved with a family...never wanted to expose himself to the hurt and pain that might be waiting for them around the corner. She couldn't make him do this for her, and she couldn't walk into that hospital with someone who might bail on her at any moment. It was better to do this now, end things here, and know exactly where she stood, exactly who she could rely on as she walked into the hospital.

'I'll come in with you, Lily. You shouldn't have to do this by yourself.'

But she didn't want him there out of duty or obligation—didn't want him there against his better judgement. She wanted him there because he was part of her, part of Rosie. Because they were a family. He was offering half-measures, and that just wasn't good enough. Not for her, and not for Rosie.

'No!' Lily shouted this time, the tears finally spilling onto her cheeks. 'We're better off on our own,' she blurted. 'And not just today. We made a mistake, Nic. This was never going to work. We're better off accepting that now, before it goes any further. You know I'm right. You know that you don't want to be inside that hospital with us. I'm sorry, but it's for the best. It's over, Nic.'

As they came to an abrupt halt Lily grabbed for Rosie, lifting her out of the car seat. The driver opened the door behind her and she ran from the car, focussing on Rosie's face, refusing to look back.

CHAPTER FIFTEEN

LILY UNLOCKED THE door to Kate's flat one-handed while Rosie slept peacefully at last in the crook of her arm. She'd never used her friend's key without asking before, but with her own place still a building site and her relationship with Nic in tatters she had nowhere else to go.

It had been a long couple of days. She wished she could curl up like Rosie, block out the world and sleep through the day. The last seventy-two hours had consisted of nail-biting terror and endless waiting while doctors drew blood, ran tests, muttered together in corners.

Until this morning, when a smiling junior doctor had come to give her the news—all clear. They had been worried about meningitis, they'd told her when she'd arrived at the hospital, and had run a slew of tests. But every one had come back negative. It seemed that Rosie had been battling a nasty case of flu, and after three days of topping her up with fluids and paracetamol they were happy for her to be discharged.

After settling Rosie in her carrycot she plugged in her phone, dreading what might be waiting for her there. Nic had called a couple of times, and then passed the baton on to Kate. But Lily had found that she didn't know what to say. She'd breathed a sigh of relief when the phone's battery had died and she'd not had to think about it any more.

But now that she was back, and Rosie was on the mend, she knew that she had some thinking to do. And—she suspected—some apologising. Kate, for one, would be furious that she'd been incommunicado for more than twenty-four hours. And Nic...?

She had no idea what she could expect from him— if anything. Looking back at that car journey, she was ashamed of the way she had behaved, and saw in her behaviour a reflection of his, of everything she had criticised him for that very morning. She'd not talked about what was scaring her; she'd not tried to explain. Instead she'd decided that she had to do things on her own, in her own way, and left him out in the cold while she got on with it.

But the thing really twisting the knife in her stomach was the fact that she knew he had been hurting already. Seeing Rosie sick, the trip to the hospital, the not knowing what was happening... It must have brought back so many memories. And instead of trying to help, or even to understand, she'd pushed him away.

Just as she was putting on the kettle, hoping that coffee would make this awful day better, a key turned in the front door. Kate, home from work. Or Nic? she thought suddenly, with a stab of guilt in her belly. Did he have a key to his sister's place?

She thought for a moment about trying to sneak out the back way. But her best friend and her brother had stood by her these last few weeks—the most challenging of her life—and it would be cruel of her to push them away now. The thought of facing Nic's hurt and Kate's disapproval was terrifying, but it couldn't be put off for ever, she knew.

She breathed a sigh of relief when Kate's curls appeared around the door.

'Lily!' she exclaimed with a double-take. 'You scared me half to death. What are you doing here?'

The blunt words were muffled as her face was trapped in a cloud of curly hair and she was squeezed in a tight hug.

Pulling back, Kate held her at arm's distance as she gave her an assessing look.

'Of course you're here—stupid of me. How are you doing?' she asked, though Lily knew from her tone that she wasn't expecting an answer. 'Not great, I imagine, from everything that I've heard. Rosie okay?'

Lily nodded, unable to speak after being shown such kindness when she'd been expecting the opposite.

'Now, I need coffee, and I need some sort of baked goods, and then we're going to talk,' Kate carried on, steering Lily back into the kitchen and pulling mugs from the cupboard as the kettle came to the boil. 'That brother of mine has been walking around with a face like a month of wet Sundays, and you're not looking much better yourself. And as it seems like neither of you knows how to operate a telephone or carry out a conversation—despite you having clocked up almost sixty years on this planet between you—an intervention is required.'

Lily dropped onto a stool and opened her mouth to speak.

But Kate stopped her with a pointed finger. 'Uh-uh. I'm talking first. You're sitting like a good girl and listening while I tell you just why *you're* an idiot for pushing my brother away, and *he's* an idiot for letting you and for somehow managing to screw up a romantic whirlwind trip to Rome. And then you're *both* going to apologise and find a way to make this work before your twin glum faces drive me mad. Am I clear?'

Lily didn't know what else to do but nod and accept the coffee that Kate placed in front of her, some of the hot black liquid sloshing over the side of her cup with her enthusiasm.

Despite her rousing sentiments, and her insistence on speaking first, Kate sat and listened quietly as Lily gave her a summed-up version of what had happened in Rome—skirting very quickly round the 'sex with your brother' part and instead focussing on the 'thinking we were falling for each other and then he freaked out and left' part.

Not for the first time she wished she could have fallen for someone else—anyone other than her best friend's brother. Maybe then she could have just spilled out all her worst pain, everything Nic had done wrong, every way he had hurt her and upset her. But knowing how much Kate loved him, how much she knew that he was really a good guy, she couldn't do it.

She couldn't explain what had happened without seeing for herself how much responsibility they both carried for the way things had fallen apart. No, Nic *shouldn't* have left with barely a word the morning after they had made love for the first time. But she should have given him the space he'd needed. Recognised that grieving was a long process, full of setbacks and surprises. That he must have been as taken aback by the turn of events that morning as she had.

And she couldn't deny that pushing him away when he must have been every bit as frightened for Rosie as she had been had been cruel. She just hoped that it wasn't unforgivable.

'So you're both idiots—that's what you're telling me?'

Once again Kate had managed to find a way to compress their entire torturous, complicated lives into one simple sentence.

Lily nodded. 'Though I'm pretty sure I'm the bigger one.'

'You both want to make this up. You're both sitting at home moping rather than doing something about it. Seems pretty equal to me. You know that he wouldn't leave the hospital, right? Slept that first night across a couple of chairs in the A&E waiting room? It wasn't until you texted me that Rosie was fine and I passed it on to him that he would leave. He wanted to be there... just in case.'

Lily dropped her head into her hands, her heart swelling and breaking a little at the same time, ashamed of the way she had behaved, but pleased at this demonstration of Nic's commitment to her —and to Rosie.

'So what do I do about it?'

'Do you want him back? Really?'

She was surprised Kate could ask her that after everything that had just been said—after she'd explained how much she felt for him, how stupid she had been. But in the words she could hear more than a hint of sisterly protection, and Lily knew that she was crossing some sort of rubicon. Say yes now and she wasn't just committing to Nic, she was committing to his family. She was promising not one but two of the people she cared for most in the world that she was committed to them, that she wouldn't hurt them.

'I do,' she said seriously. 'I want us to try again.'

Kate leaned over and gave her a hug with uncharacteristic gentleness, both in her body and her words. 'Glad to hear it. Now, you go borrow my room and get some sleep—you look hideous—and we'll talk again tomorrow.'

Lily felt her body growing heavier. The lack of sleep these past days was catching up with her, and she knew that Kate was right. She needed rest, needed to recharge. And then, when Rosie was better, she'd call Nic, beg his forgiveness, and see if there was any way to rescue what they had so briefly found in Rome.

A few days later Lily reached across to the coffee table, trying to grab her phone without disturbing Rosie, who was asleep on her lap.

It was a message from Kate.

I have a plan. I'll be home in an hour—make sure you're in.

Lily glanced down at the sleeping baby and thought for the millionth time how lucky she was to have her safe and well in her arms—the doctors had given her a clean bill of health, her temperature was gone, and she was feeding and sleeping as normal. The only reason she was being cuddled to sleep instead of drifting off on her own in her cot was because Lily was still nervous of letting her go, still haunted by her worst fears.

It was how Nic must feel every day, she thought, unable to shake the unease of knowing how easily a child could be lost, how impossible it would be to fill the void she would leave.

The doorbell rang, and Lily softly cursed Kate. How could a grown woman, a successful barrister, forget her own house keys on a daily basis?

She set Rosie down, careful not to wake her, and picked her way across the living room. She threw open the door, and had already half turned back when she realised what was wrong with the scene. Kate's slight shoulders wouldn't block the sunshine, wouldn't cast a shadow that was solid and masculine and...

'Nic?'

CHAPTER SIXTEEN

'Hi.'

In that moment he knew he'd done the right thing: 'borrowing' his sister's phone, sending that text, coming to see her. Her voice brought memories flooding back...their one night in Rome, their walks around the city, the way she'd heard him confess his darkest fears about his character and told him that she still trusted him. What they'd found together was too important to let it go without a fight.

But maybe Lily was tired of fighting. She looked tired: black bags under her eyes, her shirt unironed, her skin pale. But none of that mattered. Because all he could see was what made her beautiful to him.

How had they managed to get it all so wrong? He thought back to that night in Rome—he couldn't even remember how long ago that was. Four nights? Five? It felt like a lifetime... Everything had seemed right with the world. He'd had the woman he loved, relaxed and happy and contented in his arms. He'd felt peaceful at last, after a decade of running from his memories.

And then in a half waking moment of confusion he'd pushed her away. That one push had spiralled and had a butterfly effect on everything—until he hadn't even recognised who they were to each other any more.

He'd been in so much pain—watching her suffer, watching Rosie suffer—and utterly paralysed with fear that he would lose them both. He should have argued when she'd told him that she wanted to face it alone. Should have told her that he *knew* this pain, *knew* this fear, and that they would be stronger if they faced it together. All he'd been able to do was wait, haunt the hospital waiting room until he'd known that Rosie was going to be okay.

'Come in,' she said, though her voice was hesitant.

He followed her through to the kitchen anyway. He couldn't bear the thought of leaving without things between them being back where they had been. Without her knowing what he'd realised as he'd sat in the hospital, waiting for news, wanting to be nearby just in case she needed him. He loved her. That was why he hadn't been able to go home to his huge, empty apartment. It was why his heart had felt empty for days— why he hadn't been able to sleep or think straight until he'd made the decision to come here and fight for what he wanted. He just hoped it was what she wanted too.

He took a moment to watch her, to refamiliarise himself with her features, with the colour of her hair, the line of her nose and the angle of her smile. Did she know how much he had missed her? How he had missed Rosie as well? Missed the mess and the noise of the two of them at home?

Lily was hovering by the table, and he realised that in his eagerness to look at them both he'd not yet spoken. She looked uncertain, as if she might bolt at any moment, and with that his anger towards her dissipated.

He'd been furious for a while that she wouldn't even answer his texts, that she had left him sitting and wondering whether Rosie was even alive, but seeing her now, seeing the evidence of the emotional toll of the past few days, he found that he couldn't add his anger to her list of troubles.

'The text was from you?' she asked, her voice tremulous.

'I wasn't sure you'd see me. I'm sorry.'

'I would have,' she said. 'I wanted to call…to talk. But after the way I behaved I…I couldn't.'

'You *could*,' he told her. 'That's what you've been trying to show me, isn't it? That we should be finding ways to support each other? I'd have supported you, Lily, if you'd let me. So how is she?' he asked at last, and suddenly his arms felt empty, light, as if they needed the weight of the baby in them to know that she was okay.

Lily wasn't the only one who'd become part of his heart, and he knew that could never be undone.

Never mind his arms, his heart had felt empty these last few days, missing its other half, missing that which made him whole. At first he'd thought it was just the memories making him sad—the thought of another funeral, another tiny white coffin. But when the feeling had persisted long after he'd known that Rosie was in the clear he'd known there was another cause.

Knowing how that felt, knowing what it was to be without her, it suddenly seemed stupid of him to be angry, to hold a grudge. Why jeopardise this? Why risk the chance of being happy?

He met her eyes and tried to show her everything with that look. Everything that he had felt and thought and hoped and feared since he'd last seen her. But it wasn't enough. He had to be sure that she understood.

'I'm sorry,' he said. 'I'm sorry for leaving that morning. I'm sorry that you didn't think you could rely on me when Rosie was sick. I'm sorry it's taken me all week for us to get to this point. I love you, Lily, and I want us to fix this.'

She stared at him for a moment. He wasn't sure what she'd been expecting, but it was clear from her expression that it hadn't been this.

'*I'm* the one who should be apologising,' she said. 'I shouldn't have judged you so harshly when we were in Rome. I shouldn't have pushed you away when Rosie was sick because I was still angry with you.'

'You don't have to apologise,' he said, reaching for her hand and allowing himself a small smile when she didn't pull back. 'You were so worried about her—you had to do what you thought was right at the time.'

'It doesn't make the way I acted any better.'

Nic shrugged. 'We can't change what happened— what we said or did. But if you still want to we can forgive each other. See if we can try harder, do better.'

She smiled, although it still looked tentative. 'I'd like that.'

'I can't promise that I won't have another day like that one in Rome,' he warned. 'There will be times when I feel sad. When I look at Rosie and remember Max. Things might not be smooth sailing just because we want them to be.'

Lily nodded. 'And I can't promise I'm not going to make mistakes, either. It's quite a lot to get used to, this parenting thing. I might need help. Sometimes I might need space.'

'I *can* promise that I will always love you, though. That I will always want you—want you both—in my life.'

'Then I can promise to remember that. Even when I'm upset and angry. I love you, Nic.'

A tear sneaked from the corner of her eye and he reached out with his thumb to wipe it away. The last tear she would shed over him, he hoped.

Rosie started to stir in the bedroom and Nic smiled. 'Can I?' he asked.

Lily nodded and he went to pick the baby up, moved himself beside Lily on the sofa.

'She's really okay?' he asked.

'Right as rain. They were just being cautious. Absolutely the right thing, of course. But it did give me seventy-two hours I'd very much like to wipe from my memory.'

'Just as long as she's okay. And as long as *we* are.'

He placed a tentative arm around her shoulders and his whole body relaxed when she turned into him, burying her face in his neck for a long moment and taking a deep breath. He wished they were at home, that there wasn't a chance his sister might walk through the door at any moment.

Taking advantage of the privacy, temporary as it might be, he dropped a kiss on the top of Lily's head. When she looked up at him he caught her lips with his, holding her there in a long kiss, pouring all the emotion of the last week into it. She moaned as she opened her mouth, and he sensed her longing, her love for him.

As they leaned back in the sofa, nestling together, their little family of three, a thought came to him—and a question…

EPILOGUE

LILY LOOKED IN the mirror. As with pretty much everything else in her life, this wasn't exactly what she'd had in mind. She had always thought she would walk down the aisle on her wedding day looking like something out of one of those bridal magazines. She had never expected to do it eight months pregnant.

The day she'd found out she was expecting their baby had been one of the happiest of their lives. But when they'd sat down and worked out the due date they'd realised that, as always, things were a little complicated. The church and the venue had been booked, and everything had been planned for months. It had seemed silly and vain to change the date of their wedding just so that Lily could buy a gown in the size that she wanted.

After the briefest knock on the door Kate appeared, Rosie propped on one hip and a grin on her face. 'How's the blushing bride getting on?' she asked. 'Better than my brother, I hope. The poor guy's so nervous he can't even eat. Don't know what he's worrying about, personally. Not like you can run very fast in your condition. If you tried to ditch him he'd catch up with you and drag you back.'

'And hi to you too.' Lily laughed, accepting a glass of something sparkling and a kiss on the cheek. 'I'm fine. Better than fine. I'm flippin' brilliant and I cannot wait to be officially your sister. How long have I got?'

Kate checked the time on her phone. 'Three minutes. Right—have we got everything? Old, new, borrowed, blue?'

Lily nodded. Not that she needed any of those things. As long as she had her family she had everything she wanted.

'Let's get you hitched, then.'

She walked into the church and saw Nic waiting for her at the end of the aisle. Any nerves she might have been hiding fell away. She had never felt so happy and in love and safe and secure in her life.

As she turned to look at her guests she saw Helen in the second row, a tissue pressed to her eyes. Her sister looked well, *really* well, better than she'd seen her for a long time. She was making tentative steps to get to know Rosie, and focussing on looking after her own health.

Rosie, still in Kate's arms, went ahead of her up the aisle, so when she reached Nic her little family was all together. Looking around her, Lily felt more lucky than she ever had, and knew as she said 'I do' that nothing could make this moment more perfect.

* * * * *

COMING SOON!

We really hope you enjoyed reading this book. If you're looking for more romance, be sure to head to the shops when new books are available on

Thursday 28th June

To see which titles are coming soon, please visit **millsandboon.co.uk**

LET'S TALK
Romance

For exclusive extracts, competitions
and special offers, find us online:

f facebook.com/millsandboon

⊙ @millsandboonuk

𝕏 @millsandboon

Or get in touch on 0844 844 1351*

For all the latest titles coming soon, visit
millsandboon.co.uk/nextmonth